THE FORGOTTEN GOD

ANDREW RYLANDS

ISBN: 978-1-914505-00-3
[or ISBN 978-1-914505-01-0 for paperback]

Illustration and design by: Kelly Carter

www.andrewrylands.com

For Sue

who gave them their names

and asked me to tell their story.

CHAPTER 1

THE LOST CONTINENT

THE CAT was older than the rocks on which he sat. Apart from the crossed paws, he resembled a misplaced sphinx, carved from the landscape, immobile and unchanging. Nobody lives forever, they say. Yet this small sphinx, though still, was very much alive. The rays of the setting sun illuminated a handsome ginger face, his fur streaked with darker stripes above the eyes; a tiger in miniature. Below his chin, his chest and belly were white, as were his paws. He lay beneath a cypress tree enjoying the late summer heat. With thoughts lost on paths far away, he gazed toward the horizon. Golden irises reflected the glow of the setting sun, his pupils narrowed to a slit.

He had long come to accept this small body; it no longer concerned him—it was what it was. Once, he bestrode the heavens, manipulated matter, shaped the world. He helped mould its inhabitants, and wielded a power he could no longer imagine. Once, by thought alone, he could change the course of history. Now, in this state of blissful selective amnesia, he barely knew his name. He'd been like this so long it no longer mattered. These days, he was just a cat, nothing more. Relinquishing responsibility was liberating, after a fashion; let humans carry the burden for a change; it's what they'd always wanted. As felines, he and his kind were safely out of the mainstream, inconspicuous and retired. At least he could no longer do them any harm, as he used to...

1

His seclusion was deliberate, here at the former epicentre of his cult and the source of his fame. It was an appropriate place to retire to once he had finally mastered the turmoil in his soul; the anguish that threatened to tear his mind apart. Carefully over time, he wove spells of forgetfulness, creating a web of amnesia and indifference, layer after layer, strand upon strand, to seal off the world outside. Behind his invisible wall he lived a simple life with others of his new kind, among the ancient stones. Cut off from their former home, several of his family accompanied him, spending their days on the slopes of Parnassos in tranquil retirement. But for Apollo, deep in his soul, at the core of his being, the uneasy restlessness remained.

THE DAYS blended into one another while he mingled with his companions and ceased to care. Time didn't flow there like elsewhere. In their temporal bubble, out of sight and out of mind, playing their little games and scheming their little schemes, they forgot and were forgotten by everyone. Everyone that mattered. Out there, beyond those self-imposed boundaries, things happened. Events took place, attitudes changed, bold plans were hatched and men of ambition pursued their place in history. They dreamed of tomorrow.

On this hillside, they strove to stay the same. Nothing changed. They were slaves to the slow-turning wheel of the seasons, nothing more; a pride of feral cats, keeping watch over the ancient dream of Delphi. Animals were born and animals died, but for the others among them, nothing much happened. With one exception. A ghost from the past sent to haunt him, or test him; unfinished business from the time of legend. Blissfully unaware of their past life, just as he had forgotten the ancient barb in his heart,

2

the shot that pierced his soul. Suddenly restless, it stirred once more. Someone didn't want him to rest easy.

He amused himself by showing humans around the site in return for something to his liking from the cafe where he ended his tours. Few could resist; it was one of his few remaining powers. They came to discover their past; he escorted them around while forgetting his own. His impulsive need to tell visitors about this place slammed into a growing frustration as his recollections faded. When he walked the Sacred Way, he was certain he could once read the inscriptions on the stones. Now they were just meaningless scratchings.

ACROSS THIS landscape, beautiful and ancient, a strange torpor had settled long ago. Memory seeped into the stones. Delphi was just another dream of a distant and opaque past. Waiting. Sleeping. Apollo settled into a daily routine of guiding, sleeping, and eating, then socialising with his friends or hunting in the dusk. The days streamed past, and the seasons came and went. Throughout this long drowse little changed other than his companions, and all those comings and goings wrapped yet more layers of sadness around his soul; more than he could count. It was better to forget. Forgetfulness helped him stay sane. Behind meticulously constructed fog banks of amnesia he screened off the horrors of his past. In doing so he also lost much more but, thankfully, the past became a lost continent, never to be explored. It was better that way.

There, on the mountainside, he was safe. Ambition was abandoned, life was uncomplicated. This day was the same as the one before, and no doubt would be the same as the one after. He didn't care; the pain had gone.

Until the car ate his friend, and everything changed.

CHAPTER 2

DELPHI

A NEW morning, bright and hot. Apollo spent it wandering around the less frequented lower part of the Sanctuary. This was where he tended to find his most willing guests, the ones with a deeper interest in the past, rather than those who alighted from tour busses to hit the Sacred Way and theatre, as quickly as possible, en route to the museum gift shop. Down here, below the level of the road, was off the oft-beaten track. You could hear yourself think. You came across a more thoughtful kind of pilgrim. But this day hadn't gone as well as he'd hoped. He felt distracted, somehow. He had led them back to the café by the roadside too early for lunch, and his visitors headed straight to the museum, rather than stop for refreshments.

"Losing your touch?" Olympia exhibited her usual sarcasm. Usually, he enjoyed jousting with her. Theirs was a cosy relationship founded on friendly bickering, but today he wasn't in the mood.

"I let them go. It was too early for lunch, anyway." He relented, not wanting to allow her the petty victory of seeing him riled. Lovers they may be, but their intimacy only granted her so much leeway. Apollo caught her glance, then lowered his head and bunted gently against her to show there were no hard feelings.

"We could get together this afternoon?" she suggested. "It's been a while."

He was noncommittal. "Maybe."

She followed his eyes across the road and saw Daphne's hindquarters disappearing behind a tree. His latest infatuation. "Oh well, I can see you've got better things to do."

He looked at her. "It's not that…"

Now it was her turn to sound irritated. "Don't worry. I know my place. I'm just the fallback." She turned to go. He could have said something, but didn't. Theirs was a casual arrangement, nothing more. She had no claim on him. Instead, he hopped onto a nearby flat-topped wall to people-watch for a while to calm his mood.

Daphne, meanwhile, was walking up the hillside enjoying time alone. History held no interest for her, but the funny-shaped stones and ruined buildings from long ago that littered the slopes made for interesting places to explore once the tourists had all gone. Trees provided defense from the summer heat, but she was used to it, just as she was used to the chilling snows of winter. A stray and, thus, a recent arrival to the clan, she'd soon become accepted as if she'd always known them. She loved this place. It was as if Delphi had always been entwined within her soul.

A young cat with an easy-going personality, she enjoyed the company of the others, but was happy to explore by herself. Her natural effervescence teased the boys and even had the old toms wistfully glancing her way while they dreamed of their days of glory. Daphne was a free spirit, wild at heart, gentle by nature, and in no hurry to have a litter of kittens to tie her down, unlike some of her peers. So she kept her distance from most of them. Except for one, the ginger one with the white markings; Apollo. He was one of the older ones, but he didn't talk down, and he was kind; more thoughtful than most, and good company. He had something her younger suitors lacked. She couldn't put a claw on it; if pushed she would have said it was a kind of gravitas, but he didn't act old, or aloof. Daphne felt comfortable with him, and he was never boring. Sometimes they would play games of chase around the stones or down in the olive groves just like an adolescent, but he never pushed things too far. She never stopped to wonder why, she just enjoyed the companionship.

She didn't dislike the others. Far from it; Daphne had many friends; but the attention could sometimes be a bit... exhausting. Perhaps her fluffy fur, longer than most, lent an air of playfulness. Even the tourists couldn't leave her alone if she got too close; they seemed unable to resist her amber, black and white colouring. So she kept her distance, reluctant to for them to touch her, unlike some she could mention, who would sell their soul for a ham sandwich.

HER FELLOW females, on the other paw, exerted pressure of a different kind. "Isn't it time you became a mother and settled down? What about lover-boy? We can see the way he looks at you, follows you about." Not yet; she valued her freedom. She saw what was happening with her friend Olympia. Olympia was older and liked to pretend she was more worldly wise, but Daphne knew it was all a front. Olympia didn't know half as much as she thought, despite her tours.

Yes, the 'tours'. She'd borrowed the idea from Apollo, as had some others. He seemed, somehow, to just know stuff. He liked to guide tourists around the site, past the bigger jumbles of stones, and the ones that stood on end, miaowing at them, telling them things. Things Daphne couldn't guess about. She was in awe of his imagination, making up all those stories. What the humans made of it all she had no idea, but it worked. They often made a fuss of him at the cafe by the road; fed him bits of meat from their sandwiches or platters, tried to befriend him. At those times she liked him least; the attention-seeking seemed so tawdry. She wouldn't say no to the titbits, though. They were a nice supplement to their otherwise frugal diet of locally hunted rodents and the dry food set out at the back of the museum by some well-meaning humans. Daphne wasn't above a bit of scavenging from the café herself, but she wouldn't go as far as her friend.

Olympia also spent time with Apollo, listening to his stories, and tried to copy his tours, but with far less success. The humans were less inclined to follow her. Maybe it was because her stories weren't so good, perhaps it was something else, but Daphne admired her persistence. It helped pass the days. That they were both competing for Apollo's attentions didn't bother her. She liked Olympia, and looked up to her, but all was fair in love and war. For the moment she just enjoyed teasing him along; it gave her a tiny thrill of power.

What would she do this afternoon? The sun was at its zenith, the earth hot beneath her pads. She thought about finding Apollo and spending some time with him in the shade somewhere. He could tell her about the view and the places only he seemed to know. She liked that; her mind would wander while he held forth, then she would drift off to sleep to the accompanying vibration of his purrs. Instead, she saw Jason. Grey-with-white-stripes Jason, a nice guy but a bit too eager and still a little young for her liking. He was well meaning, but not quite her type, and he looked to have far too much energy for a warm day like this. At the moment she didn't feel like being chased across the hillside or engaging in a friendly rough-and-tumble. She sighed. It might take a while to shake him off.

There was a sudden commotion. Loud miaows from down by the road. What was going on? A rustle in the bushes was followed by the sight of a ginger streak speeding up the hillside. Daphne couldn't remember ever seeing Apollo move so fast. One or two cats emerged in his wake, ambling as if wakening from sleep, looking around in bewilderment.

"What's happening? What's wrong?" she shouted.

"It's Olympia," came a voice. "She's been eaten by a car."

CHAPTER 3

KIDNAP

A SUPER-SIZED woman with loud jewelery had popped her into a sack, like a piece of garbage, then fed it into the rear mouth of the large car. Her partner did nothing to intervene. In fact, he'd given her the bag. Apollo saw it all from his perch on the wall by the café. He was horrified; this took customer dissatisfaction to an excessive level. Abducting the guide was totally unacceptable: did these people have no honour?

The callous brute got into the front, followed by his heartless wife and the monstrous shiny black metal beast reversed into the road and set off. Apollo's outrage grew. Olympia's tour might have been bad, but not so bad, surely. They had to do something, but what? He felt powerless. He needed to tell someone, at least. He decided to start at the top.

Apollo hurtled across the road, through a gap in the railings, and scrambled up the hillside in search of his father. Regardless of the quality of her tourist spiel, Olympia was a friend. A bit more than a friend, in fact. A sometime confidante, occasional playmate, and someone he'd spent a lot of time with, watching the world and the dumb tourists go by. He shadowed the well-trodden Sacred Way, following his own route. There should be a council of war about this.

Zeus was snoozing in a shady spot overlooking the remains of the temple. Apollo skidded to a halt, creating a small cloud of dust. The older cat's nostrils contracted in annoyance, and he raised his head, eyeing his son with suspicion.

"What?"

"One of those metal beasts has eaten Olympia and headed off down the road. You've got to do something, punish it, whatever. This is an outrageous attack. We shouldn't tolerate it."

Zeus studied him while Apollo looked away, his frustration increasing. He stretched a foreleg languorously, studied a pebble just beyond his paw. It was a lovely late summer's day. The heat reflecting from the stones, and the hypnotic accompanying buzz of the crickets, made it impossible to stay awake. This interruption was not welcome.

"You do realise they're not alive, you know? They're metal automatons. Machines." Zeus spat the word out, lowered his head onto his paws again, and settled down to sleep. Apollo stared at him in mute frustration. His father had as little time for the modern world and the current actions of humankind as he did, but this was different.

"She's a friend."

Zeus raised his head a fraction.

"Cats go missing all the time. It happens. Accept it and move on. You've got other friends. Tell them to be more careful. You know what humans are like; often stupid, yes, but some of them are vicious as well. You need to learn to tell them apart; sort the wheat from the chaff."

He lay his head down again and closed his eyes, satisfied with his pronouncement. Apollo studied him, a pool of dark, russet-coloured fur in irritation. He circled around, trying to organise his thoughts before he said something he would regret.

"Do you suggest we give in? Let it go? Give up on a

friend? Is that all?" He tried to keep his voice level; in some distant part of his mind a residual echo warned him not to provoke the older animal, although he no longer knew why. "I thought you were the leader of our group? Ignoring her sets a terrible example. Makes it look like we don't care. Anyway, she's a friend, like I said. I like her. I spend time with her..." His voice trailed off.

The older animal opened his eyes to a slit.

"This level of care for a mere mortal is not like you. She's not your only girlfriend, is she? I see you a lot more in the company of that other one, the little one with the longer fur; Daphne. I thought she was your 'special friend' these days? What am I missing?"

Apollo squirmed beneath his unflinching and menacing stare. Zeus was right, Daphne was more than just a friend, but she wasn't yet a mate. A wave of intense annoyance washed across him. Were his thoughts so transparent? Had he become their source of entertainment, the gossip of the pack? His ear twitched, and he had an almost irresistible desire to scratch it. To take his mind off it, he looked away, pretending to study the view.

"I like her, that's all. I don't give up on my friends so easily."

A fly buzzed between them: the older cat fixed it with a glare. He sighed. What an irritating start to the week.

CHAPTER 4

PYTHIA

INFURIATED BY his conversation with Zeus, Apollo passed through the sanctuary, rounding up as many of the elders as he could, but his spirits sank further. The more he thought about it, the less convinced he was that they could help. There had to be a way of finding Olympia and mounting a rescue; someone must have an idea? He fantasised about what he would do to the humans if he caught them but, without knowing where they had taken her, he was powerless. Someone should be punished for treating his friend like that. Who did they think they were? In the past he'd exacted violent, deadly revenge for a single disrespectful word or deed… hadn't he? He shook his head. Of course not; what a crazy idea. He was a cat.

Most of the elders were equally if not more disgruntled than Zeus at having their peace disturbed. Their attitude did little to lift Apollo's mood. He arrived at the clearing below the ruined temple which served as their meeting place, to find at least twenty cats had already assembled. They sat there, chuntering among themselves. Hera was grumpy.

"This had better be good," she muttered for the benefit of anyone nearby and staring across at Leto as if it was her fault. Their feud had lasted more years than either could remember and wasn't about to end. Some younger cats, who were usually out exploring at this time of day, were also arriving to find out what all the fuss was about. Out of respect, they stayed on the fringe of the gathering. Their leader emerged, standing on a low wall at the side of the clearing.

"We appear to have a problem," Zeus started. "There is a story that young Olympia is missing—has anyone seen her recently?" He gave Apollo a sidelong glance. The ginger cat could not contain his impatience. Giving Zeus a venomous glare, he stepped into their midst.

"They kidnapped her!" he miaowed at the top of his voice, his fury clear. "I saw it. Two humans, showing her no respect." Her, and by extension me, was what he meant. Who were these people to act so high-handedly? "They bundled her into a bag and put her in their car and went away. Up that way," pointing with his nose. "We need to mount a rescue." The older cats stared at him, then averted their gaze. There was an abrupt silence as if they didn't know what to make of this sudden rather embarrassing outburst. A murmur of conversation started.

"He sounds way too excitable to my mind," said one old boy. "He's lost all decorum."

"She should have taken more care," muttered a female.

"What was she thinking? She must have brought this on herself," agreed another. "Some of these youngsters are far too friendly."

"Too late to do anything about it now," grumbled an elderly black-and-white tom. "She's gone, and that's that."

"Stop it. Listen to me!" Apollo could not contain his exasperation. "This is a crime against us. One of our family. It might happen again, to anyone. We stick together—we always have. We must do something."

"What can we do? She was an idiot!" came a heated retort from the crowd. Tempers rose and arguments became

13

heated. Zeus imposed his authority.

"Silence!" That had an effect. After giving the assembled group a threatening stare, he turned to Apollo.

"You have no right to make demands of this group. They are not your subjects, but your companions, relatives, and friends." His son received his sternest expression. Apollo held his tongue, but his resentment was mounting.

"You have told us what happened, but what do you suggest we do? We cannot chase after her; she might be anywhere. We cannot move with a speed to match their metal chariots. There is nothing we can do."

Apollo stood his ground, glaring into the distance. Some older cats got to their feet, glancing at one another as if relieved to be leaving. Some younger ones started talking about assembling search parties with groups of them hitching lifts in other cars.

"Let us hear what Pythia says," Zeus said, turning to the old priestess who had arrived later than most, unnoticed by the majority. Perhaps the dotty old seer would bamboozle Apollo into silence.

Pythia rose stiffly to her feet and jumped onto a fallen stone at the edge of their clearing. From her perch, she looked down at the assembled group, and the angry animal in their midst, savouring the moment. She paused for effect, closed her eyes in concentration, and summoned the essence of Gaia. Raising her face toward the sky, she started speaking in a high-pitched monotone.

"While Old Zeus stares at his navel, chaos is unleashed and storm clouds gather. Doom will arrive from the north. The fortune of Athens is in ruins that only great intellect can release, but love, twice renounced, will be lost," she declared.

After a pause, she opened her eyes and a fleeting look of disquiet crossed her face. The other cats stared at each other in amazement, impressed; the old seer had outdone herself. No one had a clue what she meant. There was an awkward silence. At least her pronouncement diffused the tension as they all grappled to interpret her words. Zeus, however, looked outraged.

"It's sad, but she's really lost it," said Hera to her neighbour.

"Maybe," the other replied, "but you've got to admire her timing. It was like something out of the old stories!"

Apollo stared at the elderly cat, bewildered. What did she mean? He stepped forward to question her further, but she gave him a warning look, turned tail and disappeared. While the others argued among themselves about what she meant, he slipped out of the ring unnoticed, and pursued her. She circled the remains of the temple and followed a narrow track beside the ancient theatre. Above this she zig-zagged onto higher ground, skirting the stadium and out on the open mountainside. He followed at a distance. Finally she stepped aside onto a patch of level ground beside some low-growing bushes and turned to await him. He stood next to her, taking in the view. He hadn't been this high up the mountainside for years and had almost forgotten how far you could see. Mountain ridges receded into the distance in different shades of blue and grey. In a gap between them, the sea sparkled.

Pythia was in no hurry to fill the silence and continued enjoying the view. This was her favourite place, little visited by the rest, quiet and discreet. One of the oldest cats in the group, she had no offspring of her own. She avoided the others, keeping herself to herself, wandering around the upper ruins and into the deep cleft in the mountain where the spring emerged. It was rumoured she had explored the caves up in the hills where few of the group dared to venture.

Among all the Delphi cats, she was the only one Apollo avoided. When in her company she always seemed to scrutinise and judge him. Now, perhaps, she was the only one who might give him any answers.

"What am I supposed to make of that?"

"Do you know how many asked me, or my predecessors, that question down the years?"

Something squirmed in his brain; a deep knowledge long-suppressed stirred from sleep. Long forgotten names stirred like undead spirits rising from their graves. With them came the memory that wars and revolutions had started, and dynasties risen and fallen according to interpretations of the priestess's utterances, delivered from the depths of her trance.

"I am only a mouthpiece," she declared. "I say what the Spirit tells me. It is for others to decide what it means."

"The temple has fallen. The Oracle is dead."

"No. You forgot to look for it."

He studied her. How long had she known, and why had no one told him? If it lived still, why did he not feel it in every fibre of his being? His thoughts veered between anger and delight, but doubt assailed him. As if in answer, Pythia turned, pushed past the lower branches of two bushes and disappeared. He followed and found himself at the entrance to a narrow opening in the mountainside, beneath a high cliff. There was no sign of the other cat. With a deep breath, he plunged into the dark.

Instant night swallowed him. After a few steps he was blind, relying on his other senses. Faint air movement detected by his whiskers told him he was in a confined but open-ended space, most likely a passage. He advanced. It was broadly straight with only a few minor turns, and fortunately the ground was even. His nostrils told him

Pythia was a short distance ahead. She must have been here before; he could sense her scent on the walls to either side. If he concentrated, he could hear her faint padding steps.

Onward he went, wondering how far into the mountain this fissure led. Progress was slow, but after a long while, a more distant echo of footprints told him he was entering a larger space. He turned a corner and saw the faintest shaft of light, grey against the blackness. It was too dim to illuminate any walls, but within it, he saw curling and coiling, vapours rising from a crack in the cavern floor. It was warmer here. The gasses hissed as they escaped and there was a pungent, almost metallic odour in the air, with a hint of sulphur. Silhouetted in front of the twisting pillar of gas was Pythia. He approached cautiously. Without looking at him, she spoke.

"You see? The Oracle still lives. It's just harder to find."

He stared, scarcely able to take it in. Was it true? Something he'd believed forever lost? His sanctuary's foundation; his reason for being here? All those wasted years. Resentment boiled within him, but then, like the impact of a cold shower of rain, it evaporated. His followers had deserted him long ago. There was no point anymore. The Oracle had ceased to speak, and his temple had fallen into ruin. He was forgotten, his advice no longer sought. He had become irrelevant to them, a piece of folklore, nothing more.

"This is useless." He turned to go.

"I brought you here so you could ask your question."

He hesitated, torn. His indecisiveness itself annoyed him he never used to feel this way. With a suspicious glare toward Pythia, Apollo stepped into the column of smoke and closed his eyes.

CHAPTER 5

THE ORACLE

ONE STEP and he left the world behind. Blackness. Nothing. No senses, no sight, sound, smell or direction. No up, no down. Just floating. What was this place? There was no scale; nothing to measure. How big was it? Did it extend just beyond his reach, or did it go on forever? It was the absence of everything, a void; the opposite of existence. Did Chronos know of this place, or was it beyond his ken? Was this all there is, all there will ever be: the well of creation, or its grave? What was his purpose here? So many questions. His mind probed for answers, but the dark held no fear. Instead, on the fringes of his awareness, there was a vague familiarity; he had been here before.

Faintly at first but growing rapidly, colours and shapes appeared. They swirled around, forming and dissipating in constant motion, changing hue, altering their shape, increasing in solidity before evaporating into ribbons of gossamer only to appear again somewhere else. At least they brought some sense of scale, but with it the sensation of nausea. With an effort, he suppressed the desire to vomit.

Then came the sounds, not so varied at first, creaks and moans like wind moving through an old deserted building. They ebbed and flowed, solidifying then fading like an invisible storm. Then laughter; not joyous, but mocking and belittling, unpleasant, questioning, and cold.

A shape formed within the mass of colour. A man,

perfect and chiselled like the finest statue, his skin golden, his dark eyes piercing but his expression unreadable, a reflection of what he once was before the Transformation. Light shimmered around him. But what was this? The face changed, hardening to fury, chest and arms and hands red as if he had bathed in blood; it smeared his face, dribbled down his chin. Vivid and terrifying, he faded into mist, and the mocking laughter swelled once more before morphing into speech.

"What is it you want?"

A simple question, but it caught him out. He had no straightforward answer. What did he want? So many questions raced around his mind and he struggled to form a response, but blurted out, "I want to find Olympia." It was a manifesto, not an answer. Shame overwhelmed him. Shame he had allowed them to take her; shame at his neglect.

The laughter resumed, but more knowing now and more measured. He sensed he was being weighed in the scales, his fate uncertain while he hung there in the blackness, inert, waiting. Once outrage would have consumed him, now there was nothing. He was a blank canvas awaiting the artist.

Has mighty Apollo slumbered so long amid Delphi's dreams,
His soul so polluted that all the water in Castalia cannot cleanse?
Can an unclean god ever rescue his legacy?

The mocking laughter returned and gradually faded to be replaced by a swirl of visions in his mind's eye. They rushed past at increasing velocity. Some he recognised, others were opaque. Some were ancient, some recent, and others he could not place. There were visions of violence and scenes of destruction. Vistas of temples and ceremony

19

mingled with riot and bitter despair. Others were impossible to categorise; a blue-grey cat on the quayside of a small harbour, scenes of butchery and horror in a grimy nondescript room, screams cut short by the fall of a blade. An ancient city sacked and burning then standing once more; vast and proud. Prometheus chained, his gaoler laughing as he tightened the bolts fixing him to the rock, his sweat trickling down the stone. Then someone he thought he knew; kittens playing amid old stones tenderly watched by their tortoiseshell mother; surely Olympia? Before he could look deeper, other scenes of horror flashed toward him: an animal tortured, its eyes wide and terrified; a broad shallow river twisting through a mountainous wooded landscape under a blue sky, an old man in a cloak with a staff beneath a dark rocky roof, a boat crossing a black river and then, oh no, could it be? No, no, no, not that, not him, the one memory he kept locked away. Apollo fought with renewed vigour, but no matter how hard he struggled his sight zoomed in toward a rustic barn in a small village in a lonely mountain valley.

With one last effort of will, he hurled himself backward and into the world of rock and air, panting, stunned, sickened, and feeling drained. What had he become? He was supposed to help, not punish. Was there enough water or blood in all the world to purify him now?

He fell backwards, blind, nauseous, numb. Somehow, he found the passage and, ricocheting from wall to wall, staggered, and stumbled toward the light and fell onto the grass, gasping for air.

One thing was clear: his doom was set. He had no choice but to rescue Olympia. She was pregnant.

CHAPTER 6

OBSERVATIONS

THE LARGE grey cat lay under the shade of a low, gnarled tree on a comfortable bed of pine needles. To her right she could see the tops of the white columns of the restored Stoa of Attalos above the trees, to her left the classical outline of the Temple of Hephaestus. Behind her was Areopagus Hill, a vantage point thronged by tourists, jousting with their selfie-sticks for the best view of the Acropolis. From her hiding place Athena could observe the comings and goings of both the tourists and the other animals that moved within the archeological park of the modern Agora. It was a pale echo of its millennia-old heyday when, as the city's main open space, it served as meeting place, entertainment venue, its beating commercial heart, and the primary location for worship and ceremony. If only the stones, unearthed over the last century or so with such painstaking care, could speak what stories they would tell. If only she could remember. If only they could remind her.

It was a quiet morning with few people about. Most of her acolytes, the select group of female feline followers who lived with her under the trees in this urban woodland, were out and about seeking news or in search of breakfast. She would meet with them later on to share information about the day's comings and goings. For now, she was watching. And occasionally napping. Then watching once more. Things were coming to a head. She knew it in her heart and sensed it on the sluggish morning breeze. There was change afoot, but she could not yet tell how it would pan out. It seemed likely that the activities of the humans down on the edge of the Agora had something to do with it.

Athena was impatient for their excavations to bear fruit. In recent weeks her followers had delivered tidings of increasing unrest among various tribes across the city, and even of disquiet among other species resident in Athens, but she remained uninterested. She had tried to keep the peace in this city for longer than she cared to remember, and she had grown weary of politics. Let them let off steam for a while; they would be back in line before long. It might take a bit more effort with her chief enforcer and ally missing, but not impossible; she could be very persuasive when the time came, as could her followers.

At the moment her focus was on the activities of the human animals, and in particular this little group digging among the ancient stones. They were on the point of uncovering something important; she knew it. Something she'd lost; had been taken from her. She couldn't remember what it was, but she was certain she'd know it when she saw it, and that it would change everything. But how? So far such knowledge eluded her, and her frustration grew. It had taken them years to clear the ground and start digging, rediscovering their past one pebble at a time. Archeology took forever, but her confidence was growing that her long wait was about to end. She could feel it in the tips of her whiskers. But when?

A languorous stretch and it was time to have another look, as she had done yesterday and the day before that. She got up and walked across the park, skirting the ancient ruins to the gate where humans came and went. It was a warm day; there was no need to hurry. Athena attracted little attention as she strolled out through the gate and down onto pedestrianised Adrianou Street. On the far side of this narrow thoroughfare was a row of restaurants and cafés, and behind them another set of railings overlooking the archeological dig site. She made for her favourite café and hung around for a while, glaring at selected members of the clientele until they caved in and shared their food— few could resist the piercing gaze of those bright emerald green eyes; they gave the subtle hint of retribution, should the subject fail to comply.

It wasn't health food from the feline perspective, but Athena had developed quite a taste for baklava, and who was there to reprimand her? Hunger pangs sated, she found a quiet spot beneath an unoccupied table and observed the activity in the sunken space below. The dig had removed several strata of the city's more recent history to uncover foundations and debris of a building from a much older era, and everything built over this space in between. It was like looking back in time, and it fascinated the grey cat. Her gaze flicked from one person to another. She wouldn't have paid them any more attention had they been prey.

A part-excavated pit between the base of two columns absorbed most of her attention. The earth at the back was different in colour and texture, not stratified like elsewhere, more jumbled. It looked like the site of an old well. Many things were cast into wells in the old days. Could it be in there? At the back of her mind whirled the faint, fleeting echo of cries, flames, burning buildings and smoke against a dark sky, people running everywhere, shouting, screaming, some carrying spears and swords, others their belongings and babies. An image of panic and slaughter and chaos. It faded as quickly as it had come, leaving her puzzled. Was it a memory, an echo from the stones, or something else?

She shook her head and renewed her focus on the scene below, but now she had another thought; this place must remain secret from all other cat tribes and gangs of the city. What if some opportunist got wind of her interest in it? What if the precious object she sought fell into the wrong paws? It was imperative that the excavation, and her interest in it, be kept secret. Her followers must maintain a close watch and repel intruders. She must be ready to act when the time was right, and before anyone else. It was a delicate matter.

Athena turned and retraced her route back into the wooded hillside above the Agora, thinking all the while, then called her followers to her and addressed them.

"Ladies, we are on the cusp of important developments, of which I cannot speak as yet. However, change is on the way which should benefit all of our kind across this great city—I feel it. But the period just before this revelation is the most dangerous. If I am correct, they are about to uncover a tool that, if it falls into the wrong paws, will spread division and dissent. We have to place a cordon around the site where the humans are digging. It must be made secure. No cat is to be allowed through. You are the instruments of my authority in this; my gatekeepers. You have my permission to use whatever force is necessary to deter intruders."

The demure sisterhood studied her with appropriate gravitas, despite their misgivings. They left it to one of their most experienced members, Herse, to voice their concerns.

"There is trouble brewing across the city. Our spies are hearing rumours of attacks, war between the gangs, and more. Surely, we should be going out, speaking to them, trying to prevent violence between our kin, not turning our backs or hiding away?"

The grey cat studied her. "This is more important. War among the clans comes and goes. They're always squabbling over territory. What I'm talking about will affect all of us for the rest of our lives. You have to trust me on this; that's all I will say."

She looked across all the gathered cats. All averted their gaze and none spoke up, even though most shared Herse's views.

"You know what you have to do. We will set a perimeter at the gates where humans and some of our kind get through, on both ends of Adrianou Street and on Astiggos, at the corners of Thisiou and Agiou Fillipou. This area is to be cordoned off. No cats to enter under pain of death until I have recovered the artefact I seek. We must maintain the watch day and night." She turned to one of her senior followers. "Penelope, you will organise the changing of guards at appropriate intervals." She turned back to the others. "No one is to breathe a word to anyone. Is that clear?"

Several of them exchanged wary glances, but there were no other dissenting voices. With the meeting over, they turned and went to their various watch posts, prepared to carry out the instructions of their leader to the letter.

YANNIS AND his informant crouched on the edge of a flat roof, looking over a low parapet. They peered down into the fenced-off excavation of the Stoa Poikile. It was slow going. Nothing seemed to change day after day. Yannis was bored with the stakeout after only ten minutes.

"Wait a minute, you'll see her," his contact informed him. "She's usually here around now."

He was right. After a few minutes a cat appeared behind

the railings opposite, about 50 metres away. It was a large animal, its colour difficult to determine given the angle of the sun, but Yannis was sure it was her. He studied her for a while. She wasn't as large as the boss, but she was larger than most cats he knew. A bit more supple, he guessed, but not as strong. She was staring at one particular human labouring down below. He followed her gaze. The subject of her scrutiny was scratching at the earth with a small trowel. In its other hand, it held a brush which it used periodically to clean dust or small particles away from whatever it was it was trying to dig out of the ground.

He watched for a few minutes more, then looked up to his fellow observer opposite. Every movement below entranced her. Was this it, he thought? The object she sought? He had no way of knowing, but he'd better tell the boss, just in case. He and his companion crept back from the edge of the roof and out of sight. He looked thoughtful; not a frequent occurrence.

"You'd better keep a close watch on her. Let me know as soon as anything happens. I want to know if she makes a move, any move, OK?"

"But I can't watch round the clock! I need to sleep," the other cat protested.

Yannis looked at him in exasperation. "Get your friends to help. You must have some?" he sneered.

The other cat looked doubtful, but consented. In fact, he had very few friends, just a few acquaintances, and most of them he could barely tolerate. He anticipated the response if he asked them to keep watch on a dull patch of earth for hours at a time. He'd be a laughingstock. But getting on the wrong side of Yannis and his colleagues wouldn't do much for his health either. He sighed and hoped nothing much happened while he was asleep.

CHAPTER 7

ENTRAILS

AT THE edge of their territory, by the perimeter fence of the disused factory, the Botrys Gang had an admittedly pretty dirty rat surrounded. It was dead. In fact, it had been dead for a week, lying here under a dusty bush in the summer heat, and it stank. The cats gave it as wide a berth as possible, apart from one whose mission had brought them here: the Seer, Melanippus. He had the unenviable job of reading its entrails, and they would lap up every word. A lot hinged on his interpretation; were the Fates with or against them in their proposed war? What would be their leader's reaction? If the portents were bad, it could be disastrous.

Kratos watched the seer impassively, giving no outward sign of impatience; no twitch of the ear, flick of the tail, or movement of any kind. His inscrutability came laden with menace, and he stared at Melanippus with an intensity only reserved for small rodents. This rat, however, was something else. Kratos knew it was a sign; knew its entrails must be read, and he'd brought just the animal for the job, but he wanted results. The right results. This reading was the last piece in the jigsaw, Melanippus's chance to shine, his moment in the spotlight.

Melanippus had the strong suspicion his immediate future health depended on a successful reading. Here on the front line, well inside the olfactory event horizon, the aroma was far from therapeutic, and his stomach already in rebellion. He approached the corpse. One wrong move might cause him to vomit; an omen he could do without. He swallowed, trying to bite down on the bile already threatening his throat. He was aware of his heart pounding against his ribs and the prickle of sweat on his pelt. With eyes half-closed, he raked his claws down the distended belly of the animal from nose to tail. Its flesh split easily like over-ripe fruit, and the stench of putrefaction released had a near physical impact. He had to get this over with, and quickly. The contents of his own stomach were lurching around, and he was in danger of losing the battle to keep them still. Concentrate!

Scents tell their own story and sometimes hold important messages; who was last here, what they'd had for breakfast, how long ago, and so on? He could do it, he knew, but right now, facing sensory overload, he couldn't think straight. Don't faint, don't squirm, just do it. He stared down at the body and its spilled innards in acute discomfort. He did not lack evidence; getting close to it was the problem. He closed his eyes.

"You've had long enough."

The encouragement he didn't want. His mind went blank. Oh no, what does all this mean? What to say. Despite the assault on his senses, a new unwelcome sensation; a dry mouth. He opened it without the faintest idea what would come out.

"Er..."

He sensed, rather than saw, the impatient twitch of a tail behind him. Eyes boring into the back of his head. Where was his Sight? Don't desert me. Not now. Calm, calm. Try to stay calm.

"Well, it's very clear...."

"What's clear?"

"Er, this, this is the liver, and you can tell a lot from the liver, obviously." He chanced a glance at his leader, trying to buy time, but instantly regretted it. Kratos cocked his head to one side, waiting. Oh well, in for a penny, "... such as the diet of the deceased, for example, and what the weather was like when they passed away, of course." He looked around, desperate for support. There was none. Melanippus looked down again and once more struggled to avoid being sick. "You see that?" he squeaked excitedly, noticing something for the first time. "That's a kidney, and it's... it's facing over there to that building which means...." He stopped, groping for words. Almost imperceptibly, Kratos adjusted his position. If this joker was lying, there would be hell to pay, and he felt like making a deposit. Melanippus saw the subtle movement and speeded up his analysis. His voice squeaked up a notch.

"So, it clearly means whatever danger is coming is going to come from over there." He nodded to the south, and the building he'd been referring to, and glanced up, hoping it was enough. The look on the large animal's face showed he expected more. He tried to swallow but had no saliva, so he stared down again in desperation at the unfortunate rodent. The Sight arrived at last.

"Look, look," he cried excitedly, treading the ground with his front paws and almost hopping up and down on the spot. "His nose is pointing north, which must mean a vital portent is going to arrive from that direction soon, and, and..." He again paused but this time his eyes widened in shock as the distended stomach of the rat twitched. It was as if it contained a seething mass of snakes—something was in there. With a sickening movement, the lining burst and three fat, juicy maggots emerged, wriggling to freedom. Melanippus took an involuntary step backward, both fascinated and horrified at the same time, his own stomach lurched alarmingly.

"And there you have it," he croaked, his throat constricted as he tried to keep everything down. "Danger from the south and three important portents from the north." He looked up at Kratos triumphantly. Kratos stared back. He needed more. "Or three messages of importance," equivocated the Seer. "Or something like that; three of them anyway." He realised he might have to identify and interpret these portents whatever they might be, so he'd better gain a little wriggle room. He looked down again where the maggots were now enjoying plenty of wriggle room of their own, wished he hadn't, and turned and retched explosively. The other cats politely averted their eyes. Most of them were grateful to have an excuse to back off. They exchanged glances, impressed by the analysis. It was cutting-edge stuff. They could interpret and discuss and reassess this for weeks.

The dark-coloured cat looked thoughtful. He looked around at the retreating cats, gave Melanippus one last suspicious glare, and languidly made his way back to the centre of his lair. This abandoned factory had been their home for years and had so far avoided demolition and redevelopment. Its high walls still stood, but the roof over the main hall had long since gone. Within this larger open space, nowadays trees grew, providing excellent cover and protection from prying eyes from above. An important consideration regarding his enemy. It had the added advantage of providing lots of shady resting places on hot days. It, and the fenced-off wasteland on which it stood, made an excellent base, and crucially it was free from humans, apart from the watchman in his little hut by the road, but he didn't bother them. This fortunate circumstance provided the Botrys

Gang not just with their home and safe ground, but also plenty of space in which to relax between their thieving and intimidation exercises in the neighbourhood. It also provided excellent hunting opportunities, attracting mice and rats from the surrounding area, to meet their doom.

The Lord of this domain was Kratos, a large burly cat of amber and black colouring. He was no ordinary suburban thug and opportunist; Kratos was different. Kratos thought bigger. Kratos had ambition. Kratos held grudges, often for centuries. Kratos was a Titan. Driven by a malign but cunning intellect, scarred from a hundred fights and well versed in the art of intimidation, Kratos ruled through fear. Huge, bulky, and formidably strong, he resembled nothing more than a fur-covered boulder, but when this rock started to roll no-one wanted to jive, not even the many sons and daughters he had spawned, the semi-divine who with their arrogance and cruelty formed the malevolent core of the gang and helped maintain its rigorous discipline. A discipline that made them feared by their peers across the city. They called themselves the Botrys Gang after the disused factory they used as their base, and in addition to Kratos' extended family, they comprised a motley crew of ruffians and outcasts from across the neighbourhood and beyond. Their territory covered a large swathe of northern Athens. Most other beasts in those parts lived in fear of getting on the wrong side of the Botrys Gang.

They were no ordinary gaggle of thugs, though. What marked them out from other groups of feral opportunists in the city was their organisation and purpose. Kratos held absolute authority and had done since before any of them could remember; they bowed to the power of his will. A slow burning sense of injustice and relentless desire for revenge drove him. First kindled a long time ago, and fueled by resentment at his lot in life, it came to possess his waking thoughts, an unshakable sense that he'd been overlooked and made unwelcome, pushed to the fringes by what passed for the ruling authority in the city. He felt unappreciated by them, and by one animal in particular, the arrogant daughter of Zeus. Once he and his siblings served at the Sky Father's right hand; now he despised the very name.

Kratos could no longer pinpoint the origin of his hatred, but it consumed him. Once he was allied, a member of the Olympus hierarchy. Once he had been the most faithful of followers. He'd sat at the top table, a loyal servant with power and influence on the inside, but something had happened. They had cast him aside, and now, disdained by the pompous self-centred hypocrites from Olympus, he'd been left to scavenge for living space here on the fringes of the city, kept distant from its ancient heart like an exile of old. The hurt was almost physical. He resented this exile. He had striven over the years to build his power anew, and now he wanted vengeance.

His plans were coming together, but before he could act, before he could goad his disciples, supine and intimidated as they were, he needed conclusive proof; a clear and compelling interpretation of the signs to show them fate was on their side, and they were unbeatable. It would cement his power over them. Divination was the ultimate piece of the jigsaw, and there was enough in the seer's rambling analysis to confirm his belief that the time was ripe to launch an attack. It was obvious that danger lay to the south, that was where their enemy resided. The nonsense about 'portents from the north' he could live with; there were no meaningful gangs up there, no one with any force to trouble him. No reading was ever perfect; that part was a red herring. He should set one of them to watch the sky for birds travelling in threesomes, but there was no need to go overboard. Everything else stacked up, and there were no further omens. Nothing could now stop him. The time for action was nigh. There was one last component to slot into place, and that would happen very soon.

Back in the centre of his domain Kratos called Yannis over for an update on the dig. He had no idea what was the source of her obsession, but whatever it was, he had to have it. Not for its own sake, but because it would be the final insult, her treasure stolen from under her nose. It would be the clearest demonstration yet of her waning powers. He would shatter Athena's influence for good, and drive her out of her home. He ordered his lieutenant to redouble the watch and went to his sleeping quarters.

CHAPTER 8

THE QUEST BEGINS

AFTER A few moments spent gathering his thoughts, Apollo rose and set off down the hill without a backward glance. Pythia watched him go but said nothing. It was still mid-afternoon, the sun high in the sky. A new sense of purpose guided his footsteps and lifted his head higher, although he still had little idea how to execute his search. Again he followed his own path, avoiding the tourists thronging the Sacred Way. At a small clearing in the pine trees near the entrance, Daphne and Jason were waiting.

"We heard all those things they said earlier, and we didn't want you to sneak off without us," Daphne said, by way of greeting.

"We're going to help," Jason added.

He looked at them, grateful for their support. At least someone in this place cared. His heart went out in gratitude to both of them. They sat in the shade of the trees for a while to talk.

"Olympia's one of us. We've got to do something," said Jason.

Apollo paused, unsure what to say. Did Jason really care about her enough to want to help? He looked into the other cat's face. Once he could read what was in men's hearts in an instant, but the power eluded him now. Besides, he didn't want to spurn any offer of help.

"She's my best friend, just tell us what we need to do,"

added Daphne. Apollo was glad she was here, her presence always lifted his spirits in a way no one else could.

"That's the trouble, I don't know what to do," he admitted. "All we know is that she's in Athens. Probably."

Daphne broke the silence. "What did Pythia mean? I've heard of Athens; it's a big city, isn't it? But they say it's a long way away. How do we get there?"

Like all their tribe they knew Delphi was sometimes called the 'navel of the world', but why would Zeus be gazing at it? None of the rest of Pythia's pronouncement made any sense to them. It was impossible to disentangle. After a while, they stopped trying to interpret the crazy old cat's announcement and thought back to how they could find Olympia.

"Athens, Athens," Apollo muttered to himself, turning the word over in his mind. Again, the name was so familiar. He must have been there before, but when? It was as if his brain consisted of cotton-wool and his memories hovered just out of reach. The modern world was as much a mystery as trying to recall the true location of the Minotaur's labyrinth.

"If Athens is a big place, how do we find her when we get there?" asked Jason.

They were at a loss until Daphne brightened and sat up, her tail twitching as an idea formed. "We must tell the police," she said.

Apollo looked doubtful. "But how will Sergeant Papadopolous help? He can't understand us."

"None of them are good at our language," Jason agreed. "They can only just manage 'feed me.'"

"Not Sergeant Papadopolous, silly," Daphne cried. "I mean Hector the police dog."

The other two thought about it for a while. Hector was

a large, somewhat overweight German Shepherd avoided, as far as possible, by the other animals in the village. He was bad-tempered, had a vicious bark, and was rumoured to bite those who dared to talk back. He was particularly hostile to the cats of the Sanctuary. They weren't 'respectable;' in fact he regarded them as little more than outlaws or brigands.

"He won't help us," said Jason. "He hates us."

"He'll listen to me," said Daphne. She sat up, her back rigid with determination. Apollo watched her in admiration, loving her attitude; in fact, pretty much everything about her. Her fearlessness was one of the qualities he admired most. With Daphne around, anything seemed possible.

He forced his mind back to the task in hand. "OK," he said. "Let's give it a go. We've got no other ideas and we have to do something."

They set off, slipping through a gap in the railings and darting along the pavement toward the village. It was a sultry afternoon and very few tourists were walking in their direction, but even so the three cats hugged the wall and did their best to stay out of reach of those they saw, darting past them as quickly as possible. The kidnap of one of their friends had shaken their trust in humans.

The place modern humans call Delphi is a short walk from the ancient site, hidden around a bending road. It is familiar to all the cats of the Sanctuary. Most of them scavenge for food from customers of the cafés on the edge of the village from time to time. The Police Station was nearby. More specifically, it was Sergeant Papadopolous's house (and Hector's residence), the front room of which doubled as his office and operational centre. The house was set a couple of meters back from the pavement, behind a dusty and rusty set of iron railings that had once been painted olive green. The cats slowed as they approached, keeping an eye out for both Hector and the villagers, and in particular the smaller humans who could be surprisingly fast and determined to make friends with them whether they liked it or not.

Hector's reactions might be slower than theirs, but he was big and strong, had a very loud, intimidating bark, and was quite short-tempered. They spotted him sleeping under a wooden bench beside the front door. Apollo stopped at the gate, struck by indecision, but Daphne brushed past him and boldly approached the large dog, her tail rising in polite greeting like a furry flagpole. Hector slumbered on, snuffling and snoring. She tried mewing at him, pushing her face close to his.

"Hello," she said. "We need help."

Hector stirred as her scent filled his nostrils, triggering a response deep within his sleeping brain. He opened his eyes, focusing on a fuzzy amber and black face in front of him, then started and jerked upright, banging his head on the underside of the bench. He barked at the sharp pain and lunged forward sluggishly.

Daphne jumped back, the fur on her back standing upright, but held her ground. "We need your help," she said again, flicking a glance from side to side, to check her exit was clear if she needed to run. Hector lumbered to his feet. Apollo studied her perky little ears, rather than pay attention to the unfolding conversation. How did she maintain such poise in front of the big dog many times her size? Mortals could still surprise, and this one melted his heart, his affection melding into something stronger.

Hector looked poised to launch into a long bad-tempered tirade, but it died in his throat when he saw Daphne had not yet fled. As he hesitated, she regained a measure of confidence and slowly, deliberately sat down in front of him, appearing to study the walls and door of the police station while watching him out of the corner of her eye. Her fur was still fluffed out and her heart beating fast, but she attempted to keep a semblance of feline coolness. She hoped the dog would understand the subtleties of her body language.

"We have an emergency," she said. "One of us has been stolen."

"Kidnapped by humans," Apollo added, snapping into the present and approaching.

Hector turned to him, still angry at being disturbed. There was a long pause. Curiosity got the better of him. "What do you mean, 'stolen'?" He addressed Daphne, but Apollo cut across her.

"Two humans put her in a sack and took her away in a large car. Just after she had given them a lovely tour of the sanctuary."

"Maybe they took a shine to her, wanted a companion animal?" the police dog said.

"No, they were very rough with her. They didn't look nice," Apollo said, edging closer. "And besides, we don't play well as 'companion animals.' We value our freedom." He couldn't keep an element of sarcasm from his voice.

"And you know the prophesy," Jason said. He stepped forward, reciting from memory. "The cats of Delphi have guarded the Sanctuary since time out of mind. If anything happens to us, if we ever leave, then the world will crumble."

Hector was as familiar with old superstitious rubbish as any animal in the village, but he had never paid it any attention. "Load of nonsense," he growled. He shared the sentiment of many of the village animals; the annoying cats at the Sanctuary might have been there forever, but it didn't mean he had to like them. Still, no matter how much he begrudged the fact, he had to admit they were citizens of Delphi and therefore under the protection of the police. Also, there was a sincerity about these three in particular that seemed to show they were telling the truth. If so, it appeared one of Delphi's animal citizens had been abducted, and that was a crime. He sat down.

"So what do you want me to do about it?" he asked.

"We need to find out where they've taken her," Apollo said.

"They took her this morning," Daphne added.

"They went that way," Apollo said, pointing with his nose toward Arachova.

"She won't be there," said Hector. "I know Clytemnestra, the police dog at Arachova, and she says the visitor cars never stop there, they go on down into the plains towards Athens."

"That's what we thought," Apollo said. "That's where we have to go. To Athens. To find her and bring her home." He looked around at the others.

"Athens is huge," Hector told him. "Even if you get there, you'll never find her."

Daphne turned to face him. "If there are cats in Athens, we will find her," she said. Hector doubted it, but said nothing.

"Where's Athens?" asked Jason. They all looked at him. "I mean, I've heard of it 'n all, but…"

"Follow me," said Hector, turning and going into the police station. The cats followed, hesitant and sniffing for hidden dangers. Curiosity overcame their natural suspicion of enclosed spaces. They found a room filled by an enormous desk that faced the door and had some chairs in front. Against the walls were lots of cupboards and filing cabinets. The whole room smelled of vinyl seat covers and furniture polish, mingled with paper and dust. At another time it could have kept them busy for hours. On one wall was an enormous picture. Hector stopped in front of it, looking up.

"Wow" said Jason, craning his neck to see it. "That's huge. What is it?"

"This is a map," Hector told him. "Of Greece," he added. He pointed his snout toward a large red plastic spot stuck on it. "We are there," he said, "and the large black blob where all the lines join up is Athens."

The cats surveyed the map, with its pleasant colours and zig-zag lines, but it meant nothing to them. Apollo jumped up on the desk to get a better look. He glanced down at Hector.

"So how do we get there? Is it far to walk?"

The police dog snorted.

"For a start, you can get down from there," he said. "That's police property. It's not for walking on." Apollo ignored him. Hector pretended not to notice, and after a moment, continued. "You need to get a bus. There's one every afternoon to Athens," he said. "It leaves from the café at the end of the village at 4pm."

"When is that?" they chorused.

"A bit later on, halfway to sunset," the dog said. He turned away from the enormous clock on the wall, hoping the cats wouldn't notice it; his ability to read the time was a bit hit-and-miss. He was in luck; none of them knew what the big round thing on the wall was for.

A door opened at the back of the room and Sergeant Papadopolous stepped through, having finished his lunch. He stopped in his tracks when he spotted the cats. Apollo was still on the desk. "Scram," he shouted, waving his arms around and advancing. The cats darted outside and ran down the street. He gave Hector an accusing look.

"What did you let them in for?" he said, his voice raised. "Stupid boy." He went to smack the dog, but Hector stepped back out of reach, bowing his head and wagging his tail. He gave an apologetic whine. Grumpy, and muttering a few oaths, the police officer sat down at his desk and looked through a file of crime reports. Hector, feeling guilty, slunk back outside, and reproached himself for being taken in by those damn cats.

By now Apollo, Jason, and Daphne were approaching the café at the end of the village main street. They slowed down.

"I've seen these busses," said Apollo, "but I've never noticed where they stop."

"We'd better wait here until it comes," said Jason.

They looked for suitable spots, in the shade, out of the way of clumsy human feet. Underneath parked cars was good—hidden from casual observers, but allowing them to monitor what was happening. Other cats would spot them, but with any luck, leave them alone.

The afternoon dragged on. An occasional vehicle passed by. Some tourists paused at the café over the road for a cool drink and something to eat. They considered heading over the road in search of titbits, but several warning glares from the café owner's cats made them think twice. A mutual hostility existed between the cats of the village and those of the Sanctuary, and vice versa. Scavenging for food on their patch didn't go down well, even though almost all the Sanctuary cats had done it.

"I'm bored." Daphne had her head on her paws and her eyes closed, and was trying to take her mind off food.

"I'm hungry," said Jason, trying to avoid looking at the café. The food scents spreading on the still air were enticing, despite being mixed with the aroma of oil and grease from the underside of the car. "They can't be so bad, can they? I bet I could make friends with them?"

"We're on a rescue mission," Apollo reminded him. "We can't afford to get distracted."

Jason was about to argue when they heard a bus coming down the main street. At the café, people collected their bags and gather on the pavement. The bus appeared and stopped at the roadside near the cats' hiding place with a loud hiss from its brakes. They gathered themselves. Apollo gave the others a warning look.

"Ready?"

Humans were milling everywhere, most of them carrying huge bags and suitcases. There were two doors, one at the front and another halfway down, but around each a scrum of people gathered, jostling to climb onboard. The cats tensed, waiting beneath their car, watching intently.

"How are we going to get on?" asked Daphne.

"It's a nightmare," groaned Jason. "We'll get trampled to death." Apollo wondered if his companion was having second thoughts about this adventure.

The bus driver clambered down the front steps, parting the crowd and opening the luggage hatches along the sides of the bus. People surged forward, handing him bags which he flung into the dark hold. The crowd thinned as more people got onboard, and the number with cases went down. Apollo spotted an opportunity.

"When he's looking the other way, we'll get past him and into the hold with the bags," he told the others. They circled toward the back of the bus and edged closer. No one noticed them; they were focused on making sure the driver took their luggage, then scrambling to get a seat. The driver started arguing with one of the passengers, giving the cats their chance. They shot behind him and dived into the dark of the hold, out of reach. They were in luck; no one noticed them, except for old Kostas back at the café.

"Hey!" he shouted across to the bus driver, "you've got stowaways!" but the driver ignored him; he was too busy arguing.

Apollo, Jason, and Daphne scrambled out of sight behind and between suitcases and backpacks. There was plenty of space to hide, but as they were settling down the hatch slammed shut and they were in pitch dark. Cats have excellent night vision, but this was different; there was no light at all.

There was a slight but detectable tremor in Jason's voice. "Oh no, this was a bad idea. I don't like this." Daphne was whimpering nearby. Apollo somehow found her in the dark, butted his head against hers and purred reassurance. Despite the noise and vibration of the engine, the other two could hear it, or sense it and the powerful calming influence it exerted.

"We'll be OK," Apollo said, "they have to open the door sometime." This huge vehicle they had boarded, with its swerving movements, vibrations and constant background engine thrum, seemed almost alive, but so did he. With every passing mile the fog that shrouded his thinking seemed to thin, and he became more confident of his decision to leave. He couldn't remember the last time he had been away from Delphi, but at the outset of this quest, and in contrast to his companions, Apollo experienced a strange exhilaration.

They tried to settle down, but as the bus lurched around corners luggage sometimes shifted around them, forcing them to adjust position. After some time the road became less twisty and such movements ceased. Afternoon passed into evening, but for the travellers it remained dark, airless, and hot and the journey seemed endless.

It was mid-evening before the bus arrived at the terminus. As soon as the engine cut out its rumble was replaced by the shuffling and stamping of feet above them as the passengers stood up and gathered their belongings. In the dark the cats tensed, waiting for the luggage compartments to open, bringing them the opportunity to escape.

After a few moments, the driver released the catches and lifted the luggage compartment doors, admitting a little extra light from the dim streetlights. He started hauling out luggage while a throng of impatient passengers gathered.

"We run as fast as we can to get away from this bus," Apollo whispered to his companions. "Wait for my signal, then we go. We'll meet by those trees over there." He pointed them out with his nose. The others could just see them as they peered past the forest of human legs toward the far side of the tarmac. The driver worked his way closer, removing their cover. As soon as there was space in front of him, Apollo made a bolt for it, streaking out of the hold, followed by his companions. The driver pulled back in shock, and several people jumped aside as the cats darted past, swerving around and between them, dodging suitcases and backpacks and the occasional grabbing hand. One or two laughed or exclaimed to see such enterprising stowaways. Several wondered aloud whether they'd ripped their bags open, or worse. A couple expressed concern about their welfare in the big city. Apollo, Jason, and Daphne weren't listening, they were free and running, relieved to be out of the horrible hot and claustrophobic bus and into the open air. Wherever it was.

INTERLUDE

STORIES OF THE DISAPPEARED 1

OLYMPIA SAT in misery, head bowed, in a wire-mesh cage, one of many in a yard at the back of a building. She couldn't tell how long she'd been there, but it seemed interminable. The other cages were mostly populated by cats, but some contained dogs, either expecting or with a new litter of puppies. The filth and the stench were offensive to her eyes and nose. The place was never cleaned. She wondered how long they'd keep her here and tried not to think what might happen after.

To provide a distraction, Olympia tried talking to the small cat in the neighbouring compartment. She was unresponsive at first, but as trust grew, she spilled out her story.

"It happened while I was out burgling. I was looking for socks. Anything small and made of fabric, really. The boss likes that kind of stuff. It's his 'thing'—he likes to rub his nose into them, roll around on them and soak up the scent of all the sweaty humans who've worn them. To each his own, I guess." She caught Olympia's look and tried to explain. "The good thing is in return for a bit of thievery I get a safe bed, a fair share of the hunting spoils, and I'm a respected member of the gang. We look out for one another."

She paused, lost in thought. "Or at least we did until I got nabbed. I suppose I got too cocky. I'd found an empty flat on the ground floor with the window open just wide enough for me to squeeze in. I had the run of the place. I found a basket where they dump their laundry." She looked up, with a gleam in her eye. "It was like a gold mine. I had the pick of anything. Of course, a lot of it was too big to carry, but there was plenty of underwear too. 'Smalls' I've heard them called. 'Bigs' for someone my size, but whatever. I got a mouthful of knickers and headed back out. It was all going well until I went round the corner into Kalama Street. I was concentrating on not tripping up, so I forgot to pay proper attention. It was a kitten's mistake." She sounded philosophical. "She came out from behind a parked car, all friendly like. Made some cooing noises. I was suspicious right from the start and backed away. I didn't want to let go of my prize, but there was something about this human that felt wrong. She was trying too hard to be friendly."

Olympia looked up. This human sounded all too familiar. Her companion continued, now only too happy to relay her story.

"I paused to think. That was my undoing. Thinking. I should have just dropped the pants and run. But I'd put a lot of effort into getting them that far and I wanted to please the boss. I wanted to get the praise, to feel a bit special. I still wanted to take them with me. I might've got to share his den for the night. I could even get to join the inner circle with all the important ones." She looked at Olympia, seeking understanding. She didn't need to worry, Olympia knew the politics of feral cat communities very well, with their jealousies and petty rivalries, but she was grateful that at Delphi there had been no one of such a thuggish nature in charge. Theirs had been a far more benign society. Her neighbour continued.

"That's what did for me. Too many useless thoughts.

She had something behind her back. A net. She was quick with it for something her size. Once it had landed on me, that was it. I struggled but just got tangled up worse and worse. It was no use. I snarled at her, let her have a piece of my mind, but she put me in some kind of bag and bundled me into one of those cars they all have. So I ended up here." She looked around, disdainful. "There must be cats in here from every gang in the city, some civilians too. Not that I want to talk to them." She turned to Olympia once more. "At least you're not like them, bleating all the time about how unfair it all is. I don't trust them." She cast her eyes down, bitterness in her voice. "Thinking. It's over-rated."

CHAPTER 9

ATHENA AND HERSE

BENEATH THE twisted olive trees on the hill above the Agora, Athena was deep in conversation with Herse. The dusty coloured cat with her darker brown ears and tail was making another attempt to get her mistress to take the latest threat from the gangs seriously.

"The unrest is growing. My contacts among the citizens are getting edgy. They see many more comings and goings within the criminal community, and lots of them are feeling intimidated."

"We mustn't refer to them as criminals," Athena corrected. "They're 'wilder,' they live off their wits. They aren't all criminally inclined."

"I haven't met one yet that isn't a qualified burglar."

"Yes, but that applies to almost all our kind. We call it 'opportunism' when it is performed by one of our own."

Herse tried again. "Things are getting out of hand. We've got reports of mass raids on market stalls, particularly fishmongers, large-scale fights on waste ground and sometimes in respectable neighbourhood parks, increased theft—basically anything shiny is a target—and lots more including intimidation. I'm also getting feedback that quite a few cats are disappearing. It's serious."

The grey cat was dismissive. "This sort of thing happens now and then. It's cyclical. The gang leaders get big ideas, they throw their weight about a bit, have a few run-ins with their rivals. It all settles down after a while. We're in the middle of the worst phase at the moment. It'll change. It always does." She licked her paw and started washing her face.

Exasperated, Herse looked away. In previous years they had been much more proactive. They had gone out and knocked sense into the wayward souls out there until they got the message. Sitting here on the hill behind a screen of sentries and doing nothing seemed like an evasion of duty.

Athena had a good go at her right ear, then paused. "You should relax more," she said. "Spend some time with that young boy of yours. What's his name, Erichthonious? Check up on him, see who he's hanging out with. Take some time to enjoy the Plaka. Have some fun."

Herse couldn't believe her ears. She was being told to take a break, relax, go away for a while, stop pestering. She'd never heard Athena like this before; it seemed un-natural. The thought of being effectively cast out made her shudder. This part of the city, beneath and among the trees adorning the ancient Agora, was her home. She belonged here. Away from the twisting narrow streets of the Plaka in the Acropolis's shadow, the heart of old Athens. It was the neighbourhood she'd grown up in, where she'd learned to jostle and fight with every other scruffy kitty for at-tention and food. She didn't want to go back. She'd been little more than an adolescent when the older toms started paying her too much attention, and too small to fight them off. As a result, worn down and abused and hating the experience, she'd had a litter of kittens, few of whom had survived. As soon as she felt able, Herse escaped; left them to fend for themselves within the gang. It was a selfish act, but one she'd needed so she could survive. Or so she justified it.

49

Herse hated thinking back to her earlier life, but now she was being instructed to go there and, recurrent nightmares permitting, relax. It wasn't her current idea of fun. At least she was older, wiser, and stronger now; better equipped to fight off unwanted suitors, or accept them on her terms, although there was little room in her life for desire any more. Under the guidance and protection of Athena, the sisterhood lived a chaste life and the worldly bickering and petty jealousies of the cats of the Plaka held little appeal. Herse followed a higher calling these days: maintaining order throughout the entire city, a mission identified and pursued relentlessly by her mistress and leader, Athena, for as long as she could remember. Under their leader's guidance, The Sisterhood kept the feline population in line.

Her old life seemed small and pointless by comparison. But given her responsibilities and those of her chosen clan, the thought of leaving without being on official business seemed like desertion. Herse had become used to travelling the city poking her nose into other animals' affairs in an official capacity on behalf of her higher calling. What would it feel like to be free? To have no cares, no responsibilities? To shake off the woes of the world, even if only for a short time? She was so used to minding everyone else's business, she found it hard to imagine. A tingle of apprehension ran down her spine. There was only one benefit she could think of: catching up with her son, her beloved Erichthonius, as far as she was aware, the only survivor of her brood. She'd seen him around occasionally, prowling the streets of the Plaka, sniffing out the shops and bars and dodging the tourists, but she'd always kept her distance. Herse always kept an ear attuned for news of him. She heard it he was popular, and bright; she had high hopes for him, but he had his own life now. Still, it would be nice to see him again, to see if he remembered her. The anticipation made her nervous.

Still, being instructed to take time out, to unwind and relax, was so unlike her leader it felt like a slap in the face. She searched her mind for Athena's possible motivations. It required little effort: her watch on the archeological dig was the only thing consuming her attention these days. It had become an obsession and she would brook no distractions.

Herse ventured a direct question. "What is it you're hoping the humans find with all their digging?"

Athena didn't reply. She stopped her grooming and looked out across the city. "I'm not sure," she admitted, "but I think it's going to be something important. If I were to hazard a guess, I'd say it is something stolen from me many, many years ago."

This made no sense to Herse. Yes, Athena was old; she might be ten, perhaps even older. How could something stolen from her be hidden so far underground? She could only conclude that her mentor was getting a little soft in the head. She was sprightly for a ten-year-old, but her obsession with the dig might be a symptom of a larger problem. The thought worried her. She shuddered. Perhaps it was a good time to take a break and test the temperature down in the real world amid the hustle and bustle of other animals. At least it would get her away from this obsession with things long dead and buried. Herse got up and stretched.

"You may be right. I'll take a day or two off and check in with my son." She sauntered off. Athena resumed washing.

THE SLEEK silver-white cat strolled in a leisurely fashion through the side streets of the Plaka. He was in no hurry, taking time to check out interesting scents here and there, exchanging pleasantries with the local cats, and occasionally basking for a few minutes in a patch of sunlight to watch passers-by. Today he had no particular errands, no important calls on his time; he was just taking the pulse of the neighbourhood. It was surprising what you could pick up from these informal visits. Investigators and inquisitors such as those who lived on Filopappou Hill and Areopagus Hill always went in through the proverbial front door; too direct, too harsh. A more subtle, low-key approach often paid dividends.

He was enjoying watching the back and forth of people and animals along the street when he saw something unusual, one of the Sisterhood sauntering towards him. Herse, if he wasn't mistaken. He prided himself on his prodigious memory; all those names and faces down the years. What was Herse doing here? She was one of the High Command, Athena's closest advisers. She rarely left the sanctuary. Looking at her, it seemed clear she wasn't in a hurry, but her kind never came down here to pass the time of day. There must be something going on. Curiosity piqued, it was important he find out. Information and gossip were his trade, his currency. He followed, maintaining a discreet distance.

Trailing her proved trickier than he expected; she often stopped in her tracks to consider a fragrance or odour or make a detour. Exasperated, he headed diagonally across the street to intercept her.

"Hi, er, Herse, isn't it? What brings you down among the mere mortals of the Plaka?"

"Hermes, hello. How nice to see you." She kept it polite, but he detected her irritation at bumping into him, a common-enough reaction among those he interacted with; they often tried, but failed to shield their business from him.

"I'm taking a little break," she admitted. "Catching up with a few old friends and my son."

"Ah yes, Erichthonious, if my memory serves me. A fine young animal, I seem to remember. And how are things up on the hill? Is Athena keeping you all busy?"

She hesitated. "Well, yes, we're a bit stretched to be honest; I feel guilty taking time off."

Hermes shared an interest in a passing scent, making a play of sniffing the air.

"Mmm?"

She watched him from the corner of her eye. "Oh, it's probably nothing, just business as usual, but it's keeping us on our toes," she said a little too breezily. "You know, the gangs are in a ferment, the sky's falling in, that sort of thing."

Hermes exuded an air of indifference. He ambled down the street, expecting her to follow, which she inevitably did, ostensibly out of politeness until, like so many before, she couldn't resist seeking his opinions, worldly wise as he was.

"I hear all sorts of rumours about Kratos and his mob wanting to grow their territory, and the Gizi Gang is getting so out of hand. The raid on the market last week was shocking. What do you think?"

Hermes considered her question, then answered with one of his own. "Well, the more important thing is what Athena thinks? She must be a bit worried, surely?" He noticed his companion looking a little flustered, as if unsure how much to reveal.

"Er, no, no, she's not too bothered. Says it will all blow over."

"That's most unlike her, is it not?" He waited for Herse to say something, but she remained silent. After a while he went on, answering his own question. "Ah well, I expect she has her reasons." He gave her a sidelong glance. "I'm sure she'll be back to business-as-usual before long."

He read the subtle signs from her body language. She seemed tense, uncertain, twisting on the horns of a dilemma. Hermes waited for the revelation; they all cracked in the end.

"I'm sure it will once we've got this current obsession out of the way."

Hermes looked up and saw in her reaction the worry she'd said too much. "Oh, she's got a special project, has she? How interesting. Now I understand why you can't say anything. Don't worry. Your secret will be safe with me." He was at his most conspiratorial, inviting her into his confidence. He saw her bewilderment, knowing the offer to share his innermost thoughts would be too inviting to turn down. Like a practiced angler, he played out the line, letting her wrestle with her conscience. Hermes knew full well Athena tried to shield her business from him. She schooled her protegés to avoid him and warned them against sharing confidences. It made Herse's inner turmoil even more delicious. He relished this minor victory, proof that despite her best efforts Athena couldn't train her followers well enough to keep him at bay.

He was right. At that point, Herse made her mistake. She looked into his eyes and was lost in unguessable distance. Beneath her feet, the street lurched as if it was floating, and her head spun. She experienced a fleeting sensation of panic, leaving her stomach feeling small and knotted, but she couldn't break his stare. Those blue eyes bored right through her, splitting her thoughts into fragments, a colourful kaleidoscope, swirling and dancing in a kind of inner space. Behind them, through them, she sensed something much more strange and unsettling, something incomprehensible and vast beyond her imagination; a hint of terrifying power that could crush her with just a thought, if it so wished. Herse was defenceless, her thoughts plucked, unpeeled, and weighed in the scales by some invisible judge. She had no secrets anymore, only the horrible sensation that she was no longer alone in her own head. Startled, she heard herself speaking, as if from a great distance. At least it sounded like her voice, but trapped in this mental vise it felt as if the conversation outside was taking place between two completely different beings in another place entirely. Her captive mind bore horrified, silent witness to the things her physical body was saying out loud, things she had wanted to keep to herself.

"Well, she said something odd earlier today. Made me wonder if she might be losing her marbles."

"It's not that Elgin chap again, is it?" There was a sympathetic chuckle as if, out there, an inconsequential conversation was taking place between friends. Imprisoned in this inner space it sounded a million miles away and false, and there was no humour; the scrutiny intensified.

"What? No, she said, they were going to dig up something she'd had stolen years ago. That doesn't make any sense, does it?"

He let her go, broke the bond, and looked down the street. She staggered, and a wave of nausea passed over her, but at least she was back on solid ground, alone once more with her thoughts. She stared, wide-eyed, in relief at the flagstones under her feet, and tried to regain her balance.

"No. Very odd," he muttered, as if to himself. "She hasn't said what it is then?"

Herse shook her head, feeling confused again, not daring to meet his eye; now desperate to escape.

"You'd better keep a close watch on her in case of any

other signs, and if there are, let me know." Orders issued, he turned his attention to a nearby plant growing in a pot. She was dismissed. "Well, it's been nice seeing you. Pass on my regards to your youngster."

The spell was broken, leaving Herse feeling flustered. What had she done, what confidence had she betrayed?

"You won't tell anyone, will you?" she pleaded. "I shouldn't have said anything. I don't want to get her into trouble."

Hermes turned his head and flashed his most reassuring look. "Of course not," he replied. "It'll go no further." He paused as if a thought had just occurred to him. "But if you are worried about her behaviour, I think I know how to get her back to the straight and narrow. I know someone who can help. I'll get a message to you." He set off before she could respond. Never had the promise of help sounded so sinister, but her overriding emotion was relief to see him go.

A SHORT distance across town, Herse's colleague Rena watched the comings and goings at the corner of Thisiou and Astiggos Street. The morning had been long, and she was bored. How long did she have to do this for? The sun wasn't yet overhead. It would be late before her shift ended. The street was at least traffic-free, but the number of pedestrians was increasing. She kept a wary eye out for members of her own species. Dogs could pass, they were accompanying humans as often as not, but cats could go no further. She had turned four away already this morning, but the arguments were tiresome, and she hoped there wouldn't be too many more.

Her spirits sank as she spotted three more heading towards her, gang members by the look of it. They might be tricky to turn aside. She glanced down the street to her right, but there was no sign of Trixie, her backup. The newcomers marched straight up to her, and without breaking stride, they attacked. She screeched in pain and surprise, but was overpowered, and dragged into a nearby alley by the scruff of her neck.

"You can't do this," she said, before further blows rained down. Then one of them got her in a chokehold and darkness descended.

She came to in a filthy back-alley well away from the main thoroughfare, behind the bins and rubbish bags piled up at the back of a larger store. The place stank, debris accumulating in the gutter, strange coloured liquids puddling in cracks on the ground. She didn't like to think what they might be. Yannis leaned toward her.

"Tell us what we want, and we might let you go," he leered.

She looked around, terrified, but there was no escape. The three of them had her boxed into a corner. Her eyes darted around, seeking an escape route, a hiding place, anything, but there was none. She was trapped.

"I don't know anything," she pleaded.

Her captors exchanged knowing glances.

"Course you do. You just need to get it off your chest," their leader insisted.

She tried reasoning. "What is it you want to know?"

"Your leader, Her Ladyship; what's she so interested in? What are you guarding?"

Rena's fear increased. "I don't know. She doesn't tell us anything. You've got to believe me."

A swipe across her face, drawing blood, told her they didn't. It loosened her tongue. All thoughts of holding out against these thugs vanished. She just wanted to survive.

"She said it's an artefact, whatever one of those is. It

has power. We have to stop anyone getting near it. That's all she's told us. That's all we know." She was desperate now, sobbing, pleading. "There, I've told you everything, let me go."

They didn't.

CHAPTER 10

THE BOTRYS GANG

THE TERMINUS was next to a metro station north of the city centre. The cats ran beneath and around busses and then across a road to find temporary cover beneath bushes on the verge at the far side. Apollo would have liked to go further through, but a high chain-link fence blocked further progress. He halted to catch his breath. Jason, and then Daphne, who had had to make a longer detour to avoid people, arrived.

"Made it," he said, still out of breath. "Now all we have to do is find Olympia." As soon as he said it, the enormity of the task sank in. They had seen little so far, but Athens smelled different, and he sensed it was bigger than anything he had imagined. Peering out from their hiding place, they looked about them. All they could see was a road and on the far side several busses and a now diminishing throng of people, most of whom were heading into a large building behind. There were lots of streetlights, and strange scents in the air of diesel, different plants and cooking somewhere in the distance. It was all a bit frightening.

"Where are we going to start?" said Jason. "This place looks enormous, and we don't know anyone."

"I'm not doing anything without a proper rest," said Daphne. "I felt sick inside that horrible bus and I couldn't sleep, it was so hot. We need to find a safe place for the night, then we can make plans."

None of them fancied sleeping where they were. It was too close to the bus station, and someone might still come looking for them.

"Let's move then," said Apollo, turning to survey the fence. Its design made it difficult to climb, so they walked along beside it. Soon they came to a small gap where the wires had been cut and bent aside. Once through, they came to the side of a quiet road. They crossed and followed a short side street, keen to put as much distance between themselves and the bus station as they could. Before long they found themselves on the side of a major thoroughfare. At this time of the evening, the traffic was sparse, but it was still far busier than anything they had experienced in Delphi. They stood on the pavement watching in dismay as vehicles thundered past their noses.

"It's no good, we've got to get across." Apollo said, raising his voice so they could hear him. The others glanced at him in horror. Cross this? It looked like suicide. They pawed the ground and walked back and forth, as their nerves took hold. "Let's look for a gap and then run," he added. He gave Daphne his best reassuring look, then glanced across at Jason who was absorbed in following the traffic. He waited, calm and still, until he had their attention. "Watch me and run the moment I move."

Jason swallowed and agreed, his eyes still following the cars. Daphne paid him closer attention. Apollo regarded the traffic once more. After a while, he sensed a longer space between vehicles.

"Now!" he shouted and ran. Jason and Daphne followed, trusting his instinct. They made it, and stopped on the other side, panting from fear as much as exertion. A few moments later they were ready to continue. Eager to find somewhere quieter, they headed along a smaller, but still busy side road. They crossed railway tracks and continued along a narrow pavement between tall buildings and parked cars. The buildings and roads seemed to go on forever. The size of the city was dawning on them. Finding Olympia here would take a lot more than guesswork or luck.

First, they needed somewhere to rest for the night. They came to a piece of waste ground surrounding several old, abandoned buildings. It was difficult to make out in the dark, but they could see no sign of human habitation. The site seemed vacant. A badly maintained wire mesh fence separated it from the road. They wanted somewhere to hide and rest, out of sight of potentially hostile humans, and this location seemed ideal. A place where they could rest and take stock of the situation. In the centre of the overgrown waste ground were the high walls of a large building. They looked intact, although few of the high windows had any glass. Next to it, a tall chimney prodded into the dark sky. Most of the roof was missing, and they could see the tops of trees poking above the brickwork. It was by far the best-looking place to hide that they had yet seen. They found a gap in the fence and headed toward it.

"It's not like the ruins back home," said Jason.

"It looks lovely," Daphne ventured. "I like the trees. I wonder what it looks like in the daytime? Perhaps we could stay here while we try to find Olympia?"

The first item on Apollo's agenda was eating. "I wonder if there are any mice or voles here? It could be a good place for mouse-hunting."

They passed through a doorway into an empty room, debris from old broken furniture still littering the floor. Turning a corner, they found themselves in a large, dark, tree-filled space surrounded by high walls. Almost no light from the nearby streetlamps penetrated here. They hesitated at the entrance, while their eyes adjusted.

The trees were tall, many overtopping the walls. The place must have been deserted for a long time. They could see a few stars in the small gaps between leaves, but little light reached ground level. As his eyes adjusted, Apollo sensed movement to his right. He spun around and saw the outline of a very large cat standing on a pile of rubble, a metre above them, a shadow against an even darker background. It edged closer, and as some faint light fell on its face Apollo thought it the fiercest and ugliest cat he'd ever seen. He could make out a nasty-looking scar below its left eye, running down almost to its jaw. It bristled with hostility, every movement tight and tense.

"Well, well, what have we here?" it growled. "Who are you, and what do you think you're up to? This is our turf. As if you didn't already know."

Apollo suppressed a sigh and adopted his most reassuring persona. He glanced around nonchalantly, noticing movement all around them as cats appeared from almost every crevice and nook.

"Just as well I didn't nip over there for a snooze," murmured Daphne. Unfriendly-looking animals soon surrounded them. Apollo turned back to their inquisitor. He maintained the confident demeanour of a tourist on a sightseeing jaunt, exuding friendliness.

"Nice place you have here," he said. "Very spacious and secluded. I like it." His companions said nothing, but stood very still, watching the shadows.

"Like it, do you? Fancy moving in, eh?" sneered the big ugly brute. It was obvious he was the leader of this gang. "Well, it's not for sale. And we're not planning of moving out." He glanced around, checking the gang members were in position. "But we could do with some fresh meat," he snarled, his voice low and threatening. Nerves sent a shiver down Daphne's spine. She could feel her heart pumping harder. Apollo seemed unconcerned. He took another moment to glance around, which only provoked the big cat further.

"We are the Botrys Gang, and this is our territory. No one comes in here without our leave, and no little sneak-thief intruder gets out in one piece." His voice became lower and softer, which only made him sound more threatening. All around, members of the gang edged forward toward the Delphi cats. They looked hungry for blood; heavily outnumbered, Apollo, Jason, and Daphne instinctively edged closer together.

"Well, there's no need to take offence. We mean you no harm, we're just visiting. We're looking for somewhere we could sleep tonight. Perhaps a quiet corner? We'll be off before dawn." Apollo was the epitome of calm reason.

Neither Jason nor Daphne could believe the cool approach their friend was taking, and neither wanted to sample the hospitality of this mob. Quite the opposite. They wanted to get as far away as possible. Their eyes darted left and right, looking for escape routes. Meanwhile, Apollo's calm assurance seemed to have some effect on his wider audience. There were one or two blinks and murmurs of agreement among the observing gang members. This interloper seemed to have a good point. He sounded alright, even reasonable. Surely there wouldn't be any problem letting him stay overnight.

Kratos jumped down from his platform and advanced until his snout was almost touching Apollo's. Apollo didn't move, but despite the gloom, looked back into his eyes, calm and unflinching. As the two stared at each other, the seconds seemed to stretch, and the others held their breath.

"So, you want to make friends? Oh well, that's all right then!" Bile ladened the gangster's voice. He stepped back, playing to his admirers in the gallery, exuding a fragile and menacing bonhomie. His followers breathed a sigh of relief. They would welcome the newcomers; everything would be fine. Apollo remained statue-still, his eyes following every move the other cat made. Kratos spun around and in the same movement, a pawful of razor-sharp claws flashed toward Apollo's face. The ginger cat jumped backwards, but not quite fast enough to prevent a nasty slash across the nose. As if released from a dream, the other gang members followed their boss's lead and, yowling and squealing, they attacked in a blur of teeth and claws. They were wiry and streetwise, hardened by years of fighting like this, but their momentary confusion dulled the edge of their attack. The Delphi cats had far less experience of combat. Relying on instinct, they were fighting for their lives.

The big cat pounced on Apollo, trying to grapple with him and drag him to the ground, but found himself evenly matched. Despite the unprovoked attack, Apollo still felt reluctant to fight. He experienced a flush of dislocation while he wrestled with the big bully, as if his waking mind struggled to accept what had happened. It shouldn't be like this. He was also shocked at the power of the other animal; he was far stronger than Apollo anticipated, but the over-whelming reaction was disappointment that his message had failed to chime. Why was that the case? He could not hold off the gang leader much longer, but despite the growing urgency, he still had little appetite for the fight. His own bites lacked venom, his claws remained sheathed.

His enemy, in contrast, aggressive and experienced, used every means available to bring down his enemy, targeting his vulnerabilities with deadly intent. Apollo experienced genuine pain from the claw marks on his shoulder and back and felt his skin pierced by the monster's sharp incisors, yet he struggled to shake off the torpor. He was still musing on why his peaceful request for help had carried so little weight. It was disheartening; had they no idea who he was? Shouldn't they be paying him some respect? The demise of his cult hit hard afresh, but even bereft of followers such an unprovoked assault was more than rude, it was sacrilege. It wasn't only Olympia's captors who needed to be taught a lesson.

He put the thought aside; he'd done enough punishing to last many lifetimes. Instead, belatedly, he tried to push back at his opponent, but it was like trying to push a boulder uphill. As they tussled, his hind paws slipped on the loose ground and he fell sideways, the brute on top of him. This was not a good position. Kratos reinforced his grip, sensing victory.

Around them gang members strove to attack Daphne and Jason, pouncing, biting, snarling, and slashing for all their worth, but in their eagerness, they often got in each other's way. Daphne and Jason were desperate to stay on their feet. If one of them went down under a larger attacker, it could be fatal. The screeches of a dozen fighting cats filled the still night air, and a light came on in the night watchman's hut.

Things looked hopeless, but the Delphi cats fought with a desperation that surprised their attackers. Daphne was nimble and quick-witted enough to use the trees as bounce-boards and balletically spring over their heads. They looked slow and clumsy as they twisted and turned to keep up with her. Jason, larger, stronger but more earthbound, preferred to use the trees for cover as he dodged attacks. But quick as they were, they could not hold out against these odds.

Torchlight swung in their direction, surprising all the combatants and bringing salvation. A human voice yelled at them to shut up. The night watchman resented having his peace being disturbed by yowling fighting felines.

As the light fell on him, Kratos loosened his grip and looked over his shoulder. With his attention diverted, Apollo squirmed out from under him. At that instant a shower of gravel flung by the human landed in their midst, accompanied by some choice words. Cats scattered in different directions. Jason freed himself from the brute who had his leg in his mouth and scrambled toward a panting Apollo. Daphne, on hind paws shadow-boxing with her attacker, broke off and joined them. Together they charged away from the fight zone between piles of rubble and the detritus of the abandoned factory until they saw a gap in the wall. Onward they ran across more waste ground toward another fence, looking neither left nor right. They burst through one of the many gaps, relieved to be out in the open once more. The road on this southern side of the site was busier, but they darted across, heedless of any cars, and reached a quieter pavement on the other side. Without breaking stride, they headed on down a narrow street lined with tall buildings. At a junction, they turned into another similar street. There they paused, panting, looking back and listening for signs of pursuit. No one was following.

"That was… intense," muttered Jason.

Daphne agreed. "Scary." She spat out a mouthful of her enemy's dusty fur. Her entire body trembled with nervous energy. Apollo said nothing, just caught his breath until his heart rate subsided. His wounds felt raw, the pain searing, but rather than lick them he stared into the distance, trying to remember when he had last received such a reception. Standards of hospitality had lapsed since he was last abroad. How much else had changed? He walked between his friends, convivially butting and rubbing against them, offering unspoken reassurance. They sensed rather than heard him purr. The shared experience brought the three of them closer, creating bonds that would forever bind them, even as the enormity and danger of their quest became clearer.

Apollo gave his companions an appreciative look, and their fear subsided, but as the effects of adrenaline wore off, they were all sore and weary. All had suffered scratches and bites, some quite savage and deep. Jason's leg was oozing blood from a deep bite. The pain was getting worse, and he was limping. Daphne had nasty bite marks on her neck and ear and was sore all over. Apollo's nose, back, and neck bore deep wounds, but they already seemed to be healing. Jason gave him a quizzical look.

"You played it pretty cool back there."

"Did I?"

"Yes, you didn't shout back at him, tell him what you'd do to him, you know? I thought you'd threaten him a bit. Instead, you just tried talking to him."

"I hoped he'd listen to reason. Violence is never the answer, despite what our friend might think." The words felt automatic, and he wondered if, in his innermost self, he still believed them. He shook his head and tried to quell such regressive thoughts; they belonged in the far distant past, if anywhere. The gang leader's resistance to the potency of his call to reason disturbed him. Would it be the case with everyone he met? Worst of all was his strength; he hadn't come up against such power for as long as he could remember. The realisation left him subdued. "Come on," he said after a while, "we'd better find somewhere to rest."

They were in a narrow street lined with many tall

buildings. Every so often there was a gap between them, sometimes filled with parking spaces for cars, sometimes fenced off, concealing small gardens. They soon came across one such patch of vegetation screened by a low wall surmounted by railings.

"In here," Apollo said, feeling dispirited and more tired than he could ever remember. They crawled between the railings and gathered together on the other side, looking around. They were in a small space filled with trees and large plants. In the centre was a plastic table and several chairs topped by a sunshade umbrella on a small piece of grass. Screened from the street, they felt safe and started to relax. Too soon.

CHAPTER 11

ACHELOIS

"I GATHER you're new around here," drawled a low voice from the darkness above them. They looked up, fearful again. A white face peered down from the flat roof of a small shack that stood beside the tall building. The owner of the voice jumped elegantly down onto the grass beside them. "You don't look very threatening," it added. "I'm Achelois, by the way, Lois for short. Pleased to meet you."

"What do you mean we're not threatening... how do you…" Jason was unsure whether to feel worried or insulted.

"It's obvious what was happening, my dears, I could hear you little scuffle a mile off. If it's any comfort, you're not the first upcountry victims of the Botrys gang."

"How do you know we're new around here?" Jason asked, calming down a little. Lois looked him up and down.

"Well, you don't speak like an Athenian, for a start. And you don't seem to know much about this neighbourhood." She circled around him and noticed his leg wound. "The more civilised among us around here give the hoodlums from Botrys a wide berth. They, and especially their leader Kratos, are trouble."

"We come from Delphi," said Apollo, stepping forward. "I'm Apollo, this is Daphne and Jason." He glanced toward his companions. "We're here to rescue a friend. We didn't want to start a fight. We're not here to claim territory."

Lois stopped walking and sat down to study them.

"From Delphi, you say." She gave him a long look. "How interesting. You've come a long way, this friend of yours must be awfully important."

"She's just one of us," said Daphne, "the cats of the Sanctuary. We're a big tribe; a family. We stick together."

There was silence while Lois absorbed this information. Then she stood.

"Follow me." She led them along a path around the side of the apartment block to a larger enclosed space at the rear, bathed in bright silver moonlight. They could make out tall apartment buildings on all sides. There was a meagre patch of grass surrounded by a few trees and bushes. "You will be safe here. You may rest until morning, but before you sleep, let me have a look at those wounds." She told Jason to lie down and inspected his leg. Jason didn't know how she could see, even with the moon this bright, but Lois took some time in her examination, delicately sniffing at the wound before licking it. The sensation was pleasant and soothing, and before long his pain and discomfort receded. She repeated her actions with Daphne's various bites and then approached Apollo.

"I'm alright," he said. "It's just a few scratches, I heal quickly." She looked but couldn't see any visible marks on him, then paused and studied his face for a moment. She stepped back, her expression unreadable.

"There are humans here who leave water and food for me. You can share it this evening."

"What about you? Won't you be hungry?"

Lois looked at him, her tail swaying as she thought. "It's a beautiful night; I'll hunt for something. I haven't enjoyed the taste of a fresh mouse for a while. Get plenty of rest; we shall speak again in the morning." She turned to go.

As soon as she had left, the cats crowded around the

71

bowl and devoured the food, jostling for position like new-borns scrambling for an empty teat. They had forgotten how hungry they were. Once they'd licked the bowl clean, they studied their surroundings again to find a good place to sleep, settling on the edge of the grass just under an overhanging bush. There they snuggled together in a jumble of fur, each falling rapidly into a deep sleep.

Apollo's dream was vivid.

THE SUN was scorching, and he sensed the danger with every fibre of his being. They were being hunted by a monster: his mother, sister, and himself. Anxiously he watched the seas from the summit of Mount Cynthus, day after day, but of the monster, there was no sign. He tired of waiting.

"We cannot stay here, we're like rabbits in a trap," he told his mother.

"We're safer here than out on the open sea," she replied.

His agitation grew. Finally, he could bear it no more and took matters into his own hands. He leaped into the sea, transforming into a dolphin, and swam swiftly toward his enemy's domain. Below the slopes of Parnassus, he emerged and strode through the olive groves to the rift in the earth where Gaia's breath emerged.

Seeing him approach, Python, the mightiest serpent ever to have lived, emerged to do battle. He wounded it with many arrows until it turned and fled back into the cavernous shrine. There he pursued it until, at last, he put an arrow through its eye, then with a sword, cut off its head. The body he sliced into many pieces and burned on a massive pyre, the column of smoke a warning to Heaven.

The shrine he would take as his own. His father's punishment was nothing. He had found his home.

In this way was his legend born.

STIRRING FROM his troubled sleep, Apollo opened an eye. It was still dark. Above him, sitting on a roof, silhouetted against the moon, was the dark shape of a cat sitting upright, perfectly still and darkest black, as if carved from the night sky. He turned over and went back to sleep.

Dawn arrived, and they slept on. Between the tall apartment blocks, it took time for the full light of day to penetrate beneath the trees. The sun had been climbing into the sky for a couple of hours before they stirred. A nearby buzzing insect made Apollo open his eyes. He yawned and stretched, and for a moment wondered where he was. The tattered remains of his dream drifted through his head, then vanished. Then he remembered the events of the previous evening and stood up.

"Good morning," came a now familiar voice. Lois was curled on a cushion on a garden seat nearby, a favourite perch. "There is more food, if you'd like to eat." Apollo saw the re-filled bowls, shocked that he had heard no human arrive and replenish them. How could he have slept through it? His hostess appeared to read his mind. "You looked exhausted after your exertions yesterday."

Apollo shook his head to banish the last remnants of slumber and sat down for a quick wash. By now the others were also waking up and studying their surroundings. The space between the apartment blocks made a snug communal garden. It was little more than a small patch of grass and bare earth with some trees and shrubs for shade and cover, but it seemed like heaven in this strange, unwelcoming city. Despite its spartan appearance, there were some beautiful scented flowers that Daphne would have liked to sniff at. But first things first. With a grateful glance toward Achelois, they approached the food and water bowls again and once more had their fill.

"You have been so kind, thank you," Apollo said, sitting in front of his hostess. "We'd better be on our way." Although he realised he had no idea where they should go next, or how to begin their search.

"Do you know where you're going? Have any of you got the slightest idea how you're going to find this friend of yours?" Lois gave each of them a brief glance. They looked at each other. Athens was huge, and they hadn't a clue where to look for Olympia.

CHAPTER 12

DEBRIEF

IN THE early morning light, in a clear patch of ground within one of the deserted buildings, the Botrys gang assembled. Kratos was in a foul mood. Two dozen or more cats sat or lay down on the ground or on mounds of rubble or disused machinery, most of them trying to keep a safe distance from him. In a clearing at the center, their leader slowly paced back and forth, his tail slashing from side to side, as he tried to control his temper. His eyes blazed in fury.

"Last night was a disgrace," he said, struggling to control his temper. They averted their eyes. This was uncomfortable. "I am disgusted with you. Where were the sentries? Asleep? You just let total strangers come and go in the heart of our headquarters! And three moronic yokels fresh from the farmyard at that. At the very least, we should have taught them a lesson they would never forget; made an example of them. It's the minimum I demand!" He glowered at them. "But you lot just let them waltz in and walk all over us," he added, warming to his theme. He may have been mixing his metaphors, but none of the gang were going to pick him up on grammar. Nor did they doubt the menace in his voice.

"And as for their cocksure leader, I should have ripped his throat out! But you lot let him go," he added in a low voice. He licked his lips, staring around at them. They looked away or down, unable to bear the terrible weight of his glance. Several of them tried and failed to suppress shudders. The morning chill did nothing to ease the tension in the air. None of them wanted to feel the sting of an angry claw-swipe.

Kratos circled once more.

"Let me remind you. This is our headquarters. Our secure secret place. No outsiders allowed unless we bring them here, but what do you do? You let them scamper right through bold as brass." He spun around again, a savage grimace on his face. Those nearest shrank back. "And instead of making an example of Mr Superior and his friends, you let them go." He ignored the fact that he was as guilty as any of them.

"We wouldn't have but for the big human with the light," ventured Demetrios. A cuff across the side of the face was enough to show that his intervention had been rash. Kratos stood before him, a low growl at the back of his throat. The smaller cat backed away a couple of steps, not daring to take his eyes off his leader. Kratos' eyes burning with fury rooted him to the spot. In earlier times a muttered curse and such a look would have turned the recipient into stone as a permanent reminder of the folly of misplaced words. Nowadays, Demetrios was petrified in name only, but he could not break the connection. He was all too aware of the raw power the other animal possessed; power that could crush him like a bug beneath his paw.

"It's all the big human's fault, is it?" Kratos enquired. He turned to the rest. "So where was the chase? How come you yellow bellies scattered and let them off the hook? You should have captured them and brought to justice. My justice. You're going soft. You seem to forget we rule this part of town. No cat in north Athens dares stand against us, and the dogs stay out of our way. We say what goes on around here. We come and go as we wish; we steal what we want, we eat what we want, we take anything we fancy from those soft house pets and their dim-witted human slaves." He turned to one of the smaller females perched on some rusting machinery. "Here, Magda, when was the last time you brought me some socks or underwear to pad out my bed or a little of their twinkly jewelry? How long is it since you got me something infused with catnip? Now that's what I call proper thieving. Call yourself a cat-burglar? You've gone soft—you all have." She mumbled an excuse, but Kratos wasn't listening; he'd turned away. "Last night those three mongrels insulted our name and our honour," he growled. "We need to teach them a lesson. It's time to remember who we are: the Botrys Gang. We rule around here, and soon we'll rule this city. We don't let a few mangy strays from the countryside come and go as they please."

There was an awkward pause. The gang members glanced at one another. No one knew what to say next. No one, except Melanippus, the one animal in the entire group feeling good about himself. "At least it shows I was right!" The others looked at one another, scrambling to remember his reading of the entrails the other day. Kratos stopped dead in his tracks.

"Spies," he said. "And from the north. The portents were correct; we've been infiltrated by filthy spies!" His fury redoubled. He paced back and forth, his tail slashing even more wildly. With a conscious effort, he forced himself to be calmer. He had to think; the incident had been more serious than he'd thought. It was no accident; the Seer had foreseen it all.

He addressed them again, his voice menacing. "I want them hunted down, and an example made. They're going to regret the day they marched in here, especially the ginger one." He looked around, staring into their faces. "Got it?" he added. He called two of his most trusted subordinates over.

"You can lead the intelligence gathering. Yannis, get a few of your best guys and scout out Avalos Street up to the north. Rea, do the same to the south. I want spies and sniffers out, pronto. Use Menelaos, he's our best tracker, but it shouldn't be too difficult—you should easily smell the goat dung on their paws. Question the local citizens. Use a little muscle if you need to, they'll cave in soon enough. Someone knows where they are. And when we find out, I want you to track them down and arrange a nasty little surprise for them. And anyone that's been hiding them. Question, then kill. Whatever it takes, no one walks in here and gets away with it."

Yannis looked pained. "Menelaos is missing."

"What?" Kratos sounded incredulous. He stared at his lieutenant as if it was his fault.

"Disappeared. Can't find him anywhere. I've sent out some guys to look for him. We've even quizzed the locals, but there's nothing. Not a jot of information anywhere. Can't even pick up a scent."

"It's like what happened to Martha last week," Rea interjected, trying to defuse the situation.

Kratos turned his discomforting stare to her. She couldn't stop herself from squirming. When he resumed speaking, his voice contained shards of cold fury.

"This is her doing. I know it. No more velvet; it's time to unsheath our claws." He addressed Yannis once more. "Change of plan. I don't care who you take but get a group together and get down there. I want the place staked out. Squeeze the locals for all they're worth. I want to know her plans." He looked at Rea. "It's time for action. Get over to Gizi and talk to Zelus. Tell him what's happened. It's time to coordinate our attack. Find out the earliest he can get his guys moving."

He called a third cat over. "Kostas, get a hunting party together and track those three down. I want them punished. Dead or alive, it's up to you. But if you let them live, you'd better have a good excuse." The other animal bowed his head and left.

Kratos considered his plans. This intrusion was foretold, so it must be part of a wider pre-ordained chain of events. It was time to accelerate his plans. He looked around at them, still under his spell and hanging on his every word.

"What are you waiting for?" he shouted. "Get moving."

They scattered to carry out his orders while he retreated to his favourite place to bask in the warming morning sun. It was time for a snooze until the troops returned with information. Then it would be time for action. 'You can't escape,' he thought to himself. The gang members set off on their allotted duties, scouting the nearby streets, sniffing for clues, and heading off to intimidate some fat dozy local drones, or 'pets' as certain humans liked to call them.

CHAPTER 13

INTO ATHENS

ACHELOIS HOPPED down to the ground and gathered them together. She sat in front of them. "Tell me about your friend, and what you hope to do." After a moment's hesitation, Apollo recounted the story of Olympia's capture and their mission to rescue her. He left out much of the detail but concluded with their escape from the gang.

"If it wasn't for the human with the bright light, I'm not sure what would have happened." The events of the previous night still consumed his thoughts. Being friendly and open hadn't worked. Maybe modern-day mortals were different, and not so easily influenced. Perhaps he'd been too naïve. But there was something unsettling about the big bully of a gang leader.

Daphne's concern was about the practical matters to do with finding Olympia. "Do you know where she might be?"

Lois' eyes widened, a feline look of incredulity. "Have you any idea how big Athens is? It goes on for kilometre after kilometre. I wouldn't have the faintest idea where to look," she said. Daphne slumped, her eyes downcast. She'd hoped for clues, a sign, anything. This was going to be a hard search, maybe impossible. Lois felt sympathy. "I know someone who might help. He knows a lot of what goes on in this city, and he might have heard of something. It's quite a walk to where he lives, and if the Botrys Gang will be out looking for you, there's no time to waste. You should set off immediately."

"Will you take us?" asked Jason.

"No, it's too far for me to go, but I will start you off on your journey and point you in the right direction." She looked at them. "We'd better go." She stood up and headed to the opposite side of the garden from where they had entered. In the corner was a narrow passage between two apartment blocks with a tall gate at the end. It presented no barrier to four agile cats, however, and they dropped onto the pavement beyond. Lois took a glance up and down the street, but saw nothing unusual. She trotted south, keeping close to the buildings. The Delphi cats followed her.

At this time of day, the streets were quiet. Old Leda lay dozing in the warm sun on a balcony. She opened an eye as they passed, briefly wondering why four cats should be out together and where her neighbour would be leading them, then forgot about it and went to sleep.

Yannis's spies were sweeping the nearby streets. They had picked up some suspicious scents, but nothing conclusive, and had threatened a couple of residents, but neither of them knew anything. They searched the neighbourhood, street by street, looking under cars, down alleys, and on side streets. The intruders couldn't hide forever.

For Apollo, Daphne, and Jason, the stifling heat of the city streets proved energy-sapping. Their guide led them further toward the centre, hugging walls and staying on the quiet side of the street. They used parked cars as screens against prying eyes and changed direction several times at intersections. In no time the Delphi cats were lost, as the city's true scale unfolded. The endless warren of roads seemed to be without end. At midday they came to a square, shocked by the intensity of the traffic crossing it. They had experienced nothing like it. It was hot and noisy; from their perspective at tail pipe level the dust and fumes were overpowering. They didn't want to stay here very long. Achelois drew to a halt.

"This is where I must leave you," she said, shouting over the noise of the traffic, "but let me show you where you need to go." She led them to the corner of a wide street. Across a busy junction, it continued into the distance. "You must carry on down there," she indicated. "Do you see that hill in the distance? That is Mount Lycabettus. On its summit live more of our kind with their leader Hermes. If anyone in the city can provide you with help to find your friend, it is them." Apollo looked up at the name. She caught his eye but misread his thoughts. "They are not like the Botrys gang," she reassured him. "They are more welcoming toward strangers, and if anyone knows what goes on in Athens, it is Hermes. He gets news from all over the city and sometimes beyond; he is more likely than anyone to know what has happened to your friend. But it is too far for me to journey—I don't like to venture so far from my home."

Apollo, Jason, and Daphne looked down the long street to the steep-sided hill at its end. It looked a long way away. Jason and Daphne were reluctant to part from Achelois. She had provided so much help; they felt secure in her company. Somehow her treatment had gone a long way toward healing their wounds. They didn't want to lose her calm assurance and advice.

Apollo was keen to get going. "Thank you for all your help."

She paused and looked at them, concerned about their welfare. She gave them a last piece of advice. "You must take great care crossing these roads. These metal chariots move very fast. Don't be frightened of the noise they make, but be sure to keep your wits about you. I've seen too many young friends die under their wheels. Once you have crossed the junction, keep going straight ahead and always head toward the hill. That is where you should find news. If any of them question you, tell them I sent you. Go now, don't tarry, but take care." With one last look, she turned and left them. They were alone once more.

"It's still quite far away." Apollo was voicing their thoughts.

"And we've been on the road for ages already," groaned Jason. Despite his leg being better, it still ached a bit, and he didn't want to go too far.

Daphne mewed in sympathy. "Well, we'd better get started." She was trying to sound braver than she felt.

They studied the road junction in front of them, but it was so confusing. Traffic seemed to come from all directions. Busses, trucks, and cars hurtled by but stopped periodically for no reason the cats could deduce, before roaring into life and sprinting off again. The pauses offered no respite; other vehicles from different directions immediately filled the gap. Adding to their confusion, some of them went straight ahead while others veered off right or left. From their point of view, it was chaos and getting to the other side in one piece would be a lottery.

"Ooh, this is horrible," Daphne muttered to herself. The junction was perhaps the most terrifying place she'd ever been.

After a while, there was a brief pause in the traffic flow.

"Now," cried Apollo and shot off into the middle of the road. The others, nerves on edge, followed as fast as they dared. They could do this—it wasn't too far. A screech of brakes startled them from behind as a large truck, coming from a direction they hadn't expected, shuddered to a halt.

Behind it, horns started honking. "Fucking cats!" yelled the driver from his open window, but they were gone, startled and scattering as they crossed the last few busy lanes. With engines roaring, vehicles were moving once more.

With the kerb in sight, Daphne froze as out of the corner of her eye she saw a large bus coming toward her. With her body flattened, she closed her eyes, and it passed over her head. The instant it was gone she bolted across the last stretch of tarmac at top speed, hurdled the kerb, and ran for the first safe place she could find, a narrow gap between a chained-up bicycle and a wall. Panting, and close to panic, she closed her eyes and tried to calm down; she'd made it, but where were the others?

Despite his limp, Jason kept running when Daphne halted. He cleared the last lane of traffic, a taxi missing him by the length of a tail, and hurtled down the street ahead towards Lycabettus as if three-headed Cerberus were after him. Fifty metres down the road, the shock subsided, and he slowed down. He looked around but caught no sight of the others. They couldn't be far behind. He ducked under a parked car to wait for them.

Apollo took a different line to his comrades, darting across a second road, then veering past some human pedestrians. He ran between them, dodging around their legs as they crossed the road, and ended up on the opposite side of the street to Jason. It was the street they had been targeting, but he could no longer see his friends. Where had they got to? He hoped they were safe.

"Where are you?" His frustrated miaow, lost in the noise of the traffic, got no reply. For a while, he stood in the middle of the pavement as humans came and went on either side. Some had to swerve around him, swearing and giving him fierce looks, but most ignored him as just another obstacle. Apollo experienced an instant of pure indecision. One human bent down to scoop him up, which stirred him into action. He needed to find somewhere to think; to get his head straight and plan his next move. Darting through the crowd, he spotted an open door. It seemed quiet inside so he entered and found himself in a small shop with two aisles each lined with tall shelves reaching up as far as he could see, all stocked with the items humans seemed to value, in tins, boxes, bottles or packets all lined up in tightly packed rows. There was a gap under the bottom shelf which was just large enough for him to squeeze into. He tucked himself away to collect his thoughts.

A flash of memory caught him by surprise, recalling an indestructible invulnerability and the chance to move where he would with nothing more than a thought: the ability to solidify or evaporate into the aether at will. It vanished, leaving just the faintest imprint in his mind's eye. That was no longer him. He was trapped in a far smaller body, admittedly agile, but vulnerable, and prone to weariness and pain, something that had once been merely concepts. There was no escaping the fact he was footsore and tired. He dismissed the thought and focused once more on his friends' whereabouts.

Should he go back and search for signs of them at the junction? No, it was pointless; there was no way they would hang around near the chaotic junction. They must have moved on together, he hoped, following the directions Lois had given them. His thoughts lingered on Daphne. It might have been unfair to let her come on this quest. He should never have endangered her so. Daydreams of lazy afternoons in her company, ranging the hillside in Delphi, distracted him. Memories of chasing one another, lying together in the shade in tranquility, far away from this frantic place. Was it unfair that he worried about her far more than Jason? He suppressed a pang of jealousy at the thought of the two of them being together. Logic dictated they must have passed him and gone on ahead. It was time to get moving and catch them up. Perhaps he would meet them at Mount Lycabettus. Had Hermes changed much? Would he recognise him? He couldn't remember the last time they'd met.

Apollo sensed movement from the back of the shop. Not sluggish, oafish human movement, but stealthy, supple, feline tracking kind of movement. Then he saw it: a large, well-fed (the unkind might have said overweight) grey and white cat.

"Who are you and what are you doing in my shop?" it demanded. Apollo suppressed a wave of intense irritation and tried to be diplomatic.

"I just popped in for a rest."

"Oh, 'I'm only resting,'" the other mocked. "Well, rest out on the street, you scrawny little mongrel. No one comes into Stavros's Convenience Store without my permission."

Apollo sighed; what was the problem with these Athenians? Why were they so hostile, but of more concern, why were they oblivious to his powers of persuasion? He noticed two humans enter the shop and walk down the aisle in front of him. "Have they asked permission?" he enquired, his voice dripping with sarcasm. Rather than wait for an answer, he left, ignoring the jeers that followed him out onto the street. Once there, he paused to take stock. The trees that lined each sidewalk limited his view, but he was certain enough of the direction he needed to travel. It was a long time since he'd last been abroad, but he felt sure that the last time he was in these parts the ground he was now standing on had been a mixture of fields and woodland punctuated by the villas of the wealthy and the humble cottages of their farmworkers and servants. Concrete, asphalt, and paving slabs were a poor upgrade. He set off slowly. Apollo was used to cars, busses, and the occasional truck at Delphi, but the profusion of vehicles was alarming and almost overwhelming. How many people lived here, he wondered, and who was their leader? He kept close to the buildings, out of the way of the pedestrians who rushed past in both directions, and passed a low plate-glass window. A ginger cat was walking along in the same direction as himself. He paused to study it, before realising it was his own reflection. How many centuries had he spent in this body, yet it still caught him out? He stopped and looked at his reflection again. The shadows above and dark interior made the shop front a mirror. He explored the face, the whiskers, the ears, and then, looking deeper into the dark well of the pupil, he caught the faintest glimpse of something else; the echo of what he once was. He peered more closely, but no, it was gone, leaving just the fading impression on his retinas of something long lost, as if he'd been caught in a camera's flash and had to close his eyes tight. No amount of staring would bring it back. He walked on.

A little further on he came to a large paved area, like a small agora, but without the market stalls, or hustlers, or orators. What's more, it was far away from where he thought the centre of the city should be. The road he'd been following took a large detour around the edge, before resuming its course on the far side. Apollo stopped in his tracks. Ahead of him, in the centre of this space, jets of water rose from the ground, squirting high into

87

the air before falling back. What strange magic was this? He approached with caution. The jets of water formed a circle, all those on the perimeter pointing inwards, those in the centre ascending vertically to a great height. He watched, entranced, as the fountain played, the height of the jets altering according to a pattern. It was fascinating. Keeping to the grass surround, he skirted the water, then decided it would be nice to try some different tunes. How high could they shoot? The jets changed their pattern, and the water played a new intricate dance. Some water jets intertwined about each other in an ascending spiral; others played different gravity-defying games, changing direction in midair. Globes of water burst from the ground in staccato rhythm before exploding and cascading down to soak passers-by. The central jet climbed to an impossible height, casting a veil of spray as far as the perimeter of the square. People stopped, aghast, and stared. Apollo ignored it and casually walked past them toward the tree-lined street leading toward Lycabettus.

Another distraction caught his eye, a portal to some underground cavern. Confused, he studied it. Could this be an entrance to the Underworld? It seemed too obvious, not well enough hidden, and in any case, humans were emerging from the depths: Hades would never let them go. He drew closer, and saw the moving stairs leading down into the depths, and next to them, another set rising. Curiosity piqued, he made a detour, descending to a brightly lit hall criss-crossed by many pedestrians. He remembered his mission; he couldn't afford to be distracted. Further exploration would have to wait. A second moving staircase took him back toward daylight like any other commuter, but smaller. It was, he reasoned, another thing to add to his growing catalogue of strange contraptions the human race had developed while he slept.

DAPHNE COWERED in the gap between the bicycle and the wall. The noise and sudden movement of those huge vehicles had been terrifying, and she felt lucky to have escaped in one piece. Her body was rigid with fear. She closed her eyes and tried to take a few deep breaths to calm down. After a few minutes, the terror eased, but relief evaporated when she found she couldn't see the others anywhere.

'What's happened to them, and where am I?' Her heart still raced; her breath came in ragged bursts. Confused, she stared straight ahead, her eyes focused on a tall lamppost by the side of the road, but she didn't see it as she struggled to calm her feelings. Her mind was elsewhere. Traffic fumes washed over her, dust filled her nostrils, but in the unmoving air and barely audible, she heard the faint voices of the trees that lined the nearby streets. She closed her eyes to concentrate, trying to make out their thin, distant, echoing voices.

Poor thing, she's lost.

So far from home.

What are you doing here?

Go back, back to where you came from, go before it's too late.

An itch catapulted her into the present, and she lost the thread. While she scratched her neck Daphne recognised her breathing had slowed, and her panic had subsided. She was calmer now, and able to think. Where had they gone? Why hadn't they waited for her? Irritation replaced bewilderment. Looking around she could see no sign of them at all, which she supposed meant they weren't injured, but with so many humans around, and the horrible noisy traffic just a few meters away, she didn't feel safe. Someone was bound to spot her, and then what? She didn't trust them at all. What had Lois told them? They should cross the busy junction and then go down a street to a hill. Perhaps the others were already on their way. Maybe she could catch up with them.

They might have waited, she grumbled, but another thought struck: which street? Daphne had a choice, the one to the left of her, or the other to the right, but how could she tell which was correct? She couldn't miss something as big as a hill, she thought. She left her hiding place and walked around the corner to the street on her right, hoping to see her destination ahead. But she had no such luck. Instead, she found a street lined with trees on each side. Between them and the tall buildings that seemed to close in on her, she could barely see the sky. With a deep sigh, she set off, trying to stay out of reach of pedestrians and keeping an eye out for dogs, just a small amber, black, and white cat minding its own business on this hot afternoon. She brightened up a little. There must be a few friendly cats around here who kept humans for pets and who might give her directions if she got lost? Buoyed by such positive thoughts, she headed down the street.

JASON SAT under the car, unnerved and trying to regain his composure. He was appreciating the scale of the challenge they had undertaken in trying to navigate this enormous city, let alone find Olympia. He would need to keep his wits about him; Athens was so alien to everything he knew. This area, nearer to the centre, was much busier than the neighbourhood they had passed through earlier. What now? He pondered the question for a while, but a new one replaced it: where have they gone? Looking up and down the street from his hideout, he couldn't see his companions anywhere. He decided he'd better go back and look for them. A horrible thought hit him—what if one of them was hit by one of those big metal things! He suddenly felt sick, but there was nothing else for it. He would have to go back and find out, one way or another.

Steeling himself, he crawled out from under the car, and keeping close to the kerb, he trotted back to the junction. At the corner he paused, looking around. It was a relief not to detect any dead or injured cats, but neither could he see them anywhere.

What would they do? Lois told us to find Hermes, and he lives on top of a mountain, he recalled, so that's what we have to do. He looked around the square and down the roads nearby and wished he'd paid more attention to her directions. After the trauma of the road crossing, he'd lost his bearings, and the more he circled around, the worse it got. Trees lined the road behind, but to his left was a long straight avenue with, at its far end, a kind of flat-topped hill with steep sides and an old building on top of it. They reminded him of home. That must be it. Having a firm destination to aim for lifted his mood. But first, there was the matter of another road to cross. This time Jason spent time studying his surroundings. He noticed the humans waited for a while on the pavement until the metal chariots all stopped before they crossed. Pleased with this insight, and confident of safety in numbers, he crossed the road with them, dodging feet and dashing ahead once safe on the far side. More alert now, he made his way south.

ACHELOIS WALKED home through the heat of the afternoon along deserted residential streets. She ambled back, in no mood to hurry, taking her time to enjoy watching the occasional butterfly darting between flowers, or investigate the multitude of overlapping stories hidden within the more interesting scents she came across. Along the way, she mused about the three visitors from Delphi. She also worried about them; they seemed so innocent of the big city. They understood nothing about the place or how it worked. She wondered if sending them to Hermes was the right thing to do? Maybe she should have…

She was so deep in thought as she turned a corner that she almost walked straight into Rea. The russet-coloured thug slashed her tail from side to side and uttered a low, threatening growl from the back of her throat. Lois felt the fur rising along her spine. She normally stayed well clear of Rea and her associates.

"So, what have you been up to?" the gangster sneered, unable to hide her contempt. "Been acting the 'tour guide' for our little out-of-towners, have you? Leda told me you'd brought them down here."

"What does it matter to you?" It was unsurprising that Rea had extracted information from her elderly neighbour. She seemed even more hostile than usual. It would be difficult to get out of this encounter without a fight, and she wasn't as young or as fast as she used to be.

"Where have you taken the little toe-rags?" Rea demanded. "What did you do with them?"

Achelois crept backward as the other inched forwards, trying to maintain the distance between them while looking for an escape route: a gateway, a car she could get under, a fence to jump over, anything. But there was no shelter in her immediate vicinity. She tried to play for time.

"Why are you so interested in them? They're well gone now and they won't be back. They're no threat to your gang."

"They're spies, and I think you know who for. They left

without paying their dues and we can't let that happen, can we? We're going to make them pay, just like anyone else who crosses us. So you'd better tell me where you sent them."

"Asleep, were you?" Achelois taunted. "What happened to your lookouts? Kratos has really let things slip."

Rea snarled, saliva dripping from her jaw. "No one gets past our guards without special skills and training. We're going to teach them the last lesson they'll ever learn, and then we're going after their masters. Or mistress, more like. And we won't let collaborators like you off the hook."

Lois froze; what had the intruders done to get under their skin so much? She'd never seen gang members so on edge, even one as vicious as Rea. She saw a car coming down the road toward her and thought about darting in front of it to put some distance between them. Rea noticed the flick of her eyes and attacked. Lois could only react, but she wasn't used to fighting, whereas the younger cat was a practiced warrior. Lois was no pushover, but she was no match for the other cat and she suffered a beating, covered in painful bites and deep scratches. One of her eyes was closed and bloodied, an ear notched and ragged. She didn't have the strength or speed to get away, and there was, in any case, nowhere to hide. Rea stopped. She stood over her opponent, gloating, unable to resist a boast.

"Times are changing. The fat cats of the Plaka and the Agora have had their day. Soon we'll rule Athens, then you'll pay your dues. All of you," she shouted to any animals within earshot, then stared down with contempt at the older cat struggling for breath at her feet. "But it looks like you won't survive long enough to tell them."

With arrogance befitting her gangland reputation, she turned tail and set off back to the factory with her news. Rea had a good idea now where the young cats were going—they were off to report back to Her Ladyship and her gaggle of interfering do-gooders hiding in the woods. She must have sent them to infiltrate their lair, test their defences, and find out their numbers. 'But all she's done is hasten the end,' she thought. The thought exhilarated her. War was coming. Kratos would soon gather the troops. It was time to march. A new thought hit her: 'and if he doesn't survive the engagement…. well then, that would be an interesting development, wouldn't it?'

Lois lay badly injured and struggling for breath. Her head was swimming and she couldn't see properly. In pain from head to tail, with blood oozing from her wounds, she felt a strange relief it was over. She didn't have the strength to crawl to find shade or shelter, she just lay there drifting in and out of consciousness. She had been aware of her enemy's rant, but hadn't been listening; they were all the same, these petty megalomaniacs. Along the deserted street, insects buzzed and the distant traffic noise continued, but the immediate vicinity was quiet. The cat lay still; funnily the pain subsided as she felt her life draining away. How interesting, she thought; she should tell someone. Sadly, she never got the opportunity.

CHAPTER 14

DAVAKI PARK

IN DAVAKI Park, Bia and her followers sat together under the trees in the eastern corner, close to the fountain. The park was shut at this time of night, but despite the hour, the traffic on Thiseos Street never stopped. As long-term residents they had become used to it; at least the closed gates gave them respite from human pedestrians for a few hours. Having tested and overcome the psychological defences of diners at a number of nearby restaurants, many of the cats had had their fill and were sleepy, but not all. Several gang members remained on the prowl. One or two were raiding the dwellings of some of the more easily intimidated local citizens via open windows or (a luxury item around here) cat-flaps. The still, warm night air which encouraged people to keep their windows ajar aided their efforts.

Bia herself was feeling very relaxed and content. She had carved out a nice territory south of the Acropolis. It was a good district with plenty of pickings for the gentlewoman cat-burglar and her followers, and bounded by a busy dual carriageway to the east, and a warehouse-dominated business quarter to the west, there were few territorial disputes with other gangs. It was true they occasionally had trouble from the stray dogs who roamed the business quarter, but when they became a problem, the city authorities wasted no time rounding them up. The cats of Davaki Park found it paid to keep a low profile and look as cute as possible.

On this particular night, Bia was struggling to sleep. She was pondering the latest intelligence her followers had brought back from an expedition up to Filopappou Hill near the Acropolis. This wooded central area provided excellent hunting opportunities but was little inhabited by felines, with the odd exception or two. They told her of some excitement among the humans at the ongoing excavations in the nearby Agora. The human diggers seemed to have unearthed some interesting (for them) finds including a stash of bright circular metal discs, such as they often used to buy things in shops. Evidently, these examples were old. They were dull and soil-encrusted when dug up, but her spies noticed that they scrubbed up nicely, and looked quite charming—and collectable. Bia wondered where the humans hid them and if there were any more just waiting there to be dug up. She might have to engage in a little burglary or excavation of her own. She had a little pit that she had dug in a quiet corner of the park where she kept some of her valuables, and it might be nice to add to her collection. It would also enhance her prestige and influence within Athenian feline society.

However, the most intriguing thing was what they said about the other watchers. They had spotted an owl in a tree overlooking the dig site and thought they glimpsed another cat observing from the shadows further away. What's more, they stayed on, watching long after the humans had packed up and gone away for the night, and most mysteriously of all, the cat then went nosing around the dig site itself. They couldn't tell who the observer was, but it was likely to be one of the Agora cats, she thought, and Bia knew what that meant. She wondered whether she should take the opportunity for some serious one-upmanship; mounting a raid on the dig and nicking whatever was there for under her nose? It was an appealing idea.

She was in the middle of planning the logistics when a flash of silver-white to her right caught her attention. There, circling the marble fountain, picked out in the moonlight, was a large, white, sleekly muscled cat. She gave it her full attention. Where had he come from, damn him, and what did he want? Hermes approached. Mr Superior always put in an appearance when she least wanted. What would it be this time? Well, he'd just have to wait. She was in no mood to play along with his little games.

"What a pleasant evening," he offered, looking around. Then, as if to wind her up some more, he hopped lightly onto a nearby stone bench and settled down. Bia was doubly annoyed. Not only had he barged in uninvited, but now she had to look up at him like some young kitten receiving instruction from an elder. She tried to ignore him. The silence grew, and with it her frustration. Eventually, she cracked.

"To what do I owe the pleasure of your company?" She tried to sound as sarcastic as possible, but in reality, she might as well have just come out with "whaddya want?" He'd never given a straight answer to a straight question in all the time she'd known him, so she suspected he wouldn't start now. Time to begin the verbal chess.

"Just passing by. Thought I'd see how you were doing." A likely story. He always wanted something, and she knew she'd have to be on her guard not to let something slip out, even more so with half the gang listening in. She didn't want to share her plans with the King of Gossip. At least he had the decency to get down off his ridiculous perch. He hunched down nearby, curling his tail neatly around his side, and glanced at the cats nearby, most of whom had heard his greeting and were now just pretending to sleep while keeping a nearly-closed eye on proceedings. Bia's frustration grew. What was worse, she could tell he was relishing her discomfort.

"So, what news from up on the hill?" she said, at last. "Are those buffoons in the north keeping their noses clean?" She knew the answer without asking. "Still doing your bidding?"

Hermes lent towards her, "I can't imagine what you're on about." He flashed her a sidelong glance. "Actually, I have some news that might just interest you. How you use it is entirely up to you, of course." He paused for effect, looking straight at her. Bia shifted position, aware he was trying to goad her into questioning him, and determined not to fall into his trap. She could wait for a long time, if that was the game he wanted to play. After a lengthy pause, he continued. "They're getting rather belligerent at the moment. In fact, I'd go so far as to say things might be about to get a little out of control."

"She must be slipping," Bia ventured. "Or you're losing your touch."

Hermes looked into the distance.

"That's as may be, it's not for me to say. However, the situation appears to be getting a little dangerous. A war is brewing between the northern gangs and those in the Plaka, and then there is a rumour something interesting may soon be uncovered by our two-legged companions. It's just speculation, of course, but there is a suggestion it could be a powerful object last seen centuries ago, back in the mists of history, and I suspect you might know where that line of thought leads?"

This was more interesting. Was this what was attracting the watcher's interest? Something from the distant past? She rarely thought about it these days; it was too painful to remember what she once had, but she dredged through her memories. What had been lost that was so interesting to her rival? Did she really think they were about to rediscover the Luck of Athens? She'd heard the name, but she didn't know what it looked like. An object of reverence and power, they said, but what was it, and what use could it be, beyond some memento of times long gone? She tried to recall snippets of old legends. It was said to bestow its owner great fortune in battle, she seemed to remember. Perhaps even to render them unbeatable? With an artefact like that under her control, she would rule all Athens! Bia's thoughts ran wild. Think of the power and influence. Think of all the retribution she could deliver. The fur along her spine rose in her excitement. But apart from not knowing what it looked like, how would she use it, assuming it was this thing. How could she tell? She looked directly at Hermes, suspicious.

"Why are you telling me this?" she said.

Serious now, he lowered his voice so no one could eavesdrop. "Let us assume it is, indeed, this item known as the Luck of Athens. You don't need me to spell out what it would mean if those two goons from the other side of town got hold of it. If the rumours are only half true, life for the rest of us would be very miserable." He looked around, checking no one could overhear them, and continued in a more conspiratorial tone. "I'm looking for someone responsible to hold on to it. Someone who wouldn't let it go to their head. I've been keeping an eye on you, and the way you run this neighbourhood. It works. If a war seems inevitable, as it seems to be, then I think you might be a far better keeper than either Kratos or Zelus." He stopped, watching her closely. Bia wasn't taken in for a second.

"What's in it for you?"

Hermes leaned back. He looked hurt. "Why, I trust you to look after me; to make sure no harm comes my way. Of course, I like to look after those in the business of thievery, it's a skill which is not respected as much as it should be, and one appreciates an artist. I like to champion their abilities. On the other hand, in the case of certain animals I could mention, criminal behaviour has become intertwined with more violent strains of activity, and *that* I do not condone. Should this object be what it purports to be, then I shudder to think what would happen if it fell into the wrong paws." He fell silent. Bia's suspicions remained.

"Why don't you take it for yourself?" she asked.

Hermes looked into the distance. He said nothing for a long while, then, "I've mused on that, and it has some appeal, I don't deny." He turned his shining blue eyes on her, and she had to look away. "But as you know, I don't have a huge number of followers and I like to keep on the move. I suspect I wouldn't be able to hold on to it for long unless I watched it night and day. And of course, I wouldn't like the responsibility; I'm not after power for its own sake. My currency is gossip. News."

"And what about her?"

"You know what a fearsome reputation she has as a warrior, and to have it dramatically enhanced is the last thing I want. And if she were to enlist the help of her brutish oaf of a brother, goodness knows what havoc they would unleash. No one would be safe. Fortunately, no one seems to have seen him for some time, so maybe he's no longer on the scene."

Bia fell silent. She remained suspicious, but she couldn't think of anything to add—her own opinions of them matched his. Perhaps, just perhaps, he was telling the truth. She shuddered. It seemed impossible, but here he was, offering her dominion over the entire city and beyond. The dream was tantalisingly close and with it a chance to look down on her 'betters' after all these years; the Olympians who loved to belittle her and her kind. It would be such a pleasure. She allowed herself to dream a little. If she could unlock the power of this legendary object, she might even bend dogs to her will, which would increase her authority immeasurably. The thought was intoxicating.

Hermes stood and arched his back in a long stretch. He glanced at her one last time.

"There is one problem: you must act soon. Tomorrow night at the latest, I suspect. The humans are making progress with their digging and you-know-who is likely to make her move soon. If you are going to act, I know someone who might help. One of her followers, in fact. Someone more than a little disillusioned."

"How do I find her?"

"Astiggos Street. Approach from the west. Get there an hour before dawn. Her name is Herse. I'll warn her to expect you. Right, I'll be off." He made to depart, then halted. "Anything else?"

"No," she replied, then hesitated. Hermes waited. "It's probably nothing, but when I'm over to the west, I hear dogs yapping on about being imprisoned."

"What do you mean 'imprisoned?'"

"It's quite faint, but that's what I think they're saying. Of course, dogs like to big things up, they're all drama queens, and their accents are a bit funny. Maybe I didn't understand them right. You don't think the humans are doing something to round up strays? You don't think they'll start on us?"

Hermes appeared unconcerned. "Who knows? Anyway, a few less stray dogs around the place is hardly a problem, is it? I don't think they'd start on cats. Where would they keep us all?"

Bia studied the ground in front of her nose and regretted asking the question; she hated hinting vulnerability. Hermes watched her for a second longer, then turned away and was gone.

CHAPTER 15

THE CHASE

APOLLO TURNED his thoughts back to his mission and walked on. He crossed a square and continued along the tree-lined street. He paid little attention to his immediate surroundings; the streets all looked the same to him. The hill ahead of him was all that mattered. He had to find Hermes. Gaining his help in his search looked like Apollo's best, perhaps only, hope of finding Olympia in this enormous bewildering city.

From the corner of his eye, he detected movement. He glanced across. On the opposite sidewalk, another cat was walking in time with him, in the same direction. It focused ahead and avoided eye contact. Apollo wondered whether it too was seeking Hermes, and what it might want from him? Did Hermes grant wishes? He trudged on. He and his companion across the street appeared to be going against the flow of pedestrians. Most two-legged traffic was heading past him, lured by the escalator in the square he'd left, and the subterranean world it led to. After several minutes of dodging pedestrians, Apollo glanced across the road once more to see what progress his fellow traveler was making and noticed the other animal now had a companion, both of them keeping pace with him. Both seemed determined to avoid looking at him. Interesting. Apollo slowed down, sauntering along the pavement and meandering in pursuit of interesting scents. He sniffed at some litter by the kerb. When he looked up, he found that his shadows were also dawdling, waiting for him to move.

He set off again with a more purposeful stride. They matched him. A junction with a minor side street came and went, and they continued on their parallel courses. Then Apollo sensed movement, a change in direction from one of them. Dispensing with subtlety, he looked across the street. One of his stalkers was marching across the road to get ahead of him, the other taking a more direct route toward him. Apollo considered the options. Should he challenge them, find out what they want? He thought about turning back, and looked over his shoulder only to spot a third, scrawny looking cat with dark mottled fur, following him. It seemed to stare right through him, but the look on its face was none too friendly. He was being led into a trap. Why? The next corner was approaching. He quickened his pace, then bolted as fast as he could down the side street.

"Get him, stop the spy!" yelled the cat behind him. The other two arrowed toward him just too late to pounce, but the chase was on. His pursuers weren't as coordinated as they should have been. Taking the initiative bought Apollo a few metres' head start, but nothing more.

Luckily, down this street, there were fewer humans to impede him. Unluckily, down this street, there were fewer humans to impede his pursuers. Apollo sped on, not heeding his surroundings. He sought new turnings to try to shake them off, and careered around corners as if pursued by the hounds of hell. But they knew this place too well, and he couldn't lose them. At least he managed to stay ahead, for now, at any rate.

Once again the cats of Athens had become aggressive, but why? Was it related to last night's encounter? Could he stand up to all three of them? After his previous encounter he wasn't so sure, and he didn't feel like finding out. The most annoying thing was he couldn't outpace his pursuers, but to his relief, they didn't seem able to close the gap. It was going to be a test of endurance. How long could he keep going? As the adrenaline surged through him, he shot across a multi-lane highway, vaulting the low fence in the central reservation, heedless of the traffic. He dodged busses and cars by a whisker's length and hoped his pursuers weren't so fortunate, but they were just as adept at avoiding those metal chariots of death as he was.

The longer the chase continued, the more anxiety clouded his mind. The relentless pursuit was most unusual. What was driving them? Was it fear? Was it anger? If so, what had he done to annoy them? Up ahead he saw trees to his left. A park, maybe. He hoped it might provide some extra cover. At least the trees would give some shade from the punishing heat and get him away from cars and exhaust fumes. He swerved to pass beneath the arching branches, and as he did so, he could hear his pursuers almost snatching at his tail. In the distance a dog barked at the sight of the chase and made a beeline toward them, its human guardian trying but failing to call it to heel.

He ran on. His breath never seemed to carry enough air to his aching lungs. His paws, his legs, his muscles; all were hurting. It was impossible to keep this pace up, and he had to slow down to something more sustainable. Would it be fast enough? Surely his pursuers must also be suffering, but from the pounding he could hear behind him, there was no sign of them slacking. Their persistence seemed almost supernatural and a horrible thought entered his head: what if they could outrun him? Apollo wondered how much further he could go. His lungs ached for him to stop. Sheer willpower was all he now had to drive him on.

Something strange happened. The weariness eased, and he felt he could keep going as long as he wanted. His body felt stronger, lighter. Was this what they call second wind, or was it something else? The self-doubt which had been stalking his thoughts fell away and his thoughts became clearer, but the pursuit continued as the chasers found new reserves of their own.

Apollo started changing direction at random, to try to force mistakes. He swerved around trees, through and between the objects in children's playgrounds, over or under park benches, anything that might cause one of them to stumble. But he was out of luck; the park ended far too soon, and he found himself at a roundabout where four roads met. To his good fortune, they were quiet at this time of day. He darted across and up a road opposite. A flimsy metal archway stretched across, and enormous gates stood open at each side. He passed them without thinking, but something in the air changed. Something he couldn't put a claw on. There was no longer any sound of pursuit.

He dared to look behind and saw his pursuers had stopped on the far side of the gate, their bodies heaving as they panted for breath. Apollo turned to face them. They glared at him across the invisible divide with raw hostility. He couldn't understand why they'd stopped; like many things today, it made little sense.

"Don't think you'll escape us for long," one of them sneered, "and don't expect her to keep you out of our clutches."

"You can't hide there forever. We'll find you. We'll get you," snarled another.

The third just uttered a guttural growl, deep in its throat. Apollo glanced at the flimsy arch. It wasn't designed for defence; it was just a simple barrier for cars. Why were they afraid to pass underneath? It seemed unlikely, given the risks they'd taken chasing him here.

"Who are you?" he shouted. In reply, they just jeered at him but said no more. After a minute, they turned and grudgingly departed.

Apollo stood there for a while, watching them go and letting his heart rate return to normal. He had no idea where he was, and worse still, he couldn't see any sign of Mount Lycabettus. He sat down, feeling deflated, wondering who or what was behind them. Someone far more frightening to them than he was. A deep frustration replaced the exhilaration he'd felt at evading his pursuers. He was being blocked at every turn. So far he'd been attacked and wounded, lost his friends, then stalked, and chased halfway across the city, and he was no further forward in his quest. Being the prey of some mindless thugs seemed like the ultimate insult. He'd been pinning everything on meeting Hermes and enlisting his help, but someone was trying to prevent it. Who? Could it be his attacker from yesterday? It seemed unlikely; why would he bear such a grudge? He thought about retracing his steps, but he wasn't confident enough to take on all three of them and however many more there might be. How could he ever find Hermes now? There was no one in this alien city he trusted to ask for help, and his word no longer seemed to carry any weight with mortals. He was alone, for perhaps the first time. He had no answers, he couldn't see a way forward. Uppermost in his mind was the feeling he'd let Olympia down. Time was dragging and his quest had stalled. Poor Olympia. He had no idea how to find her and was no further forward than when he'd arrived in Athens.

He couldn't just sit on the side of the road forever; he

had to go somewhere. Weary, he stood and turned to scan his surroundings. Behind him, the road curved upwards and soon passed out of sight. It was in a cutting; wooded slopes rose on each side. To his immediate left, a short rocky bank climbed a few meters and then levelled off. It seemed as good a direction as any. At least he would have the advantage of height over any fresh pursuers and allow him to see them coming. Apollo didn't have complete trust they had given up the chase. He paused once more and looked over his shoulder, thinking of Daphne and again wrapped in guilt. He hoped she was alright. Jason too, of course, but Daphne, well, losing her was more than just misplacing a companion; she was his inspiration. He wanted her by his side when they finally found their friend. Olympia might be his most recent ex, but Daphne was his future. He wondered where she was.

Weary and more dispirited than he could remember, in laboured fashion made his way up the steep slope onto the gentler gradient behind, lost in thought, and paying little attention to his surroundings. 'Spy,' his pursuers had called him. He thought back to his encounter with the gang. The leader was quite a character. Impervious to reason, bitter and full of anger. What made him so? Just trying to have a conversation seemed to aggravate him. Was he the one who sent the chasers? Why was he so paranoid and who did he think they were spying for? What did he think they might find? He must have mistaken him for someone else. Apollo's concerns for his friends grew. If they'd tracked him, then they too would be in danger. It was an alarming thought. He hoped they'd managed to avoid capture. Apollo halted and looked over his shoulder, tempted to go back and try to find them, one leg hovering in midair as he was gripped by indecision.

"Few dare venture through my gate," purred a low female voice above him. He turned and saw a large black cat perched on the trunk of a fallen tree not far ahead. Apollo's hackles rose. Who was this, and what did she want from him? His patience with Athenians was wearing thin. He studied her. The cat talking to him was black from nose to tail with no other visible colouring. Yellow eyes surveyed him coolly.

"I'm lost."

"That much is obvious," she said. "I don't get many casual visitors."

Apollo looked around with fresh interest. His surroundings didn't seem special or distinctive, other than he was in a quiet patch of woodland within the midst of a huge bustling city. How quiet it was here. He could hear no vehicles; even the birds were sotto voce in this glade. He sniffed the air and caught the scent of vegetation and earth rather than the exhaust fumes and other pollution he'd become used to in Athens. The abrupt change was welcome, but startling. Ahead of him was a long slope, the top veiled by trees. More of them stretched out to either side, while below, at the foot of the slope, was the road with the mysterious gate. Why were his pursuers so scared of this strange black cat? He looked anew at his surroundings with narrowed eyes, trying to spot anything unusual.

"What is this place?" he asked, voicing his thoughts.

"It's just my domain," she said. "My little kingdom. Enter at your peril."

Apollo felt hot in his fur. She was mocking him. "And who are you?"

She gave him a long look, then jumped to the ground and sauntered up the hill between the trees. Apollo watched her go, hypnotised by the languid sway of her hindquarters as she sashayed away. She had a dangerous walk. He weighed up his options. To return the way he'd come, with the likelihood of bumping into those three gangsters again, held no appeal. The only alternative was to venture on into the lair of this mysterious and slightly sinister creature who seemed to exert a strange power over this territory. He gave her a suspicious look and followed.

CHAPTER 16

DAPHNE ALONE

DAPHNE CONTINUED down the street, wondering where Apollo and Jason could have got to. Her worry increased with every step. Surely nothing horrible could have happened to them, could it? If that wasn't bad enough, she still wasn't totally convinced she was heading in the right direction. If only she could get an unobstructed view down the street past these trees. I've never been great with directions, she thought. But what was getting to her most was the length of this interminable quest and their lack of progress. How long had she expected it to take? Her naivete appeared incredible from what she now knew. Athens was proving a difficult education. Her thoughts turned back to Olympia, hoping she was alright.

Her legs ached. She had been walking across this enormous city all day, or so it seemed, and she'd had enough. Her paws were aching, and she wanted a nap. Somewhere nice and quiet and maybe a little something to nibble, she thought, skirting an old plastic bag and looking at her drab surroundings. The street she was walking down was quite a busy thoroughfare lined with shops on both sides. Cars, busses, vans, and trucks rushed down the central tarmac strip, but she learned to ignore them. Provided she didn't antagonize them by trying to go toward them, they appeared happy to keep out of her way. None of the shops looked like suitable places to rest up. She wondered about side streets. What she needed were some houses or apartments, but to find somewhere like that would mean deviating from the route she had determined. If she left it, she would soon be lost.

As she plodded on, worry turned to dread, and hunger began to gnaw. She felt footsore and weary and frustrated that she still couldn't get a proper sight of her destination. With every step away from the square where she had lost her companions, her self-doubt grew. If only she had paid more attention to the directions.

She arrived at a crossing. The street she had been following ended at a wider, busier road. On the opposite side she could see her street (as she thought of it) continuing, narrower and free of vehicles. But how could she get there? The prospect of another dangerous crossing filled her with dread, and the noise and bustle of the road before her was terrifying. Not wanting to repeat her previous experience, she waited for a gap in the traffic. And waited. And waited some more. Sometimes the vehicles seemed to stop from one direction, but it only slowed down from the other. Then without warning it all speeded up again.

Despair increasing, she paced up and down the sidewalk, wondering what to do. Then she noticed some bright lights on posts that kept changing colour and stopped. They seemed to be attractive to humans; maybe a shrine? Now and then the humans gathered beside the posts and after waiting to, she assumed, pray or something, risked crossing the street. In homage to their piety, the noisy traffic stopped and waited. Daphne didn't associate their behaviour with the colour of the lights, just that they seemed to signify the place where this strange ritual took place. She approached, hesitant until she could be sure that they wouldn't chase her away. Then, still keeping as much distance as possible, she waited until they began to cross and screwed up her courage to run for it, her heart in her mouth. The relief she felt at having survived was almost worth the risk.

A little of her confidence crept back. Daphne made her way to the traffic-free street she had seen and turned into it, feeling better. Her reward was the sight of several restaurants, their tables covering much of the street. Some had people sitting at them. This was more like it; she could handle begging for food—she'd done it occasionally at the café in Delphi. She knew the ropes; have a quick wash to look presentable, look toward the humans sweetly, perhaps cocking a head a little to make it look like she understood what they were saying, pretend to be friendly, even allowing the odd pat on the head, watch like a hawk and pounce on anything dropped before any rivals could steal it away. If it amounted to more than one mouthful, be prepared to fight to defend it. Simple, provided there wasn't too much competition. Daphne surveyed her surroundings. Not too bad. Her chief rivals seemed to be a mother and kitten combination. She would have to watch out for the older cat, but the youngster wouldn't be too much of a threat. Apart from the cuteness aspect, of course. But Daphne was young and good-looking, just a few months beyond being a kitten herself. She could do 'cute' as well as anyone; it was the streetwise mother who would be a problem. Would she share her pitch?

Daphne settled down in a prominent position near a promising-looking table. She maintained a reasonable distance from her rivals and kept a weather-eye out in case anyone else was tempted to join them. At this hour of the day, she was in luck. The occasional titbit came her way, and she could eat for the first time since early morning. A few mouthfuls reminded her just how hungry she was, so she spent the next few hours on watch, moving among the tables as people came and went, seeking the best scavenging opportunities. Now and then a waiter would shoo her and her rivals away, but they would soon be back at post, waiting for the next opportunity, eyeing the diners, and assessing the odds of them sharing a mouthful or two—a nibble of souvlaki (her favourite) here, a piece of kebab there; she felt better. Daphne wondered how her companions were getting on, supposing they would have arrived with Hermes by now, and felt envious. It would be nice to be together again. She missed them, particularly Jason, but hunger wouldn't allow her to reflect for long. She concentrated on the diners once more.

In the heart of the city, surrounded by tall buildings, it was difficult to tell if shadows were lengthening, but eventually, Daphne noticed that afternoon was turning into evening, and it was time to move on. Before leaving, she tried to thank the other adult cat for allowing her to share.

"Don't worry, I won't stay here, I was just hungry. You can have your restaurant back."

"You're new here, aren't you?" replied the other, looking at her in suspicion. "How do I know you won't be back? This has been our place for as long as I can remember. My mother used to bring me here when I was a kitten. I only let you stay because there was enough to go round, but I might not be so generous next time."

"Thank you," said Daphne. "I understand, but I'm from Delphi, not around here, and I'm trying to find my friend, Olympia. Perhaps you might have heard about her? Humans kidnapped her and brought here in a big car."

The other cat was unimpressed. "Have you seen that road down there?" She glanced at the street Daphne had crossed. "How many cars go down there every day? How am I supposed to know if there're any cats in them?" she snorted. "If you ask me, your friend's history. They might be OK here," she indicated to the diners, "but some of them hate our kind, and like nothing better than to do away with us, or sell us to others who might do the same or worse. Forget her, and get back to your 'Delfi', or whatever it's called."

Daphne suppressed a shudder of revulsion, but her anxiety for her friend returned. Where could Olympia be in this immense city, and how might she be able to find her, and would she have time before something dreadful happened? Her spirits sank. After a while, she tried a different subject.

"Do you know a place where I can get a proper rest around here?"

Her companion stared into space for a while, thinking.

"I'm not showing you my nesting place, but if you're in luck, you might find somewhere down there." She indicated down the street in the direction Daphne was planning to go, anyway. "Past the end of this bit there are some quiet back streets where the humans live, and some of them might have left a window open." She said no more, instead turning her attention to the kitten, which was chasing a piece of paper blown around by the breeze. Daphne waited a while, but the other cat continued to ignore her, so she left, raising her tail in brief, silent thanks.

At its end, another road crossed the short, pedestrianised street, but this one was much less busy. Daphne crossed without bother and continued up the street opposite. Absorbed in her thoughts, she didn't notice it headed in a slightly different direction. It had been a little demeaning to beg for food (and she was glad someone left bowls for her and her extended family at the sanctuary in Delphi), but it was a relief to realise she could survive on the streets of this never-ending city.

Away from the street with the restaurants, it was far quieter. She had entered a part of town where humans lived. There were few shops. Instead, apartment blocks lined the street, most with their windows shuttered against the summer heat. Here and there, Daphne noticed that upper floor apartments had balconies and on some of these windows were open. In frustration, she noticed they were just out of reach, even for a young cat like her. But her luck was about to change. The street ascended. She followed until she reached a corner where there was a building with its ground floor set partially into the hillside, and a first-floor balcony she could reach with ease. Once there, she found an open window. She hesitated a while, listening for any sounds from inside, but there were none.

Feeling braver than ever before, she leaped inside, landing on a small cabinet with a polished wood surface. Daphne skated across it, sending an ornament spinning into space to smash with a tinkling sound on the floor. She froze for a second, shocked at the noise, but there was no new sound. She jumped to the floor, skirting the remains of the thing she had displaced, and started to nose around. Unused to the dwellings of humans, she failed to appreciate that she was in a neat, but sparsely furnished living room with a small settee and a couple of armchairs. A table stood against a wall. The chairs looked inviting. One of them might do for a snooze, but she decided to explore further. Through a doorway Daphne found an even darker hallway with several doors and was pleased to find the first one she pushed opened, taking her into a bedroom filled with the largest bed she had ever seen. When she jumped onto it, her paws sank deep into the soft duvet.

This was as pleasurable as it was unexpected. Daphne

congratulated herself for such a marvellous reward for her bravery. She walked to the centre of the bed and curled up. It was glorious and comfortable. She felt she was in heaven. Within seconds she was asleep. Fast asleep. It is normal for cats to sleep with one ear open, instantly awake at the slightest sound, but Daphne was so tired after her long trek across town that she fell into a deep, dreamless sleep. Anyone listening would have detected the rare but delicate sound of a cat snoring.

CHAPTER 17

JASON GETS LOST

FOR THE first few blocks, Jason made excellent progress. There was still no sight of the others, and that left a nagging doubt. Perhaps I'll get there first, he thought, although it raised the whole question of where 'there' actually was. He pondered this as he dodged pedestrians along the sidewalk. He decided it must be the big temple-thing on the top of the flat-topped hill. After an hour, with only a few minor pauses to investigate interesting scents along the way, he reached the end of the street, but to his dismay came across one of the busiest junctions he had yet seen. The street before him was narrow but very busy. On the other side was a large open paved area, a reward for surviving the immediate danger. Getting there required all his powers of concentration.

Having navigated the road, Jason arrived in a large irregular square which people were crossing in all directions. Momentarily he lost his sense of direction, but then he looked up at the skyline and saw the rocky mass of the Acropolis before him. He marched across the square, making a beeline for it, and wondered how he was going to climb it. The cliff faces looked sheer and impassable. Of more immediate concern was avoiding getting trodden on or kicked by the myriad of humans milling around. The square was extremely busy in the late afternoon as people emerged from work and tourists went in search of refreshment following a busy day's sightseeing. Though he didn't make the connection, Jason had similar motivations; all he wanted was somewhere to rest and lie low for a while and gather his thoughts. A pleasant drink of water would be a bonus.

He wandered around aimlessly for a few minutes thinking about his options, then noticed a patch of what looked like waste ground just beyond the square. A few humans were wandering across it for reasons best known to themselves, but it looked promising. It was fenced off by iron railings and far quieter than the main square; a good place to find a secluded corner for a nap and to de-stress after his long dusty journey.

He watched some people come and go through a gate, but decided he could just as easily squeeze between the railings. Once inside, he became insulated from the hubbub of modern-day Athens, as if transported back to an earlier, quieter time. The effect was soothing. Jason paid a little more attention to his immediate surroundings. There were a lot of old stones, some intricately carved with designs he couldn't work out. A few pillars or sections of wall of varying height stood here and there with bare earth or patches of grass between. One high wall had a row of extremely tall old columns in front of it. Jason had to crane his neck to see the top. He spent a few moments observing all of this, taking it in and looking for a good place for a rest. In a sunny spot on the far side of the site, a couple of cats were sitting while a gaggle of kittens played on some grass, alternately play-fighting and chasing their tails.

He looked around some more and spotted a quiet corner where few people seemed to venture, with no animals visible, and headed toward it, hopping over some low ruined walls on the way. This was a lot more promising. There

119

was a wall to the rear stretching up to present-day street level above, and some old ruins before it surrounding a small patch of open ground now in shade as the shadows lengthened. He looked around briefly, then settled down and curled up to sleep. His thoughts wandered briefly to his companions. Apollo, he reasoned, could look after himself, but he worried about Daphne. She was, after all, the primary reason he was on this quest; the cause of the spur-of-the-moment decision that had taken his life in such a completely unexpected direction. He hoped she was alright. Perhaps she'd already found this Hermes character Lois had seemed to hold in such high regard. Jason hoped so. With a bit of luck, he'd make it there tomorrow and be reunited with her. At the back of his mind a slightly ungracious thought arose: what if something happened to Apollo? Not really bad; not life-threatening or a serious injury, but something to hold him up, or keep him busy elsewhere for a while so he could have her to himself? He shook his head to erase such unworthy and disloyal thoughts and tried to sleep.

It was no use; just a few minutes had passed before he was rudely interrupted by two aggressive looking cats.

"What do you think you're playing at?" asked one.

"You looking for trouble?" demanded the other.

Jason looked up wearily. He didn't need this right now.

"I'm tired," he said, "I just want a rest."

"A likely story," said the first, circling to Jason's right. His companion moved slightly in the opposite direction, making it difficult for him to keep both of them in sight at the same time. Jason briefly wondered if they would go away if he just ignored them and lowered his head onto his paws again. He was tired of having to be always on the alert in this city and longed for the simpler life he had back in Delphi.

"One more time—what are you doing here?" demanded the first cat, more aggressively this time. Jason had had enough. He raised his head and turned toward the interrogator, determined to ask a few questions of his own.

"My business is my own and nothing to do with you. What are *you* doing here? And why are you disturbing me? Are you always this rude to your visitors?" He made no other sign of moving.

The other cats looked at each other. This wasn't working out like they'd planned. They had hoped to intimidate this interloper into leaving without having to resort to violence, but he didn't show any signs of being scared, and they were both a bit out of practice. House cats were a different matter, they just wanted a quiet life and were easy to push around—especially the older ones. This guy was much younger, and by the look of him, fitter. They changed tack.

"Who do you belong to?" the second one asked. "Botrys or the Gizi mob?"

"Perhaps he's one of the nutters from the South Side," his companion ventured.

Jason said nothing.

"Who sent you?" the first cat tried again.

"No one, I'm my own animal," Jason replied, staring levelly at his questioner. He was becoming increasingly irritated and thought about taking him on. The only worry was if they had some colleagues in the area. Jason paid more attention to his wider surroundings, alert to any new arrivals.

"I reckon he's one of Kratos's losers," the second cat said to his companion, talking over Jason's head, and ignoring him.

"Nah," said his companion, "he looks too well fed to be

one of that scrawny crew."

"Maybe he's been sent to spy on us," the other cat proffered. He was about to say more, but Jason pounced, catching him unawares. There was a brief scuffle as Jason raked his claws across his opponent's nose and delivered a sharp bite to his neck. The speed of his attack had forced the other onto his back, a position of vulnerability. The second cat made as if to join in, but held back, waiting to see how the fight unfolded. Jason stood over his opponent, snarling viciously. The cowering animal in front of him looked up fearfully, all his aggression gone in an instant. His wounds stung, and he wanted to get out of this situation before it got any worse. With infinitesimal movement he backed away, his eyes still fixed on Jason. Jason let him go, still bristling with anger, but inwardly absolutely delighted with his victory. This had been far easier than he had expected.

He looked from his victim to the equally surprised other cat, now poised to flee. He noticed the other was carrying a little more weight than most of the street cats he'd seen in the city to date, and certainly more than Kratos's crew. A little more of his anxiety dissipated.

"I reckon I'm quite a bit faster than you," he said, threateningly. "So, I think it's time for you to give me some answers. Who are you losers?" He glanced dismissively at the animal at his feet. "And why are you trying to intimidate me?"

There was a pause. The first cat spoke, never taking his eyes off Jason.

"We're in the Plaka gang. This place is one of our bases. We come here to rest up between missions and before scavenging raids. We're just trying to protect our turf; you can't be too careful. These days you never know who's spying on you, and sometimes folk just go missing, know what I mean?"

Jason didn't, but he pressed on. "There aren't very many of you?" He looked around; he couldn't detect any other cats in the area. The second cat recovered its voice.

"It's still early. They'll be here soon," he said. "Perhaps you'd like us to introduce you?" he added, turning submissive and compliant. Jason looked at him, weighing up the sincerity of the offer. The first cat had said nothing, but seemed, from the minute twitch of his tail, to agree with his friend.

Jason sat and thought fast. He didn't yet trust this pair, but if what they said was true, he'd get little or no peace in this neighbourhood without agreement of safe passage from the gang who owned this territory. Better they knew him, than see him as a threat. Perhaps they could show him the best places to get food and drink. His stomach was rumbling.

"Alright then. Let's wait."

They sat in silence, the two Plaka cats trying to act as if nothing had happened, Jason still keeping a wary eye on them in case of trouble. He didn't expect any—he'd shown his dominance, but you never knew. They might feel braver when some of their companions arrived. While they waited, he went over what they'd said. Wherever they went in this city, the local cats seemed jittery and on their guard against one another. Territorial bickering was a way of life for all cat societies, but the paranoia of the cats of Athens was exhausting and far different from the life he'd known in peaceful Delphi. And what was that reference to cats disappearing? His thoughts, shrouded in guilt, wandered back to Olympia. It was a while since he'd thought about the quest, but his fixation on getting to the Acropolis, hoping to find some answers, and meeting his companions again had driven her from his mind. Lingering here was a distraction he couldn't afford. But he needed to eat and sleep, and with a bit of luck, the gang members might give him some information about what was up there, and who it was who lived there.

After around 20 minutes another cat appeared, soon followed by another, and then a third. More arrived, heading into the heart of their den. In retrospect, Jason had been quite bold to just stride in and treat it like home. He put the thought to the back of his mind as he confronted the newcomers, but before he could speak one of his initial interrogators piped up, attracting the attention of his peers.

"Hi everybody, this is… er…"

"Jason," said Jason.

"… Jason. Er, he arrived this afternoon. Well, not very long ago, actually. He's just… visiting." He looked around at Jason for help.

Jason stood up and raised his tail in what he hoped was a confident but friendly manner. "Hi," he said. "I'm just passing by. Visiting your magnificent city." He stopped, unsure what to say. Oh, why not tell them everything, he thought? "Look, it's like this," he said, starting again. "I'm here with some friends and we're on a quest to find another friend who was stolen." He sat down. The recently arrived cats sat and lay nearby, staring at him. Strangers were not unusual around here, but confident ones that who strolled into their inner sanctum unharmed were rarer than a field mouse dancing a hornpipe on their lawn. This one must have something about him to have persuaded Sergios and Theo to give him free rein to address them like this. He must have something really important to say. Then the questions started.

"How many friends?" said one.

"What do you mean, 'stolen?'" said another.

"Where have you come from?" added a third.

Jason looked around at them. "There are three of us, Apollo, Daphne, and me. We're from Delphi. We're looking for our other friend Olympia—she was taken a few days ago." He struggled to work out how long—it seemed like an eternity. Was it really only yesterday? "We think they brought her here. We have to find her." His voice trailed off.

"Well, she ain't around here, we'd 'ave seen 'er," said a gruff old male from the back of the assembly. "Any strangers round here, we see 'em off with a flea in their ear, or worse."

"It was humans. They put her in a big black car," Jason told him, raising his voice. "She's no trouble to you. None of us are. I'm just wanting news. We were told there would be some answers up there." He turned his head, pointing his nose toward the Acropolis towering above.

"No one lives up there," said another quieter voice to his left, a tabby female. She glanced at the cliffs and back toward Jason. "Someone fed you a line." She looked pleased with herself.

"We were told he lived on a hilltop," Jason replied, his temper rising. "Hermes. We were told he'd help us." The cats looked at one another and a murmur of conversation started up. Several of them were laughing. Jason was furious. The tabby turned toward him again.

"Have you no sense of direction?" she said. "Hermes lives over there on Lycabettus." She nodded in the other direction. Jason followed her eyes and noticed a much bigger hill. "No one lives on the Acropolis. We visit from time to time, but no one actually lives there."

Jason's head bowed as if the weight of this news was

pushing it down. All this way for nothing. How could he have got it so wrong? What an idiot, he thought to himself. He said nothing. No cat likes to look stupid, and he was no exception. Amid his scrambled thoughts, he tried to save face. "I must have been given the wrong information," he lied.

"So what happened to your mates then?" A questioner from the other side of the clearing.

"I—I don't know." He felt helpless. What had happened to them? He'd thought they might be ahead of him, but if this lot were adamant they'd seen no strangers in the vicinity, where could they be? He tried to look on the bright side. Perhaps they had gone in the right direction and it was just he who had got lost. He no longer had any idea what to do. He needed some time to think.

The tabby spoke up again. "You could stay with us for a while?" she offered. Several of the other cats looked at her, but there were no dissenting voices. She turned to the assembly. "Why not? He's young and strong, and as long as we teach him where the best hunting and scavenging spots are, he won't be any trouble. We can always do with new recruits." There was a general murmur of agreement. "Good, that's settled then," she said, turning back to Jason. "I'm Tabitha. Let me show you where we sleep. In the morning, I'll show you what we get up to."

Jason looked at her, lost for words. He hadn't expected this. He didn't want to join a gang, but right now he had no choice. Perhaps he could resume his journey tomorrow. With a small sigh, he followed her to their sleeping quarters.

CHAPTER 18

SANCTUARY

THE BLACK cat led the way through the trees and up the slope to a neat complex of buildings at the top. Well-maintained steps led to a paved rectangular terrace with a low wall along one side and three buildings on the other sides. Apollo climbed the steps cautiously, maintaining a careful watch. He paused briefly and looked around in surprise. Surely this was a human dwelling of some sort? How many of them lived here, and how safe was it? He couldn't see any sign of them, but he remained on alert. He had little experience of the buildings they lived in, but surely this wasn't a cat-friendly environment?

The other cat paused by a tree, planted in the middle of the terrace, its base surrounded by a low wall. She sat down in the shade and turned to face him once more.

"This is what humans call a monastery." She caught the blank look on his face. "It's where some of their religious people live." As if reading his thoughts, she carried on "I know, what am I doing living here among the followers of this new-fangled cult; me a practitioner of a far older religion; the true religion?" She paused and looked around, then turned back to him. Her tone became convivial. "The fact is, they're quite benevolent. For their species. They keep themselves to themselves, mostly. They leave offerings of food for me. It's almost as if they worship my cult alongside their own! What's not to like?"

Apollo broke off his stare lest it be thought rude. What cult? Who was she? He couldn't place her, but recognition wasn't straightforward these days. Still, he was grateful for any place of sanctuary after the day he'd had. He sat down and tried to think of something to say. Meanwhile, she was studying him closely and his discomfort grew. He was just about to remonstrate with her, when she averted her gaze, got up, and walked to the middle building. This one was the smallest of the three, a simple single room with, in place of a door, an open archway facing the courtyard, and an altar in the middle. On the threshold Apollo paused for a moment, suspicious. He looked at the contents of the room. Before him, the altar, on a raised plinth, took up most of the floor space. At the top was a painting of a man nailed to a cross, writhing in agony, or was it ecstacy? It had an ornate silver frame, and was positioned behind a large carved cross also made of silver. Above it dangled a coloured glass lantern containing a candle. There were more candles on a shelf halfway up, and on a low step at its base. To either side of the altar, alcoves retreated into darkness.

The black cat disappeared inside. Curiosity got the better of him, and Apollo followed. She disappeared behind the altar where, in a small alcove, he found two large bowls containing food and water, respectively. "Come on, there's enough to share," she said in encouragement. Apollo needed no second invitation to join her at her feast.

Afterwards, they sat once more in the courtyard enjoying the evening air. For a long time neither spoke. The black cat didn't seem inclined to start a conversation, while Apollo wrestled with whether to admit his predicament. Since he had arrived in Athens, he had mainly had to deal with suspicion and hostility. He sensed this cat was different, but he still wasn't sure he could trust her. Yet he had so many questions. Would she be able to give him any help? Somehow he doubted it. She'd hinted that she didn't move from this place, so how could she know anything of the city beyond? He took it slowly.

"Where is this place?"

"We're still in Athens," she told him. "Not far from the centre, in case you were worried. The Acropolis is over there," she pointed with her nose. He vaguely remembered the name, but couldn't visualise it. He didn't want to admit as much; it was yet another mystery to resolve.

"How come it's so quiet?"

"This is a rather special place. It's been a place of sanctuary and worship down the years. It has centuries of spells and incantations laid about its boundaries; can't you feel them?" Her eyes lit up as she talked and looked up at the canopy of trees, and through the branches the early evening stars.

Apollo remembered the change he'd noticed when he passed under the gate on the road and had to admit it did feel different: tranquil and secluded, the air heavy with the scent of pine trees. It was a relief to be away from the frantic noise and congestion of the city streets, but he couldn't afford to relax. He still had a mission to complete, no matter how impossible it seemed, and he mulled it over.

"I wish I knew what to do next," he said, scarcely aware that he had accidentally given voice to his thoughts. Slowly his head dropped toward his paws as weariness got the better of him, and he fell asleep. The black cat watched him carefully through half-closed eyes.

He awoke with a jolt. It was dark. He couldn't tell how long he'd been sleeping, but as he stretched and moved, his muscles felt stiff from being in one position for too long. He looked around. There was no sign of his hostess.

Slowly, he stood up and tentatively explored the courtyard. The moon was high and full, bright enough to cast shadows from the tree and buildings, but from one, the one where they'd eaten earlier, yellow candlelight spilled forth. Apollo approached, sniffing around the doorway. There were scents he couldn't place. They seemed familiar yet unfamiliar, as if once known but long forgotten. He stepped over the threshold of the shrine. In the shadows, he saw a dark shape. He jumped, only to realise it was the large black cat. She stared at him with an unwavering, unnerving gaze. She could penetrate his innermost thoughts, and that made him uncomfortable. How long had she been here and what was her game? If she was so interested in him, why didn't she just talk to him? He stepped forward, but before he could open his mouth, she started speaking.

"You seem confused. Not just about me, about this place." She glanced at the altar and painted ceiling briefly before training her stare back on Apollo. "It's time to find out what it is you are here for, and what you must do." Not for the first time, Apollo felt he was playing catch-up.

"What do you mean?"

"Step closer. Here," she nodded to her left. "I have some herbs gathered locally beneath the light of the moon. They will help free your thoughts so you can find some answers to your questions. Look into the flame."

Without further ado, she delicately picked up a bunch of leaves in her mouth and dropped them on top of the nearest votive candle. She stepped back but immediately started muttering an incantation in a language Apollo had never heard, her eyes focused on the burning herbs.

It was entrancing. He couldn't remember seeing anything like this before, but dimly remembered images floated in his mind. He moved a centimetre or two closer, then closer again, watching as the leaves smoked and crackled in the flame. A powerful fragrance filled the shrine, overpowering his senses. It was both delicious and intoxicating, arousing and soporific at the same time. As he watched the flame, it seemed to take over his entire field of vision. Then it seemed he was watching from a great distance down a long tube or tunnel. Then it went out.

HE FOUND himself in a dark, desolate, rocky plain that seemed to stretch on forever beneath a not-quite-black starless sky. There was just enough light to make out the landscape, but not enough to see any detail. There was no sign of any living thing in any direction. Far away he thought he could make out a ridge of low hills at an unguessable distance. There didn't seem to be any vegetation at all. There was no moon. He looked down, surprised to see that the only thing emitting any light in this place was himself—a small pool of golden light illuminated the ground around his feet before being swallowed up in the enormity of the all-encompassing darkness. As his eyes adjusted, he could see that he was standing on a road of sorts. He followed it—there was nowhere else to go. He trudged on and on. Nothing in this featureless dusty desolation seemed to get any closer or further away. He had no concept of time here. He could have been walking for minutes or days, but strangely, it didn't seem to matter.

Eventually, as seemed inevitable yet at the same time surprising, he arrived at the bank of a wide, slow-moving river. Its waters were the colour of pitch, the darkest black imaginable. He stopped. Even the pale glow emanating from him had no power to illuminate it. As he looked across, he could just make out the far bank. Could he swim? The thought horrified him, but how else could he get across? He looked to his right and saw, not far away, a small rowing boat beside which stood a tall figure in a dark hooded cloak. The man (he assumed it was a man) took no notice of him at all. He thought of approaching him, but immediately a voice came from his left, loud, deep, strong.

"I wouldn't even think about it, if I were you."

Apollo spun around and found himself confronted by a huge, vicious-looking, three-headed dog. His mouth fell open in astonishment. The beast's three heads glared at him, each mouth half open and filled with a fearsome set of savage teeth the size of daggers. It was so close that its slobber splashed on the ground just in front of Apollo's paws. He stood his ground and looked up at this creature of Hell, and strangely his fear and uncertainty were gone.

"I'm looking for someone. She may be over there; I need to find her." He looked toward the distant bank.

The three-headed dog edged closer. Two of the heads growled menacingly; the third addressed him directly.

"You can't. You're not meant to be here. Begone, lest I change my mind and make you stay forever." It made a strange, strangled sound that Apollo interpreted as laughter. The monster took another step closer, almost grinning in anticipation as the last thought played across its triple brain.

Apollo looked back at those baleful eyes, and something snapped. Instead of feeling cowed and intimidated by this monstrous, threatening beast, pure anger flared, and with it his confidence returned. He would not put up with threats anymore, no matter who the bully might be. He looked down at the creature before him, the way a lion might study a mouse. A small part of his mind stood aside, surprised at the transformation; he was now the largest lion ever seen, and the light that had been glowing from his small body, kindled by his rage, flared so brightly around him it seemed a star had landed on the banks of the Styx. Now blindingly bright and clothed in full Olympian glory, he threw back his head, shook his magnificent mane, and roared for the sheer joy and release, and the sound travelled far across the river and the dismal kingdom beyond, even to the halls of its pale king.

"Enough of threats," he growled in a voice so deep as to make the earth shake. "Answer me." Cerberus took a couple of steps back; two of his heads turned away, unable to bear the light, the third bowed, but despite this turn of events, did not yield.

"I am the guardian of this place," he said, his voice now almost apologetic. "I cannot let you pass. You must go, or else face the wrath of my master." One of his three mighty heads looked across the river into the distance.

Apollo was in no mood to back down, and the dog unable to. A fight seemed inevitable, but then he heard voices from the far side of the river.

"You're too late..."

"You should have come earlier…"

"It was so horrible…"

"Why didn't you help us?"

"Why did nobody come to rescue us?"

There were so many voices, accusing, wailing, pleading. Apollo stared across the river. Horror mixed with pity flooded his feelings. He could make out shades there, transparent disembodied shapes drifting on the far shore, imploring and shaming him at the same time.

"No one came to help us, and now it's too late."

A desperate thought struck him. He felt sick, but he had to ask.

"Olympia?" he shouted; a roar heard miles away. He got no response. Then.

"I knew her. She's not here. Not yet," cried a spirit, a small lone voice among the multitude. "But she will be soon, if you're not quick."

"Where? Where do I find her?" Apollo yelled, but there was no further reply, just the hushed moaning and chattering of the dead talking among themselves.

"Go. Now!" urged the three-headed dog, becoming visibly agitated. This intervention was unprecedented. If it went further, there would be consequences. He kept glancing across the river, fearful, as if it expected its Master to turn up at any minute.

Apollo turned toward it once more.

"You do not give me orders."

"Neither do you belong here. This is my domain, not yours."

They stared at one another. Apollo's anger had abated; as it faded so his golden light no longer burned so fiercely. He gave the three-headed dog one last withering glare. Before departing, he turned once more toward the lost souls on the far bank. Whether it was guilt or pity, or sympathy for their plight, or some combination of emotions, he couldn't afterward tell, but he had to do something for them. Softly at first, then slowly building, a beautiful music began. It seemed to grow out of the air surrounding him, and flow across the dark waters to the other shore, a symphony so moving, so beautiful, so heart-rending yet somehow comforting and ultimately, in some small way, uplifting. He created it from his thoughts, and breathed life into it, setting it free to linger on that sad shore, soothing the souls of the departed. Above all, in this dismal, forsaken place, he wanted to leave them a small gift: hope.

With one last dismissive glance at the enormous dog, he turned and padded away on paws the size of tree trunks, a more powerful presence than had been seen in those parts in aeons. After he departed the music played on, never repeating, slowly ebbing and flowing, seeping into the stones, delivering its timeless message on the miserable riverbank forever more.

In this way, he remembered he was a god.

INTERLUDE

STORIES OF THE DISAPPEARED 2

TO THE other side of Olympia they'd imprisoned a small, miserable, and uncommunicative tabby. She'd already been there when the Delphi cat arrived. At first they ignored each other, but with few other distractions, Olympia tried to break the ice. Her neighbour, introverted and shy, some-how blamed herself for the mess she'd landed in. It took a long time for Olympia to tease out her story, a tale of misery that was at once heartbreaking and familiar.

She'd never been evil, just a bit mischievous. Had stolen a few things here and there. Nicked another cat's dinner now and then, nothing bad. No, she hadn't been particu-larly friendly with humans, but she didn't hate them. She just wasn't sure about them; they were so big, so clumsy, and she found it hard to read them. It was her own fault really, she probably just needed to try harder. Have anoth-er go at making a connection. That was what started it. Trying to make a connection. The woman distracted her when she was minding her own business on the street, following some interesting scents on her way to one of her favourite places for hunting. She'd bent down, making out she wanted to be a friend in that stupid way humans do. Of course, she'd distrusted her immediately, and let it show, holding back. If she'd been sensible she'd have run away, but the woman dangled a little toy, a piece of coloured string of some sort. Oh, if only she'd had more sense, but there was something about the way it moved. It was fun and enticing. She couldn't resist chasing it, pawing at it. She'd never come across anything like it before.

In fact, she had little that could be regarded as fun in her brief life. She just got on with things, eking out a living, getting stuff for the boss, staying out of his way as much as possible, and keeping her nose clean. Sometimes it was a struggle to keep going. Not just getting on the wrong side of the boss, but dodging vicious dogs, outraged domesticated cats (every last one of them a stuck-up, self-centred, bourgeois abomination), and those horrible vehicles on the streets. But at least she'd been free. At least she'd had somewhere to sleep, and companions to pass time with.

Some humans seemed OK, but others hated them and threw things, or worse. So there she was, entranced by a twirling, dancing piece of coloured string, hypnotised by it, totally off her guard, having a little fun. Then the net dropped on top of her and her freedom was over. Then the human didn't seem so friendly. The woman had an ugly expression on her face and she lashed out at her as she dangled there, unable to escape. The attempt to shut her up only made her screech louder, but a second heavier blow stunned her, and cold fear did the rest of the job.

More days of terror followed, penned up in a little cage with hardly anything to eat. How she hated this place. Other cats came and went. She had no interest in them; conversation was stilted. She distrusted them almost as much as their captors, but at least she didn't fear them. There was something about the humans in this place that terrified her.

That was all Olympia found out. Later the same sunny day they came to her neighbor's cage, opened it and roughly picked her up, put her in a bag, took her into a nearby room, and ended her life with several blows from a heavy club.

At least it was quick. Almost. Because she was wriggling and screaming in the bag, it took four blows. Four strokes of terror and pain to end one small, ordinary life. No one would miss her; she had few friends and no-one close. There was nobody to remember her name. No, she'd never been evil, just a bit mischievous; she just wanted a bit of fun.

A week later, her coat was part of another one.

CHAPTER 19

CATNIP

DAPHNE AWOKE to the sound of a scream as a light was switched on overhead. Alert in an instant, she crouched down, trying to identify the source of the sound. It was an older female human. Daphne wasn't sure whether it was a cry of alarm, shock, or delight. The old woman just stood there in the doorway, blocking her only escape route. The two of them stared at each other; Daphne suspicious, the woman surprised. Daphne tensed, ready to spring away, but it seemed the new arrival wanted to make friends. This was unexpected; she wasn't sure how to react. She wanted to make her escape, but how quick were the human's reactions? The older ones could be slow, but Daphne didn't want to take any chances. She hesitated.

The old woman moved toward her, making no sudden moves. Her face melded into one of those human expressions Daphne interpreted as happy. She appeared pleased to have a visit from a total stranger. Wary, and ready to flee at any moment, the cat allowed the woman to stroke her between the ears. The woman made a move to pick her up, but Daphne shrank back and she stopped. The two of them surveyed each other once more. Then the woman disappeared. Daphne waited where she was for a few minutes, straining her ears to assess if she had gone, and whether it was safe to make her way back to the room with the window. She jumped down from the bed and approached the door to the hallway cautiously. The woman was nowhere in sight. Daphne darted into the living room, but skidded to a halt in dismay—the window was closed. She was trapped. She pondered her next move.

A little later the old woman reappeared in the doorway, making sounds at her. Daphne wasn't as used to understanding human speech as some of her kind, but the woman seemed to be making an attempt to be friendly. She held out a small bowl with food in it. Daphne's nostrils twitched. Fish of some kind, she was sure of it, and decent quality. It was a promising development. She might as well have a bite to eat and then leave with a full stomach. Better than going hungry. She followed the woman into her kitchen, where she placed the bowl on the floor beside the wall. Daphne looked up again and tried to read her expression. She remained suspicious, but the fish smelled too nice, and her resistance crumbled.

While she ate, her mind was racing. How long would it be before she could get out of this place, and where had she got to? She felt guilty; she was in Athens on a rescue mission; she hadn't come to meet the locals. Poor Olympia was waiting somewhere, perhaps in a place like this or maybe worse. She suppressed a shudder at the thought. While her nose was deep in the bowl, she heard a door shut. She lifted her head. Oh no, the woman had left, and she had missed a chance to run past her when the door was open. This was very annoying. She waited a while longer, but the door remained closed, so she returned to the tuna and finished the bowl, then walked into the hallway and sat facing the door. When the opportunity arose, she was going to have to execute her move with precision.

She waited and waited, but there was no sign of the elderly woman returning and the door remained stubbornly shut. Daphne was powerless and frustrated. After a while, she surveyed her surroundings once more, but she could find no evidence of another exit. In pure frustration, she scratched at the hall carpet and found it pleasantly satisfying. Being brought up in Delphi, she had never had the pleasure of carpet to scratch, and this was so much easier than bark; it was as if they'd made it for scratching. Seeing her claws ploughing grooves into the material as she vented her frustration was delightful. But she couldn't scratch all day, and as time passed her outrage at being imprisoned grew. She was a creature of the fresh air and wide-open spaces, not some lap-cat! How dare this human keep her like this? It was outrageous!

After a while, she tried to gather her thoughts. There was a chair in the hallway, opposite the door, and sitting beneath it made her feel a little better. With a sigh, she settled down once more to wait. An hour passed, and then another. Finally, there was a sound outside and the rattle of a key in the lock. The door opened. Daphne tensed, waiting for a clear gap through with she could run, but the woman's speed was annoying and she closed the door before there was enough room for Daphne to make her escape. Her frustration returned; a successful escape would require careful planning, and perfect timing, but at least she now knew what she would need to do, and how quickly to move. Her dread of being kicked or trodden on was just another operational risk to factor in. She needed to remain vigilant, then make her move next time.

The woman placed a shopping bag on the kitchen worktop. She took out a bowl and opened a tin of cat food. Daphne wouldn't be going hungry. She placed the bowl on the floor, making the encouraging noises some humans make when trying to communicate with cats. Daphne studied her with curiosity. There was no doubt the woman was trying to ingratiate her way into Daphne's affections, but why did she believe Daphne would reciprocate? Did she think she was a simpleton, ready to roll over at the first sniff of fish? Daphne remained dismissive and determined to keep her distance. She was in no mood for faux friendliness from someone she'd just met and who was trying to keep her prisoner. She remained under the chair.

The woman opened another door and entered a small room Daphne had not yet explored. The sound of running water pricked her ears. It sounded like a stream plunging into a pool. Do all human residences have such streams flowing through them? How come she hadn't heard it before? Curiosity got the better of her and she made the mistake of exploring. With a speed that belied her age and size, the human grabbed her by the scruff of the neck and lifted her. Briefly Daphne hovered over the water, then, to her horror, was thrust into it and submerged. Immediate panic: she's trying to drown me. Scrabble and twist for all you're worth. Bite, scratch, wriggle. Don't go down easily, but she won't let go. Head above water again; deep breath, relief. What's this? Smells awful. Nasty, greasy liquid, not water, smeared on fur and rubbed in. Bubbles and foam. Tastes... disgusting. Spit. Hey, that's my tail, what are you doing? How dare you! Urgh.

Daphne continued to wriggle and grapple for all she was worth, but her opponent's arthritic, bony fingers gripped her like a vice. The woman smothered the small cat in shampoo, massaged her into a frothy foam ball, dunked her several times more, then finally released her, only to gather her up and swaddle her in a thick towel then vigorously rub her down. After what seemed like an eternity in hell, Daphne was placed back on the floor, angry beyond reason.

She stood bristling with fury, glaring up at her tormentor with venom in her eyes and hate oozing from every pore, fluffier than she'd ever been, smelling faintly of pine, and very, very clean. She despised this human with a passion her enemy could never conceive, her thoughts running wild with the things she would do to her if she had the chance. What was worse, the woman didn't seem to realise the depth of the indignity she had inflicted. Instead, she scuttled back to the kitchen and rummaged around in her cavernous bag once more. Daphne, relieved to escape from the watery torture chamber, scrambled into another, hopefully safer, room, scanning for hiding places.

The woman, having retrieved another object from her bag, pursued her furious and pristine prisoner. She held out a peace offering: a small cloth bag, sewn up around the sides, and just a few centimetres across. It looked like a small pillow, if Daphne had known what a pillow was. Daphne stared at her gift with suspicion, sensing a trick, but then detected an aroma she had never before come across, and which stirred emotions she could barely contain. It played with her senses; she had to get more of this wondrous scent. Her eyes widened, and her nostrils flared. Her reservation a thing of the past, Daphne approached the woman, her nose in the air. She wanted the bag, needed it, wanted to wrap herself in it and cover every inch of her body with that wondrous aroma. If she could, she wanted to bathe in it. She had to have it. The old woman teased the cat, dangling it just out of reach. Daphne almost snarled as she waved it to and fro above her head. She lashed out with a paw, claws fully extended, but narrowly missed. All semblance of civility vanished; she crouched, ready to pounce, a wild and primeval beast, prepared to do anything to get hold of that little precious parcel. She was like an animal possessed. Possessed by the scent of... catnip.

The woman ceased her torment and threw the little bag on the floor in the centre of the room. Daphne spun and pounced on it like a mad thing, grabbing it and clutching it to her chest. She cuddled it and rubbed it all over her face, burying her nose in the heavenly aroma. The outside world ceased to exist as she rolled back and forth on the carpet, wrestling with and loving the fragrant little bag. A new world had opened up—something she had never experienced, and now she knew she could never live without it. She felt elated, joyous, drunk in aromatic heaven. She forgot all she was trying to achieve. Any thought of escape vanished, and her ambition to rescue Olympia disappeared.

CHAPTER 20

BACK ON THE TRAIL

HE WOKE in the pale light of dawn to a crushing head-ache and tried opening his eyes, but the daylight hurt. For a while he lay still, breathing hard as if he'd been running. After a few minutes, he tried to get up and struggled to his feet. He got two paces toward the door and threw up. Another few steps and it happened again. He flopped down, exhausted, and feeling awful. What had happened? Mind reeling, he could barely remember where he was. Had just one night passed, or many? And what about that dream? Was it a dream? It seemed so real, but it couldn't be. He gave up and closed his eyes.

This was no good. His head was still swimming. He had to try again. A few more minutes passed, then he read-ied himself for another effort. This time was better, and he stood up, swaying and feeling lightheaded. His mouth was dry; he needed water. Unsteady, he wove a path back into the shrine, to the alcove with the bowls, and drank. Too much too soon—waves of nausea returned. He sat down until the feeling wore off, then he felt he couldn't breathe; he needed fresh air. He returned to the courtyard and found a shady place to flop down. Gradually normality returned. 'Never again' was the thought echoing in his head. It was some time before he could sit up with a head clear enough to think about what to do next. As he did so, the black cat appeared on the wall a short distance away. She examined him with a faint air of amusement.

"Perhaps I should have warned you not to get too close, those herbs and enchantments can be quite intense. You went very deep into your trance."

Apollo said nothing. He was still trying to work out what had happened, his head gently throbbing. He looked up at the trees; the day was overcast but humid. Not the best day for a hangover, whatever caused it. He glanced across at his hostess.

"Who are you?" he asked, fixing her with a stare, his eyes narrowed. He was in no mood for deflection. She returned his stare for a long time, considering how much to reveal.

"I am Hecate," she said finally. "Among other things, I practice witchcraft."

Apollo nodded, absorbing this. "Hecate," he repeated. The name was familiar; it was ancient and signified power, he was certain, but he remembered nothing about witchcraft, nor could he remember meeting any practitioners, apart from maybe old Pythia back home, but she was a seer and that was different. "What did you do to me?"

"That is difficult for me to say." She continued to look at him. "Normally those braver mortals who dare come here are trying to gain some insights into their true nature, or to perceive the future, however imperfectly. I merely show them the way. I have no influence over what they find. Their experiences vary, but since you've been asleep for so long, I'd say your journey last night was longer and deeper than most."

He considered this. His memory was still sketchy, but fragments of his dream remained. They made little sense to him, apart from one thing.

"They said she wasn't there." He said it as much to himself as to Hecate. He looked up at her, more hopeful now. "That was it, the spirits of the dead. They said she wasn't there, but there wasn't much time."

She considered his response. "It is up to you to interpret or find meaning in your visions. They are personal to you only. I can not offer much help."

"I came to Athens to look for a friend who was kidnapped. She's called Olympia. She was taken from us by humans. We think they came from here." He looked around as if expecting to see them appear around a corner, then recognised how silly it must appear. "I don't know where though." His voice trailed off. He was not much further forward. He had no way of finding where she was.

Hecate paid close attention to his story. After he had finished, she spoke. "Few citizens ever visit me. The gangs are too frightened, and most of the other inhabitants are put off by my reputation." She looked quite proud. "As a result, I am not the best person to visit for gossip." She sounded disdainful. "However, my gifts do allow me to tap into the…" she paused, searching for the appropriate word, "… wider ambience of the city. The psychological undercurrent. And what I have detected recently is that there is a level of fear within the animal population which seems far different from before. Your friend is not the first I've heard of who has gone missing, nor will she be the last."

Apollo felt vindicated, almost relieved, but he couldn't see how this helped him. "Who is doing it? Why? Where are they being taken?"

"That I can't answer. Humans probably, but whether for sacrifice or some form of worship I can't tell. If they were being offered to me it would be a different story of course, although sacrifice of a creature from our species would be rather impudent, don't you think? Possibly sacrilegious."

She looked into the distance. "No, times have changed. It is a long time since I was offered a blood sacrifice. Food is the preferred choice these days, plus the occasional mouse." She gave him a mischievous glance.

Apollo tried to follow her conversation, but this talk of sacrifices conjured other memories. He nodded, absently. His mind was racing. More fragments of his dream from the previous night were coming back to him, but they made no sense. The one thing he clung to was the thought that Olympia was still safe, at least for now, but what was more worrying was the news that she may not have much time.

He stood up. "I have to go. They said I didn't have much time."

"And where are you going?" she asked. He stopped once more, confused. Hecate continued. "As I said, I live my own life, I am no fan of news and gossip, but there is probably one animal who can help you. If anyone knows where to find your friend, it is probably him."

Apollo anticipated her. "Hermes," he said. "I was on the way to find him when I got waylaid and chased all the way here." Chased. Me! The thought left a bitter taste. It made him feel ashamed.

She gave him a cool, appraising look which only reinforced his embarrassment. "Then you know where to find him." It was a statement rather than a question. He hesitated.

"I've rather lost my bearings, I'm not sure which direction to take," he admitted.

She stood and walked along the top of the low wall to the corner, waiting for him to follow.

"Head down here and back through the gate you passed yesterday," she told him in a businesslike fashion. "You must retrace your path to the other side of the roundabout and the park beyond. When you reach its far end, you should see the hill in front of you."

"But what if they are waiting for me?" He didn't need to spell out who he meant. She looked him up and down.

"What are you afraid of; you of all people? There was a time when I don't think they would have bothered you in the slightest." Apollo felt himself judged and found wanting. Embarrassed all over again, he chastised himself for expressing such weakness. This city and its inhabitants were testing him in ways he hadn't experienced for centuries, and that had to change. He made a silent vow; from now on Athens was going to bend to his will, not the other way round.

"For what it's worth, I think it's unlikely," she continued, "but you never know. In any case, even at the unlikeliest moment, you may meet someone who can help you. Trust your instinct and heed their advice."

Yet another riddle to unpick. It was time to leave, but he hesitated, uncertain how to thank this mysterious witch. She read him, and with an almost motherly nudge of her nose, ushered him on his way.

"No need to thank me," she said. "Just go and find your friend."

He gave her a grateful look, jumped down, and set off through the trees below. When he looked back, she had already disappeared.

CHAPTER 21

JASON IN THE PLAKA

JASON WOKE up surrounded by his newfound friends in a secluded corner of the ancient ruins on the site of Hadrian's Library. He stretched as much as he dared without punching his neighbours and rolled over against the back of the cat next to him. She grunted in her sleep but showed no sign of waking. He raised his head to peer over the top of the sleeping animals and examine his surroundings. They were lying on a rectangular patch of ground enclosed in part by the low foundations of old walls. A short distance away, most of the youngsters were already awake and engaged in their morning activities. These comprised competing for milk, play fighting, or chasing one another. They were relentless. It all looked like too much effort. Jason dropped his head and dozed off for a few minutes more.

But not for long. Cats were stirring all around him and getting ready for the new day. Some had been out and about for hours. Jason wondered what the day had in store for him. He needed to get back to the job of finding Olympia, but he was at a loss to know how. Perhaps he could persuade one of these cats to help him in his quest; he just needed to find the right time to ask. In the meantime, he needed to get to know his companions better and find some food. He meandered around the place. It had some similarities to home: ancient stones sometimes lying around, in other places standing upright, sometimes several of them balanced on top of one another. He wondered what humans saw in all this; some of them would most likely arrive soon to look around. He had enough experience to understand that they liked to do that, even though they never tidied things up. The old stones here had a fence around them to keep them apart from the rest of the city. This was nice because it kept them at a distance overnight, but he couldn't understand why these old stones were so important to them. Perhaps they worshipped them? He couldn't tell, and there was little point speculating. It was what it was, but at least it kept them from interfering for a few hours, and in his limited experience of humans he knew they did like to interfere, whether it was to tickle you, stroke you, try to pick you up, feed you something, or smack you. They were unpredictable and a little odd, and it was a good idea to keep them at a reasonable distance.

Jason sauntered around the compound, examining some unusual scents. They could tell some interesting stories, if he could have bothered to interpret them, but this morning his mind was wandering. The small tabby who had spoken up for him the previous evening approached. She hopped from paw to paw, as if nervous.

"Hi, I'm Tabitha," she purred softly. "Would you like me to show you around?"

"Yes, why not?" He gave her a quick reassuring glance, then looked away lest he appear rude. "Where shall we go first? No, wait, before we do anything, what do you do about eating round here?"

Tabitha brightened. "Oh, that's easy. There're loads of opportunities. Let's see what we can find."

They spent the rest of the morning exploring the winding back streets of the Plaka, visiting some of the best locations to find food. At this time of day, the restaurants were closed, but several cafés and bars were open, serving breakfast to their two-legged customers. There were few inclined to share, but by their back doors things were more promising. Yesterday's leftovers and unused items were bagged up and left for collection, but a little detective work with the nose followed by some surgical bag-slashing here or there when no one was looking could unearth some tasty delights. Jason was ravenous, but he soon had his fill.

Replenished, they continued Tabitha's guided tour of the neighbourhood. She showed him the best positions for watching the restaurants, the quiet residential streets where well-intentioned humans sometimes left food out, and those houses where members of the local citizenry lived with their adopted human servants. She graded them according to ease of access, should one need to break in. The cats of the Plaka gang weren't short of options when it came to dining out, so they tended not to impose on their more sedentary neighbours too much, but who could resist the temptation of an unguarded bowl of premium cat food?

Tabitha was good company, and Jason felt relaxed for the first time since he had arrived in the city. They paused often to explore interesting nooks and crannies, sniff out some beautiful flowers and plants, and just chill for a while, human-watching. By afternoon Jason's head was a whirl with all this new knowledge, and he needed a nap. Once more his little companion came up with the goods. Behind an ochre-coloured wall, in the corner of a tiny secluded garden, was a shady patch of grass overhung by a bush and just big enough for two.

It was evening before they emerged and headed back to the Library of Hadrian to rejoin the others. Tabitha left him to rejoin her friends, and for a while, Jason was at a loss. But he wasn't alone for long. A dusty-coloured adolescent male made a beeline for him. He looked about the same age as Jason and introduced himself as Erichthonious. He asked Jason if he liked football. The question baffled him; he had no idea what football was, but, intrigued, he accompanied him to find out.

They headed back toward the main street with its many bars and restaurants. It was now mid-evening; the sun hung low in the sky and lots of humans were milling around, eating, drinking, walking, talking, socialising. The two cats had to plot their course through a forest of legs. Erichthonius stopped outside a popular bar and jumped onto a low wall separating the pavement in front from a narrow passage to the side. There was a small cushion in place, as if they expected him. The brightly lit interior was busy, but large windows were pushed wide, allowing tables to spill out onto the street. They were crowded with people drinking and watching a box perched on a shelf high on the wall. Before he arrived in Athens Jason had never spent much time people-watching, so ritual behaviour such as this was a novelty. The front of the box had a screen with moving pictures. His first experience of television, which he realised must be some kind of magic, left him transfixed. Was it a religious ceremony? If so, the congregation seemed quite raucous; shouting and drinking were an essential part of the ritual. It made him nervous, but at least they weren't shouting at him. He suspected they must be members of the cult of some local deity and tried to make sense of the ceremony.

The pictures on the box showed an enormous field with a lot of humans running around in random patterns, wearing one of two types of coloured shirt. Then he noticed a small white thing in the middle. It zipped back and forth as the humans kicked it. Jason focused on it intently, his head moving as he followed its movement. How come he had never seen magic like this before? He settled down to watch more. By his side, Erichthonius had already happily settled down, his attention focused on the box. A waiter approached. Jason stiffened, ready to flee, but his companion was unfazed. He welcomed the waiter's greeting and even allowed him to tousle his ears.

"You've brought a friend," said the man who placed a small bowl of offcuts between them. He remained wary, unable to understand a word the man said, but the tone of his voice seemed friendly enough. "Don't fight over it," the man warned, and moved away. Jason hesitated, trying to read his intent. Humans were challenging to interpret; hostile one moment, welcoming the next. He needed to improve his reading of them. Turning his head, he looked at the mass sitting outside the bar, and gave up. For now, he would have to rely on the instincts of his new friend.

He realized Erichthonious was a regular here. "They're friendly, and the food's good," was his explanation. That plus the fact it showed football matches on the television. Erichthonius was a big football fan. He explained the basics of the game to Jason.

"It's Barcelona," he said. "They're the ones in purple and blue. They're fantastic. The other team is AEK, they're from Athens," he added, the pride in his voice evident. He talked and talked, but after the busy day he'd already had, Jason was struggling to absorb any more.

"How do you know all this?"

"Oh, I pick up a lot from the commentary," the other cat replied. "I learned to understand human," he added when he saw Jason didn't seem to know what he was talking about. If he had more facial muscles, Jason would have been slack-jawed in astonishment at this information. He'd never heard of anyone who could hope to understand what humans were on about with all their chitter-chatter. Body language was as far as most of his kind went, and it had always been enough for any interactions he'd had.

As he glanced over at his companion, there was a loud cheer. Startled, he looked up to see several of the humans looking extremely happy. One or two were gesticulating wildly. "It's a goal," explained Erichthonius, "AEK have scored." Jason looked blank, so he explained what the white things with nets were, and how you won the game by getting the ball inside. Lots of times, if possible. "Last month I saw a game that ended 5-2." Jason was impressed. He struggled with counting, but he knew it was the same as all of his paws AND his tail together. "That's a lot" he admitted. He reappraised his companion. This young city-living sophisticate was very intelligent, and Jason felt out of his depth. He realised how much he missed his home and his extended family, even snooty old Hera. Life was slower and a lot quieter back in Delphi, but perhaps it was no bad thing. Coming on this adventure had been the most stupid spur-of-the-moment idea he'd ever had, and by lingering here instead of trying to find the others, he'd made it worse. Guilt arose at the thought of what might have happened to Olympia while he dallied with his new friends. And then there was Daphne. He longed to find her more than anything, more even than returning to Delphi and his familiar old haunts. The trouble was, he didn't know where to even start. The scale of the city was overwhelming; he felt out of his depth, his spirits sank.

The match had just about finished. Humans were finishing their drinks and leaving. "Let's go," he said, keen to leave.

His companion followed him with a sigh. "They came close," he said, "but Barcelona is just too good." They made their way in silence back to their sleeping quarters for the night.

CHAPTER 22

LYCABETTUS

APOLLO DESCENDED the hill and retraced his steps from the previous day, passing the gate and roundabout, and entered the wooded parkland beyond. Was it only yesterday those thugs had chased him across this park? It didn't seem possible. He still wasn't certain he was heading in the right direction, but he had no choice but to follow Hecate's directions. Senses on high alert, he half-expected his enemies to reappear at any moment.

He thought about his friends and where they might be. Jason could look after himself, he was sure, but he hoped Daphne was alright. Apollo felt protective of her, possessive even. He missed her cheerful optimism and experienced more than a pang of jealousy at the thought of Jason having her all to himself. Even though their acquaintance had been brief, he now regarded Jason as a friend, but Daphne was a bit… special. She tugged at his heartstrings like no one else. He daydreamed about her as he plodded on through the trees; a sweet reunion somewhere quiet, nuzzling and purring, and finally asking that question. With reluctance, he put the thought to one side and paid more attention to his immediate surroundings.

Toward the far side of the park, the prospect of ambush arose once more, and he slowed down. He was sure his enemies would be on the lookout for him. Putting himself in their paws, where would be a good place to waylay him?

After a while, he stopped, no longer sure which direction to take.

"I wish I could fly above these trees," he muttered to himself.

A large crow, perched on the branch of a nearby tree, cocked his head, looking at him. Apollo had no more regard for birds than any of his species, and since this one was too big to eat, he ignored it. The bird shuffled along the branch until it was closer to his eye-line. Apollo glared at it, but to his surprise, instead of flying off as he expected, it spoke to him.

"Morning guv, perhaps I could be of service?" it asked, tilting its head to the other side.

"What?" he said. The bird went on.

"Well sir, I couldn't help overhearing you, if I may say so, and it seems like you've got a problem and you wants to fly to sort it out?" It studied him. Apollo stayed silent, so it continued. "Well, it's like this, perhaps I could do your flying for you, if you like. If you tell me what it is you're looking for?"

Apollo narrowed his eyes, suspicious. "Why are you offering to help me?"

The crow paused before replying. He sounded a little offended.

"We always help the Golden One," he cawed. "It's in our blood. Always has been, since before anyone can remember." He shuffled back along the branch, huffily. "But perhaps you don't need us anymore."

Apollo looked at it in astonishment, but then at the back of his mind, some vague notion clicked into place. Yes, this seemed natural, like an ancient connection clicking into place. He faced the bird, more enthusiastic now.

"Wait," he said. "You can help me."

The crow turned back toward him and shifted position again. With those golden eyes giving him their full attention, he found their power disconcerting. "You just have to ask."

"I'm looking for Hermes," Apollo told him. "But there may be some cats ahead that are trying to capture me. I need to get around them without attracting attention. Can you help? Do you know Hermes?" Was he asking the impossible?

The crow's response was reassuring. "Everyone knows the Messenger. Stay here, my lord, I'll have a look around. Back in a jiffy." It took off.

Apollo considered what had just happened. Just a few minutes, let alone days ago he would never have believed he could have a companionable chat with a bird. But then a lot of strange things had happened since he arrived in this city. The crow soon arrived back.

"There's a trio of your kind about half a kilometre ahead, they're hanging around by the road, two on this side, one on the other. They're not moving far, they're just sitting around pretending they're not with each other. Perhaps you were right to worry."

Apollo took stock. "Can you tell me how to get around them?"

"Easy," said the crow. "Follow me." Immediately it took off and flew off north-eastwards. Apollo hurried after it before it went out of sight. A moment later it reappeared, sounding apologetic. "Silly me, I forgot you can't fly. I'll go in shorter hops." It set off again.

And so they went via a circuitous route toward Lycabettus hill, arriving from the southeast. The crow was as good as its word and took care to direct Apollo via less used thoroughfares. They travelled down quiet streets, across small parks, through hospital grounds, and passed a large concert hall. The trickiest bit was crossing a large multi-lane highway, but, more used to them now, Apollo had the patience to wait until there was a gap in the traffic. On the other side, the gradient increased. A few more turns and he came to a flight of steps leading onto the hillside, leaving the buildings behind. He paused. The crow was waiting for him just ahead.

Apollo thanked it. "I think I can make it from here."

"Until next time, then." The crow took off.

Apollo looked at the slope ahead of him. The hill provides an airy viewpoint. Most human visitors ascend via a funicular, but a footpath also climbs to the summit. The path, zig-zagging upward, was just to his left, but Apollo had no desire to follow it. He preferred to arrive unannounced, and he suspected the path humans used would be watched. That would mean navigating the steep, rocky slopes above. It would be a long, hard climb, but with luck he might have a look at this Hermes fellow, and get a sense of his character before approaching him. It would be nice to be on the front paw for once.

Lycabettus, a famous viewpoint, is also home to one of the more distinctive feline communities of Athens, the Hermaeans, as they liked to call themselves, or 'that bunch of hillbilly weirdos' as some of their less kind feline neighbours described them. They were regarded in similar wary fashion to the inhabitants of the Agora, always poking their noses into other animals' business, but they were less assertive so most of the cats of Athens just left them to it. After all, everyone has a hobby of some sort.

Apollo started his climb. The oppressive heat of late afternoon made it hard work, but he was relieved to be above the city streets and away from the noise and throb of engines, and the fumes and dust that followed them. But though he was ascending, there was little or no breeze to freshen the atmosphere. He toiled on, taking as direct a route as he dared despite the increasing steepness. Above him, the hilltop was well defended by rocky outcrops, but he noticed gaps between the cliffs which looked passable. With the sun sinking toward the western horizon, he finally approached the summit. Apollo had given no thought to the possibility humans might like to visit the terrace at the hilltop to watch the sunset, but his instincts had proved correct, and by taking the harder route he had reached this point unseen by any of those thronging the terrace.

"Ah, there you are," said a calm voice above him. "Glad you made it."

Apollo halted, annoyed. He looked up, trying to find the source of the voice, and then saw, perched on the top of a pier of rock some three metres above him, the silhouette of a pair of ears surmounting two bright eyes. The voice spoke again.

"I believe you're looking for Hermes," it said, matter-of-factly. "Over here; we'd better talk." The ears disappeared. Apollo laboriously continued up the narrow cleft to the top, trying to slow his breathing and collect his thoughts. He stepped out onto a small plateau of flattened naked rock. Waiting for him, a short distance away was a silver-white male cat of medium build with ears and paws tinged with brown. But his most striking feature was his piercing, unblinking blue eyes. To his left Apollo was aware of several other cats, lounging or sitting a respectful distance away. He knew they would be observing their visitor discreetly, and judging from the number of ears facing him like an array of miniature radio telescopes, listening to everything he said.

Hot and breathless from his climb, with his plan foiled, Apollo tried not to let his irritation show. Was this the Hermes of legend or not? He'd known a Hermes once, and seemed to remember he'd been a friend, but that was so long ago he'd forgotten almost everything about him. What sort of welcome could he expect after such a long time? To date, with a couple of exceptions, the felines of Athens had not been welcoming. He stood still, trying to think of an appropriate opening gambit.

"I heard you could help me," was all he could come up with. He hated sounding so helpless, and once again embarrassment rose in the back of his mind. The other cat continued to survey him coolly. The longer this continued, the more Apollo's exasperation grew. He returned the stare; for cats of any variety, this was close to outright hostility. Long seconds passed, and neither moved a muscle. Without averting his gaze, Apollo noticed a faint silvery shimmer around the other cat. It made him look larger; more imposing. It brought him the certainty that the animal before him was the real deal.

"So you must be Apollo?" The other cat's tone was not welcoming.

"How did you…?"

"I pick up a lot of things." He was dismissive. "I thought you might be out of business, but then to my surprise, I hear you've been winding up some of our citizens. Stirring them into a bit of a frenzy. Creating discord where, frankly, we could do with a little bit of harmony." He cocked his head to one side and paused, to see how his visitor would react. Detecting no response, he went on. "So the first question on my mind is why now and why here? What is your little game? Please enlighten me—I'm all ears. We've had a broad equilibrium between our fractious little communities for years, but as soon as you arrive you stir up a hornet's nest! Who are you working for, and why?"

Apollo said nothing. He was still trying to work out how this superior-sounding fellow knew his name, let alone what he had been doing in this forsaken city. An unpleasant thought crossed his mind; was this blue-eyed silver monster an ally or friend of the big bully of a gang leader and his bunch of toe-rags? Was it a trap? His muscles stiffened, ready to fight, and he regretted all the wasted effort getting up to this miserable eyrie. A myriad of thoughts crowded his mind.

"I don't work for anybody, but that apart, what has my arrival here got to do with you?"

For the first time, Hermes looked away, affecting a faint air of amusement.

"Come, come, dear fellow, are you going to blame everything on a faulty memory? Really, I'd expected better. I realise you're going to tell me you're new to the city, but even you must have heard it said that walls, and even streets, have ears?" He turned to confront Apollo once more, affecting disappointment. "But perhaps not. No matter. Life must be a lot simpler for you rustics, up on your hillside up north, eh? Perhaps the mosquitos have sucked up your brains along with your blood?" He looked away again, seemingly losing interest in the conversation.

Apollo's anger at this pompous know-all boiled to the surface. He stepped forward, his fur ruffling around him. Whether it was the setting sun behind him or a sudden increase in the breeze, or his air of outrage, but he seemed to loom larger, and his golden eyes blazed with indignation. There was a low growl at the back of his throat. A day or two ago he might have tried reasoning and appealing to logic, but he was out of patience; his old instincts were reviving.

Several of the cats in the distance forgot their manners and turned to look at him in surprise. His voice was low, but he made no attempt to hide his disdain.

"This is the least welcoming city I've ever visited, and I don't much care for it. You may enjoy muckraking in this cesspit, but I'm close to the end of my tether, and right now harmonious relations with its inhabitants are the least of my concerns; they seem to have forgotten even the most basic rules of hospitality. I will pursue my quest with or without you. If you are unwilling to help, just say so and stay out of my way. I won't ask twice."

Hermes backed ever-so-slightly away and lowered his eyes. He changed his tone.

"Son of Zeus," he said with a minute bow of his head, "you are welcome. Please accept my apology for my greeting and apparent lack of manners, but I had to be sure you were who you said you were. My followers and I," he glanced in their direction, "are delighted to assist you as we may." His manner changed in an instant, now businesslike and friendly. "First things first, you must be hungry after your climb. Please join us in having a bite to eat. Follow me." He turned and led the way across the small summit to the back of the café.

Ready to fight one instant, treated as an honoured guest the next, Apollo was wrong-pawed once again. He exhaled, releasing the tension in his muscles, and followed his host, wondering about the purpose of the whole charade. Hermes' moods changed more quickly than the weather. He dimly recalled that his host enjoyed nothing more than verbal jousting. That and thievery. He would have to keep his wits about him. In the distance, one or two of the assembled cats rose and strode toward them with languid grace. The others resumed their business.

It reminded Apollo of home. Here, as in Delphi, some well-intentioned human placed several large feeding and drinking bowls out in a quiet space behind the restaurant. It was out of sight of the human visitors and secluded. As with the other places where cats lived wild, this was a supplement to their main diet, and it didn't negate all begging at the tables on the terrace, but it was good to have as a backup. Apollo was starving and thirsty after his long hot climb. Out of respect, the other cats gave him some space; no one tried to jostle or crowd him out as they might have done back home.

Eventually, he stepped back. Hermes had been observing him for a while from a short distance away. Saying nothing, he turned around again and sauntered across the rugged rocky hilltop, away from the buildings. He stopped on the top of a raised flat-topped boulder and hunched down. Apollo joined him. As he was settling down, he caught sight of the view. Laid out before and below him was an enormous city, its expanse far exceeding any city he'd ever seen. The scale was daunting. In every direction he could see buildings and streets, covering all the flatter ground as far as he could see, even down to the distant sea. They also climbed up the slopes of hills far away. He raised his nose and caught the faint scent of salt water on the air. Somewhere out there was Delos, a name whose significance hovered on the edge of his memory, tantalisingly out of reach. As the sun set, lights came on, illuminating the entire vista and adding a magical effect below the darkening purple sky. Above their heads, appearing almost close enough to touch, the first stars twinkled. But there was no avoiding the jewel in the crown of this vista. His eye was drawn to the southwest, to the spectacular cliffs of the Acropolis, looking like a mighty stone ship sailing on a sea of earth, stone, and concrete. Its sheer sides were bathed in light from below, and on its flat deck was the most magnificent colonnaded temple Apollo had ever seen. He stared at it, lost in thought. Hermes followed his gaze.

"The Acropolis," Hermes told him, "and the Parthenon. Stunning, isn't it, even now?"

"It's wonderful." Apollo was struggling to find words. The sight brought back emotions he'd thought long gone.

"Yes, it is quite something," Hermes continued, relishing the fact that his companion was once again a little out of his depth. "It's looking rather battered these days, but… well, you probably know." He trailed off.

Apollo glanced across at him but said nothing more. They crouched for a while in silence.

"I can't believe you came here just to stir up the locals, so tell me, why are you *really* here?" In the light of a gibbous moon rising overhead, the white cat's fur gave off a soft silver glow. Apollo sighed and returned his thoughts to the present.

"We came here to rescue our friend, kidnapped from our home a few days ago. We think humans brought her here, at least, that's what our Oracle indicated." As he was speaking, he tried to work out how long had passed. This was the third evening since Olympia had been snatched. They had been in Athens for less than 72 hours. It seemed a lot longer.

"We?"

"My friends Daphne and Jason are with me." Apollo looked down at this carpet of lights stretching as far as he could see and wondered where they were. "Well, they were, until we got separated." He experienced an acute pang of guilt at losing them. Where had they got to? He'd hoped they would have arrived here before him. The fact they hadn't nagged at him, he should have taken more care. Were they safe? Was Daphne alright?

He told the story of Olympia's kidnap, Pythia's prophecy, and their vow to find her. He recounted their confrontation with the Botrys gang. He skipped the detail of his own encounter with the Oracle, and his visit to Hecate, and the chase that led him there. Hermes said nothing until Apollo had finished.

"I'm not sure why Achelois sent you to me rather than straight to the Agora," he mused. "Unless she thought I might have some... influence," he added softly to himself. There was another long pause. The air grew more chilly. "When did you say she left you? It's taken you a while to get here."

Apollo's answer was evasive. "I'm new to the city. I got lost," he said. Hermes took it no further.

"Well," he said, standing up and stretching. "If you'll forgive me, I've got a few things to attend to, so I'll leave you in the capable paws of one of my companions who will look after you. See you in the morning." With that, he set off into the shadows and was gone.

A smaller, darker coloured cat appeared. "I'm Pandrosus," she said. "Let me show you where we sleep." She led Apollo to a small hollow just below the summit rocks. There was a dip in the ground, protected by rocks on three sides, with a gap facing toward trees on the other. Several cats were curled up together, sleeping or trying to. They included mothers and kittens of varying sizes, snuggling for warmth, and older cats as well. It reminded Apollo of home, far away but under the same stars as looked down on him now. A couple of animals moved aside to make room for him, and he settled down, content and comfortable in their midst.

Standing on the north-facing side of the hill, Hermes pondered his next move. He came to a decision and called several of his disciples to him, issuing instructions. Without speaking they bowed their heads in acknowledgement, and departed, swift and sure-footed in the night, moving unseen on their own secret paths across the city to seeking out contacts and gathering news.

Hermes himself set off north. He wanted to check out a couple of things for himself before deciding his next moves.

CHAPTER 23

CAPTURED

THE OVERWHELMINGLY sweet and heavy, all-encompassing aroma of catnip faded. In a shriveled-up corner of her mind, a small patch of sunlight found a small cat trying to make sense of what had happened to it. Daphne had no reference point. She'd experienced nothing like this before. Amid the drowsy after-effects was a dim awareness of having behaved in a strange and downright undignified manner. Had she really snarled and swiped at the old human, all claws bared? It was as if her normal self had been possessed for a time, or some wild inner spirit released. The thought was disturbing. For the first time in her life, she felt a little dirty, shredded, exposed. Had those swipes, the wild abandon, been her real self?

She shuddered a little, put a paw over her eyes, and tried to get back to sleep but the thoughts kept on cascading through her brain, and there, just across the rug, was the little aromatic bag of herbaceous temptation that had started it all. Daphne rolled over. Sleep was impossible; she had to have more. Torn, she rose to her feet, gave a feeble half-hearted stretch, and fixed her stare on the catnip. Stopping short, she circled to one side, gave it a tentative poke with her paw, then hooked it with an unfurled claw and grabbed it with renewed passion, smothering her nostrils and breathing in the heady aroma once more. For the next half hour, she was lost.

The day wore on and the pattern repeated itself; a light sleep or snooze disturbed by feelings of guilt that she couldn't quite pin down, punctuated by a catnip love-in rolling over and over and forgetting all pretence of dignity. As the day wore on, the scent lost some of its power, and some mental clarity returned. 'Olympia! What have I done?' In an instant, remorse took hold, gnawing at her mind. How much time had she lost? How could she have allowed herself to be captured so easily? What a fool she'd been. For a while she berated herself for her weakness, but that took her no further forward, so she chastised herself, instead, for being unable to come up with an escape plan. Escape was vital in order to mount a rescue, but it would mean leaving the little heady-scented bag of loveliness behind. She looked at it wistfully. Could she take it with her? A picture formed in her mind of walking through the city, her precious catnip bag in her mouth, but she realised it would be futile. She would be a target for every no-good thug and ruffian in this part of town, and they wouldn't be able to believe their luck. It would tempt even the soft, stupid domesticated pets to have a go. It would be madness. There were no hiding places out there that would screen her prize from the super-sensed nostrils of envious fellow felines, and they would stop at nothing to steal it from her.

Daphne collected her thoughts once more and focused on the matter of breaking out of the apartment. She reviewed her situation; the apartment had one main door and a second leading out to the balcony, but which appeared to be permanently shut. She had arrived through a window from that balcony, but it too was closed, as were all the windows apart from one in the bedroom, but it was only open a crack, far too narrow to squeeze through. So far she had only seen the human come and go through the main door, so it seemed the most likely way to escape unless she changed her behaviour. Daphne decided to keep it under close watch. Her inexperience with humans was a problem. When in groups they seemed to act similarly, but by themselves they appeared more erratic and difficult to predict. She had no idea what her guard was thinking, or likely to do next. The only course of action she could think of was to keep her under observation and be ready to act fast at the first opportunity. A chair in the hall provided excellent cover. She should start right now, make this her base, and keep watch. But it was quiet at the moment. So... was there time for a little more fun with the catnip first? She gave it a covetous look, then pounced on it once more.

Several hours passed before Daphne got her opportunity. In the late afternoon, a buzzer sounded, making her jump. She looked around for the source of the noise, but couldn't see anything moving. It sounded again, and this time she heard movement from the living room behind her. The elderly human laboriously clambered out of its armchair and approached the door. She opened it a crack and spoke to someone on the other side. Daphne tensed, ready to move, but the door wasn't wide enough open yet. She fretted it might close again before she got her chance.

She was in luck. The old woman opened the door wider to receive a parcel from a delivery man. This was it; this was her chance. She made a bolt for the gap, catching the old woman by surprise. The delivery man was first to spot her and moved a leg to block her path, but as he was waiting for a signature, he was neither quick nor decisive. With a cry of dismay, the householder reached down and tried to grab the cat as she darted past, but she was far too slow. Daphne swerved past the legs and out into the stairwell, scrabbling for grip on the tiled floor. She spun away from the hands reaching towards her and shot off down the stairs, reckless in her anxiety to escape. At the ground floor she came across another door; this was unexpected and unwelcome. Daphne glanced over her shoulder. How long before they arrived? Heart thumping, she could hear the heavy tread of both humans thundering down the stairs toward her. Frantically, she looked for a hiding place, zigzagging from corner to corner of the small vestibule, but to no avail. The door was the only way out.

For the second time in a few minutes, fortune favoured her. Another resident arrived before her pursuers. He turned his key in the lock and opened the door to enter, but was greeted by a desperate animal flashing past him at escape velocity, followed by an out-of-breath neighbour and a courier. In her desperation, Daphne misjudged her trajectory, and received a glancing blow from his leg which sent her sideways into the frame of the doorway, but she was through, down onto the street and into the daylight. Blinded by the bright sunlight, she turned up the street and ran as fast as she could until she was 50 meters away from the entrance. The shouts behind her faded, and she took refuge under a car to recover. The ribs on her right side were very sore where she had hit the door frame, but nothing seemed to be broken. Her breathing soon returned to normal; her emotions took a little longer to stabilise. Elation at having escaped, and satisfaction at being back on her rescue mission, mingled with anguish at having to abandon her lovely, glorious catnip.

Daphne shook her head and scratched an ear, trying to dislodge negative thoughts, and focused on what to do next. She had lost her bearings while she'd been in the apartment and was no longer sure of the way. 'I was look-ing for a tall hill,' she reminded herself. 'Hermes lives on a hilltop.' Beneath this vehicle, her view was limited, but she had hope; the street she sat on sloped upwards, and she was near the top. Peering ahead, it seemed to end in a park. The summit of a hill, perhaps? Could this be the place? At least it would allow her to get a proper view of her surroundings and find her bearings.

After a hundred metres, she arrived at the park and hopped through a gap in the fence. Amid trees and vegetation again, she felt better. Above her, the ground rose to a rocky knoll. Her heart leaped in anticipation; was this the place where Hermes lived? She set off to explore but soon realised there was no feline community here. There was, however, a trail to follow through the trees, but when she reached the top her heart sank. Daphne was in the middle of a small patch of vegetation surrounded by endless streets and houses as far as she could see in all directions. In the distance were several hills, but quite close by, towering above her, was a very steep one. It dominated the view. Daphne sat down, deflated. How could she have missed it? Lycabettus, if that was indeed her destination, was still some way away, and looked difficult to climb. Getting up there would take ages, when every minute lost in her quest was precious.

She got little time to dwell on the matter. Two cats emerged from the foliage behind her and strode in her direction. Birds chattered a warning in the trees nearby, but before she had time to think both cats sprang upon her and knocked her to the ground. Teeth and claws flashed everywhere as the three of them rolled and scrabbled in the dust. Daphne was still tender from her earlier escape and wasn't in the best shape to start with. She couldn't free herself from them. One of them had her by the throat, and she struggled to breathe. The only upside was that he blocked some of his companion's blows. Daphne punched with her hind legs for all she was worth, but her opponents were strong and streetwise, and try as she might she couldn't break free. She felt herself weakening, and she couldn't breathe at all now. Her prospects looked bleak, but her enemies stopped their attack and let go. They didn't back away, but just stood above her threateningly. Daphne lay on her side, panting, while her enemies stared down at her.

"Better not kill her," one of them said.

"Not yet, at any rate," her companion agreed. "We'd better take her to the boss—for some proper questioning."

Daphne's heart sank. *I could have stayed with the catnip,* she thought.

"On your feet," they commanded. She struggled to get up, bruised and battered as she was. There was a deep gash on her right foreleg, blood seeping into her fur, and vicious bite marks peppered her neck, but she was still just about in one piece. She tried to walk, but it was a struggle. She could just about hobble in the direction they showed. Limping and in pain, running was impossible, and there was no chance of escape. Feeling like an elderly cripple, she staggered down the slope between her captors.

They led her away down the far side of the knoll, away from Lycabettus. Anyone paying detailed attention would have seen the rare sight of a cat being painstakingly herded down the hill. In the distance, camouflaged behind low-growing shrubs, a grey and white cat stood up, watched the departing trio, stretched, then ambled downhill in the opposite direction.

The Gizi mob's base was a disused warehouse. It was the largest enclosed space Daphne had ever seen. Tall shelving units in long rows, empty of goods, covered about half or the floor, and in the remaining space several large wooden pallets littered the ground. More were stacked by a distant wall. In one corner sat an old fork-lift truck. Not that Daphne could have described it as such. She'd never seen a place like this before. Amid the pallets was an open space where she sat, nervous and trembling. Surrounding her on the ground and atop the pallets was a ring of the meanest looking cats she had ever seen. Head bowed, and in considerable pain from her various wounds, Daphne's misery was plain to see, but elicited no sympathy from those around her. She closed her eyes and tried to pretend none of it was real. The walk from the park, in the company of her two tormentors, had been hard. Several times she stumbled and almost collapsed, only to receive a nasty nip from her captors. All the time they complained about her 'playing up,' appearing to relish their sadistic little game.

After a while she heard the faint pad of footsteps and looked up to see an enormous cat approaching with purpose from the opposite end of the warehouse, his eyes fixed on her. He was taller at the shoulder than any cat she'd seen, apart from the big brute they'd come across the other night. Not as muscular, perhaps, but intimidating nevertheless. He appeared much better groomed as well, she noted, but his face had a mean pinched look and his eyes were close together. As he marched towards her, she wondered if he was going to stop, or trample her underfoot. To her relief he did halt just in front of her, gave her a dismissive look, then paced back and forth before her, as if trying to decide his approach.

Daphne closed her eyes and wondered what would come next. Her head throbbed, her multitude of cuts stung, and she ached all over. She just wanted the ordeal to be over.

None of the surrounding cats displayed the slightest sympathy; in fact, quite the opposite. She was a prize in their constant battle against external foes, real or imagined. To them she was a sign of their cunning and resilience in the face of outside provocation. One of those super spies from the oh-so-superior mob up at the Agora had finally revealed her hand and been caught, and they scented blood. They were looking forward to their leader taking this secret agent down, permanently. If any had questioned them, they might have revealed a degree of disappointment their catch didn't quite match the profile of a super-secret agent and highly trained killer they believed had been stalking them these past months. Sitting here before them she looked rather feeble, but no matter, she was what she was, and that was dangerous. And now she was theirs. And before her execution, the boss was going to make her sing.

The leader of the Gizi gang was Zelus, a thug of note in this part of the city, and second to none in the effectiveness of his rule, or so he liked to think. He ran a tight ship, rewarded loyalty, but dealt harsh punishment to any who failed to follow orders. Zelus's ambition knew no bounds; he intended to be the most powerful feline in the entire city, and he had assembled an efficient team which he managed with care. What differentiated him from his rivals was his vision and long-term strategic intent. He had no time for free-riders; they had no place in his long term mission, which was to reach the top and displace the present archaic hierarchy with its out-of-date ideas and antiquated methods. He envisaged himself lording it over his peers from the lofty heights of Filopappou Hill next to the Acropolis, a network of underlings at his beck and call, bringing constant tribute and delivering his orders across the city. From here he would spread his influence through every corner of Athens, dividing and ruling all others as was his right. This new golden age was the final step in the execution of his mission statement and strategic plan. But it was taking a little longer to deliver than he would have liked.

Zelus was determined to make an example of the small assassin that had fallen right into his paws. Having decided his approach, he walked up to his captive and without warning cuffed her across the side of her head. Her eyes still on the floor, Daphne realised she should be grateful he'd kept his claws sheathed, but her already aching head rang with the blow. She wondered if her jaw had been dislocated.

Playing to the gallery and determined to make a spectacle of the interrogation, the big cat raised his voice and began his questioning. "Who are you?" he demanded.

"Daphne." Her small voice died in the large open space. Zelus moved closer.

"Don't be shy, speak up," he prompted.

"I'm called Daphne," she answered, raising her head, but not quite looking him in the eye. Instead, she glanced at the ring of leering faces surrounding her but caught no sign of any sympathy among them; they wanted blood.

"And who might you be working for…. Daphne?" her interrogator demanded. "If that is indeed your actual name." He strode back and forth in front of his captive like a caged tiger, unable to sit still. Daphne felt faint and swayed slightly, but tried to keep her eyes on him. She was also a little confused; what else would anyone call her?

"I don't work for anyone," she replied.

Zelus turned to face her, and she wished he hadn't; she found it difficult to contemplate those eyes, but the voice, when it came, sounded almost conciliatory. "Come now, no need to lie." The pinched face moved closer and Daphne shrunk back as if she'd been struck. She tried to avoid his stare.

"I... I'm not lying," she stuttered. "I'm from Delphi. I live there." She sounded desperate. How could they not believe her? Why were these animals so cruel? What did they want her to say? At the back of her mind, she was trying to work out what, or who they thought she might be, and why they were so bothered about someone sending her here, but try as she might she failed to come up with any answers.

Zelus resumed his stalking back and forth. He moderated his tone, trying a fresh approach. "Let me recount the facts," he said, looking at his audience as if making a case before a jury, and sounding at his most reasonable. "You were found not an hour ago, deep in Gizi Gang territory, staking out our land and, no doubt, hoping to glean information about our movements. Why would someone like you," he flashed her a glance, "be in a place like that? I would suggest you were planning to meet up with a contact, perhaps to find out more about our movements?" He looked her full in the face again, his voice now lower and more dangerous. "You wouldn't be the first of your order to come here and spy on us."

There was a pause. At this point most prisoners would fill the silence with a confession, real or confected, but Daphne was struggling to understand what he meant. What 'order' and why all this nonsense about spying? Failing to get a response, her interrogation resumed.

"Now we can be reasonable about this. We can do it the civilised way, where you tell me everything you know about your operation, or I can beat it out of you." He sounded perfectly calm and businesslike; chillingly so. After a brief pause to let his threat percolate, he continued. "So, just to reiterate: my operatives intercepted you before you could meet up with your usual contact in that neighbourhood.

177

Ideally," he gave Daphne's captors a meaningful stare, "they should have waited until you made contact, but," he turned back to Daphne, brisk and businesslike once more, "in the circumstances I can understand their excitement. Now, here's what you have to do. Start talking. Now. I want names, faces, fur colouring and distinguishing marks, addresses, and full disclosure about who or what was your next target. And above all, how much does she know?" He loomed over her, huge and menacing.

Daphne's mind was racing. How could she be in this position? She was a straightforward animal. She'd been brought up to tell the truth (well, most of the time at any rate) but the truth didn't interest this brute. He wanted conspiracies and lies. She groped around in her dazed and befuddled mind for a convincing story.

"I can't tell you. She… she'll kill me," she whimpered. Zelus stepped back. This was more promising. The little mouse was about to sing.

"Who?" he demanded.

"Her Ladyship." Daphne played for time, thoughts whirling around her brain. "You know what she's like when she gets angry. She takes no prisoners." She warmed to her theme. "She sent me to find…" She groped for a name. "Alejandro. From the… from the.."

"From Strefi Hill Park!" Zelus thundered, finishing the sentence for her. "Keep going," he barked. "What did you want him for?"

"He was supposed to help me find your base." She looked around. "We were going to stake it out. See where you went. That sort of thing." Her voice trailed off.

The big cat said nothing but narrowed his eyes and stared at her. He wanted more. In her scrambled brain, Daphne made connections. What had they been talking about? Assassins, spies, agents? Had one of them been killed? Were they out for revenge? She must have unwittingly stumbled into their territory at just the wrong time, but who was this mysterious, powerful female they daren't name? A storyline formed in her head. She looked directly into her interrogator's face.

"She's obviously a little worried about you." Daphne stole a furtive glance around the assembled gang while Zelus absorbed this information. She pressed on. "Although I don't quite know why," she added, sounding dismissive.

She snapped her head around toward the gang leader again, just in time to receive another heavy blow that made it spin once more. With vision blurry, Daphne staggered but regained her balance. Zelus pushed his nose close to hers so she could taste his breath and feel it on her cheek.

"Who, who..." he insisted. All semblance of coolness had dissipated. He was on edge, agitated, impatient. "Spit it out, damn you."

"Hera," Daphne replied.

The gang leader's eyes widened, and he took a step back and sat down. This was not the response he'd expected. The encircling cats, seeing his reaction, became a mite less smug about baiting their victim. Daphne, still in pain, dizzy and swaying, held her breath. Had she gone too far?

"Hera?" Zelus echoed. He looked stunned. Delighted though she was with the reaction, Daphne wondered what could have caused it? Surely not the Hera she knew, she thought. Maybe he was thinking of someone else with the same name?

Zelus sounded confused. "But she's not here. She disappeared. Years ago. She doesn't exist anymore," he blustered, trying to convince himself as much as anything.

Daphne pressed home her advantage. Let him think

what he liked. She tried to build a legend around the rather staid busybody she knew who liked nothing better than to poke her nose into everybody else's business.

"She does," she shouted, her voice small but clear in the big space. "I saw her just the other day. She's heard about you, and she's obviously worried enough to ask me to take a look. I don't know about any assassinations she's got planned, but she doesn't tell me everything, and it wouldn't surprise me if she's got some other agents on the case." She looked around the room. "They might be closer than you think. There might be someone here now, for all I know."

The surrounding gang members looked at one another and shuffled, uncomfortable at the thought. Their confidence was evaporating, and one or two looked distinctly nervous. The atmosphere changed. Zelus tried to regain his composure and with it control of the interrogation. He addressed Daphne again, but more cautious now, as if questioning an equal rather than intimidating a spy.

"This is Athena's city. What business does Hera have here?"

Daphne looked him in the eye. "Perhaps they're in league," she said. "Maybe they're working together, and if they are, you wouldn't want to get on the wrong side of her." Feeling triumphant, Daphne wondered how he'd heard about Hera, and why he was so scared of her. Was there another Hera in these parts? A really, really angry one? She shook her head as if to clear it.

Zelus looked lost in thought. He had got a lot more from this little interrogation than he'd bargained for, and none of it was to his liking. Daphne watched him closely. He stood, and her thoughts returned to the present.

"Don't think this is over," he warned as he loomed over her, but the menace had left his voice. "Tomorrow you're coming with us as our prisoner. Try any funny business and we'll kill you on the spot. Got it? Assuming you survive, we will continue our little chat later, until I get to the bottom of your little schemes." He turned to face her captors. "Guard her carefully and don't let her out of your sight." Then he walked stiffly out of the ring of gang members and back toward his sleeping area. Daphne was grateful to have survived, for now, at least.

CHAPTER 24

OUT AND ABOUT

TRAVELLING BY secret paths known only to himself, in next to no time Hermes arrived at the Botrys factory. The gang gathered beneath the trees that now grew in the largest hall of what was once the winery, listening to Kratos brief them on his recent discussions with Zelus. He strode among them, outlining their coordinated plans for the coming attack. Hermes held back for a moment, listening, then strolled around the corner and into their midst.

"What are you doing here?" Kratos was both annoyed and alarmed that yet another intruder had walked past his sentries without being spotted or challenged.

"Is that how you welcome me, patron of thieves and tricksters and the one who's looked after your back all these years? You should watch your tone," Hermes reprimanded. His manner, mild as ever, only irked Kratos more. The big cat bristled with indignation but held his tongue. Hermes lowered his voice and continued.

"I'm just passing by and thought I'd see how you were getting on. What's the news from Botrys?" He circled the assembly, looking around as if this were his first visit, and noting the gang members present. Beams of moonlight pierced the canopy of trees, segmenting the floor into pools of silver and shade. His circuit complete, he sat down in in their midst, and washed his paws as if it were the most natural thing in the world to do, here at the heart of the gang's headquarters and in the middle of their conference. Spellbound, they all watched him. Washing was an activity Kratos had little time for. He preferred a quick roll in the dust to dampen the constant irritation of the fleas that pestered him. Watching the sleek white cat performing its ablutions in their midst without a care in the world infuriated him, but the principal cause of his ire was the condescending air his supposed 'patron' always adopted. Well, it was soon going to change, just wait. The fur on his back rose, rendering his annoyance visible to his subordinates. Kratos shifted position but remained immobile in silent frustration, as if hypnotised, waiting for the silver-white cat to finish.

Hermes halted and stared directly at him. "Come on, spit it out. Keep quiet much longer and I might think you're trying to hide something."

The command in his voice drew an audible gasp from one side; no one dared to speak to the boss in such a manner. Gang members glanced at one another; the intruder exuded an authority they'd previously only witnessed in their leader. Such a challenge veered close to public humiliation. As if released from a spell, Kratos finally spoke, apparently keen to defuse the tension.

"You caught us by surprise, that's all. Thought you might be another spy. First time we've seen you in months. I wasn't sure you were still in business." He struggled to keep a sulkiness out of his voice. Something about his visitor always put him on edge.

"Another one?" said Hermes, making another verbal jab into his exposed fraying nerves. The intruder's eye never wavered from the gang leader, but Kratos could never hold his stare for long. Irritated at the impudence of his interrogator, he looked away, his eyes narrowed as if to fend off the white cat's stare.

"Three little bleeders marched in here bold as brass a couple of nights ago," piped Rea, breaking the silence and coming to his defence, unable to contain her indignation any longer. Kratos glared at her.

Hermes turned to her in mock surprise. "And you let them go?" Now it was her turn to handle his stare. She squirmed in discomfort. To her relief, he turned his attention back to Kratos. "They must have been awfully big and strong," he added, the faintest hint of menace hanging in the still night air. Transfixed, the watching cats hardly dared to breathe.

It was the gang leader's turn to look uncomfortable. The strange impotence he felt in the presence of this infuriating white cat only deepened his anger. He averted his gaze and thrashed his tail, unable to hide his feelings. With an effort, he deflected his irritation toward his subject matter rather than his visitor. "The interrogation was interrupted. If that human oaf of a night watchman hadn't come blundering in, they'd never have escaped."

There was silence. Kratos needed to regain some leverage in this conversation and set it on a more even keel. His authority was at stake. It was often the way. Hermes would arrive at the most awkward times, ask the most irritating and difficult questions, affect a superior air of vague disappointment, and hidden knowledge or power, then disappear for months. He was never on the front paw with this master trickster, although there was nothing he could put a claw on. The most frustrating thing of all was that he was sure he could take the know-all down in a fight, but for some reason, he didn't dare.

Hermes was far from finished. "So, you never found what they were after then?" His voice was mild and disarming once more. He looked around at the assembly, but no one volunteered an answer. "Anyone?"

Rea couldn't resist the urge to fill the silence. "Said they were looking for a pal."

"Just a cover story," said Kratos, gathering his wits and stepping in before she said too much. "We know they must have been after something, coming out all this way. I'm pretty sure they work for Her Ladyship. It's certain to be her meddling again, testing our defences, checking our strength. She's always hated us, can't bear the thought of someone in this city having just as much clout as her— maybe more."

Hermes tilted his head, scrutinising him. "And what have you done about it?"

Kratos paused before replying to gather his thoughts. He ventured a glance at the white cat, keen to impress. "I put some of my best troops on it. Gave them 'kill or capture' orders. They're the most wanted animals in Athens. They'll be found and dealt with soon, you can count on it."

"So how come the ginger one came to visit me this evening?"

Kratos blinked, caught out by the news. "What do you mean?" He tried to stifle his surprise, but couldn't. His boys should have taken down the spies and left them dead in a ditch somewhere. Those had been the instructions. No wonder they hadn't dared to show their faces yet. He struggled to come up with an explanation. "She must be worried about you a lot as well," he concluded. "Sent him on another spying mission. Perhaps she thinks you're going to join us and help sort her out?" The excuse sounded lame. He wished he'd kept his mouth shut. Hermes was the last ally he wanted.

The white cat appeared to read his thoughts. "You'd be

better off keeping me out of it," he said. "I've got problems enough without having to worry about Athena."

Doubts crowded Kratos's mind. "What did you do with him then?"

"I haven't done anything yet," Hermes hissed. "My people are guarding him while I try to find out what his little game is, and more importantly if he is who he claims to be, and if so, what his true aims are."

Kratos looked at Hermes afresh. "If he's not Athena's spy, then who is he?"

Hermes gave him a sidelong glance. "I'm not yet certain he isn't her spy. From what you've told me, that looks the more likely option. But his story doesn't fit the assumption. Not completely. But if he is her poodle, then what is she trying to achieve by sending him to me?" He paused. When he continued, he sounded more reflective. "The alternative is that if she isn't his master, then indeed, what is his game, and how has he tied you to me? I'm not convinced he would have plans of his own. He doesn't look bright enough. He must be in league with someone." Hermes looked around at the assembled animals. He changed tack. "What about the other two? You must have been able to nab one of them?"

"They were a slippery little bunch," Rea admitted, sounding and feeling a little ashamed.

Hermes persisted. "Well, where are they? What has become of them?"

Kratos' mind was in a whirl with trying to second-guess his visitor. He said nothing.

"Do you think they work for one of the other gangs?" Yannis asked. "They didn't look it—too weedy by half. Too young, too pretty, not streetwise. They didn't look like fighters."

"Nah, they work for Her Ladyship, I'm certain of it," snarled Rea, unable to keep the venom from her voice. "They'll be heading back there. No doubt about it."

Hermes watched their debate.

"Yes, that's got to be it," Kratos concluded, shaking off his doubts. "We'll find 'em anyway, I've got spies all over the place. We tracked them down south, but then they separated. We got one of their local collaborators, though. Operator of a nearby safe house." He glanced at Rea. "At least we put her out of business." He sat back, hoping to put his visitor on the spot for once. "So, when did he visit you?"

Hermes avoided giving a direct answer. "Let's assume they were working for her. What could they have found out?"

"Might have noticed we're below strength," Yannis chipped in, trying to be helpful. The others stared at him. "Well, it's true. Couple of lads disappeared last week and one or two of the girls have gone as well," he said, defensively. Kratos looked displeased and shuffled his position, but said nothing.

"What do you mean, gone?" asked Hermes.

"What I say," Yannis was indignant. "One moment they're here, next you can't find them anywhere. Just vanished off the face of the earth."

"If another gang's taken them, it's an act of war," Kratos growled, "so we have to act now, you can see that." He flicked a glance at the white cat. "I'm sure it's her, and it's about time she paid us the respect we deserve."

"You're saying she assassinated them?" queried Hermes. "I know she doesn't like you, but isn't it going a bit too far?"

Kratos dared a direct glance. His eyes narrowed. "Yes, I'm saying she took them. She's always hated us. She'd like nothing better than to get rid of us. Erase us. Thinks we're a pest, a menace to her friends in high places; the humans. I've heard she's always sucking up to them. That's the word on the street. She tells them we carry diseases, make the place look untidy, breed too fast, we're out of control. All that stuff. She wants us eradicated. Pest control, they call it." The more he expounded on his long-held grievances, no matter how tenuous, the more his anger was in danger of getting the better of him.

Rea snorted her agreement. "I'd like to see what happens to the rat population if we're gone."

"So you believe she's in league with humans to destroy you?" Hermes sounded incredulous. "And what evidence do you have?"

A cunning look crossed the big cat's face. "She's up to something, everyone knows it. She's defending the area where the humans are searching, digging. It's my bet there's treasure there that she wants, and it's worth so much that she doesn't want any of the rest of us to get hold of it." He waited to see if Hermes would say something to add weight to his theory, but the white cat stayed silent.

"How do you propose to take her down?"

"We march on the Plaka," Rea announced, unable to hide the pride in her voice.

Kratos looked at his troops. "We've still got the numbers."

"Is Zelus going to help out?"

"We don't need him or his gang," Kratos replied. He didn't want to share his detailed plans with the white cat.

"What about Bia?"

"Says she's not interested." Kratos had a difficult relationship with his sister. She'd left to carve out a territory in Kallithea on the south side some years ago. They didn't get on.

"Are you sure she can't help?" Hermes persisted.

"Yup—she wouldn't lift a paw for all the socks in Greater Greece," Kratos spat. "She's a turncoat. A splitter. She's just in it for herself. The only good thing about her is that she hates the Agora crowd as much as we do."

Hermes sat still, absorbing all this news. "Still, I hear she talks to your brother now and then." He looked away, keeping Kratos in his peripheral vision.

"Told you that, did he? He wouldn't go behind my back. Wouldn't dare."

"It sounds to me like you chat quite a lot?" His enquiry sounded innocuous, but Kratos clamped his jaw shut, fuming. The white cat continued. "So, you've made your frustration clear; when are you planning this raid?"

"It's more than a raid. We're going to take over the Plaka. That'll give her something to think about." Kratos didn't elaborate; he'd already divulged more information than he'd intended.

"And Ares is going to sit back and let you do all this?" asked Hermes mildly.

"He's not around anymore." Yannis couldn't hide his excitement. "Gone AWOL, disappeared, lost the plot, done a runner, departed the neighbourhood," he crowed, pawing the ground in delight. He was beside himself with glee. "He must have realised he's past it. And with that slob gone, they've no more big hitters. They're sitting ducks." Kratos glared at him and he shut up.

"It'll all be ours." Rea sounded very pleased with herself.

"You're not expecting any resistance from the Agora?"

Rea continued, "She might try, but she hasn't got the numbers, and they're all namby-pamby types, anyway. Not a fighter among 'em. She hides behind the humans to do her work for her and they won't want to get their hands dirty chasing us all around the tourist hotspots down in the centre. As long as we do the business nice and quick, and keep a low profile, they'll be happy enough." She glanced at the boss, caught his body language, and shut up.

"What about Ares' sons?"

There was a pause while the gang members looked from one to another. Against all his better instincts, Kratos couldn't resist a jibe. "I don't care how many kittens he's spawned, they'll be feeble without their old man." He'd always hated Ares and everything to do with him. "They won't be a match for street fighters like us. There'll be no escape."

"None of them's got a reputation," added Rea. "They'd just hide behind their daddy."

"It sounds like you've got it all covered then," said Hermes smoothly. He got to his feet again.

"What are you going to do with him?" asked Kratos as an afterthought.

"Ah yes, our ginger friend." Hermes sounded unconcerned. "I'm not the violent type. I might send him off on a wild goose chase or something," he mused. "Or maybe I can arrange for him to fall into your clutches sometime. If you come across him wandering into your path somewhere in the centre of town, think of it as a little gift." He ambled through a gap in the walls, turned a corner, and disappeared out of sight. Above, out of the corner of his eye, he sensed motion. Looking up, he spotted the dark shape of an owl rising against the moonlit sky.

HIS NEXT port of call was a disused warehouse in the district of Gizi. Zelus and his leadership team were sitting in a circle discussing the findings from the prisoner's interrogation. They had bundled her to the back of the warehouse, behind some pallets with her guards keeping a constant watch. Hermes strode in, purposeful and businesslike. It was time to go fishing; he dangled a speculative hook.

"I gather you're going to support the Botrys Gang's little excursion," he announced by way of greeting, walking toward them and inspecting his surroundings as if he'd never been there.

Zelus noted the brazen invasion of their space with equanimity. He was past caring about the white cat: he was a known menace, a long-time source of annoyance. He liked to think he could rise above his pathetic little jibes.

"Ah, you'll have been chatting with my dear esteemed brother? What's he been telling you?" he said, struggling to hide his irritation that a private conversation had been shared with a third party. "My poor brother always had an issue with confidentiality."

"As long as he doesn't spill the beans to the authorities," squeaked Nestor, keen to support his boss. "He's desperate for our help." Zelus shot him a look and he shut up.

Hermes ignored the Gizi gang boss and his garrulous little subordinate, but continued strolling for a while. He inspected the tall shelving units and sniffed the air, then approached them and stopped.

"He says he doesn't need you," he said, addressing Zelus as if the others weren't there. "Thinks his mob can manage by themselves, Athena and all, and then, if you do turn up, play you off against Bia and her south-siders. I think he's got her mounting a flanking operation via Hadrian's Arch. I'd say he's even gone so far as to divide the centre up between them. She can keep most of the Plaka while he takes Monastiraki and the Agora, and whatever's found up there."

191

Zelus sat immobile, trying to remain impassive. He couldn't prevent his jaw from clenching. With an effort, he kept his voice level. "And how come you know all of this?"

Hermes looked around, taking his time before replying. "I get around a bit. I like to keep an ear to the ground, see what's going on. I don't like it if things get unbalanced. That could be dangerous, I'm sure you agree? This current plan seems a little unfair, if you've already got some sort of arrangement in place." He shot Zelus a direct look. "Of course, it's none of my business, and perhaps you're perfectly happy here? You have a nice territory, after all. Best quarter of the city, in my opinion. Apart from the centre, of course." He tilted his head, his look turning sly. "You never know, maybe I can help with your strategic planning, offer advice, we can do some brainstorming together, you can bounce some ideas off me, that sort of thing?"

Zelus swallowed, trying to think of something to say.

"Kratos has always been a troubled soul, of course," Hermes continued in confidential tones. "I often think he seems a little," he paused, considering his choice of words, "unhinged. He's got a real flea in his fur about Her Ladyship, of course. Well," he gave the assembled gang members a conspiratorial look, "we all have, she's never been the easiest to get on with. But this time it's different. I detect a genuine animosity. More than any other time I've spoken to him. He's really out to get her, and he thinks she's got something of value he can use."

"Like what?" Zelus bent his head forward, focusing on Hermes' left ear (he couldn't live with those blue eyes).

Hermes sat upright, pleased to have such an attentive audience. "I don't know yet, but whatever it is, Kratos wants it badly. Badly enough to first ask for your help and then try to double-cross you, or at least use you to keep her off his back while he goes searching himself." He stopped a while for effect and then continued in convivial tones. "Between you and me, I'd have thought he'd have mentioned it by now. I mean, it seems so important to him, and you are family. Of course, maybe it's just too precious to share. He must want to keep it for himself. Whatever it is. He's becoming very ambitious." He raised a forepaw and started cleaning between the toes, sensing the inner turmoil in his host.

"The scumbag never mentioned Bia." Zelus was struggling to maintain any semblance of calm. His voice trembled with suppressed anger. "So he's trying to get us to do all the dirty work against those fat wasters in the Plaka, while he gets all the treats up in the Agora?" Without realising, his voice was rising as his anger grew. He was almost shouting. "Doesn't he know? He'll get nowhere without us. We're not doing this to let him collect his treasure and have all the best pickings." He paused, incensed but unwilling to vent his fury any more in front of the white cat. Any trust he had in his brother's plans was evaporating fast.

Hermes paused his manicure. "Quite," he said, and settled down, folding his front paws together. He surveyed the group. There were around a dozen cats present, but at this hour many more would be out on errands and missions, causing mischief, hunting rodents or hapless birds, stealing trinkets be it clothing items or shiny objects, and intimidating house cats, all to add to the legend and influence of Zelus, who regarded himself, and not his brother, as the leading gangster in north Athens.

"Well, you need to take care and watch out, that's all I'm saying. You know what families can be like: sibling rivalry and so on, and yet, blood thicker than water and all that…" He paused, lowering his voice so that only the two of them could hear. "If you have to act alone, have you got the numbers to do it?" he asked.

"Of course we have." Zelus sounded calmer once more; back in control, confident. "What he has in brawn, he lacks in finesse, and he's far too cautious. He can't make a plan, and he fails to see the bigger picture. He might like to think he can act alone, but in reality, he needs us. Here," he looked around proudly, "I've got plenty of muscle, and the meanest, sharpest claws in all the city. Think strategically, then act quickly and decisively, that's our approach. He's forever coming up with excuses to delay. He's all bluster. When it comes down to it, he won't do anything without us."

"We've lost a couple recently though," Demitrius, his second in command ventured. Hermes looked round at him.

"Really?" His eyes widened in surprise.

"Oh, yes," Zelus cut across his deputy before he could say something stupid. His tail slashed out a warning. Demitrius and Hermes duly picked it up. "Just a couple." He tried to sound dismissive. "Nothing major."

"Five, according to my count," Denna piped up.

Zelus rounded on her. "I said nothing we can't handle." Although appearing calm, his voice carried an undercurrent. She shut up and looked away.

"Five, dear me," Hermes said. "That seems rather careless."

"Like I said, it won't affect us. We're perfectly capable of taking the Plaka ourselves, without Kratos's dubious assistance." He tried to sound calm, but couldn't help fidgeting under Hermes' scrutiny.

"What's the problem then? Is it a lack of foresight holding you back, or is it because you don't have the balls?" The other cats looked stunned; no one ever spoke to their leader like that. Zelus stood over Hermes, his eyes blazing. The white cat didn't move a muscle and maintained his relaxed pose. Rather than apologise, he doubled down on the insults. "You tell me you're keen to get going and act decisively, but from where I'm sitting, you don't look to be taking the initiative. In fact, I'd go so far as to say it looks like Kratos calls the shots and you're his tame little pet." He stared up at Zelus, unnerving the other animal, who turned full circle, trying to maintain his temper.

"You've got a nerve coming in here and saying that." He struggled to keep his voice level. "We have a plan. Jointly agreed. A pact between equal partners. He won't get anywhere without us. But I can act alone if I have to. I don't need him."

Hermes stood, taking the other cat by surprise. Zelus was unable to prevent a tiny flinch and hoped his followers wouldn't notice. The white cat looked him full in the face, inching closer until their noses almost touched. All pretence of good nature had vanished. His stare was hard as flint.

"Perhaps the time has come? It's nothing to me whether you pad along in his shadow, or take the lead; however, a little advice. Your ally's planning is more advanced than you think, and you'd better get wise to his agenda or you'll just end up as his doormat. Someone to do the dirty work while he picks up the prizes. If he needs you at all, it's just to watch his back." He made to go, then turned back. "Oh, and better keep an eye out for interested third parties. There's more going on in this city than you know. It might be a good idea to look after any extra bargaining chips you've got. You never know when they might come in useful." His eyes flicked to the corner of the warehouse.

Zelus stood transfixed and glowering. "What have they

195

found at the Agora?" he asked in a quiet voice. Hermes backed up a pace.

"Well, isn't that the exciting thing? Nobody knows. Perhaps you'll be the first to find out?" He gave the gang leader one last scornful look and sauntered out.

Zelus watched him go, his mind working overtime. Behind him the gang members stared at one another, indignant that Kratos was playing them for fools.

CHAPTER 25

A NIGHT-TIME RAID

BIA HATED being bounced into any sort of action, but she recognised this opportunity wouldn't last. A cloudy night was just what she wanted, nice and dark, no annoying patches of moonlight illuminating the place. She padded along quiet streets, using her intimate knowledge of central Athens to skirt the urban woodland and reach her destination without attracting the watchers' attention. She hugged the walls, and sought the darkest pools of night, one shadow among many.

Her route passed along quiet residential streets, avoiding major thoroughfares as much as possible. She was alone. This was a mission she trusted to no one else. If this thing fell into the wrong paws? She shivered at the thought. No, this was something she wanted for herself. To retrieve this sacred object from right under the nose of Her Snootiness would only add to her satisfaction. If half the rumours Hermes had told her were true, it would be transformational. Once she mastered it, she would become the most powerful animal in the entire city: the all-powerful Bia, Queen of Athens. They would all have to bow down to her; she could order them to do whatever she liked. She allowed herself to dream; wouldn't it be fun to get Kratos to look after the little ones while she and the other mums had a nice relaxing time away from all the mewling? How about getting Hermes to run a few errands on her behalf, maybe bring her some appealing trinkets? She could force Athena to bring catnip toys to her. Yes, how marvellous to see her crouching submissively and taking orders, watching but unable to join in. Delicious. Her tail tingled with excitement.

As she turned a corner into Astiggos Street, she snapped back into the present. She halted behind a chained-up stack of tables from a restaurant and peered down the street. She saw movement. A cat-shaped silhouette stepped out from a doorway and stared back in her direction. Bia hesitated, then moved forward a couple of paces. The other cat raised, then lowered her tail in recognition. Having to rely on support from an enemy was annoying, but then again, her accomplice's betrayal was delicious. Athena would be beside herself. Bia sniffed around, but could detect no signs of a trap. She padded forward once more, slowing as she approached her contact. In the dark, she could sense the other animal's scent rather than make out her features. The other cat bowed her head in recognition and moved off, leading her along the silent street.

They skirted a shuttered restaurant with tables chained together out front, then Herse stopped. To their right was a metal fence at least two meters high. It presented a difficult obstacle for a human, but with gaps between and below the panels it might as well not have been there at all for a cat. Bia paused beside her companion.

Herse broke the silence. "This is where they are digging," she whispered. "The area Athena seems most interested in is over there by that bank of earth." She pointed with her nose. "Just in front of it is the place where they have been most busy. That's what she focuses on. The object must be just under the surface there. A good poke around should let you get it out, I'm sure."

197

"Do we know what it is?" Bia asked. Hermes had not shared any information on its appearance.

Herse hesitated. "I'm not really sure, except Athena says she will recognise it when she sees it. It must look impressive. Or pretty. Beyond that, she hasn't said."

Bia thought for a while. Hermes had said it was an object of power but was vague about the details. All these hints seemed to indicate something unusual. She had never paid much attention to the stuff humans dug up at these sites. Most of it seemed to be little pieces of pottery they got excited about and put in museums, but she could never understand the attraction. Athena didn't seem too bothered about such stuff either, so the thing she was looking for had to be something different. It was time to take a closer look. She moved forward.

"Wait, one more thing," Herse whispered. Bia looked over her shoulder. "Be very careful down there. Athena has other followers around here on guard. They're looking outward, rather than in, but if you make any noise, they are going to hear you and investigate. Be as quiet as you can."

It was a useful reminder. The gang leader turned back to the challenge and took a moment to plot a route through the ruins toward the area Herse had showed. It looked to be partially obscured from the railings on the street opposite, but in plain sight from here. She hoped Herse's colleagues wouldn't be traipsing along this street tonight. Bia squeezed under the fence and dropped to the lower ground level, which the archeologists' work had uncovered. There were a few shallow pits, and between them the raised foundations of walls and the occasional column. Bia skirted around them as stealthily as possible, trying not to attract undue attention with sudden movements, should any passing animal take a look. Not that there should be any, if Herse was telling the truth.

She arrived at the spot her collaborator had indicated and took some time to sniff it out. Even in the low light, the most recently turned earth was clear to see, but looking at it, she could detect no clues where anything precious might be buried. She walked back and forth, thinking. What was that? At the very edge of her senses she felt; no heard; no experienced a very faint vibration. The tips of her whiskers trembled, picking it up like radar. But the signal was so faint. Bia shook her head vigorously to try to clear her thoughts, and stayed as still as possible. Yes, it was something there; right on the limit of her detecting ability, but the faintest of vibrations, a sensation she'd had never previously experienced. It told her something different lay here, right under her paws. She bowed her head toward the ground and felt it again, then she moved a meter away and detected… nothing. Bia's excitement mounted. This had to be the mystery object. She moved back to where the strange sensation was strongest and dug with her front paws, scrabbling urgently at the dirt, forgetting Herse's instruction to be quiet. Her scratching attracted the attention of an owl perched in a tree overlooking the site. He swiveled his head, watched her for a moment, then returned to mouse-spotting.

After several frantic minutes, something glinted just in front of her nose. She stepped back to inspect it. It was still very dark, but she had uncovered something promising, round, covered in earth but with a hard centre. It was circular. She scrabbled at the earth surrounding it and extracted a muddy blob, placing it on the ground next to the hole she'd dug. Then she licked it, removing as much loose earth as she could. It fell away easily. Stepping back a short distance, Bia studied it, tilting her head to see if a different angle would deliver new insight. There, the glint of something shiny beneath the dirt at the side. Was it gold? Bia loved gold. Anything golden and shiny, in fact, as long as it was metallic, and she could tell from its weight this was metal, not plastic. She cleared more dirt away with her rasping tongue. The object repaid her effort, reflecting what little light was available, and from the way it shone Bia was sure it was gold.

If truth be told, it was a little small to be so special and so powerful, but it was very old judging from the funny pictures carved onto it. It had the appearance of something important and rare, the treasure she had been searching for. It had to be. She ran through the salient points in her mind. She'd found it in the place shown, and those strange, faint vibrations had pinpointed its precise location in the ground. It was just below the surface, like Hermes and Herse had told her it would be, and where Athena was expecting it to be. True, it looked a little small for something so powerful, but size didn't mean anything of itself. She would work out how to use it once back at her base, where she had time. Bia felt exhilarated. Whilst smaller than expected, it had the advantage of being portable. She picked it up in her mouth, tasting earth mixed with metal, and looked around. No sign of watchers, good. Bia plotted her way back to her entry point into the compound and jumped back to the base of the fence. On the other side, she found Herse. The Agora cat gave her a questioning look.

"Foun' ith," said Bia. Herse looked blank. Bia dropped her precious object and cleared her throat. She looked up. "Found it," she repeated. "Now I'm going to disappear from your life, and most likely never see you again. You'd better not breathe a word."

"You don't need to worry on that score," the other replied. This entire episode was distasteful, and she regretted her decision to betray Athena's wishes. Herse inspected the other cat's prize. Was that the powerful mystery object her mistress had been obsessing about these past weeks? It was a pretty gold disk, to be sure, but what special attributes did it have? How unimpressive. She didn't want to know, she just wanted this unpleasant gang leader and her precious trinket gone from here as soon as possible, and with the minimum of fuss. "I'm hardly inclined to go bragging about this."

She led the way back along the street and watched as her companion departed back the way she'd come. Oh well, it was over. She hoped her mistress would get over it quickly and get back to more important business: dealing with those troublesome gangs to the north.

CHAPTER 26

NO FURTHER FORWARD

ONCE AGAIN Apollo had a restless night, disturbed by a dream so realistic he felt he was reliving it. This time he found himself among the olive groves on the slopes above the Corinthian Gulf, amid a chase that was nearing its end. He sensed the girl was near exhaustion, her energy spent. She would have to stop, make her stand. She was feisty, this one, no easy conquest. Not like the others who just melted in his arms. It was part of her appeal. He saw her slow and stop ahead and turn to face him. He saw, with the strange clarity of dreamsight, the defiance in her eyes, her determination not to be a victim.

Evening was approaching, the shadows deepening beneath the trees, and he was elated. Would victory have ever tasted so sweet? She was above all others, the special one, the woman who would complete him. He had to have her. It was providence; a gift so sweet. None could equal her, not even Aphrodite herself. Inside his fantasy, his emotions felt vivid and real. His passion was unrestrained; he could almost taste her exquisite lips. Soon he would lose himself in the softness of her kiss and the sweetness of her breath, feel her lithe body, with its firm young breasts, press against his. An anticipatory smile crossed his face.

And there she was, in the middle of a small clearing, facing him, standing straight, and breathing hard. Her hands were on her hips, a bold, defiant look in her eye and her chin raised in challenge in just the manner he found so enticing. He stopped. Finally, she would be his; they would become one.

"You'll never have me. I defy you. I won't be just another of your conquests. I hate you!"

He paused, admiring her spirit, lusting for her even more. Everything about her was perfect and so different; beautiful and independent of mind, confident in manner. Her defiance just deepened his ardour, if it were possible. His passion was unbounded; he would build her a palace, set her on a throne of jade encrusted with diamonds and precious stones, give her servants to wait upon her every need, and take a delight in pleasuring her in all the ways known to the divine, their union founded in bliss. Like a huntsman approaching a cornered animal, he moved a step closer and held out his hand.

"Come on, don't be like that. We can take it slowly if you like. Just talk for a while." The honeyed words fell smoothly from his lips, and the corners of his mouth turned upward to a smile. It was an approach he'd used countless times before, but never with as much resting on it as now.

"Never." It was a scream of defiance; a declaration of war. Behind it, she uttered a silent prayer to the god of the river and was answered. She closed her eyes. He stepped closer, reached out to take her wrist, and grasped… a laurel branch!

"No!"

His anguished shout echoed in his mind, around the glade and beyond. He grimaced, staring wildly around him as if trying to spot an accomplice hiding in the shadows. Someone he could vent his rage upon, someone he could split asunder like matchwood, but there was no one. Turning back, the beautiful tree trembled before him.

Beside himself with frustration, he glared at it.

"Daughter of Peneius, at the last, all trees die and return to the earth," he snarled as if it could hear. "You can't hide in there and expect to escape me forever." He looked up at the sky, his arms flung wide, shouting in a mighty voice for all to hear whether they were far across the gulf or high in the mountains. "This isn't over."

In this way, desire conquered reason.

HE WOKE in the early light of a grey dawn, an hour before sunrise, still tired. Troubled thoughts scudded through his head like storm clouds before a gale. There was no chance of further sleep. Instead, he got up, picking his way carefully past the still sleeping cats around him, pausing at the edge of the clearing to stretch then sniff the air. At this hour, before the city below awoke and resumed its daily business, the scent of the trees was strong. First things first; he needed to scratch something. He decided upon a convenient tree trunk and let rip, ears tilted back. It was good to get some frustration out of his system. Next, he decided to explore the hilltop, weaving a path between trees and rocks until he ended up near the spot where he and Hermes had chatted the previous evening. Keeping her distance, Pandrosus watched him.

As he surveyed the concrete jungle below, the enormity of his challenge struck him afresh. The city seemed to go on forever. He couldn't count the number of buildings. How could he find the one which held Olympia? And where was Daphne? And Jason? He looked around again, needing to talk to his newfound friend the crow. He saw it perched nearby and gave a slight incline of his head. The bird recognised the sign and set down in front of him.

"What can I do for you today, guv'nor?" it asked.

"I've got something else you might help me with. I'm looking for a friend." He paused. "More than one, actually." Indecision overwhelmed him; who should he look for first? An intense yearning for Daphne swamped all other thoughts. Surely it made sense to find her first, before they redoubled their efforts to rescue Olympia? While he hesitated, the bird remained still, eyeing him intently. The dream came back to him; finding Olympia was more important. He described her to the crow and told it what had happened. "I think she's somewhere down there, but I don't know where and there may not be much time." It was embarrassing to have so little information to share. How was this bird going to be of any use with just the feeble notion that she was somewhere out there, in the enormous urban sprawl below? The crow listened. Briefing over, he made ready to depart.

"It'll be a challenge and no mistake, but I'll put the word out and we'll see what turns up—there's quite a lot of us about," he said and spread his wings.

"How will you find me?" Apollo asked.

The bird looked over his shoulder as he took off.

"Don't worry, I'll spot you."

Apollo watched him go, still feeling torn. Had he made the right decision? Maybe there was a slim chance he would find Olympia, but his worries for Daphne intensified. He couldn't bear to lose both of them. It was still just one bird within a huge urban sprawl. What chance did it have? In the east, the sky was turning pink as the sun drew closer. Sunrise always lifted his mood. It was time to find something to eat and try to put his anxiety aside, at least for a while.

As he set off across the rocky plateau, he saw Hermes approaching. "What did you find out?"

"Quite a bit, as a matter of fact."

"So?" Apollo waited.

"All in good time, old chap. Shall we see if there's any food left in those bowls? I'm starving." He set off to the place where they had fed the previous evening. Apollo trailed after him, impatient for news.

They ate in silence for a few minutes, then Hermes led the way to a different perch with another spectacular view. Along the way, he nodded to another couple of cats to join them. They sat. For a while no one spoke. Apollo's frustration mounted.

Hermes scanned the scene below, as if unsure how to start. Eventually, he broke the silence. "Perhaps I'd better give you a synopsis. I visited a few old haunts last night and found out more than I expected. Things are happening at a pace." He gave Apollo a sideways glance. "You've certainly set a few hares running, so to speak."

Apollo wasn't interested in local gossip. "Did you find out anything that would help me find Olympia?" he demanded.

"Maybe, and maybe not. There is a lot of agitation among the gangs, and war seems inevitable. But while they are all preoccupied with their preparations, several of their members have defected, or gone missing." He looked at the ginger cat. "Don't get your hopes up; disappearances happen all the time. The leaders say it's not unusual, just normal staff turnover. Bit inconvenient for them, but that's life." He turned to his two lieutenants. "Did either of you pick up anything?"

Angelia spoke first. "I went east. I spoke to Hecate at her hilltop retreat." Apollo started, then glanced at his companions. He didn't feel like having to explain his visit there; he hoped Hecate felt the same way.

"The old witch?" Hermes scoffed. "Remind me, where's she hanging out these days?"

"The Monastery of St John."

"That's right, a monastery! She's changed. Has she converted?" He looked across to share the joke with Apollo, but the ginger cat gave no response.

Angelia continued. "It's a quiet spot. The priests are kind, they give her food. Nobody else seems to know that she's there."

"You're telling me. Well, I suppose I ought to pay a visit sometime. Before she puts a spell on somebody."

Apollo's agitation was growing, and this irrelevant small talk was getting them nowhere. "Can't we just get on with it—did she have anything useful to say that might help us find Olympia?"

Angelia gathered her thoughts once more, staring into the middle distance. "She did her usual thing; 'the old ways are dying, no one has any respect for the elders anymore,' et cetera, et cetera."

"She's heard nothing on the grapevine?" Hermes asked. "I suppose she's out of the loop these days, stuck out there. And she wasn't exactly the life and soul of the party in the first place."

"There was one thing. She did say that a great evil was afoot and it threatened everybody and some humans had started to farm dogs." Apollo and Hermes stared at her. Dog farming? What could she mean?

Something clicked in Hermes' memory. "Ah yes, it might explain what Bia was on about." He gave a quick, selective summary of his earlier conversation. "They're keeping her awake barking all night," he grinned. "Anything else? No? Nothing to do with us then. Seems like a bit of a dead end." He turned to Pharis, "what did you find?"

Pharis spoke more slowly. "I went south and spoke to the gangs in Ymittos and Agios Dimitrios. They reported one or two cats going missing, but they assumed they had just been run over, or victims of assault. They tended to be the younger ones." He looked around at the others. "No road sense, of course."

Apollo shuddered at the recollection of his own introduction to Athens' busy streets; it was a steep learning curve with a 'one strike and you're out' rule. He was dispirited. "So you've learned nothing," he exclaimed. "We have no idea who is taking these animals, or where they're being held. We're no further forward. This is useless."

Hermes gave him a look. "Well, I learned that there's a price on your head, you and your pals. Kratos has put the word out, and he's got animals looking for you, and they mean you harm."

"I don't care about them." Apollo was getting more frustrated by the minute.

"You shouldn't dismiss them. They're dangerous, and there are more than you might think. You should stay here until it all blows over."

"No."

"What did you do to upset them so? They're out for blood. They're sure you're spying for Athena, out to do them harm."

Apollo snorted in derision, but the white cat continued on his theme.

"They're certain you went there to test out their defences; get an idea of their strength, information that would give Athena a chance to prepare a welcome; ambush them, something like that. I must say, if that was your mission you've stirred up a hornet's nest, and maybe forced them into action sooner than they would like, and that's not good for any of us."

Apollo looked away, seething at the implication, but in the main frustrated his quest was being ignored.

Hermes persisted. "Well? What exactly were you up to? Have you passed on whatever it was you discovered? I think you owe us an explanation."

Apollo was, by now, beside himself with frustration. The point of visiting Hermes had been to get information about Olympia's whereabouts and some help. This visit had been a waste of time. He would do better by himself. He stood up, glared at his host, then pointed his nose towards the Acropolis and set off.

Hermes caught up with him.

"What are you doing?" he asked. Apollo stopped and turned to face him.

"Coming here was a mistake. I don't know why anyone advised it. You're no help at all. I'm not just going to sit on my arse all day and count flies. I'm going to go over there and start looking." He nodded in the vague direction of the Parthenon and set off once more. Below him, he could see the start of the track down the hill. Hermes caught up with him again.

"So why did you come here? So you can report back on what I'm up to? I think not!" His usual demeanour of smug superiority had vanished.

"Don't worry, as far as I'm concerned, you're doing nothing." Apollo continued walking.

Hermes tried a different tack. "It's dangerous down there. You're top of their hit list, and more to the point, you don't know where you're going."

"For one thing, they don't frighten me, and secondly, yes I do. Over there." Apollo's reply was a challenge.

"Oh, so you are working for her?" Hermes couldn't keep

the sarcasm from his voice.

"I don't know what you're talking about."

"You can stop playing the innocent. Just admit it: you're in league with Athena. You might as well spill the beans. What's her special project all about? It's got the entire city seething. If she's not careful, her precious 'Pax Athena' is going to come crashing down around her ears."

Apollo stopped in his tracks and stared at the white cat, a glint of real annoyance illuminating his golden eyes. Despite his anger, his voice was the epitome of calm reason, and even more powerful as a result. "I seem to remember I used to like you, but for an Immortal you're so full of shit. Stop playing games for once, and just get out of my way. We came here to rescue a friend, nothing more."

Hermes struggled to keep his composure. "Ah yes, ever the altruist. You and your little friend Daphne. That name rings a bell. Peneius' daughter, if I recall. The one who gave you the run around. I thought you'd got her out of your system?"

Apollo's eyes narrowed. "What are you talking about?"

"Come on, you must remember? It was quite a story back in the day. Eros was..."

"I don't have a clue what you're on about."

The white cat was unconvinced. "No? Too bad." He pretended indifference. "Because if you dared to climb down off that high plinth, you might like to know she's..."

"Look, cut it out. She's just a friend from Delphi, and she knows Olympia. She volunteered to help."

"Sounds like she's quite attached to you, though? Something must have changed."

Apollo did not respond. He had no answer. Hermes' probing left him confused. On the fringe of memory he felt he should know something, but what?

Hermes continued. "So if Daphne's just a friend, what does that make Olympia?"

The ginger cat looked at him, bewildered. He didn't want his thoughts read, but felt exposed somehow. "We were close," he said quietly.

"Close? As in 'let's have a family?'"

Apollo gave a little snort and looked the other way.

Hermes looked pleased with himself. "Ah, I see it now. You came to rescue your 'wife,' and brought your girlfriend along for the ride. Only, now they're both lost, any you don't know where to turn: do you do your duty or follow your dick?" He pushed his face closer toward the ginger cat until they were almost touching. "I knew the old Apollo was in there somewhere." He looked insufferably smug. Apollo started to hate him. But then the white cat continued his musing, as if talking to himself. "But where does that leave the other one? Jason?"

"I don't really know him. He came along for the adventure." Apollo sounded dismissive. He'd had enough of this conversation and wanted it to end.

Hermes gave him a long look followed by a tiny, pitying shake of the head. "You don't make a very good shepherd, do you? You'd only been in Athens for five minutes and you lost your flock." Apollo's resentment grew, but the other wasn't yet finished. His voice hardened. "But that's only the half of it. You show up after all this time acting the innocent, but in reality, throw a grenade into an already volatile situation, and you seriously expect me to believe it's all because you want to save a mortal?" He sounded incredulous. "What's so special about this one? How is she different from all the others? What's she got on you?"

Apollo didn't answer, he just set off down the hill.

Hermes shouted after him. "There's far more at stake

right now than the fate of your little friend. And if you think Athena is going to give you any help, you're beyond naïve. When did she ever help you? She won't be remotely interested. You'll get a better hearing from the human police. I was trying to help you, but if you don't want to know, then you can go to hell." He turned around and retreated up the slope.

Hermes' acolytes stayed well away from him when he returned. They hadn't seen him in a mood this foul for as long as any could remember. When he had calmed down a little, he sought Angelia and Pharis and indicated north.

"Head down there and get me an update on our ginger friend's pals," he ordered. "I'm pretty sure Zelus has got one, and if that insufferable ginger fool had allowed me, I would have told him. Keep tabs on her and try to find the other one. Let's see what they've got to say. And keep an ear out for any news of this so-called friend of theirs, if she exists. I want to know who she is and what makes her so special. What or who she was spying on, and whether she's survived. We're going to find out what's happened to her before he can and wipe the smug expression off his face."

CHAPTER 27

APOLLO ALONE

APOLLO CONTINUED his descent of Lycabettus hill without a clear idea where to go, let alone a plan. He was furious with Hermes. Why did the white cat have such trouble believing his story? Why did he think he knew Daphne? Apollo was sure he was holding some information back—but what?

His thoughts circled round as he marched down the slope, looking far more purposeful than he felt. He needed to control his frustration and think clearly. He had to find Athena. She alone seemed capable of helping him locate Olympia; he just hoped she would be more helpful. As with Hermes, the name was familiar, but his memory hazy. A phrase echoed in his head: 'when has she ever helped you?' It didn't give him any confidence.

As the street levelled out, he found himself by the side of the busiest road he'd yet seen, with three lanes of traffic in each direction. His attention snapped back to the present. He'd be no use to Olympia if a bus flattened him. A few minutes of concentration allowed him to spot a gap in the traffic and he darted across. At the other side, he lost his bearings. He wanted to avoid the busy thoroughfares if possible, but as a result, his route took him south instead of west across the landscaped grounds of some museums and the ancient site of Aristotle's Lyceum. He hopped over some fences and boundary markers, but at least his chosen route was unimpeded by the city's pedestrians and vehicles.

Continuing on his bearing, making sure he always headed toward the Acropolis, whenever he could see it looming behind buildings or trees, he found himself in the National Gardens, an extensive park filled with exotic plants and trees. He wondered at the enormous palm trees and sniffed around the edges of the central pond. It was all very interesting and quite a distraction. At one point he thought he saw a tortoise, but it was no big deal, there were a few at Delphi. He could have stayed all day here in this restful corner of the city, but duty nagged him back to his task. Despite the attractions of the park he made excellent progress, and emerged at the side of another busy road, the worst yet.

As he surveyed the acres of tarmac in front of him, Apollo's attention was taken by a tram, the first he'd seen, gliding down the centre of the road, between all the cars, trucks and busses; another form of transport to avoid. He froze, keeping a wary eye on it until it was past. How many more strange vehicles did the modern world of humans have, waiting to catch him out? At least this one seemed to stick to those grooves in the tarmac, which was a relief.

Fortune was on his side. He'd emerged close to a major pedestrian crossing, and taking his cue from the humans when they ventured across, he followed in their midst. His confidence was increasing, but the big city was still strange. From this far pavement, he could see Mount Lycabettus in the distance to his right (he was impressed he'd travelled so far) but ahead was a warren of narrow streets and tall buildings and he no longer had sight of the cliffs of the Acropolis to guide him. He would have to rely on instinct.

Apollo launched himself into the maze of buildings. He

had no idea how to navigate through to the Agora where the mysterious Athena was said to live, but he hoped some of the cats in this part of town could direct him. They couldn't all be as rude as most of the members of his species he'd met so far on this trip.

The further he penetrated into the urban jungle, the more disoriented he became until he was no longer sure he was heading in the right direction. The streets were narrow and winding, and he soon lost his bearings. A tour guide, pursued by a gaggle of elderly humans, approached, holding an umbrella aloft despite the warm weather. His interest piqued, Apollo couldn't resist following out of professional curiosity. This was an opportunity to learn from a leading practitioner, a bona fide expert. He became embroiled in a sea of legs as the group passed him, then, freeing himself, followed them for a while. The group trooped down the street to a large ceremonial archway where they blocked the street while the guide delivered a lecture on its history and significance. As he observed the process, Apollo recognised how lucky he was to work in Delphi. Imagine trying to shepherd a gaggle of humans this big in the city, with all of its distractions. He wondered how many she'd lose before the end.

They set off again, Apollo tagging along, his quest momentarily put to the back of his mind. They ventured down more streets, dodging the local people, but he still had no clear sense of the direction they were heading. He hoped the group might head toward the Agora and his immediate target. After a while, the buildings on the right side of the road thinned out, and to his relief, he had another sight of the Acropolis towering above, now much closer. It was to his right, which meant he was passing to the south of it instead of the north as he'd intended, but now he had a clearer idea where he was heading he was less bothered.

The group paused while the guide delivered another talk, this time about the remains of a large amphitheatre on the hillside before them. It was described as the Theatre of Dionysius, and the guide had a lot to say about it. Apollo's attention wandered. Why had they named a theatre after that waster? He sniffed at some nearby plants while reflecting on the strange motivations of the human species. The tour had become a little boring, and he considered leaving, but the group set off again so once more he followed. After a short while, they paused in front of a large building on the left. It seemed they were heading inside. Apollo saw it to be a large, low building with enormous glass windows. Inside, he could see a lot of statues. Like home but with bigger windows, he thought, then turned to go.

He continued on his way down the narrow road, occasionally glancing up at the temple on the skyline and the monuments below. This was better. It reminded him of home. His mood lifted; the sun warmed his back; he had a renewed sense of purpose; the direction was more-or-less clear and the surroundings vaguely familiar. It was a relief to leave the concrete and steel world of men, even if just for a little while. On a whim, he took a detour along the hillside in preference to the road, wandering past inscribed stones and around gnarled trees and low bushes. At one point he passed a sleeping adder, hidden in a secluded suntrap. Further along, he spotted another tortoise chewing on a ground-hugging plant. He savoured the scented vegetation of this more open landscape, another lovely contrast to the city streets.

The sound of flapping wings attracted his attention as a large black bird landed on a nearby rock. It cawed at him. "Greetings, my lord."

Apollo stopped, somewhat taken aback but not displeased by the salutation. "What have you found?" he asked.

The crow, pleased with itself, performed a little dance on top of the rock. It tilted its head to one side and addressed him again. "We've found something you might be interested in," it said, watching the cat's reaction. "After I left you, I talked to my fellows at our daily murder. They agreed to keep an eye out and get back to me if they saw anything. I got a response a bit quicker than I expected." He shuffled his feet once more, turning to the other side. Apollo waited.

"Well, a short while ago one of the guys came up to me. He said there's been talk of a lot of dogs making a racket over in Tavros, so he went to check it out."

"I'm not interested in dogs," Apollo said. He turned away, disappointed.

"No, no, wait," the crow urged. "That's not what I came to tell you. My mate did a couple of fly-pasts to get a proper look. He says there're a lot of animals down there, in a big yard at the back of a building. It's not just dogs, they've got cats as well, but there are very high fences around it. They can't get out."

Apollo's eyes narrowed as he studied the bird. Was it telling the truth? Would they have taken Olympia somewhere like this? It sounded as plausible as anything else he could think of.

"Could be worth checking out." finished the crow, pleased with itself.

Apollo thought for a moment. What should he do? His intention had been to find Athena and try to persuade her to lend him the resources to search for Olympia, but if this was indeed where she was being held then there was no time to waste. He had to rescue her, but how? There was no backup now he'd lost Jason and Daphne, and he had no faith in Hermes so there was no alternative but to find this place himself and check out the crow's story. He wondered how much he could press him and his friends for further assistance.

"You have done well," he said. "You have my thanks, but now I need you to do more. I want you to show me where this place is. I have to get there as fast as possible. How do I find it? How far is it?"

The crow flapped his wings in delight, pleased to have been so helpful. It was eager to do more. "It's not far to fly, but it's quite a long walk," he said. "I'll guide you though." He set off in a flutter of wings and alighted on a tree a hundred meters further on. Apollo gritted his teeth and set off after him at a brisk trot. He had renewed hope for the first time in days, but alongside it came an immense surge of concern. Would he be in time?

They made rapid progress across the city; the crow making short flights ahead, the cat following as quickly as he could. They left the precinct of the Acropolis, surmounted Filopappou Hill, and descended toward the Tavros district, back into the world of modern men.

CHAPTER 28

THE GANGS ADVANCE

THE GIZI gang assembled in the centre of the warehouse as the first glimmer of light touched the eastern horizon. One of Daphne's captors cuffed her awake. She struggled to her feet, her wounds and limbs aching. Her heart sank. Today was going to be difficult. She hoped they would not march her too fast, or too far, or be too rough. How much more punishment could she take?

Across the dirty concrete floor, she watched Zelus stalking among his troops, cajoling and encouraging. He had a spring in his step, as if he'd gained some renewed purpose. She hoped she wouldn't have to face any more questioning. As if reading her thoughts, he turned and walked in her direction. Her heart sank.

"No funny business. You're staying with us today, and we'll have another cosy chat this evening. We might have quite a lot to catch up on." His eyes narrowed. "Cause trouble and we'll just execute you on the spot, got that?"

Daphne avoided his eyes and stared at the floor, mute. She wasn't ready for another bout of mental sparring or worse. Zelus observed her for a moment, then turned away to cajole and encourage some of his other troops.

They moved shortly after, streaming through the quiet pre-rush hour streets in columns, silent and swift, each led by a senior lieutenant. In the grey dawn, there were few vehicles about and they could cross major roads with ease.

Daphne found it hard to keep up. A fitful sleep had left her feeling marginally better, but the beating she had endured only a few hours earlier left her in poor shape. She ached all over and her wounds hadn't healed. Her guards, the same pair who had so attacked her so brutally the previous evening, hadn't allowed her anything to eat and were merciless in urging her on.

Zelus might have shown genuine fear at the mention of Hera last night, but having recovered his composure he didn't seem too bothered if she died on this route march. She limped and struggled on, panting for breath and in constant pain. Every few minutes a jab in her flank from the snout of a guard urged her on, faster than she felt she could manage. Somehow she kept up, breath rasping in her throat, heart pounding. For the umpteenth time, she wished she'd never set out on this adventure. She could have just stayed in calm and peaceful Delphi, playing among the ruins and the trees, enjoying good company, chasing flying insects and small rodents, having fun. Instead, she was in a dungeon of concrete and asphalt, enduring endless torture.

Approaching the rendezvous with the Botrys Gang, Zelus wondered if he needed the big oaf from across town. A brother he might be, but they had never been close, and their rivalry often set them at odds. There was little trust between them. He wondered if he and his followers could take over the Plaka themselves. All Kratos had done was suggest something he'd been thinking about, anyway. He took a pride in the streetwise fighters under his command, the finest criminal outfit in the entire city in his opinion. He was certain they could take out the furry fat sluggards that populated the Plaka with no outside help. They might call themselves a firm, but they had no leader, and they were complacent. They wouldn't have a chance, but once his forces were in control, what then? The Plaka wasn't big enough for two over-sized egos, and rich though the pickings were from the tourists, holiday lets, and local home-owning citizens, he had no desire to share them with his rival. A showdown would remind Kratos who held the real power in Athens and put him in his place. Athena was becoming an irrelevance; he, Zelus, would be the boss, no, king of this city, and he would brook no rivals.

They crossed Stadiou Street and zig-zagged through narrower streets and alleys until they reached Athinaidos Street. Here Zelus called a brief halt. He waited until all the columns caught up, then gave them one last set of instructions.

"Just remember why we're here. We are going to take over this neighbourhood, right? Look around: this is our new manor. But first, we've got to turf out the slobs who live here—put the place under new management. Think of it as a hostile takeover. This place looks good; the pickings are rich, the food better. Just a minor dispute to resolve, and it's ours. Are you with me?" He looked at his assembled troops. They miaowed, nodded, and tail-signed their agreement, impatient to get started, fired up to be taking part in something that would become legendary: the day the Gizi gang took over the Plaka. They would talk about it for years. They would be famous and feared throughout the city. This was their day.

They advanced more slowly now, keeping a careful watch for any local inhabitants who might sound the alarm as they drew closer to the square and the target of their attack. Shopkeepers were opening their shutters and setting up for the day, cafés put tables out, and the motorised carts and small vans of delivery men puttered along the narrow streets. About them and between them the cats streamed past, silent, intent on their destination, oblivious to the looks they were attracting from the few surprised humans about.

As they reached the edge of the square, Zelus signaled them to slow down again. He wanted to get a measure of his enemies, ideally send a couple of scouts out to report back on their precise location, but events got ahead of him. Zinovia, forgetting his orders, spotted a local cat sauntering across the middle of the square and in her eagerness forgot any instructions. She sprinted forward on the attack, and within a few seconds, the rest of them followed her.

Zelus tried to call them back, but it was impossible; their blood was up, they were on their way. The battle of Monastiraki had started whether he liked it or not. He chased after his troops, leading from the rear like many a general over the centuries. If he had been a student of military tactics, he would have recognised that from now he could only respond to events, rather than shape them.

Daphne had no desire to take part in any fighting, and certainly not on the side of these bullies. She just wanted to keep out of it, but she was worried that she might not get the opportunity. Her minders were straining at the leash to get involved. She wondered if she might get the chance to give them the slip, but so far they were keeping a close eye on her, and she was too weak and battered to outrun them. She would have to wait. Frustrated with keeping up the rear, her guards pushed her forwards as fast as they could, nipping her if she slowed down.

A SHORT distance across town another troop of cats was heading south along Aristofanous Street, arrowing in toward Monastiraki Square from a different direction. Kratos was at the head. To the west on Agias Theklas was Rea and her column, while Yannis and the rest tracked down Athinas Street. They were making rapid progress, each vying to be the first there, above all to get ahead of their ally. Kratos regretted inviting Zelus to this little shindig. He had no desire to share this prize; it had been his idea in the first place! For the hundredth time, he wondered if he could win this war with his own forces. He would have kept the entire operation to his own gang if the omens and those verminous little spies hadn't spooked him. If he could get his paws on that bunch again, he'd make them squeak.

As his column turned into Thermidos Street, he slowed the pace. He didn't want to arrive too far ahead of his lieutenants; there were limits to even his ability to restrain a group of agitated, wound-up cats. Nor did he want to risk losing the element of surprise and attacking with less than his full force. An elementary mistake like that would give the defenders time to get themselves organised. 'Not that it'll do them any good,' he thought.

At the junction with Ermou Street, he paused, checking for Rea's group. In only a few minutes, they appeared to his right. In silence, Kratos led his cats across the street and under the cover of the modern building opposite. Rea's group joined them. There they halted to wait for Yannis's unit. As they waited, the leader struggled to contain his agitation. Though he would never admit it, tension was gnawing at him. He mulled over Hermes' visit once more, particularly his mention of the sons of Ares. Kratos would never have dared this venture if Ares himself was still around—his reputation still hung over the city like choking smog. He didn't like to admit the fact, but Hermes had spooked him. How many sons did Ares have, and were they still with the gang? On that point, his intelligence was lacking. If any of Ares' sons were here, how much of their father's prowess had they inherited? Kratos took pride in the brutal martial

223

abilities of his own offspring. If there were several of his enemy's brood still around, that might even up the odds. If they were still young, they could be eliminated with ease.

At the back of his mind was a vague recollection that they were to be feared, but surely nowhere near as much as their old man. Kratos was sure they'd never be a match for his own offspring. He glanced at them among the throng, herding the troops and keeping them in order, reminding them of their duties. Strong family ties were the spine of his outfit; they provided strength and discipline. He cast his mind to his enemies. Unless Ares had left capable deputies in charge, they were sitting ducks, but he should take care. Eliminating any potential future threat from offspring would be wise. History was littered with legends of orphaned youths seeking revenge.

While the big cat was deep in reflection, many within the group were having trouble keeping still. Returning to the present, he became concerned that one of them might inadvertently wander out into the square, giving the game away. Discipline was wavering. He grunted orders to those nearest, and they reluctantly stepped back. All were nervous—they just wanted to get on with it. Several of them used the enforced wait to disappear under parked cars and relieve themselves in preparation. Kratos gave them a sour look. He had little sympathy for signs of weakness. They had to keep it together for a little while longer.

There came a strangled cry of annoyance from behind. One of his spotters was peering around the corner of the building into the square. He turned to Kratos.

"Over there," he urged. "It's Zelus's crew, I'm sure."

Kratos followed his gaze and saw a large number of cats streaming out into the square from the far side. What was going on? "He's trying to grab it all for himself," he spluttered. All thought of waiting for Yannis and his troops was forgotten. The Gizi gang had already started; they wanted the Plaka for themselves. He turned to the animals surrounding him, most of whom were now creeping forward to watch events across the square.

"Those swine are trying to grab all the glory for themselves. Well, we're not going to let them!" he shouted. "Follow me. Attack!" Beside himself at the thought of possible treachery from his allies, Kratos charged toward the thick of the action. There would be a reckoning for this. His supposed ally had better have a good excuse for jumping the gun. The others needed no further encouragement. Rea was first to respond, overtaking her boss, eager for action as ever. Her troops were just a hair's breadth behind, spreading across the square. Glory for Botrys was at stake, if nothing else.

CHAPTER 29

○

THE BATTLE OF
MONASTIRAKI SQUARE

OLD NIKOS was meandering across the square on one of his regular morning routes. He often left the rest of the group before sunrise to enjoy this quiet hour alone, exploring the nearby streets. It proved to be a good move tactically, as it made him a familiar face for local café owners and shopkeepers when they were setting up for the day, and often a few treats were flung in his direction. He never let on to the rest of them; it was his secret.

This morning had been unremarkable. It was not a day for hurrying. He had said 'hello' to one or two of his friends from his regular round and was wondering where to head next when a sudden movement brought his head up. A cat, no, a lot of cats, streaking across the pavement of Monastiraki Square in his direction. His immediate reaction was to look over his shoulder to see what might have attracted them, but a rapid reappraisal of their trajectory left only one conclusion: they were heading for him. He turned and bolted toward home, but saw another group moving diagonally to cut off his escape. Nikos veered right in a desperate move to shake them off, hoping a long detour down nearby streets might evade them, but his pursuers were gaining. He was older than them and had lost some of his speed and stamina, but he hoped he had enough in him to reach cover, even if it meant entering a shop.

His plans came to naught. With a flying leap reminiscent of a lioness bringing down a wildebeest in the Serengeti, Rea caught his flank, raking her claws down his haunches and bowling him over. He tried to use his momentum to regain his feet, but the other pursuers were on him and he was buried beneath a seething mass of enemies that, until these last few seconds, he didn't know he had. Fortunately for Nikos, he didn't suffer long.

So began the Battle of Monastiraki Square. The Plaka cats were caught by surprise. Most were just waking up, stretching, sniffing the air, washing, and planning their day. In a matter of moments, they were fighting for their lives. One or two were picked off in the main square itself, but most of the fighting took place within the fenced-off area of the Library of Hadrian, which the Plaka cats used as their home, or in the neighbouring Roman Forum. The Botrys and Gizi gangs raced to outdo each other to get into the action first, dozens of cats streaming through or under the metal railings surrounding the site. They scented blood and an easy victory. Kratos and Zelus had wound their troops up to fever pitch, and there was a wild but purposeful fury about them. The cats of the Plaka were pitched into a fight for survival against a bewildering array of aggressive foes who outnumbered them at least two to one.

Jason was as startled as everyone else, but at least he hadn't moved far from the collective sleeping area and he was with some younger adults. His first thought was to flee; he had no argument with anyone and saw no reason to get caught up in someone else's fight, but when he looked around, his options were limited. Behind and to the left was a wall, too high to jump. The attackers were streaming toward them from the right and ahead. There would be no simple way out. The decision was made for him as a nasty-looking black and white cat, large and bulky, made for him. The only option was to stand his ground and fight. Events moved too rapidly for him to feel nervous. As the adrenaline surged, his only thought was survival.

Savage battles were taking place all around him. If he'd had time to think, he might have wondered at this unusual behaviour. Their species didn't go in for pitched battles. A brief skirmish to establish territory, over in seconds, was all. This assault was organized and planned. However, the luxury of reflection was for later. In the short term, he just reacted to events as they unfolded around him. Out of the corner of his eye, he recognised Erichthonius engaging with an amber and black attacker, but before he could help, an enormous cat leaped at him. The two animals grappled with each other, rolling in the dirt. Jason bit hard into his enemy's neck and sank a good number of punches to his opponent's stomach with his hind paws before he shifted position. The other cat's weight and power threatened to overcome him, but the fluidity of their movement allowed Jason to break free as they rolled over, and he put half a metre between them and crouched facing his opponent, paws splayed and ready to pounce. His blood was up now. He wanted retribution for this unprovoked attack; the black and white animal would pay. Feeling invulnerable, almost giddy in the heat of battle, he zoned out everything apart from his opponent. His enemy hesitated, and seizing the opportunity Jason launched himself, fury giving him the edge. His aggression told. With a more forceful leap, his enemy's hind paws slipped on the gravel, giving Jason momentum. He pushed the bigger cat backwards, putting it on the defensive, then dumped his opponent on its back. Now on top, he delivered some savage blows with his hind paws and raked his claws across his opponent's shoulders, drawing blood, oblivious to the blows he was taking in return. In the heat of battle he couldn't feel them; the pain would come later, for now, he had tunnel vision and he could hear little. This duel was all that mattered.

Once again, he broke contact and moved back just far enough to deliver several savage scratches to the other cat's face, closing one eye. With his sight limited, and unable to detect where Jason's next attacks were coming from, the larger cat howled in anguish and the tables turned. Wounded and beaten, it fled, its tail between its legs. Jason snarled after it, but had no time to bask in victory because another attacker emerged while all around him the battle was going badly for his companions.

Kratos scented victory. He'd never doubted he would win. The soft easy living of the Plaka cats made them pussies compared to his hardened street fighters. Part of him was surprised they'd put up any fight at all; he'd half expected them to slink off without raising a paw. But victory wasn't yet complete. He had one more job to do. He had to eliminate any threat, however limited, from the Sons of Ares, successors to the former leadership. He systematically tracked down younger male cats in a methodical killing spree. Young adult animals were no match for his power and size. He wanted his victory to be decisive, to sow fear among all his defeated enemies ever after. There would be no future guerrilla actions from renegades who might rally to the spawn of their former chief. He meant to snuff out the threat completely, but how many sons were there?

Standing over the body of his latest victim he spotted the youngsters in their little creche, in the corner, mewing pathetically, not knowing where to turn amid the turmoil and noise, bewildered and afraid. The females guarding them were fighting for their lives or running around, unsure what to do. He savoured the moment. This would seal his victory once and for all. He descended on them like a raging tempest, lashing out left and right. All were defenceless against him. Some tried to resist, but bewildered and far too small and feeble, they had no chance. One after another in rapid succession, their brief lives were ended with little more than a pitiful squeak or mew. A few of the older ones tried to form a group to break free, but Kratos' own offspring, fastidious and vicious in their filial duty, herded them back toward their fate. Their parents and minders were dead or scattered, all except one. A mother, reacting instinctively to the mayhem, grabbed her kitten by the scruff of the neck, somehow dodged pursuit, and leaped higher than she thought possible to escape over a wall and through railings. She set off into the maze of narrow streets, never looking back. He caught her out of the corner of his eye and barked an order, but no one was close enough to intercept.

Kratos returned to his bloody murder spree. He would make sure the fugitive would be tracked down in time. None must escape, but first things first. In the immediate vicinity, he repelled the few remaining adults who tried to come to the rescue of the little ones with ease, destroying any remaining resistance. The Infanticide of Hadrian's Library, as it came to be known among their kind, became etched in folklore as one of their darkest days.

Jason was some way across the battlefield and unaware of what was happening further afield; he was just fighting for survival. Weariness had replaced the adrenaline surge, but a dogged determination to save his newfound friends was growing, bolstered by the savage treatment they were getting all around him. He launched himself against another opponent to assist Tabitha and was pleased to see her break free and retreat, limping, to relative safety while he kept her attacker busy. Jason kept him at bay long enough to get her clear, then looked around for other animals needing help. By now he was panting, his heart pounding and fatigue taking its toll, but somehow he felt more alive than ever and in his element. For the first time in his life, he had a purpose: to help these creatures, to rally them and lead them, if possible, to glory. His wounds smarted, but the light of battle was in his eyes, and seeing his bravery, some of them were responding. He scanned the square to see who was most in need of help and stiffened as he saw someone he recognised. This duel would be a pleasure.

DAPHNE HELD back as much as she could when the attack started. In part this was because she could no longer run fast, but also to stay clear of the fighting no matter what they tried to do to her. Her captors taunted her and cuffed her to ease their frustration at not being able to grab any glory for themselves. They wanted to be in the vanguard, seeking glory, not guarding the prisoner at the rear, but they dared not leave her. As a result, they were in no mood to go easy on her. Rough and vicious, they scratched and bit in their efforts to push her towards the heaviest fighting so they could watch what was going on. Perhaps they would pick off some of those fleeing in this direction and win their spurs that way. As they got closer, they paid less and less heed of their captive.

The closer she got to the battle, the more dismayed Daphne became. She couldn't bear to watch, but neither could she look away. The squeals of the dead and dying pierced the morning air and put her on edge, but there was nothing she could do. What was worse, the wrong side was winning. She knew nothing of the Plaka cats, but she was sure they couldn't be as bad as Zelus or Kratos's gangs, and they didn't deserve this evil abuse. As if to rub it in, her captors were relishing the success of their comrades. She lost the little hope she'd had of freeing herself from there; where would she go in this strange place if all her surroundings were under their vicious control? She had no family here, nothing other than Jason and Apollo, who she'd lost days ago. Daphne hated Athens with a passion. Where were the other two? she thought miserably.

Her eyes swept across the battlefield one more time, but she could scarcely take in the carnage. Time and again Zelus's gang were defeating their opponents. The lucky ones fled; far too many didn't, their bodies slumped in the dirt. She assumed Kratos's crew were doing the same. It was awful. Then, in the distance, she caught sight of someone with familiar grey and white colouring. Was it Jason? Her heart leaped. But hope was matched by an intense fear for his safety. What was he doing here? What if he got injured, or worse still, killed? She could no longer keep still; it was as if she'd sat on an ant's nest. What could she do? She had to get close to him somehow.

She glanced at her captors, who were absorbed with the scene playing out before them. Could she, dare she, sneak away? Tentatively, she tried to shuffle backwards out of their peripheral vision. It worked; they didn't move. She became bolder, moving with more purpose. Paying full attention to them, she sidled away in slow and measured steps. Progress was painfully slow, but before long she'd put ten metres between them.

"Where do you think you're sneaking off to?" came a sneering voice behind her. She looked around. It was Yannis. His column had just arrived after their long detour across town and most of them were streaking past eager to join the fray, but their leader had spotted an opportunity to curry a little favour with Kratos by delivering back to him the pretty little spy from the other night. No doubt he would have fun extracting her story. The big cat growled down at her with almost gleeful malice. "Don't think I don't know who you are," he reminded her. "Where are you off to? Sneaking off to report back to your Mistress? Well, you can think again." He was about to leap at her when there was a shout from Daphne's guards, who had belatedly noticed her disappearance. They ran up to her.

"Oi, this one's ours," one of them shouted.

"We're guarding her," added his companion. "Zelus has plans for her."

"Not doing a very good job of looking after her then, are you?" Yannis sneered, unable to hide his contempt. "Anyway, she raided us first, and Kratos is keen to get a word."

There was a stand-off as the allies glared at one another. Caught in the middle, Daphne didn't know what to think or do. She wondered how this was going to play out. The answer arrived in the form of a grey-and-white missile that flashed across her peripheral vision and hit Yannis side on. Focused on Daphne's guards, he'd not seen Jason coming; he had no time to react. It proved his undoing. Bloodied though Jason was, he seemed possessed with maniacal energy.

His momentum sent the two of them tumbling over and over, across the polished marble flagstones. Yannis, winded and caught by surprise, was always on the defensive, unsure where the next blows were coming from. He might have been the bigger animal, but size counted for nothing against such intense rage. The sheer fury of his opponent was more than a match for his extra muscle. Daphne's captors were agape. They didn't want to get involved, but their little prisoner was edging forward to try to help her friend. Seeing her moving released them as if from a spell. She was in danger of escaping. They sprang forward, but with hope rekindled in her heart, fueled by the cruelty she had suffered at their paws, Daphne drew on reserves she didn't realise she had. She remembered; she was a Delphi cat, not a pushover; she was no pussycat. She could fight like anyone if she had to, just as her friend was doing for her. Daphne whirled round to face her tormentors. The light of battle kindled in her eyes. She bared her fangs and snarled at them, all thought for her own safety gone. She was prepared to take on both of them. They stopped in their tracks. They hadn't seen her like this before and for the first time, doubt entered their minds. Daphne prepared to spring. Taking on these two was a fight she wanted, she just had to decide which one to go for first.

Behind her, Jason held Yannis's throat in a death grasp, strangling him. One of Daphne's guards noticed and fled. He hadn't expected this. His companion wavered for a second, but in that instant, Daphne attacked, releasing a pent-up flood of rage. Though smaller and less experienced, she was irresistible, but the fight had gone out of her enemy. The cat scrabbled to break free, and once she did so, ran as fast as she could. Daphne spat out a mouthful of fur and made to follow when a familiar voice cried out behind her.

"Oh Daffers, I'm so pleased to see you."

She stopped, paused, and returned to her normal self. Hurting all over, but relieved to be free, seeing Jason again washed the pain away. She turned to face him. Slowly they walked toward each other, sniffing, watching, then tentatively, tenderly, each proffered a delicate nose-kiss, and with more confidence a long head rub. For a moment they were lost in their greetings, but in the distance, the battle was ending, and they needed to leave before the victors hunted down the remaining stragglers.

Jason raised his head, looked her in the eyes. "Just as well I was here. That's the second time I've saved you."

She tilted her head. "Second?"

"The first was when I was in the right place at the right time to get mixed up in this crazy adventure back in Delphi. How mad was that?"

She took a step back and looked him up and down. He seemed changed, somehow. More confident. A little arrogant? She wondered what had sparked this change. He moved closer and nuzzled her once more, and she forgot her concerns; she wanted him, needed him, and soon. A low growl-cum-yowl escaped her lips, and she nipped his neck with gentle urgency, then rolled over in front of him, a come-on more blatant than any she'd ever given, and not like her at all.

Instead, he raised his head and surveyed the fighting behind them. It was subsiding; the gangs had won. He feared for his friends, but there was little he could do. The whole thing had taken a matter of minutes, but it seemed like hours. He looked down at her with a deep yearning, but reason took hold.

"Not here," he said. "Come on, we'd better go. Let's find somewhere safe."

"But where?"

He looked around. The Botrys and Gizi Gangs, who were already eyeing each other up in suspicion, had control of the Plaka gang's headquarters, but the exit from the square in the opposite direction looked clear.

"Down here," he said. "Quick, before they spot us."

They hobbled across the square, past the front of the

235

metro station and down Ifestou Street, heading away from the fighting. Instinctively, they hugged the walls, seeking cover from the display stands, rails of clothing, and shelves the shopkeepers had put out. The less visible they were, the better they felt. They were heading toward the site of the archeological dig.

Close to the end of the street, at the corner of a side street, a well-groomed light brown cat stepped out from behind a rack of sunglasses and challenged them.

"This area is closed to visitors," she informed them, sounding both haughty and officious. "You must go back."

Jason's hackles rose. "You will not tell me where I can and can't go," he said, in no mood to back down.

Daphne glanced at him, admired his newfound confidence. She noticed a slight doubt in the other animal's expression. "Those terrible gangs have attacked us for no reason," she said. "They've been doing dreadful things to our friends back there. You can't make us go back—they'd kill us."

She didn't think she had enough energy to go back even if forced to. she was exhausted. She needed rest, and she needed Jason. The brown cat looked them up and down, and noted the state they were in, then looked past them down the street. She was aware of the earlier disturbance; anyone with ears and cat-like senses could hear the commotion right across town. It was obviously a major incident. Being one of Athena's security guards and followers, she was also well aware of who the combatants were, and the last thing she wanted was to attract any of the aggressors down here. Surely these two fugitives couldn't present too much of a problem. However, she couldn't let them get any closer to the archeological site. She came to a decision.

"You can head down here," she said, looking to a side

street. "At the bottom, ask for Nina and get her to direct you to the Agora. Say Thalia sent you. The Agora is safe and quiet. There's plenty of space. You should be able to find some respite."

They thanked her and followed her directions. At the end of the street, they found Nina, who was more agitated than her companion and kept glancing down the street as if expecting an imminent assault.

"Ah, more survivors," she said, studying their cuts and grazes and trying to sound reassuring. "Nothing too serious I hope?"

"We'll be fine with some rest," Daphne assured her.

"Good, good, yes, of course," the other cat replied, distracted and flustered by the morning's events. "Well, you're nearly there. Just to the left is the entrance to the Agora sanctuary. Just go under the turnstiles; don't mind the humans, they take no notice. Once you're in, you'll see plenty of spots to curl up and get your head down. You should be fine. There are already quite a few of your comrades in there. If you're wanting food later on, the restaurants further down the street usually provide pretty good pickings."

They followed her directions and were relieved to see trees, cover, shade, and lots of places to hide and recover out of the way of prying eyes. The whole place had a sense of serenity, despite the tourists wandering about. It was quiet, and they could hear insects buzz in the mid-morning heat. As they meandered across the open ground, they spotted a few other refugees who had already arrived. Jason halted to watch them. There were so few. He felt a lump in his throat. Had his friends made it? His eyes darted among them, seeking the faces he knew. He'd only known Tabitha and Erichthonius for a matter of hours, yet he already cared for them. He wanted to introduce them to Daphne.

She took over his thoughts once more. Jason looked at her and moved to close the gap between them. He needed to feel her, to inhale her smell, hear her purr. A tenderness he'd never known took hold. Perhaps it was their shared experience of danger or just this madcap journey they were on, but she had become special to him in a way different to anyone else. He needed physical contact; theirs was going to be a special bond. As he led her to a sheltered hollow beneath an ancient tree, he knew how much he'd missed her. He hadn't been aware just how much until now. It was a new sensation. His heart was jumping somersaults, and he felt a little light-headed, but above all, aroused. Daphne reciprocated; her shyness had evaporated. She wanted him, and showed it, rolling over invitingly. Playfully, he nosed and butted her with his forehead. Together they rolled in intimacy, roughly nipping and scratching each other like two small tigers. Then she rolled onto her belly and he stood astride her, pinching her neck in his teeth. She felt his hot breath in her ear as his head bent close and instinctively pawed the ground with her hind legs, her eyes half-closed in ecstasy.

The second time was gentler and slower, the release more satisfying. Afterwards, he pushed his head into hers, and they lay side by side, wrapped in one another, lost in the moment, saying nothing, enjoying the comfort of each other's body. The rest of the world faded away to insignificance. They could deal with it later.

KRATOS SURVEYED the scene of carnage with grim satisfaction. There were bodies everywhere; he'd leave it to the humans to clear them away. They did that sort of thing. Over by the far wall, a few captives were being subjected to the tender mercies of Rea. They'd survive as long as they did what they were told. Victory had been decisive, although more of the enemy had escaped than he'd have liked; they wouldn't evade him for long. Best of all, he'd eliminated any future threat of revenge from the spawn of Ares, their former leader. Victory felt good. It was just a shame he'd had to share it with Zelus. He had achieved phase one of his grand plan: the Plaka, the biggest honeypot in the city was his, but he wasn't satisfied yet. No, there was still plenty to do.

ATOP LYCABETTUS, Hermes lay on his side, failing to sleep, staring into space. Despite the distance, his sharpened senses picked up the faintest wails and screams from the battle below. He winced. Such brutality was most unnecessary. So many lives needlessly cut short, the little ones particularly harrowing. So many souls to escort. He considered whether he could have done more to prevent the carnage taking place below and sighed. Why had Athena not acted to stop them? The responsibility for this mess lay at her door. This trinket she wanted couldn't be that important, could it? How high a price was she prepared to pay? In the normal course of events he enjoyed nothing more than to mess with her plans, and he liked to think he'd been successful on this occasion as well, but this intervention appeared to have caused a lot more collateral damage than he'd expected; it seemed like a throwback to the old days. Was this a one-off or was there something else going on? Something he hadn't picked up yet? Had he inadvertently made things far, far worse?

He put the thought aside with a shudder and concentrated instead on his ginger visitor. He called himself Apollo, but he was nothing like the super-confident, somewhat arrogant Lothario he used to call a friend. This individual was far more contemplative and reserved; maybe even a touch shy. Nor did his story stack up; there was a missing twenty-four hours between his departure from Kratos' headquarters and turning up at Lycabettus. It didn't take so long to get here, and then he arrived from the wrong direction. So where had he been? That cock-and-bull story about a missing friend didn't stack up. Cats went missing all the time; his conversations with the gangs had proved it, so what was he doing? Was he really in league with Athena, and if so, why? They were never usually allied; in any case, he felt sure he would have already heard about it. And if he was here, what about the others? With reluctance he had to acknowledge the fact that his visitor may have been telling the truth. But chasing after an ordinary mortal, rather than just leaving them to their fate, was more than unusual. It would be unprecedented. It was time to get a better handle on exactly what was happening down there in chaos-ville and find out how his old friend wove into the wider tapestry of events. Warp or weft, he wondered, or something new? He stood up, pondering the subject further as he set off down the hill in the other cat's paw prints.

INTERLUDE

STORIES OF THE DISAPPEARED 3

OLYMPIA LOOKED up through the wire mesh. The sky was grey, heavy with clouds. It was as good a day to die as any, she supposed, her fragile hope long gone. Who wants to go when it's nice and sunny? That would just make it worse. She could have been lounging in the shade of a tree, having a leisurely sleep, or keeping a friend company, not preparing to meet her maker. On reflection, she'd been fortunate it wasn't her, she supposed. Not this time, at any rate.

They'd come for him mid-morning, opening his cage and marching right in. Humans are so slow and clumsy, and this one had looked no different, but when he had the black and white cat penned into the far corner, he reached down surprisingly fast. Of course, his victim had had nowhere to go. He'd put up a bit of a fight, useless of course, but good for him. They'd taken him out of the yard, still struggling, spitting, and hissing for all he was worth. She could still hear him in whatever room they took him because they'd left a window open a crack.

Olympia didn't know what they did to him, but she heard his agonizing screams for some time. Maybe it was just a botched job. She shivered. It made her go cold, but she couldn't help it, the thought that she'd find out herself one day. When it was going to be her turn, she just hoped it would be quick: that poor soul had taken too long to die. Olympia never discovered his name, and she was glad. Knowing him would have only made it worse somehow.

She looked around the dreary compound. The fear in all the pens was almost tangible. When one or more of them was taken away, it had a sobering effect on them all. How could it not? Hope had vanished a long time ago, she reflected. All they did was pace about in their little cells and await their destiny, and pray it wouldn't be too bad when it was their turn. Hearing the demise of their erstwhile colleague took away even that last small hope. Nearby some were curled up, eyes downcast, trying to sleep, but it wasn't easy with fear hanging over you, smothering you in layers of icy dread, and passing their time asleep just made the end come faster.

Olympia's attitude toward humans changed from tolerance and curiosity to dislike and even hatred. Some of their kind suck up to them and try to befriend the brutes; why, she'd never know. They're just savages, monsters. All they did was dish out pain and misery. Cats should stay well clear, she reasoned, but like idiots, many insisted on living in their midst, scavenging off the detritus surrounding them and their wasteful lives. It just put them in constant danger. They're cunning, she supposed. She'd give them that. But vicious beyond even the most savage predator. She might play with her prey, but usually she made sure it was over quickly. This endless hell was unremitting mental torture of the worst kind.

She thought about the dogs. How ironic; 'man's best friend,' they'd always claimed. Not this lot, judging by the state of them. They seemed to keep them alive, though just. They got more food than the cats, but not much. She supposed they were only there to deliver their puppies: scrawny little souls that were taken away far too soon, still yapping for their mum while they were carted off. Sold into slavery, she guessed. She wondered about them. They'd be alive, at least, but what sort of life would they have, having started out so bitter and paranoid? Didn't these humans know anything about animals? Most likely they just didn't care.

A night passed and the following morning they brought in a new arrival to occupy her former neighbour's cage. Olympia watched him. He looked bewildered and terri-fied, like everyone else. Nothing she could think of saying would make it any easier for him. They all just counted the hours until it was their turn.

CHAPTER 30

THE BEAUTY OF AN ARC

ATHENA STALKED back and forth in front of the dusty-coloured cat crouching submissively before her. Her whiskers quivered with righteous anger. She had never come across insubordination like this before.

"You did what?" she howled. She already knew the answer, of course; one of her owls had told her, but she wanted to hear the confession straight from the miserable specimen's mouth.

Herse was almost inaudible. "I'm sorry, my lady," she whimpered. She cringed. How could she have expected to get away with her foolhardy plan? It seemed so stupid now in the cold light of day. Bia was no doubt snug in her lair across the city while she was taking the rap, and what's worse was guilty as charged. She couldn't bear the humiliation, but what stung most was betraying the trust of the animal she looked up to most in the whole world, Athena herself.

All her life her loyalty had been a badge of honour, the most obedient of all her servants. Herse had never questioned anything until now. How could she allow her stupid feelings to get the better of her? That's what you got for trying to be helpful, for trying to think you knew better than the Lady herself. She'd let her stupid emotions get in the way. Her misery was complete. Herse stared at the ground just in front of her nose, her whiskers drooped.

Athena let her stew. She was angrier than she could remember.

"You let her inside the cordon, allowed her access to the excavations, and told her where to find the object I've been seeking for weeks, no, months. You betrayed me. Not just me, but all those who rely on us to impose law and order across the entire city. How could you?"

Herse said no more. It was pointless. She'd admitted her guilt; anything she said now would only make things worse. But Athena wasn't finished. She wanted all the facts. All the miserable details. She needed to know exactly what Bia had found, what she'd been waiting for herself. She demanded the other cat recount the entire sorry story.

Hesitantly and between sobs, Herse told her everything. As she spoke, Athena stood stock still, as if carved in stone, her emerald eyes boring into the animal before her. Herse never lifted her gaze from the ground in front of her paws. She didn't dare meet her stare.

The story unfolded. The actions of the gangs had worried her, she felt worse that nothing was being done, and she shared her concerns with Hermes. He told her Bia might help, so she'd ventured across town to Davaki Park to hatch the plan to steal the object. Herse had hoped that would be the end of the matter, and things would get back to normal. Even as she recounted her tale, she recognised how stupid it sounded. Since Athena had been so obsessed with this thing, of course she wouldn't just let it drop once someone had removed it. And since she was so bothered about it, of course, it must have been important. Very important. She'd ruined everything.

Herse finished. Athena's merciless stare never wavered from the wretched animal before her. There was a long, tense silence while the grey cat pondered what to do. Her immediate anger had subsided into a colder fury, part of it directed inwards, though she would never admit it. A carefully choreographed sequence of events over decades had culminated in this excavation, requiring agreement to remove modern era buildings to uncover the ancient foundations she sought, within which one of the most precious and powerful artefacts of the city's ancient past would be retrieved. Not just a treasure, a tool, an instrument designed at its creation to be aligned to her powers (and those of her kind) and used to ensure they maintain the rule of law across the city, and help keep the forces of anarchy and darkness at bay. It was something that in the right paws could do much good, but in the wrong hands could wreak havoc.

What was worse was the betrayal of trust. She had long placed implicit faith in her servants to do her bidding. They were aligned with her aims; a tightly bound sisterhood. How could one of them betray her trust? How could her authority be so undermined? She gathered herself, and in a cold voice addressed the miserable offender.

"I have no more use for you. I dismiss you from my service. Begone. Get out of my sight."

Herse staggered to her feet, her anguish uncontainable. Her mind was in turmoil; she didn't know what to do, where to go. The words stung as if she'd been whipped. She stared blankly around but could barely see her surroundings. Her sisters turned their faces away, unable or unwilling to acknowledge her; she found no comfort there. The world had rejected her. Stumbling, she left the clearing, her head hanging low, and set off for she knew not where. She wandered aimlessly up the hillside through the wood, with no idea where to go. How could she have misunderstood? Her throat felt constricted; breaths came hard, and still, the thoughts circled around and back on themselves endlessly. I just wanted to help. I didn't mean to hurt anyone. I just wanted to make things better. How could it all go so wrong?

Her meandering path led to the foot of the Propylea, the entrance to the rock of the Acropolis. She stumbled up the stairs, dodging between the human visitors. At the summit, she wove a path across the rocky plateau to the wall at its northern edge, and raised her head to look out. From here, the breeze ruffling her fur, she had an eagle's view over the city. Her city. It looked spectacular. Herse thought of all the people and animals below, and all the cats she had lived alongside, their foibles and their strengths, the squabbles and the camaraderie. She thought of her kittens, all grown up now, and making their way in the world, including her beautiful Erichthonius. With heart almost bursting with pride, she wished them well. She paused. 'It's for the best,' she thought and jumped.

CHAPTER 31

ON TORTOISES

TRACKING APOLLO was quite easy at first. He had watched him set off and assumed he intended to pay a visit to Athena, although given her security cordon, he might find it easier said than done. Vasilissis Sofias Avenue was busy as ever, but once across Hermes paused to consider the options. Which route would Apollo have taken? Following Vasilissis Sofias would have seemed, on the face of it, the most direct route, but a few hundred meters further it veered off to the north, away from the Acropolis. Would Apollo have spotted that? On the other hand, if he made a beeline toward the Acropolis, he would have to navigate through the grounds and gardens of several public buildings. He moved along the pavement, sniffing at the railings, and eventually came across a post which the other cat had rubbed against in passing. The gardens route it was then. He set off again with renewed purpose.

Crossing the Lyceum of Aristotle, now little more than a patch of scrubby grass and some exposed foundations, he came, via another road crossing, to the National Gardens, a major area of landscaped parkland in central Athens. Following Apollo's trail through here might be challenging; there were several routes he might have taken. Hermes considered Apollo's destination. In all likelihood, he was heading to find Athena, but there was a large impediment in the form of the Acropolis. Which way would he choose?

The north side meant passing through the crowded, twisting streets of the Plaka, whereas the southern route past the museum and the Odeon of Herodes Atticus was more straightforward but likely to be equally busy with pedestrians at this time of day. While traversing the gardens he automatically kept sniffing out his quarry's scent; it wasn't difficult. But having crossed the busy avenue, he promptly lost it.

On a whim, he opted for the marginally less busy southern route that looped around the south side of the rock of the Acropolis, navigating through crowds of pedestrians. At least there were no cars to think about in this quarter. There was no sign of Apollo's scent lingering on the street furniture, nor could he detect it on any vegetation. Perhaps Homer would know? He tried to recall the last time they spoke. It must have been decades ago, but tortoises live for... well, a long time, anyway. Maybe he was still around? As Hermes passed the entrance to the Acropolis Museum, a sixth sense told him it might prove profitable to wander up past the remains of the Theatre of Dionysus and along the narrower paths under the cliffs, known only to animals. Sure enough, after a few minutes, he came across an elderly tortoise sunning itself next to a low rocky outcrop. He tried to recall his last conversation with the animal, but drew a blank.

"Hi," he said nonchalantly. "Long time no see and all that. How's it going?" The tortoise showed little sign of having heard him. Hermes didn't wait for it to respond. "Let me get to the point," he said, a touch louder, wondering whether the animal was hard of hearing. "I'm looking for someone. Ginger, with some white markings on the belly, might have come through here earlier today. Have you seen anyone who might fit the bill?" He peered down at the other animal expectantly.

Homer extended his head a little further from his shell and looked up at him. "What sort of greeting's that?" he chided. "Where's the 'hello Homer old friend, how have you been keeping? What have you been up to since our last little chat?' eh?" His beady eyes were focused on the cat. "Instead, it's all crash, bang, wallop, tell me this, tell me that, then I'm off." He looked away.

Hermes sighed. He'd half expected something like this; tortoises could be notoriously touchy. Typical; just when you're in a hurry, your affinity animal gets a strop on. Why did he have to get the sodding tortoise in the first place? Why not a squirrel or bird of some type, something useful! An eagle! That would shake things up a bit. But no, he was stuck with this recalcitrant twit. He paused for a quick count and started again.

"Sorry, old friend," he said, in a more convivial tone of voice. "Got a bit carried away. Spur of the moment thing, in a bit of a hurry, you know what it's like." The thought crossed his mind that Homer probably had a totally differ-ent concept of 'hurrying,' so perhaps not. The old tortoise snorted again.

"Anyway," Hermes added, "how are you? I should pop over here more often so we can catch up properly. It's quite nice around here." He looked around appreciatively. "How d'you like that? We could sit under a nice bush like that one over there and have a good long chat, eh?" He paused, looking for a sign the tortoise's mood was softening.

"I'll believe it when I see it," was the best he got.

He tried again. "Anyway, sorry we got off on the wrong paw, but it's like this. I'm trying to find one of my col-leagues. He's been staying with me, but he doesn't know his way around town and I think he may have got lost. I

250

don't want him coming to any harm. You know what some folks around here can be like. As I said, he's mainly ginger with a few white markings. I think he might have come through here earlier, but tracking anyone along here is nigh impossible with all those humans trampling over anything that holds a scent. Do you think you might have seen him?"

"That's better," acknowledged the tortoise. "You should have started off like that—been a bit more humble. Helps you make friends and influence animals." He stopped, satisfied he had made his point.

Hermes waited, his tail twitching involuntarily in his frustration. He wondered why he put up with this insolence from someone who was supposed to be a supplicant. He briefly fantasised about zapping the thing with a borrowed thunderbolt and suppressed a sigh.

"So?" he said, somehow maintaining his most polite and attentive expression.

"I'll have to think," answered the tortoise, retracting his head most of the way into his shell.

Hermes was, by now, inwardly seething. He looked around impatiently, half tempted to leave, but to do so would only give Homer the satisfaction of seeing him off. It simply wouldn't do to let one's affinity animal, no matter how annoying, get the upper hand. Who knew where such disobedience might end? He brought his attention to bear once more on his tormentor. He was tempted to poke a stick into his shell and give him a jolt. The tortoise spoke again.

"Well, I might have," he ventured, tentatively.

Hermes' eyes widened a touch in exasperation.

"Yes, I think I have. Someone matching the description came through here about an hour ago. Thought he was a tourist at first, and maybe a bit lost as he seemed to be taking the scenic route. He passed right by me. Didn't say hello."

Hermes was relieved. His hunch had paid off.

"Great," he said encouragingly. Now for the hard part. "You wouldn't have any idea where he was going, would you?" He suspected he knew the answer, but Homer's reply threw him off-balance.

"Well, yes, as a matter of fact. A crow came down and landed just in front of him, over there." He pointed with his nose. "Had a bit of a chat, they did. 'That's unusual,' I thought, 'few cats would pass the time of day with birds. Let alone crows.' That's when I began to think there's something odd about this." He broke off, thinking. Hermes waited, suddenly taking great interest in a pebble just in front of his paws. After a moment, the tortoise continued. "I don't like eavesdropping, you understand, but they were talking so loud it was impossible not to." Hermes looked up, expectantly. "The crow was all excited. Full of himself, he was. Did a little jig. Went on about some search for dogs and cats. Said he'd found a place. Old ginger liked that, he did. Got very excited." He broke off.

Hermes was all ears but affected an air of disinterest. This wasn't what he had expected. "Hmm, sounds very strange. Whereabouts?"

The tortoise sifted its memories. "Where was it now, let me think." He bobbed his head slightly, looking into the distance. "Oh yes, they're in Tavros, that was it."

"Tavros?" Hermes mentally computed travel times, distances, routes.

"Yeah, they set off straight away. Ginger got the bird to guide him. Went off at quite a lick, like they were in a hurry. 'What's that all about?' I thought. Still, why should I care, nobody ever tells me nothing. I just potter about here, minding my own business. I mean, even you can't be bothered to say 'hello' more than once every couple of decades." He looked at the cat, expecting a response, but Hermes was distracted, his thoughts far away.

"Yes, jolly good," he said, absentmindedly. "Well, you take care." Condescension laced his icy politeness. "I'll be on my way and let you get back to doing whatever it is you do all day." He waved his paw in the general direction of a flowering shrub. *The end of labour is to gain leisure*, as someone once said." He turned to go.

"Yeah, and he was over-rated," grumbled Homer. Hermes turned back.

"What?"

"Aristotle," replied the other. "Overrated. All that wandering around pontificating. Load of old cobblers, if you ask me. Peripatetic? Peri-pathetic, more like. Now Nietzsche, he was a proper philosopher. 'God is dead' and all that, that's profound that is." He looked up at Hermes, and stopped when he saw the cat's unreadable expression but dangerous-looking body language. "Present company excepted, of course," he added hastily. Perhaps unwisely, he went on, "Anyway, back to Aristotle. Never liked him. A miserable sod if you ask me, and I met him."

Hermes felt wrong-pawed all of a sudden. He looked at the tortoise in astonishment.

"You can't have," he blurted. "He lived over two thousand years ago. You're not that old."

"Might be," grumped Homer, defensively. "I've got good genes, me. It's in the DNA, you see. Tip-top it is. Quality. Runs in the family." He paused, thinking. "Come to think about it, it might have been grandpa who knew Aristotle. Had some stories to tell, did grandpa. Always had time for a chat, no matter what." He looked accusingly at the white cat. Hermes was almost speechless. He pulled himself together.

"Aristotle had some other sayings as well that you might care to remember, including wit is educated insolence. It's a fine dividing line between banter and insubordination. Don't let your scholarship get you into trouble." He stared at the tortoise, pointedly.

"*Character is that which reveals moral purpose,*" retorted Homer, unable to let things rest. Hermes took a step forward, looming over the tortoise. Homer retreated into his shell. The cat crouched down until he could look inside.

"*The aim of the wise is not to secure pleasure, but to avoid pain,*" he said softly, almost purring, a subtle hint of menace hanging in the air. He stood up. "Enough. You have detained me too long."

He continued on his way, following in the tracks of Apollo.

IN A quiet corner of his new headquarters at the Library of Hadrian, Kratos gathered several of his sons and daughters, the hardcore of his gang. The delay he'd agreed with Zelus allowed him to step up his watch on Athena's dig. It was time to up the ante.

"Let's force the issue," he told them, issuing instructions. Tonight, they would overpower the guards and steal whatever it was she was after. If they were careful, she wouldn't be able to stop them, and Zelus wouldn't know about it until it was too late. The thought was delicious. Then I can finally have a proper look at this thing she thinks is so precious.

CHAPTER 32

SUMMONED

HERMES TOOK off toward Tavros, prepared to conduct a street-by-street search if need be. Bia's reference to dogs howling came to mind. He'd dismissed it at first, but now it seemed the Delphi cat's story did stack up, and he really didn't want Apollo to have 'told you so' bragging rights over this one. At the back of his mind, an uneasy feeling that his casual dismissal had been too hasty was brewing. Is this what guilt feels like, he wondered, then rejected the idea. 'Never say sorry, never go back' was the mantra of all his kind, wasn't it? What continued to surprise him was the ginger cat taking such an interest in a mere mortal? Now that was quite a story in itself. He was certain there was more to it than met the eye. Perhaps there's something in the water up in the mountains, he thought, and strode on.

He spotted the owl from some distance, perched on a branch overhanging the path, and groaned inwardly. What does she want now? He approached the tree and sat down, fixing the bird with a hard stare and flicking his tail in frustration, a sign he expected the bird to read and understand. He was pleased to see its growing discomfort.

"You're wanted," said the owl, trying to remain calm but feeling a little flustered. It was a while since she'd done much 'summoning' work and most of that was with animals far less self-assured than this one. Her duties had mainly comprised silent spying of late, which was much more suited to her skill set. She noticed the hostile look the cat returned and adopted a different tone. "Er, that is, My Lady requests an audience with you, sir. As soon as is convenient, if you will." The owl twisted her head to the side, relieved to avoid those blue eyes, if only for an instant. She hoped he wouldn't be difficult. You never could tell with Hermes, and she so hated taking bad news back to her mistress. Particularly so when Athena was already in a foul mood.

"Requests, or demands?" enquired the cat, determined not to let the owl off the hook.

The bird shook itself and rotated her head from right to left to give herself time to think. Getting stuck in the middle of a family squabble was the last thing she wanted.

"Requests," she said finally, "but firmly," she added. Then, "Very firmly." She hooted nervously, wondering if she'd overdone it. Hermes cocked his head slightly, enjoying the owl's discomfort. It was a shame she was just out of reach, he thought mischievously. It might be fun to ruffle her feathers a bit.

"I can do next Tuesday," he replied, noncommittally. The owl became more flustered than ever.

"It's urgent," she shrieked, and perhaps as a sign of stress, vomited a pellet of last night's undigested supper onto the path. Hermes surveyed it the way an art dealer might study an old master.

"Urgent, eh?" he said, sniffing and studying the deposit with forensic intent. "So, really more of a demand than a request?" He fixed his stare back on the frazzled owl.

"Yes, it is!" she squeaked, now totally out of her depth and desperate to get away. She flapped her wings but didn't dare leave.

Reluctantly, Hermes concluded his sport.

"Tell her I'll be there directly," he said, and stepping delicately around the pellet, walked on purposefully down the path.

CHAPTER 33

TALKS ABOUT TALKS

HE FOUND her on the summit of Pnyx Hill, surveying the city. She was aware of his arrival without having to turn around.

"Good of you to come," she said, still looking at the view. Hermes stepped up beside her, following her gaze, saying nothing. He remained wary of getting on the wrong side of Athena when she was in a grim mood, and this was not a time to be probing for points-scoring opportunities. The silence between them stretched. In the distance, he could hear the sounds of the city, traffic, the occasional siren, metro trains emerging from tunnels. They coalesced into an unabated backdrop: the soundtrack of urban life. Nearby he picked out birdsong, the buzz of insects, and the chatter of tourists. Always tourists. They love to come and gawp at the remnants of their past, but they've forgotten about us.

Pnyx Hill provides a fine view of the Acropolis and in particular the Propylea, the ceremonial stairway to the summit plateau, and the incomparable Parthenon. Athena followed his stare.

"Time was when my statue towered above that thing," she said. Hermes murmured agreement. He could remember it. A wave of irritation took over his thoughts.

"That was when you cared about this city," he said, looking her in the eye. Uncharacteristically, he let his annoyance show. He anticipated resistance, a sharp stinging response, but it didn't come.

Instead, she looked away and sighed. "Yes, I may have let things slip." This was quite an admission. The closest thing to an apology he'd ever heard from her. What was going on? Athena led the way to a more sheltered spot beneath the low spreading branches of a pine tree and settled down. She waited until he joined her.

"I've been distracted," she conceded. "I've rather let things go." She looked at him. "But you haven't exactly been helpful." There was little accusation in her voice; Hermes' nature was all too familiar. In any case, the city was her responsibility. She might step away for a while, a century or two perhaps, but it was ultimately her domain. They sat in silence.

"So, what's to be done?" the white cat enquired after a while.

"Well, we have to stop the gangs wreaking havoc," she said. "My authority," she looked at him, "our authority is being undermined, perhaps terminally. They are waking up and flexing their muscles, so to speak., and they're not finished yet."

"What do you mean?"

"I think they're venting old grievances. They seem more purposeful than ever before. I think they want to usurp me, and not just me, all of us."

"How do you know?"

The look she gave suggested he should have known better than to ask. Of course, her silent winged spies got everywhere. Hermes recounted his recent conversations with the gang leaders and wondered to what extent they had been overheard. He liked to think he had their pulse, but had they been keeping things back from him? Were there signals he'd missed? He'd known for some time they had developed a dim awareness of their past, but they'd never made an issue of it. Not to him, at any rate. They seemed largely ignorant, or uncaring, focusing instead on their little daily power-games and territorial disputes. He might have to re-evaluate.

"And you're sure about this?"

"No, not yet at any rate, but I am worried." She sighed. "I'm afraid I housed a turncoat, a double agent; and because of her treachery, something important has been taken."

The white cat waited. The story of her strange behaviour was about to unfold. He tried not to think about his own role in recent events, but what were the consequences?

Athena glanced at him, then began. "A very long time ago, I lost something. Something precious. Not just to me, but to the whole city. It was a small statuette—of me actually—a replica of the larger one that once stood yonder." She glanced over to the Acropolis, envisaging across the years, something that no longer existed. "It was lost during a sack of the city. You know, they used to occur quite often in the latter days of Roman rule. I wasn't here at the time; I'd taken a sabbatical, otherwise, I may have been able to prevent it." She was lost in thought for a while. She resumed.

"But anyway, it got lost. And it's been a problem ever since."

"What do you mean? Surely it's just an object of veneration, an old treasure. Losing it's a shame, yes, but hardly a disaster. If they dig it up, they'll just bung it in a museum to collect dust."

"That's just it." She sounded worried. "It was more than just a statue. I imbued it with a power; the ability to communicate, mind-to-mind, across the boundaries between species and across distance."

"You mean mind manipulation?" Hermes was incredulous. "How come I knew nothing about this?"

"No one did. I kept it to myself." She looked ever-so-slightly smug. "It's tuned to my thoughts specifically, but there's a risk that anyone who has some power might reconfigure it and use it for their own ends." She looked pointedly at him. There was no need to say more. In the long silence, Hermes tried to unravel the implications of what he'd heard. He had to admit she'd been right to keep it under wraps; if he'd known about this earlier, he would have taken it for himself. Any of them would.

"So anyone can use it? But what could they do with it?"

"Not just anyone; you have to have sufficient mental strength or power. In the right hands, a skilled user can project their thoughts into the mind of a target, control their emotions, plant ideas, get them to take actions they might not otherwise have thought to do." She caught his sceptical look. "It worked with Odysseus," she added. "And many more besides. A really powerful mind can control many at once. Like a large gang, or small army even."

Hermes experienced another novel emotion: shock. This was a most unusual day. At the back of his mind, he replayed his conversations with Herse and Bia and felt uncomfortable in a 'Houston-we-have-a-problem' kind of way.

"And what's worse," Athena resumed, "I think Bia has got it."

This was not good: this sounded much worse than a little territorial squabble over control of the Plaka. He might have just handed their enemies the power to unseat them all, with unforeseen consequences, none of them good. He felt sick. It might be difficult to hide his role from the others if the full cast were to be assembled and an inquiry started. He scarcely dared ask his next question.

"Do you think she knows how to use it?"

Athena gave him another sharp look. He found those implacable emerald eyes uncomfortable. For once he was on the receiving end and he didn't like it.

"I'm not sure. I'm going to pay her a visit to find out, but at least we should be prepared."

"I guess you'd like me to find that big fat slob of a brother of ours?" It would be a relief to have something different to do. He didn't fancy being an intermediary in an unpredictable conversation between two animals who disliked each other at the best of times.

"If you'd be so kind." She sounded at her most condescending, "but don't call him a slob; he has so many hidden talents, you know." It was Hermes' turn to snort. Eating being near the top of the list, he thought. He got up and left.

CHAPTER 34

PARKLIFE

IT HAD been a while since Athena had ventured down into Kallithea, but to her satisfaction, many of the shops and restaurants were still as she remembered. She had regained her composure following the regrettable dismissal of her treacherous servant. She experienced no guilt at her treatment of the unfortunate wretch. Standards had to be maintained and the stupid cat had been acting far beyond the normal scope of her responsibilities. What had she thought she was playing at? Athena just hoped the damage wasn't as great as she feared. Who could tell what manner of mischief Bia and her thuggish brothers might unleash?

She pondered the scenarios as she walked. What if Bia used the artefact to turn humans against her, or her followers; perhaps against stray cats across the city? What if she allied with her brothers to take over the Agora and force her into exile? Where might it end? She might need to consider putting out a request for reinforcements, but she couldn't bear the humiliation. It would be the option of last resort, and in any case, she no longer knew where they all lived, or how many had retired or fallen into senility. And if she did the thought of the endless barracking, the snide remarks and suppressed laughter were more than she could bear. It might last for centuries. And that was if they won. It would all be behind her back, of course; none would dare to say anything to her face. Hera would be worst. Then they'd be wanting to interfere. They were already angry enough with her. Athena valued her independence; she didn't want the rest of them meddling, not here in Athens at any rate. She shook her head violently as if trying to banish the thought and walked on.

Hopefully, things wouldn't be so bad; it would be something she could contain. It took time to master the use of these objects, she rationalised. If one didn't have the experience or the mental capacity, it could take days or weeks. Of course, Bia had more than enough mental capacity if she chose to use it; she was a Titan, a goddess even older than herself, although saddled with the limited imagination typical of her generation. Once it wouldn't have mattered, of course. Athena could have haughtily dismissed any challenge with a swipe of her thoughts. Now, in this diminished state, the extra leverage it gave was a game-changer. Athena's one hope resided in her not understanding how to release the object's full powers. Bia would need to learn how to bend it to her will, how to project her thoughts, how to focus them into the mind of the recipient. She'd need to experiment, find a willing victim to test it on. It would take time to master the technique. That would present a window of opportunity, but she would have to be quick.

Athena turned off Thiseos Street at the corner of Davaki Park and headed down Mantzagriotaki Street. It was still early. Most of Bia's gang were still out and about, with just a few venturing back from their dawn perambulations to seek some shade where they could rest during the middle of the day. Athena guessed that Bia wouldn't want to leave her treasure to the care of someone else, so would hang around the park. She crossed the road and entered via a pedestrian gate, and spotted her target sniffing at some flowers near

264

the fountain, as if without a care in the world. She made a beeline toward the gang leader and noticed her stiffen as she sensed her approach.

Athena didn't dwell on ceremony. "Let's talk," she said briskly and headed straight to a secluded patch of grass nearby, waiting for Bia to join her. The other cat sauntered after, irritated by the way her visitor had taken the initiative; this was her territory. Athena scarcely waited for her to sit down. "I've dismissed the traitor," she said.

Bia pretended to ignore her, staring into the middle distance. "None of my business," she replied. "If that's what you came to tell me, this should be a short meeting."

Athena studied an unsuspecting beetle scurrying across the ground between them. "I just thought I'd let you know, just in case you wanted to recruit her permanently." She let it hang.

"As I said, how you manage your people is entirely your own affair. It really is nothing to do with me."

"Whereas stealing from the Stoa Poikile dig clearly is," came the pointed reply.

Bia gave her a sharp look. There was no point in denial, the snitch had clearly squealed; how many beans she'd spilled was the only issue.

"It's fair game," she replied. "Exploring, discovering, unearthing, stealing—they're all legitimate activities. Any cat in Athens would agree. There's no law against it."

Athena's jaw clenched. The other cat was correct, of course. All felines acted on their wit to turn situations to their advantage, whether through stealth or cunning, or by manipulating others. The only 'crime' was that it took place under her nose at a place she'd been watching for months. Somewhere she'd set a guard around, for heaven's sake!

"Yes, you conducted a very skilled operation," she admitted. "So, enlighten me, what do you intend to do with your prize?"

Bia squealed in delight. "Aha, so this is what's bugging you? You and your blessed antiquities. You're so precious about them. Well, this one's mine, and a nice little object it is too. Finders keepers, and all that. I can see why you wanted it, it's beautiful to look at. Special, isn't it? I could feel the hum of power as I dug it out." She paused, enjoying Athena's discomfort, and continued her mockery. "Tell me, what would you like me to do? Put it on display in a glass box in the museum? Well, you can think again. It's staying with me."

Athena studied the trees for a while and watched some human children chasing each other around the fountain. Her mind was racing. Did Bia realise the significance of what she'd stolen?

"There are worse things you could do," she said, mildly.

The gang leader gave her a contemptuous look. "Do you take me for a fool? It's part of my treasure, my hoard. Perhaps the key piece. Something that I can use. Just the fact I've got it, and how I came by it, swiping it from under your nose, enhances my legend, my fame. I wouldn't be surprised if the storytellers are already telling the tale at their evening gatherings across the city. My reputation, the fame of my gang, is growing. Yours is in decline. How many followers have you got? You're a loser, and from what I hear you won't have a home for much longer." She stared aggressively at the grey cat before continuing. "Do you think for a moment that I'm going to give it all up just so the humans can put an admittedly extremely rare, extremely beautiful gold coin on display in their precious house of relics? Think again." Bia stretched, ostentatiously flaring her claws, satisfied her darts had hit home.

Athena didn't move. A long, tense pause ensued before she got to her feet. "This city's history is important to me, but given your attitude, you can keep it," she said. "I thought it would be pointless reasoning with you. I'll be on my way; I wouldn't want to delay your victory parade. When is it, by the way?" She looked around, then stiffly walked away, not waiting for a reply.

Athena left the park, jumping through a gap in the railings, crossed the road, and turned back into crowded Thiseos Street. Let her enjoy her petty victory. As she walked, she allowed a slight spring to enter her step.

Bia watched her go, feeling just a little smug. Getting one over on the stuck-up old molly felt good. 'Sooner than you think,' she thought, and recalled last night's conversation with Kratos. Things were moving fast, and soon now there would be a change of control at the very top. If she played her cards right, it could be her on top of the pile.

CHAPTER 35

PRISON

THE STREET was dusty but deserted. A few untidily parked cars filled the gaps between the stunted, scruffy trees down one side. None were moving along it. Apollo wondered what sort of place this was. Just a few minutes ago he was passing along crowded busy streets lined with shops, offices, apartment blocks, and people. A couple of turns off the main road and he was in a netherworld of shutters, graffiti-covered windowless walls, high fences, and deserted dusty streets. This was a district of warehouses and industrial yards, most of which seemed abandoned.

He plodded along as dusk turned to night, questioning the crow's intelligence. Why had it brought him to this wasteland? Did it understand who he was looking for? He turned a corner and then another as he traced a zig-zag path across the deserted quarter. Another hour passed and the roads and buildings all looked the same. He yearned for some sign of life. Then he heard it. Faint at first, but growing louder as he homed in: the barking of restless, unhappy dogs. As he drew closer he could detect, within the overall clamour, the distressed yowls of cats. His stomach felt small. Who could ignore the calls of so many distressed animals? Even the most cloth-eared two-legged passer-by should detect the pain and fear in their voices. He was fast developing a withering scorn for the stupidity of humankind and mounting anger toward those who held these animals captive. He should… no. Free the captives, forget about the humans. He couldn't afford any distraction.

Apollo drew closer, anger building with each step, and tried to not let it get the better of him. He needed to keep a clear head to plan a rescue. The crow perched on a branch of a misshapen apology for a tree just ahead of him. On the opposite side of the road was the compound containing the imprisoned animals. Apollo couldn't see in; a high wall surmounted with another metre of sturdy wire mesh fence surrounded it. He could see no foothold that would allow him to climb up. At one end was an adjacent building with an even higher wall. The other end of the wall ended in a right angle and continued down a narrow passageway. At its end was another building. Apollo followed it and found himself on a small forecourt between the building and another road. This was at the front of the compound where the dogs were wailing. The only entrance was a sturdy locked door. Grimy windows to either side were reinforced with metal bars. The owner took security seriously. He retraced his steps along the side to the back of the site, studying the wall and fence, but he could see no holes or weaknesses. At each corner, security cameras peered down on the road outside. He sat squarely in front of one, not comprehending its function, and gazed at it. Inscrutable, a black lens peered back. Apollo turned to face the wall, wishing he could see what lay behind, but it was just too high. He would have to rely on the bird. He glanced at it, but it anticipated his question.

"This is where they are. What now?"

"I need to know if my friend Olympia is in there," he said. "Can you circle overhead and tell me who is inside? What it's like?"

The crow gave him a long look. "It's dark, in case you

hadn't noticed," he said. "I won't be able to see much." Despite the misgivings, he took off and spent a few minutes flying back and forth across the compound. He perched on the edge of the next building's roof, peering into the gloom as best he could. Then he returned to the impatient cat. "Dunno," he said. "Like I said, it's dark, but it looks like there are lots of dogs and cats down there, in pens."

"How many?"

"More than five."

"How many more than five?"

"Don't know. I can only count to five."

Apollo sat down, exasperated. If only he could get up there, he could make a proper assessment. As it was, he was relying on a counting crow with limited mathematical abilities.

"Can you go up there and shout for Olympia?" he asked.

"No," replied the bird. "I can't talk to cats."

Apollo scrutinized him with a look that, even to a casual observer, gave the impression he would happily eat him.

The crow was not a casual observer and immediately recognised the significance of the focused stare. "It's not my fault," he countered.

"You can talk to me perfectly well," the cat told him, fighting to maintain a steady voice.

"You're different," said the crow. "Believe me, before I met you, I'd no sooner have dreamed I could talk to a cat than drive a car."

Apollo bit back a comment. There was no time to dwell on the shortcomings of affinity animals. He needed to find his friend. Much to the crow's relief, he broke his stare and turned toward the high wall. "Olympia," he yelled at the top of his voice.

There was a momentary silence from the animals inside the compound. No one inside there could remember anyone replying to their wails and shouts. "Who is it, and what do you want?" came a deep-voiced reply from a large-sounding dog.

"I'm looking for my friend Olympia. Is she in there?" he bellowed.

The cacophony simmered down while urgent discussions took place inside the compound. Apollo strained his ears to make it out. There seemed to be a big debate among the dogs, perhaps because they had the louder voices. They were speaking over each other, but he could make out a few comments.

"What's going on?"

"Who's he want?"

"What's it to do with us?"

"Who cares, just tell him to get us out."

"Shh, he just might be able to help us."

Eventually, the dog who had first responded to him shouted back.

"Maybe, but what's so important about her? We all want to get out of this prison. We've been stuck here for ages, just having puppies that get taken away before they're old enough. You'd never believe how fed up we are. You've got to get us out."

Apollo paced up and down, casting exasperated glances at the high wall. "What about the cats? I can hear cats in there with you. She's one of them. I want to talk to her."

"Who cares about the cats? Just get us out. We want to go home."

Apollo stopped pacing and stared hard at the wall as if willing it to collapse in a cloud of dust and rubble. He struggled to keep the frustration from his voice. "Look, I'll try to help you all, I promise, but first I need to speak to the cats."

There was further muffled discussion among the dogs, and in the background, Apollo could make out some high-pitched feline voices pitching in.

"What's going on? Shut up for a minute and let us talk to him."

The debate went on for a short while, but then the din subsided, and he heard a cat.

"Who are you, and can you help us?"

This was progress. At least he was now speaking to one of his own species.

"I'm Apollo from Delphi," he shouted. "I will try to help you, but first I need to know if there's someone called Olympia in there. I'm looking for her." Nerves knotted his stomach. So much of his hope was resting on getting a response. He could only wait while more discussions took place behind the wall. After a while, a faint but familiar voice replied.

"Well, you took your time, sweetie." His sense of relief was tangible, he'd found her.

"Olympia, I'm so pleased to hear you. I've come to rescue you."

"And how are you going to do that, darling? Have you brought the army with you?" Even in these dire straits, her natural sarcasm shone through, although she sounded strained.

"No," he faltered. "It's... just me." He felt wretched, suddenly, feeble and powerless. How could he mount a rescue all by himself? "But don't worry, I'll think of something. I'll get you out."

There was a longer pause while they digested this news. In the background, he could hear other impatient voices clamouring for news of the outside world. Some of them seemed to expect an immediate breakout. The last thing

Apollo wanted to do was for the captives to get false hope. It was now clear to him that rescuing them would take some planning.

Eventually, Olympia replied. Her voice cracked; the bravado she'd shown him was crumbling fast, and with it, her desperation was mounting. "You'd better be quick." Her voice quavered. "I don't know how long I've got. They take some of us away every day, and I think, I think..." She couldn't bring herself to say it. She started again. "It's awful in here. It's..." she paused, collecting herself. "There's hardly any space. Some in here are their own worst enemy; they stop eating, or lash out. They take them away soonest. I don't know what happens to them, but I don't think it's good. They keep the dogs for breeding. When they get too old they disappear as well, and they take the puppies before they're weaned. Everyone's desperate. There isn't much time. I can't..." Her voice trailed off.

Apollo had never heard her like this before. Olympia always had a quirky outlook, a snarky comment, or superior look. Hearing the tremor in her voice emphasised the seriousness of the situation. "You have to be quick," echoed from his dream. He shivered.

"Don't worry, I'll get you out," was the best he could come up with, but the words sounded hollow. He had no idea how he was going to do it.

There was no further response. After a while, the dogs resumed their barking. It was clear. He needed to get help.

CHAPTER 36

THE RAID

ATHENA WAITED until well after midnight before making her move. By this time there were no humans around; restaurants and bars had closed and even late-night party revelers had retired to bed and the streets were quiet. Clinging to the shadows and moving with the grace and stealth that came naturally to her kind, she approached the site of the archeological dig. She was less bothered about spies by now; even so, she didn't want to attract undue attention.

The distractions of recent days meant she could not keep as close a watch as she would like, but she was confident no other intruders had made surreptitious visits, nor did she want to wait any longer. Once news of Bia's raid got out, other opportunists might try to see what goodies they might unearth. She slipped through the fence and descended into the dig, then made her way to the spot she expected to find treasure: the place indicated by Herse at her interrogation. It underlined what she had taken from her own observations. But something was wrong. Athena stopped in her tracks, dismayed. Even by the dim light from nearby streetlamps, she could see the evidence of rough, hasty digging. Someone had scrabbled at the dirt, careless of the disturbance they were making, and had extracted something from exactly the spot she'd been focused on all these weeks.

Athena glanced around suspiciously. How had they

known where to dig? Bia was convinced she had uncovered an item of power. What had given her the impression? She bent closer to the freshly dug earth, sniffed it warily, then buried her nose further into the hole. Just on the edge of her senses, she detected the faintest vestige of energy, like static electricity. It tickled the tips of her whiskers, giving the tiniest echo that something powerful had, until recently, been there.

Stepping back, Athena studied the area more carefully, checking for any evidence that might show who the raiders were, although she had strong suspicions. At the far side of the compound, she could see signs of entry: fur jagged on the edge of a rough gap in the chain-link fence, the sign of landing on loose dirt where the invader had jumped down. Looking at the landing place more closely, she saw a couple of faint paw prints or part-prints in loose dust. The gap in the fence was the part of the compound closest to Monastiraki Square. What had happened to her guards? She couldn't blame Bia this time; this raid looked like the work of one or other of her brothers.

Rooted to the spot, she whirled through the different scenarios. After a while she slowly made her way back to the Agora. Her mind was in turmoil. After all the waiting across all the years, and despite her careful precautions, someone had stolen her prize. It was almost impossible to take in; the enormity of her loss was bad enough, but having it stolen from under her nose was far worse, and she dared not think about the consequences. Anxiety replaced the numb feeling, then a howling rage. She could not let this go; the fate of her kind depended on it.

CHAPTER 37

APOLLO IN THE AGORA

APOLLO FELT powerless and frustrated. It was clear he could do nothing by himself. Sitting staring at this high walled compound would not help those inside either. He turned to the crow, still sitting in the tree beside him.

"I need to find help," he said. "Can you keep watch?"

"Certainly, squire. In fact, I should be able to do better than that. There's a lot of us willing to help. I can rustle up some lads and lasses, and keep this place under proper surveillance, round the clock."

Apollo thought for a minute. "Us?" he queried.

"Other crows, ravens, jackdaws. All my relatives," the bird replied. "There's a lot of us about, you know."

Of course! Apollo became a little more hopeful. It might work—intense scrutiny from the air. Enough of a racket to attract the attention of even the most dim-witted of humans. If it were noisy enough, they might even investigate. The more he thought about it, the more he liked the idea.

"Round up as many of your kind as you can and keep this place under observation. It doesn't matter about the noise; in fact, make as much as you can. If anything happens, anything even remotely interesting, come and find me as quickly as possible."

"And what about you, guv?" enquired the crow.

"I'm going to get help," Apollo told him. The thought of retracing his steps across town was not pleasant, but he had no choice, tired and footsore though he was.

"OK," the bird responded. "I'll get my mates." He flew off.

Apollo turned and trotted back the way he'd come as fast as his tired body would allow. As he left the deserted quarter and reached the places where humans lived, the eastern sky lightened. His mind wandered, retracing recent events, his concern for Daphne never far from the surface, but now he'd found Olympia he was even more aware of the importance of speed. He remembered the strange dream and its ending, and without conscious thought, he imagined music, as if an orchestra was playing inside his head. It energised and even lifted his mood, just a little. As he walked, his tail swayed with the beat. A distant part of his mind wondered why he'd never done this before; at least it provided a distraction from the weariness in his paws as they trod the dusty roads and pavements.

The sun rose before him and he stared unflinching into its glare; not far to go now. He crossed railway lines, and the normally traffic-choked major roads, still quiet at this hour. Skirting the National Observatory, he left the streets and entered a wooded area, homing in on the Temple of Hephaestus. It seemed somehow familiar. He paused to get his bearings. They said Athena lived in or around the Agora? This must be the place, much changed as it was. What had happened to the bustling inhabitants and their relentless discourse? Through the trees, he spied the Acropolis and its monuments. Below it was the long roof of the Stoa of Atalos. Paying more attention to his immediate surroundings, he noticed movement beneath the trees: cats, lots of them. There must be some sort of community here. He moved closer and was confronted by a superior-looking amber and black female.

"Who are you that dares to come here?" she challenged, looking him in the eye.

Apollo halted. He hadn't expected that he would need to argue his way past guards.

"I've come to see Athena," he said, unable to keep the irritation out of his voice.

"Does she know you? Do you have an appointment?" came the smooth reply. Athena's followers were nothing if not administratively efficient, and this animal, Penelope, was one of her closest advisors, a personal secretary no less. Good diary-keeping was the very foundation of civilisation in her book, and she was one of the best. Her tail stayed firmly and impolitely down. She looked at him with ill-concealed disdain, and if he'd been minded to sympathise he might have seen her point. It was some time since he'd last had a proper wash, and he was dusty, travel-weary, and a little disheveled. Not the type of animal she would want to allow into the presence of her mistress, regardless of the circumstances, but he didn't feel like turning on the charm; her attitude annoyed him.

He returned an appraising look of his own before answering, pleased to note that she found his scrutiny a little disconcerting. "She knows me," was all he said. He was in no mood to dance to the tune of some self-important bureaucrat, or to turn on his usual charm. He detected a momentary flicker behind her eyes, and her manner softened a degree.

"I need a name." She remained the epitome of bureaucratic obstinacy.

"Tell her Phoebus Pythius Acesius is here." His eyes narrowed. That should challenge her powers of recall. If she passed the test, he had plenty of others to throw her way.

"Hmm." She looked him up and down, her doubt evident. "OK, follow me."

She wove a path between trees, over and around fallen stones, exposed ancient tree roots and modern pavements, gradually ascending the hill known as Pnyx. Halfway up, in a small clearing, on an ancient fallen altarpiece, a magnificent grey animal reclined. Aware of their approach, she turned her piercing green eyes to study the intruder accompanying her private secretary. After a brief appraisal, she addressed Penelope.

"And what have we here?"

"This is Fee, er, Pithy..."

Putting her out of her misery, Apollo stepped past her, glaring at the grey cat. Her non-existent welcome had already worsened his fragile mood.

"It's me. It may have been a while, but you can cut the attitude. I'm here to tell you about some serious wrongdoing in this city of yours, but if you're not interested, just tell me and I'll be on my way."

To his left, Athena's secretary was aghast at his lack of decorum, but he ignored her. She tried to get a word in, if only to save her from a tongue-lashing later. "He says he knows you, so I thought I'd better bring him up here, just in case."

"I seem to recall him taking better care of his appearance," the grey replied, addressing her personal assistant and looking past the ginger and white cat.

Apollo gave Penelope a scornful glance and focused all of his attention on her superior with her emerald eyes. As he looked into them, he sensed an echo of the faintest ghost of a memory: of thrones and a mountain and long white robes, and feasting and music and laughter, but also argument, rivalry, point-scoring, bickering, and conflict. It vanished as quickly as it had arrived.

"I understood you had some authority in this city," he said icily. He glanced at his surroundings. "But if this is the best you can do for a palace, perhaps I've been misinformed."

The grey cat interrupted him. "I have enough on my plate right now, and I have little need of further distraction. If you want my help, you'd better have a good story, though if you are who I believe you to be, I'm surprised you can't deal with it yourself."

The barb stung all the more because of the truth it contained. He needed to rediscover how to manipulate humans. It used to be so easy in the past when he could just seduce them or intimidate them, according to his mood, or on occasion even appeal to reason. With a conscious effort of will, he swallowed his pride and kept a lid on the resentment building inside him.

"Believe me, requesting help is the last thing I want to do, but I have no alternative." He recounted the salient points of his story, keeping it as brief as possible. He glossed over the detail of his encounter with the Botrys Gang and the chase, but he left out all mention of Hecate. He detected surprise on the grey cat's face at certain points. She was not as on top of matters as she might claim.

"So, I have located them and discovered there are lots of animals imprisoned there. I've set a watch, but I need support to get them out. I have…" he hesitated, unwilling to admit it, "… unfortunately lost the ability to converse with humans." He looked down, as if ashamed of this weakness, then met her eyes again and continued. "Time is running out, and we need them to intervene. I need backup." It was a hard thing to admit, but once he'd said it he felt, to a degree, unburdened.

Athena rose to a sitting position and gracefully curled

her tail around her paws, buying herself a little extra thinking time. "An extraordinary tale," she declared, and looked across the treetops toward the city. "And what do you think I can do about this?" Her voice was distant, she sounded almost disinterested.

Apollo refused to rise to the bait, and with an effort of will, silenced the turmoil in his head. When he next spoke, his voice carried such a calm authority and assurance that gave her no choice but to pay him full attention. She looked surprised to find herself on the receiving end of a call to reason; his case was irrefutable.

"All over Athens and beyond cats, have been snatched and held captive. Some are dying. Others are being sent to goodness knows where. Dogs and their puppies are also being mistreated, and in addition there is an undercurrent of fear throughout the animal population; even you might detect it if you cared to listen. What's more, the inhabitants of the outer regions are in a ferment of frustration and their leaders are spoiling for a fight. I thought you had a duty of care for this city? Can you maintain any pretence of control, or is your time at an end?"

The weight of the accusation was hard for her to bear and no longer possible for her to dismiss. She glared at him as if caught in a trap.

Apollo's minor victory pleased him. She wasn't used to being challenged. Was this the same creature he knew of old, he wondered? She often used to be prickly, but she'd always been receptive to reasoned argument, and most of the time, even-tempered; she could even be friendly. Perhaps something was bugging her? It was difficult to see through this current disguise.

After a pause, she appeared to have come to a decision and her tone became a little more accommodating. "Wait in this vicinity while I investigate further and organise our response. I suggest you get some rest." She turned tail and left with no further word. Penelope gave Apollo a suspicious glance and followed, leaving him alone.

Feeling deflated but still seething, weariness caught up with him. He found some nearby shade, curled up, and slept.

CHAPTER 38

AFTERMATH

KRATOS WALKED around it, peering at it from several angles, but it was no good; he couldn't make it do anything.

'What's it for?' he growled. He was in a secluded corner of the Library of Hadrian, as far away from the prying eyes of Zelus' gang as possible. The snatch squad, the four of his children who had mounted the raid, stood nearby at a respectful distance. They watched his every move as he inspected his prize. He turned to the nearest.

"Are you sure this is it?"

"Yes, sir. We've been watching her for days now. We dug it up at the exact spot she's been studying, and there was nothing else like it around; we looked."

Kratos turned back to the object and continued his inspection. It was disappointingly small for something of importance: a small statuette of a goddess holding a spear, just a few centimetres tall. It didn't look special in any way. What was he missing? It was an image of his arch-enemy; of that he was sure. What other goddess would pose in such outlandish gear, but why did she value it so? Was it just vanity? He spotted Zelus coming toward him and turned to approach him, stepping in front of the object. He had no desire to discuss it with his brother.

Zelus wasted no time getting to the point. "We need to talk."

"So, talk."

"We need to agree our next steps. I expect Athena will seek some sort of retribution, so we need to be prepared for the eventuality."

"Let her try." Kratos sounded dismissive. "She hasn't got the numbers, and the remnants of this mob," he nodded toward the small gaggle of prisoners in the far corner, "won't be up for round two." He studied the pitiful group of captives. They were few, most of them injured, which had prevented their escape. He idly wondered how many would survive the tender mercies of their handlers, given their fragile state. He turned back to the other cat. "But you're right, we need to decide how to press our advantage and finally get rid of her." He paused, appraising his ally, then addressed the issue closest to both their hearts. "And we need to divide the spoils. I started this war, so it's appropriate that I get the lion's share of the territory. My guys will take the Plaka itself, and everything on this side of the square. You can have everything on the other side." He watched for his rival's reaction. Zelus did not disappoint him.

"Not so fast," he growled. "Your undisciplined rabble would never have managed this without us. You couldn't even get here on time, and half of your unruly mob only turned up when it was all over. We will have the Plaka. You can take Syntagma Square and the streets down there. That's more than enough for you to handle."

Kratos had half expected this response, but he was confident he and his forces could see the Gizi gang off if he chose. That might be sooner rather than later, unless Zelus backed down. He didn't look likely to do so. The two of them squared up to one another, poised for a duel.

"The prisoner's escaped."

Both leaders spun to face an extremely nervous looking

cat who had just arrived. Finding itself the focus of detailed scrutiny from both, it would have liked nothing more than to just disappear, but it wasn't an option. It was the male half of the guard team Zelus had assigned to look after Daphne. His colleague hung slightly further back, stepping from paw to paw, looking even more nervous.

Zelus vented his fury on the hapless animal. "How did you let that happen, you useless fool?" He took a step forward. "You'd better have a good explanation for this."

"Yes, you being 'crack troops' and all." Kratos added sarcastically, glancing sidelong at his rival, relishing his sudden embarrassment.

The Gizi gang boss tried to ignore Kratos. He stared with laser-like intensity at his unfortunate underling, who looked like he might melt.

"We, we didn't stand a chance," he stammered. "He came from nowhere."

"Who did?" Zelus demanded.

"Never seen him before. It was this grey and white guy. A real warrior. Deadly. He took out Yannis in seconds." He shuddered at the memory.

"Then the little assassin showed her true colours," the other cat added. "She turned into a real viper. Savage."

"She looks like she's a bit of a ninja," the first cat agreed.

"But you just let her walk away?" Zelus was shaking with anger.

"What's that about Yannis?" Kratos spoke over the top of him. He was incredulous, struggling to take it in, almost shouting.

Quivering with nerves, the guard addressed him. "He wanted to take our prisoner away with him, but we said no, she belonged to Zelus. Then the grey and white guy just appeared. Took him by the throat. Killed him."

"Then the two of them turned on us," his companion added. "We only just escaped."

"You don't look as if you put up much of a fight." Zelus advanced on the pair, who both started edging backwards. Behind them, Kratos' offspring drew closer, cutting off their escape.

"Wait, a minute." Kratos' mind was racing. "Grey and white, you say. And what was your prisoner like?" They told him. "But no sign of a ginger?" They shook their heads. "Sounds like two of the spies that infiltrated our headquarters the other night." He turned to Zelus, a fresh note of urgency in his voice. "That's two of them. We need to find the ginger one and track them all down. He's the ringleader, and I've got a bone to pick with him—once I've taken him apart limb from limb. He can't be very far away." He turned back to the guards. "Where did they go?" he demanded.

"They set off down Ifestou Street, but you know where that leads..." The guard let it hang.

"Just as I expected; they do work for her. They must be special forces or something. We'd better root them out before they come back with their friends." He continued, more eager now. "It's time to take the Agora and all the scum who lurk there. We've got to get rid of Athena and her rag-tag gaggle of followers once and for all."

"How soon can you be ready?" Zelus looked as if he wanted to attack straight away.

Kratos glanced at him, his instinctive caution returning. "Wait, we need to plan for this. We don't know what powers she has got hidden in the woods, or what friends she can call on. And the guys are still recovering. We need to give them a bit of time to rest and prepare, and right now everyone's scattered around the neighbourhood."

Zelus gave him a long, calculating look. "OK, how long do you need?"

Kratos wondered about him. Why was his brother so desperate to rush in, headlong? Was he so naïve as to never make a plan? No one had ever really tested Athena's power. She might have resources they weren't aware of—how could she have effectively ruled over this city for so long otherwise? He didn't like to admit it, but those three spies or assassins or whatever they were had spooked him. Melanippus' divination had highlighted them, and it worried him they might still have a role to play. What if they were part of a much larger secret army? Still, he had to say something. "Tomorrow we gather our forces, we do a little reconnaissance and make the call."

He wondered how long his fragile alliance with his brother would last. He didn't like to admit it, but right now he needed his support.

CHAPTER 39

POOLSIDE CHAT

IN THE leafy northern suburb of Kifisia, houses are large and swimming pools de rigueur. Beside one of the more spectacular examples was a wide patio set with comfortable sun loungers and umbrellas. Bright sunlight sparkled on the still water, casting playful reflections on the whitewashed walls of the rear of the house. A glass-roofed extension enclosed an alfresco dining area and barbecue, behind which was a dark, cool interior.

The garden was deserted apart from a large russet-coloured cat which was curled up on one of the sun loungers, in the shade. He was, Hermes reflected, quite the biggest brute of a cat he'd ever seen, and judging from his recent regime, he was getting even bigger. 'There must be a lot of Maine Coon in there,' he thought, 'mixed with souvlaki and kleftiko.' It was undeniable that the beast was overweight despite its enormous frame.

"Morning," he said, gently hopping onto the adjacent sun lounger.

The big cat didn't move a muscle, but from somewhere within the depths of the mound of fur a disgruntled-sounding voice emerged. "Don't you ever knock?"

"Bit tricky with hedges," Hermes shot back. "Anyway, you know me. I always like the element of surprise."

The large cat grunted and continued snoozing. Hermes made himself comfortable and examined his surroundings.

He was in no hurry.

"Nice place you've got here," he ventured after a while.

Wearily, Ares raised his head to get a proper view of his annoying guest. The white cat wasn't going to go away, so he might as well find out what he wanted. Why was his peace being disturbed? "It's not too bad," he agreed, keeping his tone neutral. He didn't feel remotely interested in lending a paw to any of his madcap ventures. Life here was sweet.

"Yes, a very comfortable pad, if you don't mind me saying so." Hermes continued with his flattery, watching the reflections playing on the surface of the swimming pool. "I didn't know you could swim."

Ares experienced a tremor of irritation. It was like a persistent flea he couldn't quite get at. His patience was fraying. "Of course it's nice, it's my palace," he growled in a voice deeper than the sea. "I'm not going to live in a shed, am I? Or scratch a living on the top of a windswept hill," he added pointedly. He looked across at the other cat, who studiously ignored him. "I've never understood why you don't get a proper place of your own. Why don't you put your paws up occasionally, enjoy a bit of luxury? Get some servants of the human variety to run around after you. You might like it." He was warming to his theme.

Hermes felt he was straying too close to a discussion on local real estate values, so he changed tack. "Don't enjoy swimming," he replied. "Too much chlorine's bad for your fur. I'm surprised you do," he added, looking his neighbour up and down. "Thought you might sink, given that thatch!"

A rumbling sound emitted from somewhere deep inside the big cat's body. Hermes wasn't sure whether it was a growl or a laugh. "Who needs to swim? This is a great place to hang out. The food's great—lots of tuna and seafood—and I get spa treatments into the bargain. Had my claws done the other day, and I've got a great grooming service." The big cat looked across at Hermes to see if such decadent living would challenge his spartan sensibilities, but there was no reaction. Rather than wait for the next joust, he decided to clean his anus and stuck a hind paw in the air. It was a decision he immediately regretted, given his audience. His stomach was getting in the way, and it was a lot more of an effort than he'd like.

Hermes watched his struggles with growing amusement. "Enough of tittle-tattle," he said once Ares had finally got down to business. His tone became sharper, more businesslike. "You're missed. You're shirking your responsibilities. Since you disappeared to your little hideaway, the situation has changed. There is near anarchy down in town; your gang is scattered to the winds, and a lot of it is your fault. If you'd been there, they would never have been brave enough to attack." He conveniently ignored his own role in stirring the pot.

Ares stopped washing and looked up. This was all news to him; he was clearly out of the loop.

"Whaddya mean 'my fault?'" Hermes' jibe had hit the mark. "I'm not responsible for every cat in this city." The accusation that he was somehow shirking his duty infuriated him. He paused and calmed down a bit. "I'm just taking a break. It's perfectly reasonable."

Hermes looked around the garden. "Unfortunately, your timing wasn't great. Kratos and Zelus have taken advantage of your absence. They mounted a raid on the Plaka and have taken over."

"What's happened to my boys and girls?" demanded the big cat, suddenly concerned.

Hermes caught his eye. "Decimated, unfortunately.

It was carnage. Quite a few killed, several badly injured. Some escaped, but not the kittens." Ares went still, waiting for more. Hermes hesitated. "Kratos seemed to be targeting them, so I've heard. He particularly relished getting rid of the youngsters. He's making room for his own foul brood." He broke eye contact.

Silence fell between the two cats. Ares filled it.

"Disgusting beast," he spat. He stared into the distance. "I'm going to enjoy giving him his comeuppance." He thought for a while. "Why didn't Athena do something?" he asked.

Hermes paused, unsure what to say. "She's been acting strangely lately. Watching the archeologists near the Agora. From what I've been able to find, she's waiting for a statue or artefact to be dug up. Apparently, it's important to her. It's become something of an obsession, but I have to say it just means she's taken her eye off the ball elsewhere. She's just ignored other events and didn't even raise a paw to intervene. It's most unlike her. In the end, Bia seems to have nabbed it from under her nose." He stopped, reluctant to share what he now knew of its significance and capabilities, let alone his own role in its disappearance.

Ares harrumphed. He stared into space for a while, thinking.

"Statue you say? Little one, was it?" Hermes nodded. "Where have they been looking?" Hermes told him. He reflected some more. "Oh well, bound to turn up sometime." He sounded dismissive. Hermes gave him a quizzical stare. Ares looked back at him. "I think I dropped it there. A while ago," he added, seeing Hermes look. He ruminated further. "I think it was the Vandals, or maybe the Herulians. I dunno, a long time ago. Anyway, whoever it was, they sacked Athens, and I decided to join in, have a bit of fun.

Well, why not?" he exclaimed defensively, seeing his companion's accusatory look. "They'd stopped worshipping us, they'd gone soft. Temples were being allowed to go to ruin. Offerings had ceased. Things were slipping. They deserved a kick up the backside, so when the opportunity arose for a bit of mayhem, well, I couldn't resist. I found it, if memory serves me right, in a side alcove in the Parthenon. I knew it was precious to her, but she wasn't around, so I nicked it. But it was just a trinket. After a while I decided I didn't want to be found red-handed, so to speak, so I dropped it in a well in one of the stoas down by the Agora." He finished and gave his companion a defiant look. "Didn't know she'd go all dewy-eyed about it, did I?"

Hermes considered the story. It explained a lot. Mostly it explained that even Ares was nervous of a wrathful Athena in her full glory. "And that was your idea of a bit of 'fun?'" he demurred, "you and your famous sense of humour. You should do some stand-up, you'd have 'em rolling in the aisles."

"Minus their heads, if they're going to laugh," came the reply.

Hermes looked to the heavens. Time to change the subject. "Well then," he said briskly, "time to get moving, eh?"

"Not so fast," Ares growled. "I need something more to go on. What's the situation on the ground? Who has control of what? Where are they basing themselves, and what is their strength? Above all, what is Her Ladyship going to do, or is she still planning to sit this one out? And what about our oh-so-superior Titaness, Bia? Is she going to join the fun, or is she content to leave it to her brothers?"

Hermes sighed.

"Zelus and Kratos and their forces have control of the Plaka. They've got at least sixty, maybe more. They've taken over the site of the Library of Hadrian, your old HQ." He glanced at the other cat. "As for Athena, who knows? At least she does now seem a bit more bothered about things, so she will probably want to join in. Regarding Bia, I don't have a clue. If I were a betting animal I'd say yes, she'd join in." He looked at Ares, levelly. "There, that enough to be going on with? Oh, and one more thing," he added. "Apollo's in town and he's searching for a missing friend." He paused. "He doesn't seem his usual self. Not bothered with local events at all. He's acting a bit strange." He looked up. "I think that covers it."

"Apollo?" Ares sounded surprised. He didn't really get on with the golden one. "Haven't seen him in centuries. What's dragged his prissy little ass here? Missing person investigation? Give me a break. Probably just wants to deliver a lecture or two, hook up with as many of the girls as he can get his paws on, and act all smug and superior to the rest of us." Ares distrusted anyone with intellectual pretensions. He much preferred the company of animals of action. Heroes, that kind of folk. You knew where you were with warriors and plain, straightforward enemies.

"Bit harsh," Hermes countered. He got up. "Anyway, time is of the essence; let's get going."

"Hang on, hang on," Ares grumbled. "I'm not going anywhere without some victuals on-board first." He looked expectantly at the rear of the house. As if on cue, a woman appeared carrying an enormous bowl of food. She looked across at them.

"Mr Tubs, it's lunchtime. Here you go." She carefully placed the bowl down and went back inside.

For the second time that morning, Hermes felt his jaw dropping. He turned to his companion, poised to say something, but the other cat cut him off.

"One word," he warned, his voice rolling like thunder in the distant hills. "Just one word, and I'll rip your tail off and ram it down your throat. Got it?" Without waiting for a reply, he jumped down and waddled toward the food. Hermes watched him for a long moment, then sauntered behind.

"Thinking about preparations, it might be useful to bring your boys along."

Ares grunted his assent. He stopped and glanced around at the shrubbery at the far end of the garden. "Phobos, Deimos, you're needed," he shouted. "We've got a job to do down in town, so you'd better get your backsides into gear." He turned his attention back to his meal.

The bushes parted and two sleek young cats appeared, almost mirror images of each other. One was largely black with white markings, including a patch over one eye. His companion was mainly white, with black markings and an eye patch. They sauntered over; tails raised in greeting. Hermes watched them approach and glanced toward their father.

"Are you sure they're *yours*?"

CHAPTER 40

THE SLEEPERS

ONCE MORE unwelcome dreams invaded his sleep, this time more vivid than ever before; so real it seemed he could touch the figures involved, if he only reached out.

It wasn't his first murder, and it wouldn't be his last, but it was, perhaps, his most flamboyant, and his biggest regret. He never could remember the name of the place, deep in its remote valley in the mountains. It was little more than a village, though every hamlet was a kingdom in those days. This one came complete with a rustic hall, packed with the local townsfolk, their king, and his retinue, all gathered to watch the arrogant musician beat the best Olympus could deliver.

It is never wise to summon a god without good reason, and this could certainly not be described as such. In fact, Marsayas might have been drunk at the time. No matter; he exuded confidence, certain he could live up to his claim. It is true; his musical ability was sublime. The dreamer floated through the hall, observing both participants and the audience and judges. He saw the god in question, natural radiance veiled and his form scaled to little more than that of a man (but still suffused with a subtle golden glow) standing at the side of the stage, the ageless epitome of youthful masculine perfection. The dreamer studied him. As patron of the arts, this particular god was in his element, yet he dressed for the occasion in simple attire: tunic and sandals, a cord tied at the waist; modest yet elegant. As befitted his role as 'educator,' he had, of course, brought the necessary tools.

Marsayas stepped forth and bowed before his admirers. From the wings, his opponent observed every movement in minute detail, noted the subtle and less than subtle scents lingering in the evening air, picked up the sounds of lowing cattle nearby and the melody of the crickets in the woods across the fields. He sensed the rustle in the undergrowth across town that attracted the falcon's beady eye and heard the air move beneath the wings of an owl, taking all of this in and more, but mostly he studied the puffed-up virtuoso preening himself before his admirers. Floating through the hall, the dreamer regarded the man once again. So self-important and confident of his impending victory was he that to him the contest had already been won, and the laurel wreath awarded. Knowing what was to come, with a growing disquiet, the dreamer let him enjoy this fleeting moment, before his exposure, like some counterfeit Icarus, to the full glare of the sun.

Solemnly, the man waited for the adulation to subside and silence to fall, then put his lips to the mouthpiece of his woodwind and began. He played his piece with skill and verve, and very nice it was too. The audience gasped at his accomplishment, hypnotised by every move as his fingers flew to cover and uncover the tone holes in his complicated instrument. There was no doubting his skill, but as ever with mortals, it was his ego that sealed his fate, the look of pompous self-satisfaction. He couldn't resist a smug, almost condescending, sideways glance at his watching opponent.

The dreamer saw Apollo grin back, recognising the idiot for what he was, and saw with dreadful certainty the brutal intent behind. All semblance of friendly rivalry had drained away. He didn't have any intention of losing, and it was unwise in the extreme to take him for a fool: maybe that lingering look was when his challenger got his first inkling.

The musician finished his performance and bowed ostentatiously, first to the king, then the rest of the audience, then to the Muses who sat in judgement of this little contest. The adulation was complete, and the crowd on their feet, clapping and shouting for all they were worth. He stood centre stage, soaking up the applause. They were certain, as was he, that nothing could surpass such a display. The judges gave cautious but considered support, applauding and nodding and carefully avoiding his eye. It was deserved. He was indeed highly skilled, a master of his instrument, of composition and performance. He had wrought every last drop of emotion from his tune. None could doubt he was a consummate musician, a maestro even. The dreamer's non-existent stomach felt tied in a knot; the mouth he didn't possess was dry.

While the imbecile continued to milk the rapturous applause of his fans, his competitor stepped forward and his presence filled the room. A hush fell. The air was thick and cloying, catching in their throats. Anticipation grew; something special was going to happen tonight. They held their breath while the dreamer heard himself groan. The Olympian looked sidelong at his challenger, his eyebrow arched. For the first time, Apollo spoke.

"So, can you do this then?"

With unhurried grace he moved toward the stool that appeared centre-stage and in the act of sitting, casually flipped up his lyre high toward the rafters. He caught the inverted instrument and, still holding it upside down, started to play. Slowly it started, a lilting piece of exquisite beauty, building up layer by layer; a tune of his own invention. At its heart was a melody of heartbreaking simplicity but intense emotional depth; crescendos waxing then waning, before ascending once more. Then he sang, his rich baritone filling the hall. The audience gasped. They had never heard this tune, but the refrain was so enticing and the rhythm so infectious they couldn't help but hum along and tap their feet. He had them in the palm of his hand. This was artistry, the like of which they'd never witnessed for a player of a stringed instrument.

Apollo finished and basked in the applause before turning to his challenger.

"Surely, for one who claims to be the greatest, equaling such a feat is well within your capabilities?"

His voice was mild and quiet, but the mockery within the simple statement hit the musician hard. He blanched, a scintilla of doubt behind his eyes. 'Run, you fool,' thought the dreamer, though certain that no human runner could ever escape this opponent. For a moment, a sliver of opportunity existed for the man to find a way out of the rapidly closing jaws of his fate. A bow and humble acknowledgement he had met his match would have sufficed. He could have given in with grace and followed up by making an appropriate sacrifice and obeisance recognising the futility of his boast. The dreamer urged him in a silent scream to take the opportunity, but his shriek was never heard. The musician's hubris knew no bounds, and the window of opportunity slammed shut. He was beside himself, infuriated by the injustice of it all. Blindly, he careered on down the path to his own destruction.

"Ridiculous buffoonery. A clown's trick. How can a serious, self-respecting artiste such as myself be taken seriously if I am expected to emulate such circus tricks? Any idiot knows the aulos cannot be played back to front; it is an insult to suggest it."

That was it. The Muses looked down, studying their clasped hands, giving their judgement the appearance of objectivity, then solemnly declared Apollo the winner. His opponent howled in indignation. Had they ears of cloth? Did they know true artistry when they heard it? Could they differentiate between a supreme performer such as himself and a tavern drunk strumming a few bum notes on an old guitar?

The god let the musician blather on for a while, then fixed him with a stare.

"It's time for your runner-up prize, but just remember, this is on your head. It was you who summoned me to this contest with your boastful bragging. Do you think your little skills surpass mine? You think you can over-step a god?"

The musician knew his fate then. His protest stalled in his throat. He tried to back away. The dreamer wanted desperately to look away, but couldn't, even though he knew, with appalling certainty, what was coming next. Setting his lyre aside, the god took out a fine paring knife from a fold in the waist of his tunic.

"No, no…. Please." Terror widened the man's eyes, and fear was dripping from every pore. Once more the god fixed him with a humourless grin. There was no mercy there; vengeance was due; the lesson would proceed.

It was said the musician's screams could be heard across the breadth of the valley and as far as the next town. Apollo left his victim's skin hanging on the branch of a nearby tree, dripping wetly onto the bare earth. He pinned the rest of him to a barn door with a spear wrenched from the grasp of a dumb-struck soldier. At least that ended it for him. Let it be a warning to them all.

The Muses had long since departed.

The dreamer bowed his head, tears streaming down his face, his sanity dissolving like dust in the wind.

In this way, he recognised anew the darkness in his soul that lay, forever, on the fringes of the light, and the monster that lurked therein.

APOLLO WOKE up still aching from his previous exertions, but sweating and troubled by the vestiges of his nightmare. He felt weary, but the thought of further sleep brought only fear. He stumbled to his feet to find out how plans were progressing, anything rather than dwell on those unwelcome fragments of memory.

Instead, he turned his thoughts to the time; how long did Olympia have? Then there was the question of his travelling companions: where were they? Restless and impatient, he set off in search of answers. The size of the Agora and its wooded hinterland surprised him; nothing looked familiar. Where in all this district did Athena reside? He continued his perambulations, hoping to find her. Her followers kept their distance, regarding him with suspicion, but avoiding eye contact. He spotted small groups of other cats here and there among the trees, all looking sorry for themselves, beaten down and dejected. Apollo spoke to some of them to find out what was going on and how this place was run. He found he was talking to refugees from the Plaka gang, exiled in their own city.

Over several conversations he pieced together the story of the battle at Monastiraki square, the unprovoked attack of Kratos and Zelus, and their merciless brutality, most evident in the massacre of the innocents. There were tales of heroic defenders overwhelmed by the sheer number of attackers and others who held off the attackers and so bought time for others to escape. He understood their anger and sorrow; they had suffered so much. But amid their tales, he heard mention of a brave grey and white stranger who rallied to their cause and who even took down one of the most savage attackers. Could it be Jason? Excited, he asked about his friends. Had anyone seen Daphne? He needed to find out; the need to see her, be with her, was tangible, a physical ache. At last he found someone who thought they'd seen them, hiding under the trees with the others. Apollo searched with renewed urgency.

He found them curled up together in comfortable companionship. Shared adventures had brought them closer and woven a kind of magic around them. Apollo looked down at the sleepers, their bodies entwined, their breathing synchronised. At peace. In love. His own emotions tumbled through his head, confusing and conflicted. He was almost overwhelmed by desperate envy, and an equally strong yearning for her. But here she was, wrapped in the embrace of another. However much he wanted to, he couldn't break their bond.

Something inside him broke. A little snap rather than a huge fracture, but a break nevertheless. A tiny snap that presaged a larger crack in the dam he'd so carefully constructed. A few memories trickled through and nothing now could hold them back. The knowledge he'd so long tried to suppress. The knowledge of what it was to be him.

The moment stretched and twisted while unwanted recollections tumbled around and tormented his waking mind until it seemed his head would burst. Daphne and Jason looked as if they were meant for each other and always had been. Them. Not him. He was an outsider. The eternal outsider to their love story. Envy mingled with desire, consuming every corner of his soul.

Still, he stood over them, observing the rise and fall of their ribs, sensing their togetherness in their fleeting hour of tranquility, and he saw with all the certainty of his own divination that it was the most transient of moments, like the twinkle of a distant star or the flicker of a candle flame soon to be swallowed by the long dark night. He listened to their gentle purrs. Sadness overwhelmed him; the sleepers would wake soon and their lives would change forever. He mourned not only the futility of his unrequited love, but the wasted years and the emptiness still to come. Did she know? Did she now resent him? He hoped not: that, at least, would be a small blessing. He bowed his head. He could not save them all. Couldn't someone let the lovers linger longer in their bliss? Apollo recognised the futility of the question even before he posed it.

He stirred, looked up. The struggle to recognise and be the master of his thoughts, hidden for so long behind his carefully constructed barrier, was beginning anew. Once he could look deep into the hearts of men, hoping to guide them to a better path. Toward a better fate than that Marsayas wrought, at any rate. He almost choked as his own hypocrisy snagged in his throat. What sort of shepherd was he? Hermes had been right. He swallowed hard, bit down on the bile, and forced his thoughts elsewhere. Over the course of his too-long life he'd made mistakes, plenty of them, and learning to forgive himself was still a work in progress. He gave the sleepers one last look, his golden eyes a mask of tenderness and sorrow, and left to walk alone beneath the trees.

Once the fate of mortals never bothered him. Perhaps it was his age, a softness stealthily encroaching with the years like a creeping twisting vine wrapping itself around his soul, but now their struggles against so many injustices felt raw. There was a need to correct the flow. They needed help. He had no cure, no wand to wave, but he could no longer hide. He began once more to feel their pain alongside his own. The destiny of humankind was beyond him for now, but he could still make a difference elsewhere. There was no option but to try; to hide was to give up and looking forever inwards would test his sanity.

DAPHNE RELISHED the drowsy warmth of this little nest they had made beneath the cypress trees. Jason's paw was across her shoulder. It was nice, pressing down like that. A long loving night had cemented their ties. She felt safe. She yawned; an itchy ear troubled her. A quick scratch with a hind paw and she was comfortable again. She nestled closer in against him, not wanting to wake. Wouldn't it be nice if this moment lasted forever? She detected movement nearby, opened her eyes, and raised her head, and saw a retreating cat, ginger with a hint of white.

"A... Apollo?"

There was no answer. 'Must be mistaken,' she thought and resumed her slumber.

CHAPTER 41

THE AWAKENING

KRATOS RETURNED to his prize and looked for a suitable spot to lie down. This new headquarters wasn't yet a home, in his preferred sense. He'd had to leave his comfortable bed of stolen socks and underwear behind, and despite instructions to the troops, they had yet to amass any kind of haul to pad out his new surroundings with creature comforts. It would come, but for now, his quarters looked decidedly spartan.

Curled up against a wall, head on his paws, he peered at his acquisition, but his thoughts were on recent news. Yannis had been a reliable lieutenant, obedient and ruthless. Kratos would miss him. His death was another crime to add to the growing charge list against the three spies. When he got hold of them, punishment would be sweet. What was it the guard had said? The smaller one had been their captive? He should have explored that more. What had Zelus wrung out of her? It should have been him asking the questions; he'd have made her squeak alright. It had been dark the night of their raid, but he still had a vague recollection of her. He pictured her in his mind's eye: patchwork colouring, diminutive but confident despite being outnumbered and surrounded, agile, a formidable little assassin indeed.

Just what were you after? he thought, glaring at the statue, and experienced a strange brief sensation of falling as if he'd broken through some invisible barrier and into a deep, deep hole, dissipating into space. His perspective changed, his mind's eye taking control of his waking thoughts. He was looking out from under a tree somewhere. Where? In front of his paws was loose soil, except they weren't his paws, they were white. What was happening?

"What's this?" a voice sounded in his head. It wasn't his.

"Who are you?"

"What do you mean? Who are you?"

Kratos concentrated hard. He didn't know what was happening, but he was talking to someone as if he was in their head. They seemed bewildered. From somewhere among his brooding web of thoughts, he gathered an idea of who this might be. If he was right, this was an encounter he would relish.

"You're one of her spies, aren't you? I know all about you," he lied, pressing his advantage. In his imagination he loomed over the small, hapless animal, as if made to a different scale, intimidating it with his sheer size. It seemed to have some effect.

"Aargh, my head hurts, stop it, stop it."

"All in due course, little one. Once you've told me all about yourself and what you've been up to." A sense of exhilaration filled the space behind his foremost thoughts, which suddenly seemed to sound small and far away, as if spoken aloud in an enormous open space. Kratos shut his mind to such distractions and concentrated on his target.

"Ow, ow, help. I can't think, my head's splitting," the other cat was groaning, giving a good impression of being in real discomfort, if not pain. Kratos relished the fact. He wanted to torture it and make it suffer, but he didn't want to break it. Not yet anyway; he needed information. He pulled back a little.

"I'll stop it hurting, but only when you've told me everything you know."

There was a brief pause while his target took a breath. He could sense it panting, as if it had been running. While it recovered, Kratos reveled in his discovery and the joy it brought him. He couldn't remember the last time he'd been able to exercise this kind of mental power over a subject, if at all. The strange sensation of unfolding the true scale of his mind was disconcerting, but marvellous; the possibilities were endless.

He had the disorienting sensation of his thoughts expanding into an infinite space that opened before him. Ideas flooded in, visions floated within reach, memories long suppressed emerged, jostling for attention. He perceived himself anew, understanding, or was it relearning, his place in the universe. He felt he was floating above the world. Looking down he could see the human multitudes and billions of other creatures crawling, running, flying and scurrying across its surface, tiny and fragile: a world in ferment. With a thrill he sensed how easy it would be to manipulate them and eagerly grasped for the levers that would empower him. How long had the Olympians plotted against him and his kind; sneered at them, kept them down, servile and ignorant? He and his siblings were Zeus's allies, his adopted ones. The children of Styx, herself the honoured guardian of oaths. How could they treat him like this? The treachery of Zeus's spawn enraged him. What sacred oaths had they broken?

From his lofty position he looked across the city and far beyond, saw the brief flashes of their immortal souls lit up at a distance like tiny beacons lurking in their respective bolt-holes. You have no hiding places any more. I will find you all. Find and destroy you. Suspicions long held bubbled up in his consciousness anew, a burning sense of injustice he'd long carried without knowing why. But it was no lie, and now he knew precisely why he'd carried the grudge. From this distance, without focus, he couldn't tell who was who. It could wait. He would take his time and plot a strategy. When retribution arrived, he would relish it anew.

Kratos' thoughts continued to unfold and spread. This wonderful object gave him a glimpse of his true unshielded power. It was valuable beyond measure, a way to turn the tables and reclaim his true strength. No more would he or his kind pay dues to the squeaking, mewing gods of Olympus. It was time for a New Age, a Titan Age. To put an end to their tyranny. He would be subordinate no more. His thoughts extended across the city and its human population for the first time; he wanted them as followers, obedient servants, slaves to do his will, just like his gang but on a far larger scale and with enormous power. An army that would bend to his will, driven and cowed. He would teach them to obey or face oblivion.

A fit of anger allowed him to test his new powers. On the fringes of his consciousness, he encountered strange things he'd not come across before: fresh energies, electricity and the engines it drove, and the things it powered, other systems and networks, intricate, interconnected but with so many weak points. Kratos flexed mental muscles long unused and tested his power. Across the city, there were power surges and grid outages. Blocks and neighbourhoods lost electricity. Traffic lights flicked off with the resulting chaos of collisions and confusion, mayhem, and death. On opposite sides of the city, two gas explosions turned houses to rubble and triggered panic. Water mains ruptured, flooding streets. Kratos observed the destruction and the panicky human response with satisfaction and turned his mind to more mundane and familiar items, stone and metal. Railway lines twisted like spaghetti, and derailed trains, smashing them into tunnel walls or adjacent buildings. Further chaos. The cables of the Lycabettus Funicular snapped, leaving passengers praying the failsafe mechanism held. Death, destruction, mayhem: a small foretaste of what was to come once he learned to use this power. They would fear him and obey. For the time being he withdrew, satisfied with his experiment, while across Athens sirens were wailing as the emergency services tried to restore order.

Kratos' thoughts turned inwards. How long had they had imprisoned him in this small body with all of its limitations, and why? A dim recollection of a pact, a plot to limit the power of his kind, delivered as a strange fruit for all to eat. It had been a trick. A crime. He had to undo it, and eject the poison from his system, but how? This object was useful, but could it help him discover the antidote to that dread apple, and regain his correct form? Did the tree still exist? There was so much to consider, but all in good time. First, he had to establish his power over those whining Olympians and pompous Athena in particular. He pondered what to do with the spy, who wriggled and squirmed under the influence of his thought. Observing her as if she were a specimen under a microscope, he recognised a simple spirit of streams and woodland groves, a nymph, the lowest of the immortal low, almost powerless, a servant to his mighty kindred. A minion but possessing just enough mental capacity to put up some feeble resistance to his efforts to control her mind. Once more he gave her his full attention.

"Tell me everything you know. Tell me all about your mistress."

"I'm not a spy, I've already told you everything," she pleaded. "Please, just let me go."

Kratos flexed his newfound mental muscles again and heard the squeal at the receiving end. "That's a little reminder of what I can do. Now, let's pretend you haven't told me anything. Start from the beginning. When did she recruit you?"

"She didn't, no one did. I just wanted to help Apollo."

Kratos stopped, wrong-footed. He probed further into his target's mind but met unexpected dead-ends; there was still a lot to learn about this device and how to use it, particularly the fine-tuning necessary to probe and unpick individual thoughts.

"Better come and tell me all about it then," he told her, wrapping velvet around his mental cosh. He threatened her in his most condescending voice. "Come and see your old friend Kratos. We'll have a cosy little chat and you can tell me all about this boyfriend of yours." Next, he tried to control her muscles and if possible, with difficulty, move her limbs. The connection was haphazard at first, his target jerking like a marionette, and he felt her fighting him, but she was puny, and as he worked at it, his control improved and her movements became smoother and she was powerless to stop him. Looking out of her eyes, he saw an unfamiliar view through trees of open ground sloping down to a gateway and pavement beyond. He decided that must be the way toward his headquarters. His victim's head bobbed up and down, making his vision shake, as he forced her forward in a robotic walk. It would take time before he mastered a smoother form of mind control; for the moment this would do, despite the rough edges.

Jason returned to the little nest under the cypress tree that he and Daphne had made their own just in time to see her leaving. He stopped in his tracks and watched. The way she was moving was unlike anything he'd ever seen. He shouted to her, but she didn't reply, didn't even move her head. He bounded over and stood in her line of vision, shouting her name. Looking through her eyes, Kratos noted the interloper with relish. This was the other accomplice, the grey and white one who'd killed Yannis. He'd deal with him in due course. First, he wanted to get his prey somewhere safe so he could get to the bottom of all this, even if it meant stripping her down to her muscle fibres.

Jason ran in circles around her, trying but failing to understand what she was doing. Daphne just ignored him and kept moving in the strange jerky walk, right past him. He raced around and stood in front of her, but she just barged him aside, still saying nothing, her eyes glazed and fixed straight ahead, her path unswerving. Jason watched her for a moment, then jumped at her, side on, knocking her down. Hating himself, he delivered a sharp bite to her neck.

"Ow," she said, and went limp. The sharp jolt of pain sent a shock-wave through her nervous system into her brain and broke the connection. Kratos sensed it and opened his eyes, losing his focus and his viewpoint. He tried to re-establish the connection, but back in this smaller container his thoughts fell away and he found it difficult to concentrate, distracted as he was by the remnants of what he'd just experienced. He fumbled, became too hasty, and grew frustrated. Kratos glared at the statuette and attempted to relax, but sensed movement in his peripheral vision. One of his lieutenants had arrived to deliver a report on the afternoon's scavenging activities. Kratos listened to him with only half an ear. His mind was elsewhere, still trying to understand the revelation he'd just received.

After his subordinate had left, he looked at the statuette

in a new light and marveled at it. Before him was a device of astonishing subtlety and power. Not only had it had enabled him to make the mental connection with the spy, but it had given him a glimpse of his true self and enabled him to wield power of a kind he could barely remember. He'd been able to manipulate material and systems across the city, and do it with ease. It had revealed his true nature and hidden power, but with that knowledge arose an even greater bitterness toward the creature that had imprisoned him in this tiny constrained body, with her evil tricks and spells. What had they done to him, Athena and her co-conspirators? Why had he agreed? It must have been against his will, the result of trickery and deceit, the devious behaviour for which the inhabitants of Olympus were famous. Trapped in this body for so long, no wonder it had melted his mind and eroded his memories.

For the moment he had to put aside his burning resentment and find out how to regain his true form permanently, so putting an end to the injustice. Questions piled upon questions. He'd always resented Athena, but now he had reason anew to despise her and all her kind. She had been keeping him, all of them, cooped up like this for centuries. It was time to forge a new future, one free of all Olympians. A future with himself and his peers in charge and humanity slave to their will. Where were they now, mighty Atlas, bold Crius, powerful Oceanus, bright Helios, and all the rest, individuals he'd all but forgotten: the older gods? He had a new mission: set them free and then make war on their feeble successors, scattering them to the winds, or worse.

There remained unfinished business with the spy, but she was just the start. A stepping-stone on the path to glory. Kratos started planning his next moves.

CHAPTER 42

ORDINARY ANIMALS
HAVE NO CHANCE

"WHAT IF he tries again?"

"I don't know." Daphne was frightened, but Jason was no help. The episode had shaken them both. They were sitting beneath their favourite tree trying to understand what had just happened. For the umpteenth time, Daphne tried to make sense of it. She'd been snoozing in the middle of the day, then suddenly she had the most awful crushing headache as her head was filled with someone else's thoughts. Not just anyone, but the brute who'd attacked them the other night at the disused factory. Then, worst of all, he tried to make her walk. He nearly succeeded. She stared, unseeing, into the distance, scared and helpless.

"What was it like?" asked Jason yet again.

"I can't describe it. He was just in my head, asking me questions. Then he tried to make me go to him." She shuddered.

Jason came to a decision. "I'm going to see if I can find help. There must be someone around here who knows what's going on." He bounded off up the hillside. Daphne didn't move. She didn't see how anyone could help, but she had no other ideas. She tried to compose herself; her heart was still racing. After a little while he returned with Thalia, the cat they'd met when they fled from the battle.

She studied Daphne, both curious and concerned. "I've

never heard of anything like it." She looked blank. "I don't know what to suggest." Daphne and Jason looked at one another helplessly. Thalia looked at them in turn. "Maybe, just maybe, my lady would know what to do?" Immediately she turned tail and set off without further explanation. Jason looked exasperated. He set off after her, trying to get answers.

None the wiser, and more frightened than ever, Daphne racked her brains to think why Kratos had such an interest in her. He must have talked to Zelus, she supposed. One interrogation had been bad enough; she couldn't face another. They were both obsessed with spying, which seemed odd. Then she remembered how frightened Zelus had appeared when she mentioned Hera. And Kratos seemed a little spooked to hear Apollo's name. Why? How come he'd heard of Apollo? Had he ever been to Delphi? Someone would have mentioned it, surely? Questions crowded her mind, but who could give her the answers, and where had Jason and Thalia got to? She got up and set off into the woods. Anything was better than sitting here waiting to be summoned by that evil monster.

She wandered the hillside in search of them, but they remained elusive. After an hour of wandering, she was on the point of giving up when she heard voices. It sounded like Jason, but who was he talking to?

"... What do you mean, possessed?"

"It's like there was someone in her head. At least that's what she told me, and I believe her."

"That's impossible. You need to tell her to calm down. It must have been a bad dream or something."

"I saw her! It was no dream. She was walking, but she didn't seem to be in control of her legs. She couldn't hear me. I was there." He was almost shouting.

"Enough. I've told you, it's impossible. It sounds as if you're both getting a little hysterical. I'll come and see her in due course, but first you need to tell her to calm down. Relax. She's been through a lot recently with the battle, and her imprisonment. She's probably just suffering the aftereffects of all the trauma."

Crouching down, Daphne edged as close as she could. She could see Jason, but a low bush hid the animal he was talking to. He was glaring at her, but he seemed unable to come up with anything else to add. Abruptly he turned and left. Daphne didn't move a muscle. After a moment another cat appeared: Athena's assistant, Penelope.

"I suppose you heard that?"

"Most of it, my lady, but I'm not sure I understand any of it."

There was a long pause. Daphne suddenly had a desperate urge to scratch an itch behind her ear, but she dared not move.

"It's worse than I feared," Athena said, eventually. She sounded tired. "It appears our enemy has somehow found out what it can do. Some of it, anyway. You've heard the sirens across the city? The human population thinks it's under attack, but his real target is probably me." Daphne held her breath. She looked through the branches at Penelope. The other cat was agape.

"So the story you told me is true?"

"You didn't believe me?" Athena sounded indignant.

"No, it's, I..." Penelope struggled and failed to correct her faux pas. "It just seemed incredible."

"Well it's true." There was a hint of satisfaction in the grey cat's voice. "However, it is now imperative that we retrieve the object before he uses it to cause even more harm. If he's learned to use it properly, it may be too late. I need to speak to Hermes again; can you send an owl? Better see if you can find Apollo as well." Penelope hesitated. "What now?"

"It's just, well… what can you do if he uses it against you?" There was a tremor in her voice.

"Very little. Only the powerful can truly defend themselves against a concerted direct attack, and only then with difficulty. I'm afraid ordinary animals have no chance." She must have seen the shocked look on her assistant's face and softened her voice. "Don't worry. If he's going to use it against you, he needs to know your name or at least have a good mental image of you first. The statuette is an amplifier and focus. It strengthens thought waves and also projects them powerfully into the mind of the recipient, but when used against an individual it needs a known target to aim for, otherwise it's useless." Penelope looked relieved. She left on her errand. Shortly after, Athena followed her.

Daphne was dumbstruck. She tried to absorb what she'd just heard. Not only had Kratos had a look at her the other night, but she'd told Zelus her name. That had been a mistake. She turned the other details over in her mind. 'Only the powerful can defend themselves… ordinary animals have no chance.' She'd never thought of herself as special, but she was not prepared to be dismissed as 'ordinary.' At least she now had an idea what had happened. How could she defend herself against another attack? Fear knotted her stomach. She supposed her only defence was what she'd always done when someone tried to persuade her to act against her better judgement: be stubborn as hell.

CHAPTER 43

A TIMELY THEFT

KRATOS FINISHED speaking with the last of his officers. Evening drew near, and he was impatient to have another go with his new toy. He didn't want to let it out of his sight, so he issued orders for his subordinates to come to him, rather than visiting them on his rounds as usual. He had to find a good hiding place for his new treasure, but for now fear of retribution for any who went near it would have to suffice. As his last lieutenant left, he issued instructions not to be disturbed, and resumed his study of the artefact. He settled down in front of it. He was building a list of targets and projects, but first it was imperative he concluded the unfinished business with the spy. Kratos closed his eyes and conjured her image in his mind, then projected an instruction.

Daphne was still on the hillside when the new attack came. She jerked and struggled as hard as she could to block the invasion, but he was too powerful and his thoughts overwhelmed her. Experience proved some defence; his control was not as complete as the first time, and the accompanying headache a little more manageable, at least at first. She tried to slow her movements as best she could.

"I don't believe we'd finished our discussion?" A simple command followed the unwelcome greeting. "Walk."

Daphne had no choice but to comply. He was too powerful, but in the small corner of her mind she could still call her own she experimented with some tiny adjustments here and there, to soften the impact. It was only the tiniest act of rebellion, but it was something, although she didn't see how it would help in the long run.

Kratos concentrated on moving her in the direction he wanted. It proved easier than last time; he must be growing more familiar with the control mechanisms. He sensed her putting up a token resistance, but it was feeble and point-less. He settled back to enjoy the view as she trudged out of the Agora and along Adrianou Street. She would soon be with him.

'Right through the front gate,' he thought grimly.

ATOP THE walls of the Acropolis, Apollo looked out at the city. Wrapped up in his thoughts, he'd arrived here as if by accident. Now, as he looked once more at the sea of buildings below, he marvelled at the speed and endeavour of humanity in the years he'd been asleep. Before him were countless buildings and within and between them, thou-sands of people went about their business, criss-crossing the squares and pavements, en route to he knew not where. He envied them. They had a purpose, whereas he felt lost and out of place. Lonely and bereft, he was struggling to keep those friends he had. Idly he scanned the scene below, watching the interplay of vehicles and humans. Something caught his eye. He stiffened, taking in the scene in minute detail despite the distance.

For an instant he froze, and in a moment of clarity he saw alternate futures come tantalisingly close. So close they almost mingled, almost gave him a chance, but then his vision failed, lost in a fog. Could he do it? Could he save both of them? No matter how small the chance, he had to try. The voice echoed in his head once more, like an actor in an empty theatre: 'can an unclean god ever rescue his legacy?' Silently he made a vow: whatever the outcome, he would most certainly purify his soul. In blood.

Apollo turned and flew, faster than the wind, toward the Propylea. Arrow-straight, he sprinted across the uneven rock-strewn plateau, his belly skimming the stones as he vaulted them. At the gap where the grand ceremonial staircase once stood, he didn't slow, but bypassed the steps built for tourists, oblivious to their startled looks, and leaped down in huge bounds from boulder to ledge to slab, each precise landing inch-perfect and true. He streaked through the gate and into the woodland beyond, arcing his trajectory downward toward the Agora.

Jason, looking for Daphne and asking around but getting no replies, saw the golden cat hurtling toward, then past him. Apollo? He watched him go, then followed slowly behind.

UNDER HER enemy's control, Daphne could do little but try to smooth her passage. Her body was no longer her own: the sensation was most odd. She attempted to work with the flow of his instructions rather than against them, smoothing the effect rather than stopping him. As a result, her movements were slightly less stilted than before, but it was only a matter of degree. It did nothing to prevent her feeling like a prisoner in her own head.

Soon she saw the entrance to Kratos' new headquarters. The human gatekeeper paid her little attention as her staccato movement took her past him. She went deeper into the lion's den. Those gang members who were not out and about on raids, or pestering tourists for treats, looked up when they saw her approach. A small crowd soon gathered around her, following her progress as she made a beeline toward their leader. Finally, she was there. The source of her problems was lounging on a small scrubby patch of dry grass, next to a little stone thing. She glanced at it from the corner of her eye, but couldn't make it out properly. Why was it here? More importantly, why was she here? She could guess, but she didn't like any of the answers she could come up with.

After a while his mental grip relaxed slightly, allowing her a little free movement on her own accord. She looked at her surroundings as best she could, but then had to snap back to attention as he issued a new command.

"Sit." Inside she bristled at this new humiliation. This was how you spoke to a dog! Futile anger flickered briefly in the small space of her thoughts she still controlled. Kratos stood up and skirted the object to inspect her more closely. Around them a crowd gathered, gleeful to watch the latest example of their leader's cunning and might, and eager to see him despatch a new unwilling victim.

"We could continue this interview in our private little thought bubble, thanks to my new toy. Do you like it, by the way? Pretty, I think you'd agree." He glanced at the strange object to his right. "But perhaps my devoted followers deserve to hear what you have to say."

Suddenly it stopped, and Daphne staggered slightly. She took a deep breath but remained silent. Kratos looked at the crowd assembling around them. He would take his time to play to the gallery, but in this trial, there would be only one verdict, and justice would be administered swiftly.

"Let's pick up where we left off the other night before we were so rudely interrupted."

She glanced at the thing he was so proud of, a little statuette. How odd. She'd seen nothing like it, even in Delphi, but then she'd never been into the museum—that was for humans. They were very keen to keep cats out.

"I think we can guess what your mission was, but before we hear your confession, tell me about your companions the other night." Suddenly he was in her head again. "Yes, spit it out, all of it, or else."

"Or else what?" she said out loud. There was an audible ripple through the crowd.

"You have courage, I'll grant you that." The little puffs of dust that arose as he paced around her took her attention. She wondered what he wanted to hear, and whether there was any point playing for time. A thought germinated at the back of her mind, so ludicrous she couldn't take it seriously, but just maybe…

"Come on." There was an urgency now. He didn't like to be kept waiting.

"One is called Jason." She paused. He glared at her. "The other is Apollo." The stare he gave her felt almost physical in its intensity. She had to look away.

"More."

"There weren't any more."

She readied herself for a blow. Again, she heard him inside her head.

"No funny games or I will prolong your agony as long as possible, believe me."

She concentrated on the ground in front of her and swallowed.

"We're from Delphi. That's all. We're looking for a friend…"

"I'm not interested in your cover story. Tell me about this colleague of yours. The ginger one."

"Apollo? He's just someone I know. There's nothing else to say. We're friends."

"And how long have you been friends with him, daughter of Peneius?" He caught the confusion in her eyes. "Yes, I've done you the honour of thinking about you. I know more about you than you think. There's no point lying to me anymore. At what point did you put aside your hate? Or is there more to your story? Another twist that you want to share? Someone else in the mix?"

Daphne faltered. A fleeting image passed into her thoughts, of a chase, or a hunt. Maybe. No; desperate flight, a frantic escape, just in time, from a man, beautiful and golden. It vanished, leaving her feeling confused.

A shout went up from her right. Someone on the edge of the crowd. The commotion grew. Kratos looked up, impatient at the interruption. What he saw seemed to enrage him. He stepped back, then with a screech of anger, departed. Daphne watched as her tormentors turned and followed.

STRAIGHT THROUGH the entrance to the Library of Hadrian, Apollo ran. Inside were a few gang members, the stragglers and latecomers finally on their way to see the execution of the spy, but even so his reckless attack seemed suicidal. Kratos was holding court over on the northern side of the site, behind the ancient wall, and that was his target. He caught the gang members totally by surprise, descending on them like a lion among docile antelope. Cries for help went up, and in the distance, some of their colleagues at the back of the crowd turned to see what the fuss was about. A few, led by one of their boldest, sprang into action, closing the ground fast as they sought to rebuff this surprise attack. Apollo saw them coming. He singled out the leader and leapt at him, taking him in mid-air. A sickening rip followed a strangle grip to the throat as his claws opened his enemy's body from his neck to his belly in a spray of red. The gangster fell dying while the ginger cat moved to his next target, nostrils flared, a ferocious light kindled in his eyes. As the noise grew, more of Kratos' mob heard the fight and the cacophony reached the ears of their leader. He paused in delivery of his verdict, his attention diverted. Many of the gang hesitated. Should they wait for his command, or take the initiative and rebuff this lunatic attacker? As confusion grew, many had little choice other than to fight or die. More of them turned to repulse the attacker, others to flee.

Despite his initial success, the odds were now turning against him. Apollo stood over the body of his latest victim and looked up to see many more charging toward him; unfortunately, the animal he wanted most was not among them. He still lingered at the rear. The numbers confronting him were overwhelming. He had done what he could, but there was a limit to what he could achieve alone. It was time to retreat. Past the startled gatekeeper he ran, back onto the street, then turned to the right and fled toward the square. A large contingent of Kratos and Zelus's combined troops pursued him. He passed the entrance to the metro station and turned on to Ermou Street, dodging human traffic and staying well clear of vehicles. In his fury traffic lights fused and a fire hydrant burst from its mooring, a jet of water climbing into the sky. Cars screeched to a halt at the gridlocked junction. Apollo didn't care; he ran on, slowing now as the pursuit dwindled, then stopped. He looked back. He'd wanted the big bully dead, but he had failed in his objective. Hopefully he had, at least, bought her a little time, but now his legacy called. There would be no waiting for others to act. He'd abased himself to ask for help, but it was not forthcoming, and he wouldn't ask again. He was on his own, and the freedom was invigorating.

JASON FOLLOWED Apollo as quickly as he dared, but paused short of the entrance to Hadrian's Library. He watched, astonished at his friend's bravery, or stupidity more like, and paid little heed to the pedestrians dodging around him. There was nothing he could do. It was a relief to see Apollo escape unscathed, but disappointing that he left in another direction. Jason was keen to talk to him and ask him about Daphne's strange behaviour. It would have to wait. Instead, he retraced his steps to the Agora, trying to find anyone who might have seen her.

IN THE growing noise and confusion, they forgot Daphne. Amid the distraction and without pausing for thought, she picked up the statuette in her mouth and ran in the opposite direction. She thought she'd seen an entrance there into the outside world; it was the only chance she had. She'd not gone more than half a dozen paces when a cry went up behind her. Someone had been paying attention.

The gang was split. Many continued toward Apollo to join the fray and see off this impudent intruder. But Kratos heard the alert and turned, remembering his captive. He flew after her, eating up the ground. Dozens of gang members followed his lead.

Daphne had only a few metres' lead. She darted toward the nearby gate and hurled herself at the gap between the railings. It was just wide enough for a small animal like her to fit through, but it wouldn't be easy for anyone larger. There was an instant logjam behind her as her pursuers got in each other's way in their eagerness to follow. Kratos, large as he was, struggled to squeeze between the railings, costing him valuable time. Daphne sped on as fast as she could, not daring to look behind, but extending her advantage. She ran straight ahead down a short street, then came to the corner of a plaza with a lot of restaurant tables beneath large sunshades. Veering sharply right, she ran among them, hoping the obstacle course would further delay her pursuers. Dodging between waiters and around seated customers and their bags slowed her down more than she liked.

Once through the gate, the pursuers were gaining on her. In and out of legs, of both the human and table variety, they sped, homing in on their prey. Daphne could sense them gaining. At the edge of her vision, she glimpsed her tormentor. He had almost caught up. In desperation, she darted right once more and headed for the entrance to the nearest restaurant. Her pursuers hadn't expected the move but instantly changed course, concentrating more on their target than what was in front of them. Kratos and two other gang members ran into the legs of a waiter carrying a large tray of food at shoulder height, knocking him off balance. As he struggled to stay upright, other cats got under his feet and he fell sideways onto the nearest diner. The tray and its content clattered into the middle of a table, smashing plates and glasses, spilling drinks, and splattering food all over those nearby. People jumped to their feet, covered in meat, salad, sauces, dips, juice, and beer. Cats streamed past, oblivious to the outrage, still focused on their pursuit. Other waiters and angry customers kicked out at them, sending some flying into other customers, adding to the mayhem. Someone slammed the restaurant door shut, blocking many of her chasers, but Daphne, Kratos, and half a dozen of her fastest pursuers were already inside. She bolted through a doorway at the end of the bar, a whisker ahead of the gang leader.

The kitchen was small, hot, and crowded. Gas burners were lit and occupied; pans filled with bubbling liquids, or frying calamari or chicken, sat on every ring. Chefs and assistants moved between stations with rapid precision, preparing ingredients, filling or emptying pans, ovens, and larders, assembling meals onto plates, all amid the paraphernalia of a busy lunchtime service. Daphne hurtled into the midst of this ordered activity, adding a huge dollop of chaos to the mix. She twisted and turned, dodging chefs and waiters alike, looking for an escape route, while they tried to block her progress or kick her into submission.

At first, there seemed no way out, and she was close to panic. Hard on her tail, Kratos tried to anticipate her moves and pounce. Mentally she braced herself for the impact, but then she saw the back door open as a staff member came in from the yard beyond. The hydraulic hinge closed, and the door swung shut, but she made it, squeezing through as it slammed behind her. She took a blow to her side as a result, the impact spinning her over and partially winding her. The statuette went flying into the gutter. Daphne was in a back alley, and free, although she feared the pursuit would resume any second. Feeling sore from the impact of the door, she hobbled over to the object and picked it up again. It was slimy with both her saliva and whatever it had just fallen in. She couldn't afford to think about that. She was desperate to put distance between her and her pursuers.

She walked on, limping a little as she caught her breath. The alley was short, and Daphne soon arrived at a narrow, busy thoroughfare. She turned left, in a direction she hoped would take her away from the gang's headquarters, dodging shoppers and keeping an eye out for cats.

In the kitchen, chaos ruled. In his pursuit, Kratos had to veer around annoying humans while his target seemed to slip straight past them. The delay prevented him from following her through the back door. He charged into it, but it was just too heavy, even for his size and bulk. He made a tour of the kitchen, looking for another way out, a window, anything, oblivious to the furious gesticulations of chefs and other staff as they waved dangerous-looking knives and cleavers in his direction. Someone opened the front doors once more, allowing some of his companions an escape route, but that was no good. Kratos looked to see if he could spot an open window.

While he paused, a cook gave him a hefty kick, sending him sideways into a storage rack. Pans and dished clattered around him, but Kratos ignored them. He fixed his eyes on the startled looking man and ran straight at him, leaping upward powerfully. He used the jutting handle of a pan as a springboard and launched himself at the man's face, a mass of teeth and claws. The force of his leap dislodged the pan, tipping its boiling contents into the cook's crotch just as the furious animal reached his face. In shock and sudden pain, the man dropped everything and fell backwards, screaming in agony from both the cat and the liquid scalding his groin and legs, scrabbling to get the frenzied animal off him. In later years the memory of the searing pain faded, but the image of the malevolent intelligence in the animal's eyes remained etched in his brain. The cook's momentum pitched him into the door, forcing it open as he fell backwards into the street. Kratos forgot about his human victim and raced down the alley, back on the trail.

Moving more slowly now, Daphne took a right then left turn, hoping trackers wouldn't be able to follow her scent amid the thronging tourists and shops. She was weary and sore, and the bulky thing she carried made her jaw ache. She was desperate to keep it out of her pursuer's paws if it was as powerful as she'd heard. Emerging onto yet another much quieter street, she felt bewildered. She'd lost her bearings amid the labyrinth of narrow, twisting streets. Ahead, at the end of this one, was the rock wall of the Acropolis, deep in afternoon shadow. At first, she feared she was trapped in a dead end, but then Daphne noticed some steps leading up from the end of the road. She dropped the statuette to exercise her aching jaw and ease the stiffness, but immediately she heard a shout from behind, and the scrabble of paws. Looking over her shoulder Daphne's spirits sank; Kratos, somehow reunited with three of his thugs, had spotted her and was hurtling forward with renewed intent. Terror lent her new reserves of energy. She picked up her treasure and bounded forward. The street rose toward the flight of steps, and the climb made her lungs ache. Daphne was at the limit of her endurance, and the chasers were closing fast.

At the top of the steps, following an instinct, she turned sharp right, relieved that this new road was flat. She accelerated once more, but the chasers were reining her in and the object in her mouth made breathing difficult. Past the last house she flew, and then on their right, she saw railings. There was no time to think. She darted through, barely breaking stride. Panic was the only remaining source of energy driving her forward now, but at least she was heading downhill between trees. She had come in a circle behind and above the Agora, and safety lay tantalisingly close. Behind her, Kratos slid to a halt, frustrated. He was near the heart of his enemy's territory, but he didn't yet dare to venture further with so few followers. It would come sooner rather than later. His prize had been stolen, and he wanted it back. Badly.

CHAPTER 44

A NEW BEGINNING

ADRENALINE AND thoughts of revenge coursed through him. Athena had failed to come up with any kind of solution, and there was no other help available. It was time to act. Apollo chastised himself for failing to realise it from the outset. If you want something done, best do it yourself. A vision of the prison compound fixed in his mind's eye, he set off at a run, determined to see this through.

The bus driver saw him late, a ginger streak running out in front of his bus, far too late to stop. In the end, he didn't have to do anything; his bus stopped anyway with a loud bang even before he could stamp on the brake pedal. He was lucky he had the wheel to stop his momentum, although it jabbed him in the stomach. Fortunately, he hadn't been going so fast. Behind him the passengers weren't so lucky; some painfully crashed into the back of the seat in front, those standing stumbled over buggies and shopping bags or went sprawling on the floor, groceries and other belongings spilled down the aisle. There were angry shouts and wailing babies, but the driver ignored them. He was struggling to take it in; the road had been clear. What had he hit to cause such damage? It couldn't be just a cat? The smashed windscreen and deep vertical indentation up the entire front of the vehicle was the sort of damage you would get if you'd hit a lamppost at speed.

But he had come to a shuddering halt in the middle of the carriageway, not on the verge. The v-shaped dent buckled the floor and warped the passenger entrance. He was lucky his feet didn't get trapped in the wreckage. Mangled plastic and metal meant his steering wheel was out of alignment, the dashboard smashed and the pedals twisted. Somehow he'd escaped injury, but the door of his cab into the bus wouldn't open; he had to exit via the side door.

When he stood in front and observed the damage, he just scratched his head. There was no sign of a body, in fact, no tangible obstacle anywhere. The front of the bus looked even worse from outside, but he was at a loss to understand what could have caused such damage. It was incapable of moving, but with no sign of an impediment the driver wondered what he would put on the accident report.

BLACKNESS ALTERNATED with light, and strange visions flooded his thoughts. Sounds, amplified and distorted, drifted across his consciousness; snatches of a conversation far away, traffic, the song of birds, the backdrop of everyday life.

He stood on a promontory looking across a turbulent sea. The day was bright, but the wind and the currents were always strong here. Waves broke in blue and green, and white spindrift spun from their crests. Behind him lay a small city of temples and squares interspersed with fine houses. In the distance a theatre, to his right boats bobbed up and down by the quayside. People went about their business. This was a prosperous place, a place of commerce and pilgrimage. His island. But no one acknowledged him as he walked among them. No one seemed to see him or hear his friendly greeting. It was puzzling. Was this death, finally? The idea was almost thrilling. He'd never realised he could die, but…

Maybe it was some form of purgatory? He'd heard people talk about it in solemn tones, but never paid too much attention; it was somebody else's religion, not his. If he was dead, why wasn't he in the halls of his uncle, an honoured guest in his dread realm? Nothing made sense, and now his vision shifted. He was floating above an unremarkable patch of scrubby yellowing grass in the middle of a city. It was criss-crossed by paths and dotted with the occasional feebly struggling bush or stunted tree. Beneath a park bench was a body, one of the innumerable feral cats that infested this place. Thin, wasted, misshapen, with its limbs at odd angles. Dried blood caked the mouth. Mucus dripped below an eye. Flies had gathered, but there was still the faintest of breath, so they dared not feast or lay their eggs yet. No passers-by paid it any attention. It was just one of many. The park-keepers would clear it away before long.

The realisation grew that what he was looking at, on the ground below, was his body; his travel cloak, the shroud he wore in this version of reality, the vehicle in which they'd trapped him all these centuries since he foolishly agreed to their hasty transformation. Observing it dispassionately, he had to admit it had seen better days, but the dead all look like lifeless clay once the vital spark has gone. Was it the case here? The idea had some appeal. He didn't know what came next; perhaps a long dreamless sleep? It wouldn't be so bad—he felt tired enough to sleep forever. Perhaps fresh adventures awaited in some far distant realm? He was still musing on the possibilities when the pain returned, exquisite and agonising. Its intensity appalled him, but with a pang of regret, it forced him to acknowledge he was still alive. With this awareness returned the all too familiar concerns and emotions: guilt, worry, anxiety, anger. He already missed being dead, if that's what it had been. He'd had no worries. The experience had been soothing, peaceful even. Now, he lay beneath the bench in the middle of a small park, more dead than alive, but wracked with pain and consumed by anguish at this additional delay in his race to rescue Olympia. He was losing time, time she couldn't afford, and nobody, not even himself with his full powers, could pause Chronos in his count.

The floating sensation ceased. His eyes flickered open and feebly, he licked his lips, tasting the congealed blood. It was far too soon to move any limbs; he had too much healing to do. Fortunately, it was one of his skills. He concentrated on knitting bones back together and weaving snapped sinews, healing punctured organs and closing wounds. With a tiny sigh, he knew he would ache for a long time, but put the thought from his mind. His mistreated body would just have to cope while its pilot rediscovered his form. For now, a brief sleep would help; he was still too weak to stand.

ANGER COURSED through him, icy fire flowing through his veins. Zeus had taken his beloved son, Asclepius, a favourite among all his children, killed by a thunderbolt and sent to the land of the dead. His crime? To heal the sick and prolong their lives, keeping them out of Hades' jealous clutches for longer than the Lord of the Dead deemed reasonable. His son didn't deserve to die; he was the noblest of them all. He'd brought humanity such riches: knowledge of healing, an understanding of disease, the foundation of medicine, gifts beyond price.

With deadly purpose he tracked down the Cyclops, Zeus's armourers, the one-eyed giants who forged his thunderbolts, those super-weapons that ensured the Sky

Father's invincibility, and in revenge, slew them one by one. This time he'd gone too far. This time his father was beside himself. This time he felt the heat of his wrath. They glared at each other, each filled with righteous fury, neither prepared to back down, but Zeus was still the stronger and the others stood by his side; he faced an eternity in Tartarus. Hades grinned and held the gates open himself. To his lasting shame his mother, on her knees, pleaded his case and the sentence was reduced: a year's hard labour at the Court of King Admetus.

Over time, as he carried out his sentence, he reflected on his sins and the constant turmoil in his soul. A ferocious temper sat uncomfortably alongside his peaceful intent, the aspect of himself he sought to promote. No matter how hard he tried, he'd always struggled to master the constant war between them in his heart, the curse of so many artists ever since. But control it, he must. He made a solemn vow to change his ways. He was never prone to self-analysis, but as he considered the two sides of his nature, a phrase sprang into his mind. It would look good, he thought, carved into the lintel of his temple at Delphi, above the entrance, a lesson to his followers down the years: know thyself.

In this way, he rediscovered the beginnings of wisdom.

NIGHT HAD long been swallowed by the dawn of a new day before he opened his eyes again and tried to move. To his slight surprise, his limbs obeyed their orders. He rolled onto his stomach, and with the trembling unsteadiness of the newborn, slowly stood. Bones cracked and sinews creaked, but they held firm. He walked around, tentative at first, then stretching and experimenting until he was confident of his movement once more. Then he sat and had a thorough wash. Today would be a red day, a

331

day of heroism and dread, haunted by the spectre of death, leavened by the chance to save lives. He was ready.

Apollo was still a stranger in this modern city, but he knew his destination with absolute certainty and nothing now would stop him. The wind of his passing stirred the leaves on the trees.

CHAPTER 45

SECOND LIEUTENANT SAMARAS

DAPHNE STOOD before Athena. She dropped the statuette on the ground between them.

"I believe you wanted this."

The grey cat looked at her. Against all expectations, this most unassuming creature had delivered her prize back to her. The object she'd craved for so long lay on its side in the dust between them, covered in saliva and bearing a couple of new scratches, but remarkably well preserved considering the journey it had just endured.

"Thank you." It was an inadequate way to convey the thanks and relief she felt, but she hardly knew where to begin, and in any case, she'd rarely had occasion to be thankful to mortals. There was something unusual about this young animal; something she couldn't put a claw on. "You have hidden depths," was all she could come up with. Daphne, grateful to find someone who could look after this dangerous object and keep it safe and hidden from her nemesis, didn't mind. "Now, if you'll forgive me, I have things to do." Athena looked askance at the grubby statuette, but picked it up in her mouth and made her way into the trees, up the hill.

Her destination was not a great distance away. She skirted Areopagus Hill and bypassed Pnyx, heading toward the streets to the south of the National Observatory, making for an area of neat houses next to the woods. She turned into them, took a couple of turns, and approached a modest but well-maintained property. Treating her possession with care, she slipped through the fence and went around to the rear where there was a cat flap built into a door. Without hesitating, she stepped through and into the room beyond: her secret sanctuary.

Athena shared this house with her human servant, a divorced middle-aged man whose children had long since left home. His job as a police officer meant he kept irregular hours and given the cat would sometimes disappear for days, the arrangement suited them both. He enjoyed her company when she was there, and as long as he kept a well-stocked cupboard, she was happy enough. From Athena's point of view, this was a place she could retreat to when she needed time to think, or when she became bored with the petty politics of Athenian feline society. She kept it hidden from even the closest of her acolytes.

She placed the statuette in the middle of the floor and stepped back to admire it once more. It was still a bit muddy, but she could clean it up later. First, it was time to reacquaint herself with its ancient mechanisms. She settled down on a nearby cushion and stared at it. Then she closed her eyes and studied it in her mind's eye. Once fixed there, she projected her thoughts toward it, using them to probe and examine it. At first she couldn't remember what to do, so out of practice was she, and the old pathways seemed overgrown. But with persistence and time, she was confident she could reopen them once more. Impatience slowed her progress. After another miscue, she opened her eyes and glared at the artefact in annoyance. The last time she'd used this thing, she was her old self: as a cat, reviving a connection might take longer than she'd like. It was just as well the detective wasn't at home. She didn't want any distractions. As the evening drew on, she made some progress but found it tiring. After a while, she hid it behind a bookcase and fell into so deep a sleep that she didn't hear him return.

Athena woke in the grey light before dawn and returned to her practice, finally making the breakthrough she sought: the 'muscle memory' of her mind began to renew acquaintance with the device. Elated, she wandered through the house, irritated that the man was not yet awake. Should she force the matter? She pushed at the bedroom door but saw he was still asleep. She considered jumping on him, but with reluctance rejected the idea as potentially counterproductive, and returned downstairs to wait.

How convenient it would be if she could simply reveal her true self to him, as she once could? That was no longer possible, and she had no desire to revisit the source of that particular grievance, so instead she decided that projecting an image of herself through the artefact would be an acceptable alternative. She considered its range. In olden times she had used it to communicate with humans right across the Aegean without having to leave her palatial home, and she wondered if she still had the ability, but right now there was no one she felt like contacting. Not yet, at any rate.

Waiting upon a human was intensely annoying for any deity, and her frustration mounted. She vented it by ploughing furrows in the carpet. At last, she heard him stirring upstairs, but it still took him an interminable amount of time to descend for the strong black coffee which usually passed as breakfast. Athena composed herself and watched him intently as he entered the room. He gave her an affectionate greeting, but as he approached to tickle her between the ears, something incredible happened. To his surprise, he and the cat were no longer alone; to his left, glowing brightly and filling the room, stood a tall warrior woman in a shining breastplate, her tall helmet and tip of her spear brushing the ceiling. His eyes widened in astonishment and he fell back into an armchair.

Dazzling green eyes surveyed him judgementally, carrying more than a hint of disdain. He groped for words, but before he could react, she spoke, her voice melodious but powerful.

"Mortal, well met. I am Athena, daughter of Zeus, Patron of this city. I have a task for you."

After being kept waiting so long, Athena was in no mood for pleasantries. She gave the man an enquiring look.

Her host/servant appeared thunderstruck. He just sat there, his jaw moving but no words issuing forth. This was not the reaction she expected or wanted. She wondered if he was a bit of a simpleton, but with a small sigh, she reflected that today's generation was a little out of practice in greeting deities. She had little choice but to grant him some leeway. If he'd known better, of course, he would kneel or preferably be lying flat on his belly, eyes to the ground, awaiting her gracious invitation to speak or stand. He would have brought a goat or lamb to sacrifice at her altar, killing it according to the appropriate ritual before sprinkling its blood and burning some meat as an offering, chanting an appropriate incantation as the smoke rose heavenwards in her honour, but times had changed. At least he had cleansed himself before approaching her, she supposed; it certainly took long enough.

The man was lost for words. He stared at the bright apparition before him, then at the cat, sitting on its cushion and also giving him a piercing stare, then back at the woman. He cleared his throat.

"Er…"

She waited, her patience growing thin. Were today's humans even more stupid than their ancestors? Trying to regain some sense of dignity, the man clambered to his feet, but even at his full height, she towered above him.

"Greetings my lady, welcome," he finally offered, gradually coming back to his senses. Samaras needed coffee, anything, to help make sense of this weird situation.

A thought struck him. "Are you the real Athena?" he blurted. "The goddess Athena?" Suddenly he felt awed, stunned, and bewildered all at once. Were the old legends true?

"The same," she replied, a little icily. This seemed to be the closest she would get to supplication this morning, so she might as well get down to business. "I need you to do something for me."

Second Lieutenant Samaras gawped at her again, his eyes like saucers. She found it vaguely disconcerting.

"There has been some criminal activity…"

Now he was on solid ground. "You don't need to tell me, I…"

"Silence!" She glared at him. He stopped mid-sentence. "… Concerning cats. In the western districts a band of brigands has captured many animals, both cats and dogs, and is using them for nefarious purposes. Puppies are being bred for sale, some cats as well. Others are disappearing, presumably killed for reasons I have yet to discern. You must stop this barbaric behaviour. You are with the Athens police. It falls upon you to carry out my will. I require you to apprehend, eliminate, or banish the culprits according to your preference, and free the animals." She softened her tone, leaning toward him and carrying on in a far more convivial manner. "Do this small thing for me, and I will look favourably on you. I will advance your career as a detective. You will go on to greatness." She stood back, imperious again. "Thwart me and you will forever languish in obscurity, filing traffic reports, forgotten." She glared at him, her eyes burning with intensity.

The Lieutenant shrank back into his chair, not wanting to get on the wrong side of this strange woman, goddess or not. "Well, um, I'll have a look, of course, but with all this suspected terrorist activity…" He wavered before the intensity of her stare. For a moment her aura intensified before she brought it under control. She did not like being rebuffed. Athena arched an eyebrow. "I'll get onto it immediately," he added, wondering if her spear was as sharp as it looked. Samaras tried to give her an encouraging smile.

The goddess gave him an appraising look. "Don't disappoint me," she said, and promptly vanished.

He slumped back down in his chair. What had happened? He ran his fingers through his hair and rubbed his face as if to wake up, then looked up again to check she'd truly gone, and let out a long breath of relief. Then he noticed the grey cat. It had not moved and was giving him a very persistent appraising stare. It made him uncomfortable.

"I know, I know, I'll look into it, I promise," he told it and got up. It surprised him by giving a low growl in response. "OK, OK, urgently. Today. Keep your fur on." It gave him a suspicious look. He went to the small kitchen area and tried to collect his thoughts. Coffee, that was it. He really needed coffee. Strong and black. An inquiring chirruping miaow followed him. "It's OK, I think I've got some tuna," he shouted over his shoulder, then stopped himself. Had he ever had such a frank exchange with his cat before? She seemed to understand every word. He must be going mad. Behind him, he heard a loud purr.

CHAPTER 46

RESCUE

AT HIS desk, Police Second Lieutenant Samaras hung the jacket of his uniform over the back of his chair, and tried to put the morning's episode to the back of his mind. In the bright light of day here at work, it seemed too incredible to have happened. His caseload was already too long. A wild goose chase to somewhere in western Athens to search for some stray cats and dogs wouldn't win him any favours with his boss. It was the last thing he needed.

She didn't even give me an address, he grumbled to himself. He sighed and tried to concentrate. Most of his colleagues were chasing leads, no matter how tenuous, on the terror attacks that had struck without warning across the city to devastating effect. Samaras felt overlooked. His bosses had assigned almost everyone to the new investigations except him. He was one of a small remnant expected to take over and keep on top of existing investigations. What did it say about his promotion prospects?

A new report had landed on his desk, passed across from one of his recently reassigned neighbors. Samaras scanned the cover page and summery with little enthusiasm, unable to shake off a nagging resentment that the really interesting work was passing him by. He attempted to concentrate. An informant had told his handler about an illegal fur-farming operation up north. Garments were being passed off as being of exotic pelts, but analysis showed they were made from lower-quality materials. Samaras frowned at it, weighing up its importance. It was at the other end of the country, surely one to pass on to colleagues in Thessaloniki. He put it to one side and moved to the next item.

The duty officer from the front desk stopped next to him and handed Samaras a handwritten note. "One of the patrol cars was doing the rounds in Tavros first thing, and they've reported something strange. A warehouse is being mobbed by an unusual number of birds."

The detective glanced at the note. "What do you mean, 'unusual'?"

"A huge number, they said. Hundreds. Crows and ravens mainly, not seabirds. They said they didn't know so many lived in the city. It's like they're staking it out. I wondered if you'd have time to take a closer look?"

"Why didn't they stop at the time?"

"They got a call to assist at the scene of the derailment at Lefka, and now their shift's ended, but they think someone ought to look." He gave the detective an apologetic look. "You never know, with all the strange stuff that's been happening."

Detective Samaras wasn't prepared to give in easily. "What are they doing—the birds I mean?"

The sergeant wrinkled his nose, thinking. "Well, they said that they're perching on the roof, and they keep flying over it, making a hell of a racket. It's just as well it's not a residential neighbourhood, but the local businesses will probably send in complaints if this keeps up, and there could be public hygiene aspects. I've never heard of anything like it, and the thought crossed my mind that these are all carrion birds, if you take my meaning?"

The detective gave him a long, appraising look. "As if I've not got enough to do?" he sighed. "Alright, leave it with me, I'll head out there. I could do with some fresh air."

IT WAS satisfying to see the birds still flocking above the place when he arrived. Apollo paused on the road before the front entrance. A large 4x4 and a van were parked either side of the door. As if on cue, it opened and a man stepped out carrying a large plastic crate with a briefcase balanced on top. For an instant, their eyes met. Something in the cat's eye made the man drop the crate, but he didn't have time to react. In the same instant, the animal's jaws clamped around his throat, huge claws ripping his shoulders and neck. He fell backward with a truncated scream.

The sound brought his companions to the entrance, but the instant they stepped outside they came under attack from wave after wave of crows, jackdaws, and ravens swooping down from above. Any exposed flesh was a target as they darted in, pecked viciously, and retreated for another turn while their place was taken by another. With no chance of rescuing their fallen colleague, the men struggled to defend themselves and regain the building.

TAVROS WAS such a short drive from the police station that Samaras felt guilty taking the car, but he supposed he'd better. His initial doubts faded as soon as he saw the birds; he'd seen nothing like it. The number of large black carrion birds thronging the compound below and perched on adjacent rooftops was astonishing. It surprised him people hadn't complained, starting with the owners of nearby buildings, but then with the recession, many of them in this district were closed or abandoned. But surely anyone within earshot would want this avian menace dealt with? Most pertinently though, what was attracting them?

He stopped a hundred metres short and got out of his

car to have a better look. The cawing was cacophonous, as if they were trying to bring as much attention to themselves as possible, but there was a blur of action by the entrance. Some kind of fight seemed to be underway, with figures scrambling on the ground. He couldn't make them out; they were just a blur. Behind, two or three men were trying to retreat into the doorway beneath a concerted attack from above. Samaras climbed back into his car and got on the radio to call for support.

A SHORT while later, in rather dramatic fashion, three police cars and a van, arriving from both ends of the street, drew up outside the building behind Second Lieutenant Samaras's car. The assault ceased, leaving a man's inert body between the vehicles, eyes staring sightlessly into the sky. He averted his eyes; it was not a pretty sight. The victim lay in a pool of blood, his throat ripped out, and his head and neck covered in bite wounds and deep gashes. A police officer brought a blanket to cover the body while others entered the building. The remaining humans had been arrested and driven away in a police van. A veterinary officer approached the detective. She looked wary.

"We need to keep a lookout."

"For what?"

As if to demonstrate, the woman looked past Samaras and down the street. "A large predator, possibly a lion or something similar."

A dismissive remark died on his lips as the detective saw she wasn't joking. "What do you mean?" She looked down at the body beneath the sheet, its feet poking out the end.

"The marks on his neck and head. I've never seen any-thing like it, but the severity of the claw marks, the size of the puncture wounds, and so on, they're different. I don't have a lot of experience with large predators, but to me they look like the kind of wounds you might get from a big cat." She looked him in the eye, saw his scepticism. "I mean a really big cat, a lion or a tiger, something like that."

"But I was here; I would have seen it."

She shrugged and went inside. He reconsidered. After the morning he'd had, Second Lieutenant Samaras was prepared to believe just about anything.

Police and animal protection personnel were soon swarming all over the building and the yard beyond. In their midst Apollo stepped, unnoticed. The interior of the compound was like a war zone. The number of captives was higher than he'd expected, and many were in a poor condition, physically malnourished, or suffering from severe mental stress and anxiety, or both. They might never recover. Apollo's outrage grew with every step. He weaved a path between the cages until he came to one at the back in the corner. There, looking thinner than he'd ever seen her, was Olympia. Relief almost overwhelmed the ginger cat. He pushed against the wire mesh. On the other side, Olympia did likewise as they attempted to butt their heads together. For several minutes he could do nothing more than give her reassurances the ordeal was finally over.

Getting her out was going to demand quick movement and good timing. Humans were everywhere, taking photographs, making notes, opening cages, and stepping in to treat the worst affected. Olympia's pen was one of the last to be opened. A young woman with latex gloves stepped in to collect animals to place into a rescue-branded carry-case. Olympia waited until she had hold of her cell-companion.

"Now!" Apollo yelled, and she ran for the door. The woman cursed, annoyed she hadn't closed it, but she didn't want to drop her charge. Olympia shot past. Following

Apollo, she swerved and dodged past human legs and other obstacles across the yard and down the corridor. Fortunately, the front entrance had been wedged open as people came and went, so they could easily break through into the street. They took a right turn and headed up the road. No one paid any attention; there were too many serious cases to deal with.

A hundred meters down the road, they stopped. Olympia was struggling, breathing hard. She had lost weight during her captivity and looked weak, swaying slightly on her feet. Apollo studied her with concern and searched her face. He could see the haunted look of someone who has witnessed too much horror and wasn't quite able to believe she was free, and held her in his gaze. She scanned his face, searching for hope, for a sign that the terror was over, but inside her head, the film kept playing on repeat; the noises, the smells, the underlying fear, and the terror of those taken away.

Instinctively he pressed his forehead into hers, stood close to her, body to body, purring gently. He nuzzled an ear. It was a simple instinctive gesture, but he put all of his healing power into it. Guilt was his overriding emotion. Guilt about the time it had taken to rescue her, but above all with the disloyalty that had guided his thoughts; he'd let his dreams of Daphne rule him all this time. She'd been the one driving his feelings, and Olympia had become merely an afterthought. Apollo didn't love Olympia. Not really, not deeply, and certainly not in the way she'd hoped, but he owed her a debt of gratitude for her companionship, if nothing else, and for the litter of kittens she was carrying: his legacy. He closed his eyes and concentrated his thoughts. It was a start, but she would need a lot more time to be anything like her usual self.

On a practical level, they had to take it steadily.

Olympia's energy levels were low, but just being under an open sky once more made her feel better. Barely aware of her surroundings, she just followed his lead. As far as possible Apollo walked alongside, keeping a watchful eye on every step. His initial elation at rescuing her evaporated. Now he just wanted to get her somewhere safe, while all the time knowing he was late for his appointment with a different destiny. One that couldn't wait. They walked down the road into a deepening gloom as storm clouds gathered over the city centre.

CHAPTER 47

THE SECOND BATTLE
OF MONASTIRAKI

AS THE day wore on, the heat built, becoming more oppressive by the hour. Bright morning sunshine gave way to dull flat light, and in the city centre a sense of foreboding was building. The two sides gathered, weary but wary, everyone aware of the impending climax to their struggle. Kratos and Zelus still had the numbers, but they had a hard job to motivate their followers for one last effort. Most had expected to be resting, enjoying the rich pickings promised by their victory. Many of them grumbled when safely out of earshot of the leaders or their kin. Kratos needed to use all his assertiveness to stir them up for one last push. The brothers avoided each other as far as possible, each taking a different wing of their army. Kratos was still reeling from the theft of the artefact by the infuriating little spy. He should have crushed her when he had the chance. Thoughts of revenge filled his head, together with a steely determination to make Athena pay. He also wanted the artefact, and the power it could bestow; it was the key to all his future ambitions.

A short way across town, purposefully moving in file, was another gang with Bia at their head. As Hermes had foreseen, she had circled the Acropolis and Athena's unknown forces, to rendezvous with her kin via the narrow winding streets of the Plaka itself. She was in no mood to let her brothers take all the spoils.

In the Agora, beneath the trees, Athena was restless. Her thoughts flicked from subject to subject, never resting for long. Once more she ran through the scenarios, weighing up the opposing forces, their experience, and motivation. Where was her damned brother? She could certainly use his uncouth brawn right now. What of Bia? Could she resist joining in, and if so, how many did she need to hold back to prevent them surprising her forces from the rear? She paced up and down, her mind's eye far away from the nervous-looking cats assembled before her. Daphne and Jason sat beside one another. Neither spoke much, just the occasional reassuring nervous purr or nuzzle. Both knew the stakes were high.

"I wish Apollo was here," muttered Jason, eventually. Daphne wasn't so sure. The images in her mind triggered by Kratos had unnerved her, and now she didn't know what to believe. Probably she was just being stupid. She tried to take her mind off him.

In Syntagma Square, a few rather battered survivors of the Plaka gang assembled. They grumbled to one another about their misfortune. Most bore barely healed wounds. Few looked in any shape to fight, yet here they were, hoping against hope for some sort of miracle, although for there to be any chance of one, they first needed to see their erstwhile leader. Their relief was great when they saw him flanked by his sons striding across the square, apparently without a care in the world. Large in person, and larger-than-life in reputation, he approached them with a swashbuckling, almost cavalier attitude.

"Well met, my friends," he rumbled in his basso profundo. He scanned them, offering a simple greeting here, delivering a hearty message there. His mere presence lifted their spirits. With Ares beside them, anything was possible. He moved among them, offering encouragement and rousing words, but inwardly he worried about their number and condition. Perhaps he had been away too long. Phobos and Deimos held back on the edge of the group. By nature cooler and more reserved than their father, they were far less emotionally engaged and more calculating. They would play their part, but they would not lead the attack. Ares addressed them all.

"Today is a great day. Today is the day we reclaim our home," he roared. "Are you with me?" He didn't wait for the answer, but turned and moved off smartly, heading toward Monastiraki Square.

The day darkened as cloud built upon cloud, towering above the city. With the sun obscured, night seemed to arrive prematurely. Oppressive, humid air trapped beneath the clouds sapped energy along with the willpower of the gangs. They were harder to motivate today. Time crawled. Kratos and Zelus watched the square from the Library of Hadrian, Zelus keen to attack, Kratos instinctively cautious. He wanted the artefact badly, but there is more than one way to win a battle, and his natural hesitancy was verging on indecision. Should he commit his forces not knowing what they were up against, or would it be better to wait and watch the enemy waste their energy on a futile attack? As he agonised over the decision, the tension around the square mounted.

A few hundred metres away, Athena was struggling with the similar thoughts. Finally, she could bear it no more. She nodded to her lieutenants, and they assembled the cats. They were too few, it was clear to see. This was a roll of the dice such as she'd not played for many a year; she just had to trust in others to play their part as had been agreed. Slowly but purposefully they made their way down Ifestou Street toward the square.

Rea was the first to see them coming. "They're here," she shouted.

Kratos looked up sharply to see Athena and her rag-tag army, and his spirits rose. "Is that all they've got?" Turning to his troops, he raised his voice."This lot's no match for us. Let's sort this rabble out once and for all," he shouted and led them into the square. They formed pods on either side, still reluctant, but cowed beneath the power of his will. Further along, Zelus's forces emulated them, shuffling forth, unsure what lay before them. For a moment there was silence; then it began.

Through the gloom and the sticky, oppressive heat, there was an intense flash as lightning hit the summit of the Acropolis, accompanied by a hideous tearing sound as if the sky was being ripped in two. It reverberated and echoed from the walls. Almost immediately, hailstones the size of marbles rained down, bouncing from the pavement, ricocheting from the roofs. Tourists caught out by the sudden downpour dived for cover in shops and restaurants. The two armies, driven by the willpower of their leaders, were focused intently on each other and took no notice. It was as if someone had fired a starting gun. They hurled themselves at one another in a mass of yelping and yowling that was drowned out by more thunder and flashes of lightning. Amidst the apocalyptic scene, duels broke out all over the square as cats fought bitterly to the death. No quarter was given or demanded; the fighting was vicious. Flesh was ripped, bones crunched between powerful jaws. Victims screamed in pain and fear, their cries lost amid the mayhem. The fighting was most intense around the leaders, Athena on the one side, Zelus and Kratos on the other. Athena strove to get to grips with one or other of the brothers, but they were kept apart by frenzied foot-soldiers flinging themselves at her and her companions, driven on by the spiteful mental grip of their overlords. She was getting nowhere.

Into the mayhem, Bia and her gang arrived. They paused at the southern tip of the square while she took in the scene before her. She soon picked out Athena surrounded by the remnant of the Plaka gang and her followers.

"So few," she scoffed. "We could have taken over years ago." Facing them in the middle of the square were her brothers. They had the numbers and the momentum. She turned to her followers. "This should be easy," she yelled. "Let's sort the old grey fool out once and for all." She led the charge.

Jason was in the thick of the fighting, Daphne nearby. He tried to keep an eye out for her, but it was impossible amid the mayhem. Daphne was just relieved the waiting was over. She pawed nervously at the ground. Small and frightened though she was, she wanted to do her part. She wouldn't let anyone down.

Lightning danced around the old town, and the walls reverberated with the sound of thunder. The hailstones gave way to torrential rain, but the combatants ignored it. Skirmishes were taking place around the square and blood flowed into the gutters. It looked bad for Athena. Kratos and Zelus, now abetted by Bia and her gang, were just too strong, and her numbers were thinning. But then, with a yowling battle cry heard even above the din of the storm, Ares and his ragged band of survivors emerged from Mitropoleos street.

Kratos looked up, shocked to see the old warlord back. For a moment his hopes wavered, but then he saw how few they were and how feeble they looked. This was still going to be his victory. He shrugged off his immediate attacker and tried to make his way toward Ares to see off the big oaf once and for all. But the new arrivals had more of an impact than their numbers suggested. Phobos and Deimos attacked on the flanks, spreading confusion, havoc, and panic wherever they went, and Ares in his fury was unstoppable, flinging the bodies of his enemies aside with a hideous, gleeful relish. For a while, the outcome hung in the balance.

Within the wider melee, duels were taking place all over the square. Jason and Daphne were in the thick of it, close to Athena. They dodged, struck, bit, wove, disengaged, reengaged, and grappled for all they were worth. Jason was desperate to even the score with the murderous Kratos. He was close to the big gang leader, but not close enough. Daphne ducked beneath an assailant and found herself face to face with him.

"Oh, it's the pretty little thief," he sneered. "Time's up."

He leaped at her in a frenzy of teeth and claws, but she surprised him, dancing backwards and sideways so that he swiped at thin air. She kept her focus on him as he turned toward her once more. Again he charged, and, like a small matador, she ducked under his blow and wove past him again, this time getting in a swipe of her own in passing. She was pleased to see a red furrow along his flank. Enraged, he spun and flew at her once more, and again she danced away, taunting him. Darting forward with a speed he could not match, she clawed his nose. Like an enraged bull he charged on and she spun away once more, but this time it went wrong. This time it didn't work. This time there was a screech of brakes and a heavy thud. Absorbed in her fight, she had danced too far into the road. This time she didn't get up.

At first, Kratos was bewildered, then delighted. He raised his head and let out a victory yowl. Jason, closer now, was struggling to take it in. He artlessly launched himself at the big cat but was effortlessly swatted aside. He tried again, but savage bites and blows left him wounded and panting for breath. The gang leader stood over him, crowing. It was all over. Most animals would have given up by now, but this was different. Jason's mind was numb with a different kind of pain; if she's gone, I don't want to be here. Head spinning, he struggled to his feet and mustered all his reserves for one last attack. He never got the chance.

A dazzling light cut across his vision, momentarily blinding him. The big cat barely saw it coming and had only just begun to adjust his position before he was knocked sideways and bowled right over by a glowing ginger and white thunderbolt. The two of them rolled over in a ferocious wrestling match. Jason crouched, trying to take it all in. A huge ginger cat had clamped his jaws around Kratos's throat and was shaking him like a rag doll. His claws raked the russet cat's neck and head. Despite his size and strength, Kratos had no response to the sheer power and venom of his attacker. He tried to break free, but couldn't. This was a force beyond nature; this was something else. Apollo's teeth held him in a chokehold that punctured his throat and would have quickly killed any lesser being. Beaten, the big cat teetered on the brink, but somehow clung to life. Apollo threw him down in disgust one last time and stood over him menacingly.

At bay, bruised, bloodied and battered, Kratos glared up at his attacker. Despite his wounds, he managed a ragged, croaking laugh, taunting him. "Here at last. Too little too late." His breathing was ragged and his words came in short bursts. Kratos cast a quick glance at the mayhem surrounding them. "It looks like you've miscalculated, Shining One, and I thought you were supposed to be the master of logic. I've won. Your time is over. Go back, this is no longer your fight." He paused, panting for breath, then continued. "You're stronger than you look, I'll grant, but still you are weak. The world respects strength today, not useless chit-chat. You are feeble. Aimless. Past it." He paused, sucking in air, while the ginger cat glared at him, then resumed his taunts. "You might have surprised me, but you can't kill me," he gasped, "I'm one of you. I'm immortal." He laughed once again, wheezing and panting but flaunting his defiance. Still, he had to avert his eyes from Apollo's scorching glare; it was like looking into the sun.

"Titan or no, I can send you back to Tartarus where you belong," the ginger cat snarled. Kratos just lay in front of him, panting. Trying to breathe was painful. Several bones were broken. His ribs ached.

"You can't," he managed, eventually. "Zeus protects me."

Apollo's glare intensified as if it would melt stone.

"We fought with him all those years ago. We were allies. Maybe you've forgotten? It was me who pinned Prometheus to the rock with those iron chains. Zeus likes me. He always has. Then, eventually, he set the rest of my kin free; all of them. Even Atlas. He's made peace with us. You cannot undo it, the sacred treaty." He dared a spiteful glance at his enemy and couldn't resist a sneer. "Even the mighty Apollo bows before Zeus."

It was as if time stopped. Apollo glared at his foe, his expression unreadable. Behind him, lightning flashed, but he took no heed. The moment stretched. Then a strange look came over his face, accompanying a memory. A picture of a rustic barn in the mountains, long ago. His mouth parted slightly into an almost wolfish grin.

"I'll argue with him later. It won't be the first time," he said and fell upon his foe, joyously embracing all the dark and righteous fury in his soul. Kratos howled in unearthly agony as ten razors slashed his pelt, helpless to stop his flesh being torn and stripped away. His screams echoed from the buildings, searing through the storm, and as they heard them all the fight went from his followers, soaking into the rain puddling around their feet. Some shook their heads as if waking from a dream; others looked at each other, wondering how it was that they were here, and why? The invisible hold he had over them, brittle as glass, shattered, and they fled. Zelus could only gawp in horror. Bia bowed her head to hide her face, the urge for conquest gone. Even Athena and Ares looked stunned. Apollo raised his head to look at them, his maw red from his bloody work, his eyes still blazing in fury undimmed. Red too were his paws and chest; at his feet an unrecognisable grizzly lump of flesh that held no life. They looked away.

Kratos' death sent shockwaves through the aether, like ripples on a still pool, unnoticed by mortals but as high and clear as the ringing of a bell on the still midnight air by those who could sense that realm. In their exile on the slopes of Parnassus, Zeus and Hera looked up sharply; deep in the woodland groves of Arcadia, a white cat paused her hunt, momentarily distracted; in a shepherd's hut high in the mountains of Thessaly a large copper-brown tabby, dozing on the hearth, looked up, his eyes narrowing in thought, and at the back of a cavernous beach bar on Mykonos beneath a banquet seat, lying amid the detritus of the previous night's party and trying to sleep off its excesses, a long-haired red tabby, the one they all tried to forget, opened a wine-dark eye to a snake-like slit, and absorbed the news. A god was dead.

CHAPTER 48

STYX

THE RAIN eased. The battle was over, but there was little joy in victory. Athena, Ares, and Hermes were slack-jawed; Zelus cowering at Ares' feet looked both horrified and indignant. Bia was already sneaking off with her supporters, back in the direction from which she'd arrived. All eyes were fixed on the ginger cat in his ferocious, bloody glory. He flung back his head, and a roar filled the square, a noise no ordinary cat could make. It was over. He looked around at them, defying any challenge, his eyes still burning with righteous fire.

Athena moved to his shoulder. Even her warrior spirit seemed unnerved by his savagery; still her proximity had a calming effect and his monumental wrath subsided. Across the square, an eerie silence fell.

"You'd better leave. Take the others and head to the Agora. I've got this," she said.

As she spoke, vans drew up at the roadside, humans clambering out and unloading wire mesh crates. Wounded stragglers from the defeated gangs tried to escape the advancing humans who deployed nets to catch them. Others advanced across the square, tending to the wounded, collecting the dead. They gave the Olympians a wide berth as if they didn't see them.

Apollo turned to the victors, most of whom seemed to be unsteady on their feet and in a state of shock. His insane

354

rage ebbed away; the returning tide brought a strange ennui. The monster was defeated, but could he endure his victory?

He locked eyes on Jason, his voice suddenly flat but gentle. "Come on, old friend. Let's go."

Jason didn't reply. He looked lost. Instead, he walked toward the road, past the human animal welfare officers. Hesitantly, he approached Daphne's lifeless body and stared at it. He felt numb. He struggled to accept the evidence of his eyes; just a few minutes ago she had been so full of life, so vital, so spirited. He couldn't believe it. Tentatively he sniffed at her body, prodded it with a paw, but there was no sign of life. He stood there, not knowing what to do, oblivious to the world going on around him. He was empty. Truly lost and alone for the first time in his life.

Olympia appeared at his side. She tenderly butted against him with her forehead reassuringly, but there was no comfort to be had. They both stared at Daphne's lifeless form.

"We ought to go," she said, gently.

"But where?" he asked, feeling helpless. "I've got nowhere to go to anymore."

She had no answer. Again, she nuzzled him, offering comfort where there was none. "Look at me," she said, more firmly. "We can't stay here. There's nothing you can do." His eyes were dull, but they masked a kind of inner pain he'd never experienced: intense and almost unendurable. Olympia turned and slowly walked away, looking over her shoulder to check he was coming. Blindly he followed, he neither knew nor cared where. Together they made their way through the easing rain toward the sanctuary of the Agora.

The victors assembled, but there was a hushed silence. They had won. The short but evil reign of the gangs was

355

over, but with the losses they had suffered in two bitter conflicts and the wounds many endured, there was little celebration, just relief. It would take a while before a merry band of misfits populated the Plaka streets again, teasing the tourists.

DAPHNE STOOD at the side of the road. She felt strange. What had happened? She'd been jousting with the horrible oaf, making him look like a fool, and then… nothing, for a moment. Then she was here. But what was that lying at her feet? It looked familiar. Tentatively she sniffed at the body, but it seemed to have no scent. She tried prodding it with her paw, but her paw seemed to go right through it. Daphne's fear verged on panic. She looked around wildly. Everything was in monotone; sounds were suppressed. What was happening? To her right, a fight went on, but it seemed strangely distant, as if she were watching it through a fog. She could make no sense of it. To her left, she made out a large silver-white cat. He turned his piercingly bright blue eyes toward her.

"Come with me," he said kindly. "Don't be afraid."

Relieved that someone appeared able to see her, she followed. They passed down paths she could not describe to a strange land. After a long or short time, she could not tell, they appeared at a river where a boat was drawn up. The white cat stopped.

"I must go no further," he told her. She jumped onto the boat, hesitating, and looked up at the hooded figure of the ferryman.

"Don't be afraid," the white cat told her one more time. He turned to the ferryman. "She is bound for Elysium."

"It is not for you to say," the other replied, in a rumbling voice, deep as the river. "It is for the judges."

"I know."

He stood on the bank for a while and watched the boat cross. Onboard, Daphne looked anxiously at the shadowy bank ahead, now more nervous than ever. As she approached the shore, she heard music, faint at first, but building. It was a beautiful melody, unlike anything she'd ever heard. She found it soothing and strangely uplifting. Behind her, the white cat turned and left.

CHAPTER 49

EAGLE

IN THE hours following the battle, the survivors could do little more than recover. There was no celebration. Feeling deflated and weary, Apollo sought out Jason. His friend was struggling, but he scarcely knew what to say.

"I'm sorry I couldn't get there in time."

Jason gave him a sharp look. "I thought your kind never said sorry."

"Well, I'm saying it now."

"And that's enough, is it, just a quick 'sorry' and move on to your next big adventure? She was special. Special to me, at any rate. I thought you liked her? Well, you were too late. And now you just want to forget it and move on. You think you're better than the rest of us? It seems like some animals are more equal than others."

"No." Apollo felt exasperated. Jason's bitterness was needling him, even though he understood it perfectly. He tried to explain himself, for perhaps the first time. "We're just different. It's not like it used to be." Inwardly, he fervently hoped he was right. "We... can change. At least, I'm trying to." He sighed and started again. "Look, no one escapes their life unscathed, not even us. We're all damaged one way or another; we all carry scars even if you can't see them. Everyone makes mistakes. Why should I be different?"

"But you don't die. I'm still just trying to get my head around it. How does it work? I thought you were one of us; normal, a friend. Someone I could trust. But you abandoned us. Your mistakes are pretty deadly. Do you really care about us, or are we just another one of your games? Is it like that all the time for you? You just tease us and prod us like we're mice to play with. How many other lives have you screwed up over the years? I thought you were a friend, but now I feel like I don't know you."

Apollo had no answer. There were so many deadly 'mistakes' along the ever-lengthening timeline of his existence, and he could no longer hide from them. The weight of the years was heavy today, and he had no escape. He envied his companion his brief existence. What time would he have to dwell on his own errors of judgement? Virtually none: here today, then gone, the weight lifted, the pain erased.

Worst of all, he'd lost Daphne, she who'd lit up his life once more without realising it. He longed to see her again, talk to her. Explain. Make her understand. Daphne, more than anyone else, had woken him from slumber and taught him that life could be worth living again, even though she'd eventually chosen Jason. He couldn't admit it to his friend, of course; he wouldn't understand. It would feel like another betrayal.

"I'm still me; the same animal you've known. I've always been around, and I always will be. Some have even been thankful to know me." He faltered and averted his eyes for a moment. When he resumed, it was as if he was talking almost to himself. "I hope you will too, one day. Perhaps you just have to wait and look for me when you're ready?"

Jason gave him a searching look, then bowed his head, lost in thought. Apollo turned to leave, but immediately he heard a small voice behind him.

"She's really gone. What can I do when all I've got is nothing but a few memories?"

He turned back to the animal, so lost in misery, and understood his pain.

"Treasure them," he said gently, and slowly walked away.

The golden eagle appeared soon after, as he knew it would. It circled overhead once, then swooped down to land on the Pnyx rock. Apollo stood before it.

"You have broken a treaty that has endured ten thousand years, and as a result they threaten war. You must accompany me and explain yourself before Zeus."

"No."

The eagle fell silent. It had not expected rejection. It tried again.

"The Titans seek retribution. They must be appeased, or war is likely. Who are you to defy the Sky Father?" The eagle stared with unblinking eyes, awaiting his response.

Apollo's chin rose almost imperceptibly. Through flared nostrils he could detect from afar the faintest scent of the trees and foliage of Delphi on its feathers; the scent of home. His eyes narrowed. The bird waited, still as a statue.

"This audience is over, you may leave." He turned away contemptuously. The eagle gave the retreating cat a long look.

"Is this your final answer?" Apollo continued on his way, the eagle's eyes boring into his back. After a long pause, it departed.

Athena emerged from behind a tree. "Wasn't that rather hasty? You know he won't let it go." She had heard the full exchange.

"Maybe, but I don't care." Apollo walked past her and into the trees. She read his mood and caught up with him a few paces on, walking alongside.

"We should talk, the four of us. I've got some ideas. Follow me."

CHAPTER 50

THE CAT INTELLIGENCE TEAM

I N A shady clearing on the upper slopes of Filopappou Hill, four cats lounged, passing the time of day. They communicated much in the flick of a tail, the scratch of an ear, or the occasional glance, whether furtive or bold. The rest they vocalised. Ares, Hermes, Apollo, and Athena were debating recent events.

"I can't believe you did that." Hermes was still trying to take it all in.

"He deserved it. I couldn't let him go," Apollo shot back. He avoided the real reason he'd acted as he did. He scarcely dared admit it to himself. It had taken him some time to make his peace with the messenger god again, but slowly fences were mending.

"Yes, and I will back you, even if they return to war." Ares' support was one thing, but all could remember the terrible ten-year war between the Titans and Olympians, and none of them wanted a return to those days. Apollo looked into the distance, deep in thought.

"What do you think he'll do?" They all knew who Hermes meant.

"I suppose he's going to get you to turn me in." Apollo looked at each of them. None could bear the weight of that golden stare for long.

"He might try," Athena admitted. There was an air of defiance in her response, which Apollo acknowledged gratefully, even though it surprised him. If Zeus had a favourite among his children, it was surely her.

"Hmm," grumbled Ares. He had a developed a grudging respect for Apollo. He admired his warrior spirit.

"Look, I can't just cut myself off from him and the rest, can I?" Hermes was at his most reasonable. "It's my very raison d'être. It needn't mean I'm against you, though."

Apollo looked at him again. "No funny business; you'll keep my whereabouts secret? You won't betray me?"

"I give you my word." Hermes locked eyes with him and held his gaze for a long moment. It seemed to satisfy the ginger cat.

"I'll have to go into exile, I guess."

"Where will you go?" Athena asked.

"I don't know, but it's best if you don't either. I'll just follow my nose. I'm sure I'll end up somewhere interesting." No sooner had he said it than he had a desire to venture abroad once more, exploring the countryside, the mountains, the coast, maybe even sail the seas. Go looking for dolphins, perhaps? He hesitated. "There is one thing you could do for me, though." Athena looked at him. "Olympia's carrying a litter. She'll be having them soon. After all this, she can't go back to Delphi." He left it hanging.

"I'll look after her," Athena reassured him.

"She can stay with us," Ares suggested. "Better for the little ones." He glanced across at Athena. "You wouldn't want them growing up among the Sisterhood. They'd turn out odd." Athena glared at him but said nothing.

"You will keep their identity secret?" Apollo added. He didn't want any divine vengeance wrought upon them.

They basked in the sun for a while, thinking. After a while Athena spoke again, changing the subject. "Are you ready to resume your duties as head of your so-called Plaka

Gang?" she asked Ares.

He mulled it over. "I suppose so."

"That's not what I'd call an enthusiastic response," piped Hermes.

Ares flicked his tail dismissively. "I don't enjoy feeling trapped."

"None of us do," Athena replied. "I don't think it's a problem to take the odd break. It's not supposed to be a prison sentence."

"I'll think about it," he grumbled and lay down flat on his side.

"Tabitha's an able deputy," Apollo suggested. "Jason speaks highly of her."

"How about Jason as deputy?" suggested Hermes.

"I don't know. Maybe. I'm not sure if he wants to go home or not, after all that's happened." Apollo was reluctant to dive into the details. "He's... taken it hard." He lay his head on his paws and fell silent.

In the distance, the rumble of city life continued, but closer to home the sounds of birds and insects prevailed, particularly the incessant buzz of crickets. A question formed in Apollo's mind. He looked around at them.

"Something has been troubling me. I remember we all agreed to the transition into this form, but why? Try though I might, I just can't remember."

Meaningful looks passed between the other three.

"It's her fault," Hermes said.

Ares turned toward Athena. Apollo followed his gaze. She looked a little uncomfortable.

"Come on, you were all there at the meeting. It was a collective decision. We all bought into it. Even the Titans."

"Hades didn't. Neither did Poseidon nor Oceanus at first," Ares reminded her.

"I wasn't there. I'm sure of it," said Apollo.

Hermes looked at him. "No, you were too busy chasing that nymph," he said. "Your consent was just assumed, but you ate the same fruit as everyone else."

Apollo felt confused, the memory still just out of reach. "Fruit?"

"From the tree," Hermes sounded exasperated. "The Tree of Demeter. The one she and Athena grew specially. I can't believe we all fell for it." He looked away in disgust; the memory was painful.

Athena shuffled her position and pretended not to notice. "Yes, there were one or two dissenters," she admitted, continuing as if she hadn't heard him. "And it probably makes little sense for them. But everyone else was up for it. We used to change shape all the time for our own various purposes, just not all together as a group; it took a lot more effort and coordination. It was difficult. But, after a lot of research and planning, Demeter and I put together a complex set of spells and enchantments and we combined them into a new species of tree."

"But why cats? And why little ones? Why not something bigger, like tigers? It's hard to think in something this small, let alone act. I feel almost powerless."

"It's like hiding in plain sight. We can live among them, eavesdrop on all their secrets, keep on top of things and influence them when we can. It could be fun. We just get on with things right under their noses." She seemed pleased with herself. "Keeps me busy, anyway. After they stopped worshipping us, I needed something else to do to stop getting bored, something that would spice things up. What else can we do? Stay involved or just fade away into the background like old wallpaper? I'd rather do this than drive a taxi." She gave them a defiant look. "Anyway, it seemed like a good idea at the time. And let's face it, they're bound to screw up sometime, and then we'll be ready to get more involved again."

"Except we can't." Hermes was accusing.

Athena looked uncomfortable. Apollo gave her an enquiring look. "Oh, all right then, I know it's my fault. You don't have to keep going on about it."

"About what?"

"About the fact we can't change back," Hermes told him.

Apollo sat back in shock. He looked in horror at Athena. "We're stuck like this? Forever?"

She gave him a long look. He couldn't read her expression. "Eating more of the fruit should allow us to change back," she said. "But we think the tree died. I don't know if there are any others. No one knows if Demeter took the seeds or any saplings."

He stared at her, uncomprehending, and echoed her words with incredulity. "We think the tree died?"

"It may have been poisoned." Ares was serious now. "There were rumours. But whatever the truth, we don't know where it is."

"Why don't we ask Demeter?"

"No one knows where she is either."

Apollo looked from one to another, the gravity of the situation becoming clear. "There's got to be another way? Surely one of you must be able to do something? Get us back to our old form?" Blank stares confronted him.

"You know the rules," Ares admonished. "One god cannot undo the charm, curse, enchantment, or spells of another. All we can do is ameliorate the situation somewhat. As and when. I could turn you into a cat-shaped constellation if you'd prefer?" he added helpfully.

Apollo knew the rule as well as anyone, but to have

to remain in this diminished state for all time, or at least until someone found Demeter and, hopefully, her tree was unwelcome news.

"Oh shit."

There was another long silence.

"What have you done with that precious artefact of yours?" asked Ares. He rolled onto his stomach and tucked his paws underneath. His ruby eyes bored into Athena. He'd never entirely trusted her with the thing.

She held his gaze, taking her time to reply. "I've made a decision," she answered. "I don't want it to go missing again," she gave him a pointed look, "so it needs to be stored securely. I've decided to donate it to the museum."

"Won't that stop you using it?" asked Hermes.

"No, I've experimented with range. I think I'll still be able to use it from a distance, as long as I know precisely where it is. It should be OK."

The others absorbed this information. All of them were jealous of her newfound powers. None were totally comfortable with Athena monopolising it. Not that they didn't trust her, but…

She read their thoughts. "Relax," she told them. "I will not use it against you. You can do what you like as far as I'm concerned, provided you don't undermine the safety and security of the city, of course." She gave the large russet-coloured cat a meaningful look. Ares was still suspicious. Apollo wasn't remotely concerned. Athena changed the subject once more. "I've been thinking about the future," she announced grandly. "I think we need a new purpose."

The others looked at each other.

"You mean a *collective* purpose?" Hermes asked.

Athena gave an imperceptible nod. "Yes," she said. "It worked out quite well, what with the rescue and everything,

I think we should capitalise on it."

Apollo gave a derisive snort. "Are you sure your policeman friend was up to it? He arrived late, and he didn't seem all there, if you ask me."

Athena defended her protege. "He took a little time to adjust," she admitted. "But he gets it now. The briefcase dropped by the man you attacked contained some crucial documents that tied this bunch to an illegal fur farming operation up north. They were passing off cat fur as mink, selling it on to foreign gangs to distribute abroad."

"Cat fur!" Hermes spat, his disgust clear.

"I'm afraid so," Athena went on. "Those animals were just held until they were needed up north at the garment factory. Then they were killed and sent on. That's why they hardly bothered to feed them. They were just waiting for slaughter."

There was silence while they absorbed the information. Even Ares was shocked at such casual brutality.

"We rescued Olympia just in time then," Apollo said to no one in particular.

Athena moved the conversation on. "Anyway, as a result of cracking this investigation, Second Lieutenant Samaras is going to be promoted to Lieutenant with greater investigative responsibilities. It's just the first step. He could go far." She sounded proud of his efforts. The others exchanged glances. *Here she goes again; she's got a new champion*, thought Ares. Before he could come up with ways to derail this beautiful new relationship, his sister started again.

"So, I think we should team up to help him," she announced brightly.

Silence.

More suspicious looks from one to another.

"Explain," Ares demanded.

Athena continued. "Well, we all seem to agree that we could do with some new purpose, something to get up in the morning for. This is it. Crime fighting. Think about it." She sat upright, tail curved around, warming to her theme. The others continued to look suspiciously at her. "We have agents everywhere! All of our followers and extended contacts represent a set of eyes out on the streets, in homes, in shops, and businesses up and down the country, even in what passes for the corridors of power in these days. It's a vast network. A massive resource. We need to connect everyone, of course, but it's achievable. Then we use our new network of 'eyes on the ground' to watch for suspicious activity and criminal behaviour and feed the information back to me. I'll tell Lieutenant Samaras, and he'll organise arrests."

"I'm not sure it's quite so simple," said Hermes, thinking it through.

"It might work," Apollo ventured, "but how do we get messages to you?"

Athena was now in full planning mode. "Well, you've got your crows and ravens. Hermes…"

"Has tortoises," interjected Ares mischievously.

"… is our messenger," Athena continued, glaring at him. "And Ares can just send one of his tribe over here to talk to me. I can send my owls out to check in with people periodically. It should all work." She gave them a triumphant look.

The others shuffled their positions. It would certainly be different. They'd hardly ever acted together before unless they were under a collective threat such as in the war against the Titans, and given that it might be on the brink of breaking out again, this could be a useful move. It would be entirely new. None of them could think of a good reason to dismiss it. Even Apollo, planning his own exile, found comfort in the idea of a supportive network behind him.

Athena took their silence as acquiescence. "That's settled then."

"What are we going to call this new outfit?" queried Ares.

"How about the 'Cat Intelligence Agency?'" suggested Apollo.

"CIA's been done." Hermes was dismissive. He yawned.

"Feline Bureau of Investigation?" Ares prompted. Hermes snorted derisively.

"United Cat Detectives?" offered Athena. No one liked it.

"Sounds like a parcel delivery service," grumbled Ares. "You might as well go for United Pussy Spies." Athena shot him a venomous look.

"Let's keep it simple," Apollo said, before a fight broke out. "How about 'Cat Intelligence Team?' Just tell it like it is. It's about teamwork, after all."

The others mulled it over. There were no objections.

"So, Cat Intelligence Team it is." Athena tried to regain her poise. She changed the subject. "Oh, and I've got a new computer," she said brightly. The other three stared at her in astonishment. She went on. "Yes, I spoke to the police officer and ordered him to get me one. I also told him I want a state-of-the-art voice synthesizer to go with it. A keyboard is such a pain with paws."

"Hmm, difficult," the others concurred, none of them entirely sure what she was talking about.

"So now I can do a website for us and boost our profile!" Silence.

"And just how many cats do you expect to google us?" queried Hermes.

"Oh, I know it's not likely, but it's just a bit of fun," she responded brightly. "We've got to move with the times."

"Athena, the first digital goddess," scoffed Ares. "Whatever next, cats in space?"

Sensing she might lose her audience, Athena turned to more earthly matters. "Anyway, as I was saying, we've solved our first case."

"And we've stopped another Titan insurgency," said Hermes.

"And probably started a war," added Ares.

"What's happening to them?" asked Apollo quickly, keen to avoid the subject at all costs.

"Well, I arranged for the city's Animal Protection Service to collect the wounded after the battle as you saw, including Zelus. Bia escaped. I believe Zelus is currently in quarantine. I've asked them to re-home him as far away from Athens as possible, on an island preferably, or up in the mountains."

"And Bia?" Ares enquired.

"I think she'll be easier to manage without her brothers around," said Athena.

"And what about Herse's boy?" Hermes asked.

Athena looked uncomfortable. That was one subject she didn't feel like discussing. "I'm going to have a chat with him," she offered.

"See that you do," Ares said. He liked the young fellow, and he didn't like to see him moping about. He got up and stretched. "Well, I'd better be off to check on the troops." He headed off.

Hermes made his apologies and left soon after. Apollo made no move. Athena sat with him. For a long time neither spoke.

"It is good to see you, after all this time," she said, at

370

last. He hadn't expected her to care. "Too many of our kin have disappeared, cut themselves off, or fallen into senility. But you've escaped that fate. How?"

For a while, he stared into the darkness beneath the trees. Did he really want to explain himself?

"For a long time, it's what I wanted too: to sleep, to forget." He looked at her, reluctant to continue. "The fact is, the past, my past, felt like a burden. It weighed me down. As the years passed, the loneliness increased until it felt unbearable. No worshippers to think about, no heroes to champion, nothing, just the growing sense of loss, of uselessness, the weight of the years and the things I wished I'd never done." He fell silent.

"So what changed?"

It was a while before he answered. He sounded puzzled, as if trying to work it out himself. "Along came this lively young creature, a small force of nature I suppose, and she woke me up. I thought I was in love again, but…" He couldn't bear to go on, the emptiness in his heart too great, the pain of her death too sharp. He looked Athena in the eye. "You know, I only ever felt that way about one other, a long, long time ago, but this? This time it was different. Deeper. More profound, maybe. But I played the slow game, took my time, let her make the first move." He stared into the distance, not seeing anything. "I was sure we'd connect, but something happened. She fell for another." He fell silent, unwilling to say more, gave her one last look, and left.

Athena stayed put, in no hurry to move. Modern life could wait. After a while, there was a rustle in the undergrowth, and a small black and white cat emerged. He ambled towards her and stood watching the spot where Apollo had disappeared.

Athena glanced up at him. "Well?"

"He still doesn't realise, does he?" The newcomer sounded surprised. "Probably just as well, but it makes me wonder if he's all there."

"You shouldn't eavesdrop." She didn't sound as disapproving as she might. "Anyway, what did you expect? It's been a long time."

The black and white cat looked down at her. "It worked though, didn't it? Woke him up, got him engaged again?"

"Maybe, but I'm still not sure it was the right thing to do. He doesn't seem at ease with himself. We may be playing with fire." She looked at the other cat for the first time, a note of caution in her eyes.

"Oh, I don't know. All's fair in love and war." He gave a barely perceptible flick of his tail, and walked away. Athena stared after him. In some ways, Eros was, perhaps, the most dangerous of them all.

CHAPTER 51

GREATEST OF ALL TIME?

SHE FOUND him on a narrow street close under the Acropolis, curled up next to a large plant pot and a wall. She approached slowly, but he didn't acknowledge her. Head on paws, he was not asleep, but staring blankly into the middle distance. He looked utterly dejected. Athena chose to respect his privacy and not sit too close. She hesitated, suddenly unsure what to say. Above them was the point Erichthonius's mother had jumped from. She chose not to look, fearing it might appear insensitive. How we have changed, she mused. Once the death of a mortal meant little to us, unless they were a hero, or our favourite.

The young cat raised his head to look at her. There was an accusatory look in his eye. She suspected he must know the story of his mother's suicide.

"You drove her to do it."

Startled at his accusation, the grey cat looked away. At least he was direct, which was a good thing, Athena hated animals who avoided difficult subjects. She regained her poise. "I wouldn't quite say that." It was an automatic response.

"Then what would you say?" the accusation came straight back.

Athena looked at him. "Your mother was…" she groped for words. "Mistaken."

The hostility in Erichthonius' stare was unsettling, even

373

for her. She went on. "Look, I didn't mean it to happen, of course I didn't. She just…" Now she was the one being evasive. She collected her thoughts and started again. "I'm sorry. Really sorry for what happened." Times were indeed changing. At the back of her mind, she tried, and failed, to recall when she'd last apologised to anyone. "It was a misunderstanding. I was angry with her, and maybe I said too much. But she took it too much to heart. I didn't know how she would react." Even as she was speaking, Athena's discomfort grew. This was a feeble excuse. In an automatic reaction, she shuffled her position. The truth was, she didn't care two hoots what Herse thought of her dressing down. She had been rightly furious with the traitorous behaviour of her servant, and dismissal was absolutely the right thing to do in the circumstances.

Her thoughts circled round again. That was how she justified her actions to herself, but could she have done something different? Could she have shown just a little empathy? The concept was alien to her. Perhaps she could have tried to be more understanding; see things from the other cat's point of view? Offer Herse a way to regain her trust? Maybe. She became aware Erichthonius was still looking at her as if reading her thoughts; he's pretty sharp for a mortal. "In fact, I didn't bother how she would react," she admitted. "I just wanted to vent my feelings. I was furious. I had been waiting for that artefact to be rediscovered for a long time."

For several long seconds Erichthonius said nothing. He remained wary of his visitor, but he was too angry to let her off the hook.

"She was worried about you, about all of us," he said. "And she was right. Just look what happened."

Athena thought about the war and the many unnecessary deaths. The murder of the kittens was heavy on her conscience. "I know," she admitted. "I know…" She said it mainly to herself and sighed. "They're with Hades now; I can't bring them back."

"I thought guilt would be an alien emotion for someone like you." Erichthonius' anger turned to sarcasm. In an earlier era, she would have turned him to stone for his impudence, but not today. In any case, he was past caring; they needed to be told, these immortals. "You can't go around playing with lives like we're pieces on a board."

His denunciation was claw-sharp. Deep down, Athena knew he was right. Our remit is to make things better, she thought, not mess them around playing games. She would repay her guilt as far as possible. She made a decision.

"You're right," she said. "Do you know, I think I might need some help? Someone who can keep me straight. Stop me from being unreasonable. Tell me when I'm going overboard?" She looked at him again. She was going to break the habit of a lifetime and admit a male into her service. More than that, she was going to make him one of her right-paw animals. "Things are changing around here, and I've been sleeping too long. There are things to do, matters to put right, like stopping the theft of antiquities, for one thing. What do you say? Would you join me, help me run this city?" She felt a little nervous as she waited for his reply.

The other cat's eyes widened as he absorbed her suggestion. Despite his anger, he knew this was an honour like none she'd given before. He didn't feel able to turn it down, but he waited before making his reply. He had her full attention, but the depth of his feelings lent him the strength to hold her stare, goddess or not. In fact it felt good to make her squirm just a little, while she waited for his reponse—he might never get the chance again.

"I will," he said, finally.

Athena purred in delight. This seemed right. This would be a new start. It would allow her to repay the debt to his mother in the way she knew best.

"Come on, let's get something to eat," she said.

A few minutes later, they were sauntering through the Plaka. Pleased with herself, Athena mused on her recruit. He would become one of her most trusted followers, she was sure. He had a sharp brain, and he wasn't afraid to speak his mind. An old quote came to her: 'I cannot teach anybody anything. I can only make them think.'

"Socrates would be proud." Accidentally, she said it out loud.

Erichthonius started. "I saw him play once." Athena looked at him in amazement. He went on. "It was at the bar down on Prytaneiou street, just before the last World Cup. They showed some films about famous old players." He stared into the distance, remembering. "He used to play for Brazil, didn't he? He was good, but I don't think he was as good as Messi."

Athena scrambled to get some purchase in this conversation, which was veering toward places she'd never been before. "Messi's quite good, isn't he?" she ventured, hoping not to appear stupid.

"Oh yes, I think he's the Greatest of All Time."

They continued for a while in companionable silence while she collected her thoughts.

"Personally, I don't think you can do better than Pele."

They walked on down the street into the sunset glow.

EPILOGUE

IN THE museum, they had opened a new gallery to house the finds from the recent excavations. There, in the centre of the room, in pride of place, was the small bronze statuette, on its own plinth, beautifully illuminated and surmounted by a glass box. A note below, written in Greek and English, described it thus.

Figurine, believed to be of the goddess Athena.
Early Classical period, circa 480 BCE

It was early evening; the museum had just closed. A large grey cat with bright emerald eyes wandered in. The entire gallery was suddenly filled with the vibration of purring, far louder than any animal her size could reasonably produce. The deep hum seemed loud and deep enough to spread across the city; it was felt rather than heard. The cat walked around the statuette, continuing to purr. Finally, a guard arrived.

"Ah, it's you again," he said. He was fond of cats, but this one in particular was special. There was something about her. "I don't know how you get in; you'll get me in trouble one day!" Athena raised her tail, pleased to see her favourite human again, one with proper reverence for the past. She wandered up to him and rubbed around his legs and followed him to a small alcove near the staff entrance where he placed a special bowl down, just for her. "Don't tell anyone," he said to her, smiling.

Later on, after he'd let her out, she padded back to the Agora. She enjoyed visiting the museum and renewing acquaintance with the old marbles, echoes of a past long gone. For a long time now the fortune of Athens had lain in its stones; memories of a glorious past. Perhaps one day she should tell them some of the real stories, she thought. But for a while she preferred to be alone here, under the trees of Pnyx Hill, overlooking the city from the splendour of the Acropolis to the memories of the Agora, the ancient market square and heart of the old city, and beyond to the present. She needed to feel the open air and the starlight at night beneath the trees. It spoke to the wildness in her soul, echoing down the centuries. It had all worked out well, in the end, thanks to those new arrivals from Delphi. Perhaps she should visit sometime. But first things first; it was time to update her contacts in Geneva.

She passed the hill, went down through the Agora, and arrived at Lieutenant Samaras' house. He wasn't at home, but she went in through the cat-flap and to the room he had set aside as instructed. There, on a low table, was a computer with screen and keyboard adapted to suit her paws plus the all-important voice synthesizer. A large crimson cushion was set before it. She sat down and, using the voice interface, opened a video link to CIT HQ, the command centre of the international Cat Intelligence Team network.

A moment passed, then the connection was made. A view of a distant room appeared on her screen, a cat at its centre.

"Geneva here," said the now familiar voice of the Swiss tortoiseshell who normally answered.

"It's Athena, Trudie, how are you?"

"I'm fine, thank you, good to speak to you. I'm glad you called." She wavered, looking aside. "Er, I'll just hand you over. There's someone who'd like to speak to you."

She jumped down and off-screen, and a magnificently

battle-scarred black cat took her place. He was huge, had a white heart-shaped patch on his chest and a white blaze down his forehead. His ears were ragged, and he appeared to have only one functioning eye; the other was multicoloured glass. But his good eye had just the kind of penetrating stare she recognised.

"Who are you?" asked Athena, a little taken aback.

"Greetings, dear lady," the black cat said in perhaps the deepest voice she'd ever heard in one of their kind. "I have long desired to meet you. I have many names, in many languages, but you can call me Odin."

THE END

If you enjoyed this, and would like to find out more about what the future holds for Apollo and his friends (and enemies) in future installments of The Reawakening series, sign up to the CIT Readers Club. It would be great to have you on board. You will be the first to know about upcoming books, and you can get a free exclusive prequel short story, The Transformation. I don't intend to pester you with frequent emails, but I will aim to provide you with occasional progress updates on upcoming projects, thoughts about the series and settings, first sight of future cover designs, and other relevant news. I'll also try to answer any questions that come my way, and I'd be delighted to hear your feedback.

Speaking of feedback, if you enjoyed The Forgotten God, I would be grateful if you left a review on Amazon, or Goodreads, or indeed anywhere. As a debut author your opinions are valuable to me, and I very much appreciate you making the effort.

Join then CIT Readers Club now and claim your free story.

Discover more about the series as it develops, and get your free story, at AndrewRylands.com.

ACKNOWLEDGEMENTS

I am hugely grateful to all the people who helped me bring this story to the wider world. Top of the list is Debi Alper for her invaluable advice and encouragement, and for her patience in introducing me to the intricacies of psyhic distance and much, much more. I am also heavily indebted to my editor Fiona McLaren who delivered pin sharp objective scrutiny and helped steer my direction. As a result of her questions and insights the final story is far stronger. Kelly Carter has managed to derive enough insight from my garbled thoughts to produce a beautiful cover, and layout. Elizabeth Thurmond's eye for detail in copy editing and proofreading provided the important finishing touches. Thanks are also due to Lucy Evans, Paul Harrald, Rosemary Scott, Kai Hopcraft, Alex Copeman, Nicola Dahlin, Lianne Dillsworth, Cyntia Ocampo, Anne Mortensen and Nick Franck for reading complete or partial early drafts and providing detailed feedback, and most importantly, the encouragement to keep going. I am particularly grateful to my son, Alex, for keeping me grounded and on track.

Finally, any native, or those who know the country, will realise that there is no police presence in modern Delphi, but with that exception all other locations depicted are real and many of them can be visited. If you find yourself walking the Sacred Way, keep a lookout for the local four-legged inhabitants who scratch a living on the margins of our world, and please treat them with due respect. After all, you don't want to get on the wrong side of Zeus.

ABOUT THE AUTHOR

Andrew lives outside Edinburgh with a cat who insists on auditioning for a part in a future story, and a teenager on the cusp of independence. He thrives on a caffeine intake that is probably too high, and wrestles with his conscience on a daily basis over the relative merits of excersise versus chocolate biscuits, usually losing. Andrew can't wait to go travelling again, especially back to Greece for another dose of inspiration from that fascinating land; to stand once more among the ancient stones, and try and pick up an echo of the stories they once witnessed.